Books by Alina

The Frost Brothers
    Eating Her Christmas Cookies
    Tasting Her Christmas Cookies
    Frosting Her Christmas Cookies
    Licking Her Christmas Cookies
    Resting Grinch Face

The Manhattan Svensson Brothers
    The Hate Date
    I Hate, I Bake, and I Don't Date!
    Hating and Dating Your Boss with Style!
    Yeah, I Hate-Ate Your Cupcake!
    Love, Hate, and Terrible Dates
    The Worst Dates Bring Chocolate Cake
    Dates I Love to Hate

The Richmond Brothers
    The Art of Awkward Affection
    The Art of Marrying Your Enemy

Check my website for the latest news:
http://alinajacobs.com/books.html

GOOD ELF GONE WRONG

A HOLIDAY ROMANTIC COMEDY

GOOD
ELF
GONE
WRONG

ALINA JACOBS

Summary: When your fiancé cheats on you with your sister on Christmas Eve, it's time to burn down the North Pole. This hilarious romantic comedy follows good-girl Gracie, accustomed to kindness and giving, who grapples with the shocking infidelity. She embraces her naughty side and recruits a rugged bad boy to help wreak havoc on her sister's wedding plans, all while navigating unexpected desires and a fake relationship. This festive and steamy romantic comedy proves that even the sweetest elves can't resist a dash of naughtiness during the holiday season.

*To anyone who's ever consumed
an entire bottle of wine and a
gingerbread house in one sitting…
this one's for you.*

Silent night, holy night
Drinking that egg nog ready to
fight...
                    –Snoop Dog

GRACIE

"*S*anta, baby, don't come down my chimney. I want you to go through the back door.*"

What in the fresh Christmas hell?

I almost dropped the Christmas-morning cinnamon rolls that I had left to proof in the oven. I glanced at the clock. It was 11:48 on the night before Christmas, and my freshly divorced grandmother was watching holiday-themed porn in the living room.

"Why can't she watch Hallmark movies like normal grandmothers?" I complained under my breath.

My parents' house was large, and Granny Murray had the TV volume in the living room turned way up on account of her hearing aids. The woman who was getting her Christmas present early was moaning loudly, accompanied by a rhythmic *slap slap* noise.

I wiped my hands. The rest of my large family was already asleep, dreaming of the big day tomorrow.

"*Yeah, Santa! Give me your huge cock,*" the porn star gasped.

I ground my teeth. Christmas was my absolute favorite holiday, and a big part of that was because it was wholesome. The yuletide season took me back to a time when things were simple, when my grandmother would host lovely Christmas dinners and not porno viewings. Now Gran was ruining it by "*making up for lost time after a waste of a marriage,*" as she put it.

"She's probably triggered that you're having the wedding of your dreams with the man of your dreams tomorrow. Cut her some slack." I tried to talk myself off the ledge as I walked quickly through the historic house.

The sex noises echoed through the decorated hallways. Granny Murray was going to wake up everyone, and I needed people well rested on Christmas, and not just for opening presents. My dream wedding was happening in fifteen hours, and it was going to be a packed day. I'd been planning my holiday wedding since I was a little girl, and nothing was going to ruin it for me.

Strangely, when I walked into the living room, Granny Murray was nowhere to be found. The room was dark, the TV off, the only light coming from the Christmas tree in front of one of the large windows.

The porno noises were loud and clear, though.

I peered in the dimly lit room. Was it a smart speaker? Was my little brother playing a prank on me?

"*Oh, Santa!*" a woman cried.

My mouth fell open.

"Kelly?" I whispered in confusion as I looked down.

My sister didn't hear me because she was getting her jolly holiday on with some guy who was half hidden by the oversized Douglas fir.

My face burned, and I stepped back, balling my hands up in fists.

"*Hit me harder, Santa!*"

My sister was going to wake up my mother, who would freak out, though probably on me for allowing my sister to bring some random guy into the house.

Ever since we were children, I had been blamed for my sister's mistakes. Kelly was the problem child—spilling juice all over the floor, coloring on the walls, sneaking out for parties, and bringing home strange men who had trashed the house and stolen my stuff. My parents had never done anything about it except tut-tut and ask me to keep a closer eye on Kelly and be a better role model for my little sister.

As if my sister could change.

This, however, was a bridge too far. It was Christmas Eve, for goodness' sake!

I straightened up. Well, not too much. I was in my Christmas PJs and braless. Things were a bit saggy, but I was going to be a married woman tomorrow, gosh darn it, and Kelly could not ruin Christmas or my wedding with her hookups.

"Kelly," I said in my best eldest sister voice, not that Kelly had ever paid it any mind. "You cannot bring strange men here, especially not on Christmas."

My sister responded by begging for her hookup to work her clit.

Said hookup was wearing a Santa hat that bobbed as he grunted rhythmically. He was partially blocked by the Christmas tree, but I could make out the slight pouch of his stomach as he increased the pace. His Rudolph boxers, custom embroidered, were down his pasty thighs. Come to think of it, those boxers looked an awful lot like the ones I'd made for James last Christmas …

"What the—"

"Fuuuuckkk!" My curse words were drowned out by James's orgasm. My fiancé groaned as he emptied his load in my sister. Yeah, no condom apparently, because we were putting all our faith in St. Nick this Christmas Eve.

"You—you're—" I stammered.

"Oh my god," my sister slurred as she orgasmed with a performative scream. "Oh my god, that was *sooooo goooood*, James!"

Her fur-lined Santa hat drooped over her head. She balanced on one arm to brush it and her hair back while my fiancé grunted.

"Damn. You're a better fuck than your sister," James wheezed as he grabbed my sister's ass. "You always give me a hell of a workout."

Kelly laughed drunkenly. Then she peered at me blearily in the soft, colorful light from the Christmas tree.

"Oh, fuck, Gracie. I thought you were asleep," my sister slurred as she tried to use the Christmas tree to pull herself upright. She tugged at her party outfit, a skimpy, glittery, wine-red dress, because of course she skipped out on the family Christmas Eve dinner to go to a club.

I stood there feeling like I was about to puke up all the Christmas cookies and milk I'd consumed earlier that evening. My mouth opened and closed.

"You always go to bed early. Why are you awake?" Kelly demanded.

"I had to check on the cinnamon rolls," I finally whispered.

James poked his head out around the Christmas tree. "Shit."

"Yeah, shit, James." My chin wobbled.

I couldn't process what I had seen, didn't want to believe it, didn't want to believe that my fiancé was just having sex with my own sister underneath the Christmas tree.

"This isn't what it looks like, muffin," he said defensively, using the pet name I secretly hated because he always liked to poke my stomach when he said it. He reached out a finger for my midsection. I slapped his hand away.

"I always made sure you had a home-cooked meal when you came back from work even though I was working too," I warbled, the tears making the lights on the Christmas tree blur and spin. "I clean the apartment, take your clothes to the dry cleaners, and hem your pants." The words were coming out in ugly, heaving gasps. "I don't understand how you could do this to me, James. I love you."

That was a lie. I did understand how he could cheat on me.

It was because of my sister.

Men always found her sexier, prettier, more exciting than me. Shoot, it wasn't just men—family, friends, even random retail workers—everyone flocked to my extroverted, pretty sister. She was my dad's favorite. Even though she ruined my stuff and had slept with my last two boyfriends and now my fiancé, I was expected to turn the other cheek, be the bigger person.

"You promised you liked me better than her," I cried to James, the words sounding small and petulant.

"Maybe if you weren't so boring and stuck-up, Gracie, you'd keep a man." My sister rolled her eyes.

"I am not stuck-up," I yelled at my sister. "You just ruin everything."

"I'm still going to marry you," James said, sounding annoyed as he pulled on his pants and tucked his shirt back in. "Don't worry."

I shuddered. He didn't even wash off his penis.

Then I had a horrible thought.

"You don't have sex with Kelly then come to bed with me, do you?"

"You're such a nag," James complained.

"Do you even shower after?" I screeched.

"Hell no," my sister scoffed, fumbling around for her clutch and pulling out a makeup compact. "He goes straight to sleep. He likes to smell me on him. Don't you, big boy?" She reached behind her to squeeze James's Christmas package.

My breath was coming out in hysterical gasps.

There were footsteps on the stairs. My family was awake.

The part of me that liked to pretend that everything was A-OK and under control just wanted to sweep my sister and fiancé off to bed and tell my parents we had only been enjoying a late-night Christmas movie and bonding.

I am supposed to get married tomorrow. Isn't it best to just pretend that this is all a bad dream?

"Who's having sex?" Granny Murray asked with way too much energy for someone in her eighties. "It smells like a strip club in here."

"*Mom*," my mother, Bethany, scolded.

My mom wrapped her robe around herself then peered at me. "Why are you down here with no clothes on, Gracie? What is all this commotion, you three?"

My dad patted me on the arm then saw my sister and rushed to give her a hug. "You're back, Kelly! I was so worried about you, out late at night."

My brother yawned. "Gracie, is the casserole ready? I'm starving."

"The breakfast casserole is for brunch. I can heat up some leftovers for you," I offered, my voice sounding far away.

Just keep the peace.

I was the eldest daughter. When the boat started to rock, I steadied it. I was the mature one, the third parent, the good child who made it all worth it.

"Did you check on those cinnamon rolls?" my mom asked. "The dough's not getting too big, is it? It could overflow in the oven."

You make one mistake when you're eight …

"Whose underwear is this?" Granny Murray asked, using a candy cane to pick up a pair of lacy black panties.

There were more footsteps on the stairs. My aunts and cousins were piling into the living room.

My cousin Dakota gave me a worried look. "Why are you crying, Gracie?"

You can still have your dream wedding, I reminded myself, trying to keep it together.

But James was no longer my dream groom.

"Gracie, are these yours?" Granny Murray waved the panties in my face.

"They're too small to be hers. Those are Kelly's," my cousin Connie said loudly.

Several of my female cousins gasped.

"Gracie," James warned.

"And I would be careful, Gran," I said, my voice taking on a shrill tone. "Those panties are a biohazard and soaked with James's fresh, hot cum."

My brother made a gagging noise. One of my aunts clapped her hands over my younger cousin's ears.

"Gracie," my mother scolded. "Why are you borrowing Kelly's underwear? You received a lot of nice pairs at your bridal shower."

Are you freaking …

St. Nick save me.

"Kelly and James were fucking under the Christmas tree," I said loudly and pointed at my sister and fiancé.

"I'm sure it was a mistake, right?" my dad asked desperately. "Too much eggnog, eh, James?"

"They've been having an affair." I sobbed.

"I'll get the shotgun," one of my uncles said with a chuckle. "We'll have roast cheater for Christmas dinner."

Finally. For once, my family was rallying around me.

But it was not meant to be.

James put his arm around Kelly.

"I just want you to know," he said, in a voice that for some reason I was just now noticing was annoyingly whiny, "that I'm sorry you all had to find out about me and Kelly this way. I think of all of you as family. We were going to wait until after Christmas season was over to tell everyone, but it's out now. Kelly and I are in love."

My sister beamed at me.

"What do you mean, after the Christmas season?" I said, hyperventilating. "We are supposed to get married tomorrow, James. You mean you were going to tell everyone *after* we got married that you were in love with another woman?"

James sighed heavily, like I was the problem here, like I was the one making things difficult and being childish.

"I was going to let you have your little Christmas wedding moment, Gracie," he said to me condescendingly, "then offer a quiet annulment."

"Bullshit!" I screamed at him. "Bullshit! You were going to keep fucking my sister behind my back until she got bored of you and bounced. Then you were going to mope around like a man-child and force me to take care of you and stroke your ego back into some semblance of function, just enough for you to attract some other pretty airhead with fake tits."

James scoffed. "Her breasts aren't fake."

"Yes, they are. My dad bought them for her for her eighteenth birthday."

"Kelly has self-esteem issues," my dad fretted.

"No. She has the issue of sleeping with someone else's fiancé." I turned on James. "I was going to marry you, you lying rat. And if I hadn't walked in on you coming in Kelly's chimney—*excuse me*, back door—then I never would have known. I would have married you and been blissfully unaware that you had no fucking respect for me."

"Gracie," my mother chastised, "can you please watch your language?"

"No, I won't, because James is a fucking asshole." I twisted the engagement ring off my finger and threw it at him. "This was supposed to be the best Christmas ever. I was supposed to get married."

"This was a very expensive ring," James scolded, bending down to pick it up.

He walked over to me, pretending like he was going to hand it back. As he did, he hissed in my ear, "Unless you want your big secret to get out, just shut the fuck up and smile."

My big secret? After the night I'd just had, having everyone know my secret was going to send me over the edge. I'd drown myself in peppermint hot chocolate.

My family looked at me in concern.

"I might have been too hasty. It is Christmas," I said weakly, feeling dizzy. "And the holidays are about family, so if James and Kelly are happy, I'm happy."

"Really?" Dakota was appalled. "Gracie. I know you're a doormat, but come on."

"I'm sorry, Dakota." My stomach was churning.

Maybe I did need to cut back on the holiday sweets.

"She's gonna puke," my brother hollered while my male cousins all freaked out.

I looked around desperately. I had just cleaned the living room rug, goddamn it, and the stockings had already been filled.

"Gracie, go outside," my mom yelled.

"Open a window!" my brother shouted as my male cousins hooted.

Granny Murray handed me a novelty ceramic Santa boot.

As I puked my guts out to cries of disgust from my family, the grandfather clock began to chime.

It was December 25th, and my life had completely imploded.

Merry freaking Christmas.

Chapter 1

GRACIE

"Only two and a half weeks until Christmas," I announced, opening up the door on my Advent calendar decorated with smiling mice celebrating the holidays, to reveal a mini wheel of brie.

Pugnog, who was my sister's reject Christmas present two years ago, woke with a snort and made grunting noises, begging for a treat.

"One of the budget airlines is offering cheap flights to the Bahamas," Dakota said to me as I took a bite of the cheese and tried to rally myself.

"I cannot spend Christmas on a beach. That's not very festive. I need snow and cold and spiced wine to recharge. A person only has so many Christmas seasons on this earth, and I want to make the best of them." I gave the pug a bite of cheese.

"There's a happy medium between going to the Caribbean for Christmas and planning and executing a yuletide wedding for your sister and your ex-fiancé. Why don't you compromise and go to a ski resort?" my cousin coaxed. "Hot cocoa, hot tubs, hot ski instructors."

"Gracie." James poked his head out of his corner office. I shrank in my seat.

"You need to rage quit," Dakota whispered. "You should have stormed out eleven months ago." She was my cousin and best friend since before I could remember, and she was angrier than I was at James and Kelly.

"It's my dad's company. He begged me to stay on and help," I reminded her.

"Then Uncle Rob needs to pay you more." She shook my chair armrest.

I made a face at my cousin then scurried into James's office. Though he did the least amount of work, James had the biggest, nicest office on the floor, with a view down to the snowy Manhattan streets.

My ex-fiancé was sitting at his desk, scrolling through tour packages for his upcoming honeymoon.

No one would admit it, but I had a sneaking suspicion he was just recycling our honeymoon plans for my sister.

You're in a work environment, I reminded myself. *Sure, it's your dad's company, but let's try to stay professional.*

"How can I help you, James?"

"Just want to make sure that everything's good to go for the next few weeks. We can't drop the ball with Roscoe Energy Solutions. They're our biggest client."

Correction. They were our only client.

"Did you have anything specific you were concerned about?" I asked James, pausing to watch him flounder for a response.

My ex had no idea what went on at EnerCheck Inc.

He waved his hand. "We just need to make sure that we're hitting the benchmarks and that we're on schedule for delivery. We can't let anything fall through the cracks over the holidays."

"We offer software monitoring solutions, and we don't have any big rollouts planned," I said to him slowly. "The last big update went out in early November. Next one is scheduled for March, so …"

James scowled at me.

"Okay, then why did you ask me if you already know?"

"You're the boss, and you called me in here," I reminded him, resisting the urge to tidy up his desk for him and pick up the empty cups of coffee.

I am not a doormat. Well, not a big doormat. I am a small one.

"I called you in here because … I need you to …" More angry floundering.

Maybe Dakota was right and I should just quit and leave him in the lurch. Unfortunately, my dad had a number of our less-success-inclined extended family members on payroll, and they relied on the money. Not to mention the eldest daughter in me couldn't just tank the company like that.

"I need you to … the maintenance guys are coming by to check the heating, and you have to make sure they have access to … what they need access to."

I glanced through the glass wall of his office, where I saw a man wearing gray coveralls and carrying a ladder. He plodded toward us through the rows of empty desks.

I opened the office door and called out, "We didn't call in a work order. You all have a glitch in your system. I told your colleague who was here last week, and he promised to get it fixed. I'm sorry you came all the way down here, but you need to leave."

"My apologies, ma'am," he said, setting down the ladder next to the door. "I called and confirmed with your boss."

"He doesn't know what goes on around here," I said, before I could stop myself.

"The assistants always run the show, don't they, man?" The maintenance worker grinned at James.

"Actually, I'm a project manager," I corrected.

The man muttered an apology and backed away.

"Just let him look around." James blew out a breath.

"I'm not letting the company get charged for work we didn't order. Merry Christmas," I told the maintenance man firmly and directed him back to the front door.

James rolled his eyes.

"You're so nitpicky."

"I'm trying to keep this business afloat."

"It's fine."

From James's point of view, the company was fine, but the rest of us employees were working overtime for no pay to keep up with the demand from the big energy company that was our bread and butter.

"Did you think about my idea for giving out Christmas bonuses?" I asked him.

"I said I'd think about it, didn't I?" My ex crossed his arms.

"You've been saying that since Halloween, and here it is, Christmas—"

"I told you that we can't afford it," he snapped.

"Actually," I said, tapping on my tablet, "we could afford it if you would just—"

"I have a wedding to worry about," James interrupted, standing up and reaching for his fancy ski jacket that was hanging on the coatrack. "Your mom wants to know what time your bus gets in. She has the big holiday party planned and needs your help."

"You know how the buses are," I said, trying to keep the annoyance out of my voice. "I'll get there when I get there."

"I'm tired of your attitude," James scolded me while I struggled to keep a professional face. "This is Kelly's big moment, and you need to be a good big sister and support her. Remember—"

"*I know.*"

A few hours after I had discovered James doing the reindeer nasty with my own sister, he had proposed to her, in front of the Christmas tree, on Christmas morning, just like he'd done with me. And I'd just sat there and taken it, pretending I was happy for them. Because the alternative was even worse humiliation.

He hadn't used the ring he'd given me. Not out of respect for me, of course. When I'd went to have the diamond ring appraised, the jeweler had told me the stone was cubic zirconia and basically worthless.

Somehow, he'd convinced my mother to let him use her great-aunt's vintage ring, the one I had wanted that he had claimed my mom wouldn't give him. My preferred ring would have been Great-Grandma Cecelia's, but that had been stolen and sold by one of her daughters in the '70s.

"I'll see you at the party, Gracie," James said. "Bethany promised you'd make my favorite lobster dip, too, so don't forget to stop at the store for what you need. I have to go. Traffic's getting bad."

He didn't even offer to drive me up to our small hometown in Rhode Island. Not that I wanted to be stuck in a car with him, but still.

I steamed as I went back to my desk. I did not have a window view and instead looked at the men's bathroom door that no one ever freaking closed.

"There was a suspicious lack of quitting," Dakota said.

"If I left, no one would manage the company," I reminded Dakota, "and your job would be toast."

"I have no problem going down with the ship after you set it on fire," she assured me.

Because of my sister's upcoming wedding, the office was empty, with the few cousins that actually did come into the office begging off with the excuse that they needed to get hair, nails, and spray tans done.

"You sure you can hold down the fort for the next few days?"

She shrugged. "Roscoe Energy Solutions slows down in December because everyone has to burn their PTO."

"Must be nice to have an actual PTO system instead of people just randomly leaving for a three-week vacation with no notice, and then when you complain, they tell your mom," I said tartly.

I sat down at my desk to compose a strongly worded email to the maintenance company about showing up at the office when I hadn't authorized any work. Then I responded to a few questions from our client and made a grocery list.

"Look," Dakota said, turning her laptop screen to me. "Two hundred dollars to fly to Switzerland. Ski resorts, fondue. You could meet a rich Swiss count."

"Or I can ride on a very slow, very smelly bus, go back to my parents' house, and make lobster dip for James."

"You have got to show some backbone," my cousin sighed.

I rubbed my forehead. It was greasy. "You know I can't."

"Your secret's not that bad."

"I just can't, okay?"

I stood up. The pug followed me to the break room.

"Seriously," Dakota said, racing after me. "You need to go scorched earth. Shoot, sabotage the wedding."

"I can't do that," I said quietly as I pulled my Advent cheese calendar out of the fridge.

I opened the paper door for tomorrow's cheese. "There, see? I'm living on the edge," I said as I shared the wedge of cheddar with Pugnog.

"Girl …"

My phone chimed with a photo from Kelly of her wedding dress, along with a list of demands from her describing, among other things, how some of the lace was fraying and she needed me to fix it because the seamstress wanted her to pay for more alterations.

"I see the theme of this wedding is holiday wedding skank. Did Kelly chop that dress up to pieces and hot glue on some silk?" Dakota asked, looking over my shoulder.

I frowned at the photo. Then FaceTime started ringing.

"Why aren't you responding?" My sister was snappish on the video call. "I'm getting married, and it's a disaster. I cannot believe that seamstress …" My sister didn't even say hello.

"I thought you were wearing Great-grandma Cecelia's dress?" Dakota interrupted.

"This is her dress." Kelly fluffed out her hair. "I upcycled it. Isn't it amazing?"

I pressed a hand to my chest and sat down heavily in a chair.

"I just made a TikTok post of the before and after." My sister texted me a link.

The first photo was a black-and-white of our great-grandmother in 1912, wearing an elegant Edwardian white wedding dress flowing with handmade lace. The classy portrait then transitioned into the holiday skanktacular.

Tears were threatening to spill.

"That was my dress, the dress I was going to wear to my wedding," I said quietly. "Everyone knew that ever since I was a little girl, I had wanted to get married in that dress. I planned my wedding around that dress."

Of course, when Kelly stole my fiancé, she also decided that she just had to be married in that dress.

"I can piece what's left together into a veil or a handkerchief or a small bag maybe," I said, trying not to panic.

"Well, you can't tear up my dress for that." Kelly made a face.

"That's fine. I'll use what's left."

"I didn't need the rest of the dress, so I tossed it."

"*Kelly, how could you?*"

"God, you're so emotional," Kelly snapped. "You didn't even fit in that dress. Besides, it's cool to upcycle. I got a ton of comments on my post."

"You don't upcycle a vintage dress," Dakota shot at her. "I can't believe you did this."

Kelly turned her nose up. "My astrologist said to expect that there were going to be people out there trying to tear me down and make me feel small because they were jealous that I was getting married. Mom already promised that you would fix my dress, Gracie, so I'm putting everything in your room. You'll see where the lace isn't attached right."

"Does Grandma Astelle know about this?" I choked out. She had jealously guarded that dress.

"Daddy talked to her and convinced her to let me upcycle it."

Ah, the life of the favorite youngest daughter of a favorite youngest son. With their powers combined, my sister would have anything she wanted.

"Kelly, do you want the red or—" I heard my mom ask.

My sister hung up abruptly to talk with her.

"Did you know?" Dakota said in alarm.

"No," I sobbed. "I didn't know she was going to destroy it."

"Maybe you can piece it back together. You know how to sew, right?" Dakota rubbed circles on my back.

"Not like that." My shoulders shook as I sobbed. "I can't believe Kelly did that."

"That fucking bitch. Sorry, I know she's your sister, but she is a fucking bitch," Dakota said defiantly. "You can't let this go. Stealing your fiancé is one thing. Honestly? James kind of sucked, and I never liked him. Kelly did you a favor. But destroy a hundred-plus-year-old dress? That bitch needs to be cunt punted into next Christmas."

"I can't." I wiped my eyes.

Pugnog pressed his cold nose against my ankle.

"Stop being such a pushover," Dakota rallied. "Shoot, I'll dump marinara sauce all over that wedding dress if you want me to. Just say the word."

I shook my head numbly.

"Seriously?" Dakota yelled, banging her hand on the table. "You're just going to let this slide?"

"No," I said, ripping open another door on the Advent calendar. "But only because I don't want whatever's left of my great-grandmother's dress to smell like oregano. Besides, Kelly deserves so much worse."

Chapter 2

GRACIE

What in all honesty could I do to Kelly?

I was her unpaid wedding planner; therefore, I knew all the vendors had already been booked, decorations ordered, catering menu approved, and cake deposit paid. There wasn't much left to sabotage.

"Just face it," I told myself angrily. "You're not going to do anything. You never do anything. You're going to eat the rest of the cheese in this Advent calendar, then you're going to go home and hide in the kitchen while your family talks shit about you losing yet another boyfriend to your sister, and then come the New Year, you'll be back at your desk doing everyone's work for them."

It wasn't fair that my sister could ruin my life over and over and everyone still loved her and catered to her and gave Kelly everything she wanted.

I blinked back tears. A long-haul bus trip was bad enough without being the crying girl.

Just my luck, it was a full bus. I wasn't even going to get a row to myself.

"Watch it!" a woman snapped at me as I pushed my way to the back of the bus, looking for an empty seat.

There was only one open seat in the back.

An angry-looking man in a worn leather jacket and heavy boots was manspreading in an aisle seat, arms crossed, reading a book. He ignored me when I stopped in front of him.

I cleared my throat.

"Excuse me."

Pugnog barked, though since he was a pug, it was more of a wheeze.

The man acted like he didn't even hear me.

"Excuse me," I said, louder this time. "Is this seat taken?"

The man, wearing a black skullcap, looked up at me, annoyed.

I shivered as his pale-gray, almost-silver eyes met mine. There was a scar on his forehead and another under his jaw.

Dakota's right. You need to grow a backbone.

"Could you scoot over so I can sit?" I asked firmly.

The man sighed in annoyance and made a big show of closing his book and standing up. He didn't even offer to put my bag up above on the rack and instead stood there, arms crossed, and watched me struggle with it.

What a dick, I thought as I wedged myself into the window seat.

The man sat down beside me and resumed his reading and manspreading.

I hugged the window as the bus rumbled to life and we turned out of the bus depot.

My seat neighbor read, I stewed, and Pugnog snored loudly and drooled as the bus drove at a snail's pace north from New York City to Rhode Island.

I bet James was halfway there already, driving the company car, because, of course, my father was going to side with my ex-fiancé over me, his firstborn child.

I didn't even get paid enough to take the train. Whenever I had asked my dad for a raise, he hemmed and hawed and said that it would mean he'd have to take money from someone else in the family. Like that was some great loss. Shoot, Kelly was on the payroll, and she barely did anything besides sleep with my fiancé. Now she'd gone and torn up that dress.

Even though I knew it was going to make me cry, I opened my phone and stared at the photo of my great-grandmother in the handmade lace wedding dress, her hair piled high on her head in an Edwardian pouf.

Dakota was right; my sister needed to pay. I'd suffered because of Kelly for the last twenty-five years. A woman had to take a stand. Lines needed to be drawn.

A plan, a plan, Gracie, you need a plan.

I fished out my Advent calendar, bumping Mr. Leather-Jacket with my elbow.

He gave me a dirty look.

"You can stay on your side of the armrest then," I muttered under my breath.

See? Growing a backbone.

I pulled out the calendar and opened another door. This one had Muenster cheese.

It wasn't fair, I thought as I angrily chewed the cheese. James wasn't even Kelly's type. I stuffed some of the cheese in Pugnog's stunted jaw, and he chewed noisily, snorting like a piglet and drooling.

I could feel the anger radiating off of my seat neighbor.

Kelly liked bad boys, guys like, well, like Mr. Manspreader over there, whose knee was practically halfway over my seat. I scrunched closer to the window, which only served to allow his legs to splay even more.

Was it too late to book a vacation? Christmas in my hometown of Maplewood Falls was my favorite time of year, but instead of being a newlywed with a baby on the way, I was going to watch my sister marry my ex while all my nosy aunts asked me when I was going to start dating again.

Tears dripped down my nose.

I ripped open another door on the Advent calendar, much to Pugnog's delight and Mr. Leather Jacket's annoyance. I took a bite of the sharp Manchego. This time next year, Kelly was going to be pregnant. I'd have to listen to everyone make comments about how they always thought I would be the one to give my parents their first grandchild because I was the one who liked to bake, sew, take care of people, and decorate. My mom would declare Kelly her favorite daughter ever, and I'd have to listen to my sister be insufferably smug about motherhood.

Bet she steals my baby name, too, and butchers the spelling, just like she did that vintage dress.

I straight up ripped off three more doors and stuffed a fistful of cheese in my mouth.

Pugnog slobbered and whined then fell backward onto the lap of Mr. Doesn't-Respect-Other-People's-Personal-Space.

"Can you control your mutant dog?" he snarled in a deep voice, deeper than I was used to after dealing with James and all the Manhattan suits all day long.

"Can you control the location of your knees?" I shrieked, cheese flying out of my mouth.

Pugnog ran for it, leaking slobber everywhere.

"This is disgusting." My seatmate's mouth twisted into a snarl.

"Take the train next time," I snapped at him.

It was very unlike me. Usually I tried to be nice to everyone, but today had been a very bad day.

Focus on your revenge.

Unfortunately, I wasn't the type of person who dreamed up elaborate revenge plots. Instead, I planned my dream house—a historic Victorian with a garden and a big fancy kitchen and lots of children.

Now all of that was going to my sister. Ten years from now, I would still be sitting on the bus with a selfish, egotistical seat neighbor while my sister waltzed through life, stomping all over my dreams and ruining my Christmas.

I cannot deal with her being pregnant next year, I decided. *It's going to trigger a mental breakdown, and who knows what I might do? I have to break up their relationship. I'm not doing it for me. I'm doing it for the world. I must find a way to stop that Christmas wedding from happening.*

And suddenly, like reindeer on a rooftop, an idea appeared. An awful idea. A wonderful, awful idea, because I was now in my Grinch season.

My sister was always boy crazy. Unlike me, who wanted to settle down with my soulmate, my sister was always looking for the next big thing, and that next big thing usually resided in the pants of a hot male, preferably one with lots of tattoos, a terrible attitude, and no respect for authority.

James was not her type. I had a hunch that she was disappointed with his bad jokes, his pudgy shortness, sweater vests, and lackluster bedroom performance. The only reason she was with him was because of the excitement of stealing something that belonged to me and the drama surrounding the whole situation.

But that was last year. As we counted down to Christmas, this was officially the longest relationship my sister had ever been in. The wedding excitement was waning. Kelly was staring down the barrel of a boring suburban life, because that's what James wanted—a housewife to take care of him, suffer through his demands, and suck his dick every once in a while. My sister wanted glam, drama, screaming fights in the middle of the street, jealous men, passionate sex, and a whirlwind romance.

All I needed to do was slide an ideal man in front of her, one who looked like he had stepped out of her wildest fantasies, a tall, muscular, tattooed bad boy who would give my father a heart attack and make James jealous. To make it extra enticing though, I needed that bad boy to be my boyfriend. My sister couldn't resist blowing up her marriage to steal something of mine.

It was the perfect plan. Muahahah!

My villain origin story, complete with a bug-eyed sidekick and all the cheese I could eat. Well…

I looked down at the empty, torn-up Advent calendar.

Some wine would be good with this.

The only problem with my epic revenge plan? I didn't have a bad boy.

Mr. I-Hate-Pugs was stoically sitting next to me, ignoring Pugnog's snorting and reading his book. He'd removed the book jacket, and I couldn't make out the title. It was probably one of those how-to-be-a-sociopath-to-pick-up-women type of books.

Don't ask him. Find someone on Craigslist or the Meat Market app. You need a professional.

I wished I'd had this brilliant idea when I was still in New York City. Then I could have hired an out-of-work actor. If I tried to hire anyone in my hometown, word would for sure get back to my sister.

I chewed on my lip and tried not to look at the tall, broad-shouldered man in the seat next to me.

He flipped a page in his book.

My mouth was dry.

Grow a spine.

I turned and studied him.

He was handsome; the scar made him seem rugged and mysterious. With the straight nose and strong jaw, he was totally my sister's type. To be fair, he might be any woman's type. Not mine, though.

I bet he's wearing that skullcap to hide a bald spot, I thought uncharitably.

Mr. Bad Boy flipped another page in his book then turned his body slightly toward me.

I quickly crossed my arms and faced the window.

You cannot ask a strange man to be your fake boyfriend, I scolded myself. *That's … well, it's rude.*

Besides, I'd have to pay him, and who knew how much money you had to pay a man to be your fake boyfriend. What was the going rate for that these days?

Maybe it wouldn't be too expensive. If he was riding a bus, then he must need money.

No, this is crazy. Just distract yourself with planning the postwedding Christmas brunch and do some knitting.

I pulled out the doggy sweater I was making. I was in the process of knitting holiday outfits for the local animal shelter to use to dress up their wards for Facebook posts and hopefully help find the dogs new homes.

The needles clacked as I knitted. Every so often, I glanced over at Mr. I-Insult-Pugs. Outside the bus window, dirty snow was piled on the side of the highway. This was the scene I was going to witness every Christmas from now until eternity, because I'd lost my one chance of getting a halfway decent boyfriend, and none of the men at that speed-dating event Dakota had dragged me to had written down that they wanted to keep talking to me, and I was going to ride in this slow, smelly, too-hot bus every Christmas forever and ever, and never have a house or a family or wear that dress.

I dropped a stitch. Dammit.

Do it.

I licked my lips; my mouth was dry.

Knitting clutched in my hands, I turned to the bad boy sitting next to me.

"Do ... um ..." I cleared my throat. "Do you have a girlfriend?"

His finger paused on the page he was turning. He fixed those pale-silver eyes on me, a dusty gray like the winter sky.

"No. Why? Are you offering?"

"Sort of. See, I kind of need to break up my sister and her boyfriend. She's dating my ex. He's a jerk. It's complicated. But I need you to be my boyfriend so I can ruin her wedding. I don't know if you do that type of work?"

I smiled hopefully.

The book closed with a loud thud.

He looked angry.

"Er, never mind," I squeaked and held up my knitting. "I'll get started on those baby socks. Forget I said anything."

But he didn't go back to his book.

"So you want a fake boyfriend."

"Um, yeah. I mean that was the plan. But plans change …"

Those ghostly eyes still locked on mine, he leaned over, his huge body crowding my space.

I scrunched against the window.

"You sure you can handle it?" he asked in a deep, gravelly voice. He smelled like leather and the winter wind.

No. No, I don't think I can.

I swallowed. The empty Advent calendar was digging into my side.

"Yes," I squawked.

"Prove it," he said, his breath cool on my cheek.

He twisted out of his jacket, the ridges of muscle under the tight gray T-shirt flexing and rippling as he shrugged off the garment.

"Give me a hand job." The baritone voice deepened. "I have my jacket on my lap. No one will know. Just go for it."

My eyes were about as big and round as Pugnog's and ready to pop out of my head.

"Unzip my fly," he breathed against my mouth, "and stroke my cock."

My stomach was flip-flopping. The air between us was supercharged, and my skin felt tight and prickly.

"I-I can't," I stammered.

He huffed out a laugh, smirked, and pulled his jacket back on, the leather creaking.

"Thought so." He sat back in his seat and opened up his book. "You're weak. You have an elaborate revenge plan all mapped out, yet you clearly can't handle having a fake boyfriend."

"I just wanted you to show up at dinner and brood and scowl." I flapped my hands.

No man had ever been that forward with me, especially not one who looked and sounded like this one.

"Have you ever planned anything more complicated than a dinner party in your life?" he asked, lip curled up derisively.

"I have a job," I protested.

"I was in the military," he retorted, "and as someone who was paid to destroy things for a living, your plan to get back at your sister sucks. You've failed before you even started."

The tears were threatening again. I blinked them back. I should have bought two cheese-filled Advent calendars.

"Tears don't win wars, Sugarplum." He opened his book.

I angrily wiped my eyes.

"You're such an asshole," I said.

Those eyes flicked up from the page. "Excuse me?"

"You're perfect," I said determinedly. "Kelly's going to love you and dump her fiancé like that." I snapped my fingers.

He snorted and continued to read his book.

I shoved the knitting in my purse that was on the floor between my knees.

In for a penny …

I flexed my fingers then leaned over and reached for his zipper.

He swore loudly and slapped my hand away.

"Don't touch me."

"I'm showing you I can do this," I said stubbornly, going for his crotch again. "I can complete the mission. I'm committed."

"I don't want you to give me a hand job in a bus," he snapped. "I just wanted to see what I was working with. Besides, you look like you give terrible hand jobs."

"You're so rude." I smiled at him. "When can you start?"

He fixed that snowy gaze on me.

"What would be your, ah, going rate?" I asked. "I'm thinking definitely I need you at the wedding kickoff party and the holiday party and to just hang around the house a few nights."

"You think I regularly date women for money?" He set his book down.

I shrugged helplessly. "The economy is rough right now. I could do a flat fee, maybe $600. Is that too low?"

I winced when he looked at me, incredulous.

"Do you take credit card?" I fumbled for my wallet.

Mr. Bad Boy took the credit card from me, face softening.

"Actually, I think we can help each other out. I have a rich grandmother I need to impress with a pretty girlfriend so I can get my billion-dollar inheritance."

"Oh, really?" I cried. "That works out perfectly then."

"No," he snarled and threw the credit card at me. "This isn't a fucking Hallmark movie, Sugarplum. I want cash: $5,000."

I sucked in a breath. "You sure you don't want that hand job?"

He gave me a wolfish smile.

"Fine. You dress up in a sexy elf outfit and let me have you however I want for a weekend, and we'll call it even."

Chapter 3

HUDSON

"**R**elax, Sugarplum, I'm just kidding," I said as she stammered. "I hate Christmas, and like I said, you look like you'd be a terrible lay. How about I put you on a payment plan? First date's free."

Grace O'Brien—Gracie as her family called her and the name she used to register for store loyalty programs, according to the file I'd put together on her—stared at me with wide brown eyes.

You pushed too hard.

I didn't allow the fear to skitter across my face; I was too well trained for that.

She's going to balk, and then you're going to have to go back to HQ, tail between your legs.

And after I'd given the other guys so much shit about getting thwarted by one dumpy little office girl and her overweight pug.

I read her file. I knew her, knew her better than she knew herself.

Trust the plan.

Gracie wavered.

I gave her a derisive look.

"Deal." She stuck her hand out. It was small and soft in mine as I shook it.

"Let's talk strategy," Gracie said, pulling out a notebook covered in green, red, and white fuzz that immediately began shedding all over my black canvas work pants.

She wrote in a loopy cursive at the top of the page:

Fake Boyfriend Operation

I grabbed the notebook from her and ripped out the page, crumpling it up.

"First rule, don't write anything down. No creative notes, no lists, no text messages, no emails."

Gracie saluted.

"Got it. No evidence, no witnesses."

"Second, you do what I say, when I say it. No questions."

"What if—"

"No questions," I interjected.

"But what's the plan?"

"The plan is total annihilation, by any means necessary."

She gulped.

"Do you want to win? Do you want to wipe the floor with your ex's corpse?" I demanded.

"Um, no. No, that is not what I hired you to do," she said, waving her hands.

"Metaphorically, I mean." I gave her a toothy smile.

She shivered.

Pugnog drooled.

"Third, you need to keep that dog away from me. He smells bad, and his eyes are pointing in two different directions. He's an affront to intelligent life."

"He didn't mean it, Pugnog." Gracie scooped up the pug and squeezed it hard.

His eyes bugged out of his head so far I thought one of them was going to pop out and start rolling around on the bus floor.

You are getting a very lucrative payday out of this, I reminded myself. *Just play the part that she wants you to play.*

Grace squirmed in her seat. "Do I need to tell you about my family, you know, give you an information download?"

"No," I said then mentally hit myself. She didn't know I'd spent the last few months digging up dirt on her family. Or trying to anyway.

"I'll know what I'm working with when we have our first family gathering together," I backtracked.

Sloppy.

"Don't worry, Sugarplum. I'll break up your sister's relationship, and you can have your ex back."

"I don't want James back," she said in a rush.

"Of course you do," I said, crossing my arms. "It eats at you that he chose her over you, that he loves her and not you, that he wants her and not you." I lowered my voice to a whisper. "You want him to wrap you in his arms, tell you you're his one and only, to beg for your forgiveness, tell you he loves you and beg you to take him back."

"No, I don't," Grace said forcefully, but the slight tremor in her voice told me she was lying.

"Don't feel bad, Sugarplum. It's because you have low self-esteem." I rubbed my thumb on her chin.

"Asshole." She faced the window.

"That's why you hired me."

I turned back to my book.

Love was a weakness. And Gracie was weak.

Unlike me.

I wasn't motivated by love. I was motivated by money. When my father left my mom and siblings to run off with the family's money one Christmas—what was left of it anyway—I saw love for the scam it was. Love made people irrational and ineffective. That was why I'd been able to wrap Gracie around my finger, because she had been weakened by her love for her ex.

I glanced over at her. She was staring dreamily out of the window, watching the snowy Rhode Island countryside pass us by. Other men would probably find her soft femininity alluring, but not me. Gracie's only attractiveness was as a means to an end.

I mentally plotted my next steps as the bus rumbled into the small town of Maplewood Falls. The bus terminal was on the wrong side of town, the side where I grew up.

I'd signed up for the military as soon as I had turned eighteen, needing to escape the town by any means necessary. Yet I had never been able to completely shake its hold on me.

Gracie, as I knew from her file, had grown up on the right side of town, gone to the good school, lived in a nice house in a desirable neighborhood. What I hadn't been able to figure out, when I'd been compiling my research, was why her parents made her take the bus home.

Guess you're about to find out.

Gracie was awkward when the bus pulled up under a 1950s-style awning. The terminal numbers had fallen off years ago, leaving only the shadow of the number five on the peeling white paint.

"I'll let you know when the first family event is," Gracie said quietly as the passengers jostled to escape the cramped bus.

"Call me," I reminded her, taking her notebook and jotting down the number of a burner phone I'd bought for this specific purpose.

"Wait," she said and looked around furtively. "What's your name?"

"Hudson," I replied, "Hudson Wynter."

"Grace O'Brien, but everyone calls me Gracie."

I knew that, of course, but said, "We'll be in touch, Gracie."

The much-smaller woman struggled to extricate herself, her dog, and all of the shit she'd brought with her.

"Aren't you going to help?" she grumbled.

"Helping is extra," I breathed in her ear, just in case someone her family knew overheard. "Besides, no one told you to pack this much. Are you moving home?"

"I haven't sunk that low yet," she muttered.

Pugnog yelped as Gracie accidentally banged him in the head with her laptop case.

I took pity on her and grabbed the overstuffed carry-on from the overhead rack then slung my rucksack on my back. I didn't have much in it—it was just for show. Everything I needed had already been stashed in town.

"You don't have more luggage than that?" Gracie asked me as she followed me off the bus, her bags thumping against the empty seat backs as she passed.

"I travel light," I replied, setting her bag on the icy sidewalk.

The bus driver was standing beside the open underbus storage, smoking a cigarette.

"I have a small animal," Gracie said defensively as she headed for the storage bay to retrieve another overstuffed bright-pink suitcase, sliding on the icy asphalt as she tried to drag it out.

I strangled a curse, stalked over, and grabbed her roughly before she and Pugnog could crash to the sidewalk.

My client was not going to be pleased if I couldn't fulfill the contract because I'd let Gracie crack her head open on the pavement.

"I'll get it," I growled.

"Oh, look. He does have manners." Gracie sounded slightly breathless.

Probably all that cheese she ate.

"You have anyone coming to get you?" I asked as I picked up both of her bags.

"They have wheels," she huffed as I carried them toward the dilapidated, small-town bus station.

I ignored her.

"My family is busy," she said, trotting after me, "but I called an Uber."

Inside the too-warm building, a bored bus station employee was watching sports on his phone. Christmas carols played, tinny over the ancient speakers in the terminal.

"An Uber," I repeated.

"Do you have anyone coming to get you?" she asked behind me.

I did, but I didn't need her to know that.

"I work around here," I lied.

"Oh." Her phone chimed with a notification from Uber.

"Come on, Pugnog, we need to go to the store." She was talking to the pug in a high-pitched voice.

I threw her bags into the trunk of the Uber then slammed the car door closed when she was safely inside.

"Call me."

"Are you …" she began in a small voice. "Are you sure you want to do this?"

"We shook on it," I said and smacked the side of the car.

As I watched her drive off, I pulled out one of my burner phones and dialed a number from memory.

"I assume you are calling me with good news." Grayson Richmond's voice was dry, emotionless.

"I'm in," I reported. "We're still on schedule."

Chapter 4

GRACIE

"There you are," my mother said, exasperated, when I stumbled through the front door, dumping my luggage on the floor.

I didn't have the budget for an Uber, but I hadn't wanted Hudson to feel like he had to babysit me. The five hours I'd been trapped next to him in the bus had been intense. All I wanted were some Christmas cookies, a glass of wine, and a hot bath.

Instead I got the holiday chaos of my family.

Two younger cousins raced by, high on sugar cookies and holiday excitement. I let Pugnog out of his carrier to join the fray.

"Did you buy the ingredients for lobster dip?" my mother asked. "Sandy, I don't want to use those plates tonight. We'll use the other ones."

"Why couldn't you convince Dakota to come?" my aunt Babs asked, coming over to me and giving me a huge hug.

"Someone has to manage the office."

Aunt Giana sniffed. "You smell." She sprayed me with Febreze, making me cough. "Why do you insist on taking the bus?"

"I don't know." My mother threw up her hands. "James offered to drive her, but she refused. I don't know why you can't forgive him, Gracie."

"No, he—"

"It's been a whole year, and he and Kelly are so in love," my mother lectured. "James is trying, Gracie. You're going to have to get over it at some point. Kelly's going to have children, and you want to have a relationship with your nieces and nephews, don't you? She wants a big family, you know."

No, *I* wanted a big family. Kelly wanted to party.

"The fish needs to go in the fridge, and can you make the custard for the Boston cream pie?" my mother continued as she shook out table runners. "Your uncle Bic asked me at the last minute if we could serve it, and I need to set up for the buffet. Oh, Gracie come here and help me figure out where to arrange the tables."

"I told you the buffet needs to go on the back wall, and we can seat people in the dining room and living room," I told her, trying to keep the annoyance out of my voice so my mom didn't scold me for having a tone.

A mopey-looking young woman in a crop top, Ugg boots, and leggings, slouched into the room, followed by my brother.

"I just wanted to make sure that there are going to be some vegan options for Piper," Logan said over my mother shouting at my aunt to not drop a goblet.

Bethany threw up her hands. "Vegan options?"

"She ate steak the last time she was over here," my uncle Eddie remarked as he and another married-in uncle moved the tables to where I directed.

"No, that wasn't Piper. That was Pippa," my brother corrected.

"Don't worry, Mom," I said before I could stop myself from volunteering. "I'll make sure Piper has something to eat."

It was a compulsion to help make my mother's life as easy as possible—the curse of being the firstborn daughter.

In an ill-fated attempt to lose the pounds accumulated in the post-being-cheated-on fog of sadness and self-loathing, I had tried to be vegan. It had lasted all of two weeks and had ended when my sister had posted photos of herself in a thong bikini on the beach with James, her engagement ring front and center.

A woman needed a cheeseburger and a bourbon milk-shake after a social media post like that.

On the bright side, I had assembled a repertoire of plant-based dishes.

"I'll make you a very tasty zucchini 'spaghetti' dish with fresh spinach, pine nuts, and other winter veggies," I promised.

"Um, I don't actually like vegetables all that much?" Piper said, twirling her hair.

"She doesn't like the texture," my brother explained. "When we go out, she always orders an Impossible burger."

"French fries, Oreos, and imitation sausage links it is then."

Piper brightened. "Sounds great!"

"Thanks, sis!" Logan hugged me. "We're heading to the park to shoot some hoops."

"Great. I'll just be here throwing a dinner for forty together," I said under my breath.

It's Christmas, I told myself firmly. *You're with family. That's what's important.*

It was Hudson, with his lack of respect for my personal space and his military metaphors and his sexually charged comments, that had put me in a bad mood.

I pulled out my great-grandmother's cookbook. It was one I had designed from a collection of her recipes that I had carefully typed up, tested, and photographed then given to the family one year as Christmas presents. It had the best custard recipe.

I opened the fridge.

"Where are all the eggs?"

"Your aunt Janet used the last of them," my mother said as she swept through the kitchen.

"You could have told me. I was just at the store."

"Gracie, don't use that tone," my mom chided. "I have a full house here. I'm trying my best."

"Don't scowl like that. You'll get wrinkles, Gracie," Aunt Sandy told me. "A single woman can't afford to get wrinkles."

"You'll have to go to the store and buy some eggs," my mom told me.

"She needs to go to the store and get a man," Granny Murray said from the doorway.

I rushed to hug her.

Granny Murray admired me. "Your tits look great."

"Really?" My mother frowned and pulled at my top. "I think your bra is too small."

"I'm too busy to date," I said to Granny Murray as I pulled self-consciously at my clothes.

Nothing seemed to fit right. No wonder Hudson wanted cash instead of a hookup. He had been positively repulsed by the idea of sleeping with me.

I felt nauseous thinking about my big plan.

He's going to balk, I assured myself. No man in his right mind was going to pretend to be the fake boyfriend of a girl he met on a bus. That was absurd. Hudson was probably just pulling my leg, passing the time. A slow bus ride makes people do crazy things. He gave me a fake number, which was no problem because I was not going to call him. Ever. Instead, I was going to pretend this whole thing never happened.

Granny Murray lowered her voice to a conspiratorial whisper.

"I heard the lesser grandma"—meaning my father's mother—"talking smack about you, saying that she would be surprised if you were even going to show your face this Christmas. You need to get a real home run of a man, shut them all up."

"It doesn't hurt my feelings," I promised Granny Murray. "I'm an adult. I can take it. And I don't need a man to be happy. That's what you said when you threw that divorce party last year, remember?"

"I'm not telling you to get married. I'm telling you to find a hot piece of tail, fuck him in the back seat of a Camaro, parade him around, and shut up that gossipy old woman."

"It will have to wait until I've gone to the store."

"I added onions and flour to your list," my mother called as she sailed through the kitchen, carrying a soup tureen into the dining room.

I picked up my coat from where I had draped it over my bags.

"Also, can you do something with that dog?" my mother added as she floated back, carrying a tablecloth to the laundry room.

One of my younger cousins, who was probably trying to be helpful, had put down a dish of water for Pugnog. The chunky pug had inadvertently tipped over and was drowning in his water bowl.

I righted him, picked up the water dish, dumped it out, and gave the dog a few whacks on the back.

"You're going to the store, Gracie?" my dad asked hopefully as I walked through the den. He was watching the football game with several of my cousins and uncles. "Could you pick up some ice cream? Pistachio if they have it, though it's not as good as yours."

Hint. Hint.

"I can make you some," I offered weakly.

It's Christmas, it's Christmas, I chanted.

"Can you pick up some chips and salsa?" another cousin asked.

"And some of those jalapeño poppers?" another added. "We need snacks for the game."

"Of course," I said, jotting it down on my quickly ballooning grocery list.

I stepped out onto the back porch and trudged through the snow to the detached garage with the mother-in-law suite above, where Granny Murray lived.

Both of my parents' cars were gone, and Granny Murray didn't have a car because she had lost her license after getting in a police chase.

"Guess we're walking," I forced out between my teeth as I grabbed the wheeled cloth grocery cart hanging on the wall of the garage.

"You need the exercise. It's a beautiful winter day. We'll walk to the store, taking in all the Christmas lights. It will be grounding, centering, meditative."

But it was no use. I felt no Christmas joy, no holiday cheer.

Twenty more days 'til Christmas.

For once in my life, I wished the Christmas season could just be over and done with already.

Chapter 5

HUDSON

"That's how we do it!" Jake whooped when I climbed into the back of Anderson's SUV.

I leaned back in the cracked leather seat, allowing myself a small smile.

"She practically crawled right in my lap. I didn't even have to use any of your idiotic pickup lines."

I could still feel the phantom touch of Gracie's fingers trailing over my zipper.

Focus.

"Women can't resist that handsome face." Jake grabbed my jaw and shook my head.

I let my little brother manhandle me for a moment then pushed him off.

"Eyes on the prize, men."

"It's going to be a good Christmas this year," Jake crowed, leaning over the center console and turning on the radio, then punched buttons until Christmas carols blared out of the speakers.

As the second to youngest, Jake preferred to shirk as many responsibilities as I, the oldest, would let him get away with, which of course wasn't a lot.

I turned off the radio.

"Thank you."

Like me, Anderson, the second-oldest Wynter brother, was not a fan of Christmas. Always seeking ways to optimize his life, Anderson had followed me into the Marines, and he'd been an asset in the military and was an asset at my company.

"You two," Jake said, turning the radio back on, "need to get in the holiday spirit. Especially you, Mr. Casanova. You're dating a Christmas-loving woman and her Christmas-loving family. Time to pack up the family trauma and rediscover your inner Frosty the Snowman."

"Never."

Anderson glanced over at me.

"You better not fuck this up. It's not just money, but our reputation is on the line. This contract has already taken longer than it should. If you have to dance around a Christmas tree in nothing but an inflatable reindeer costume to complete the mission, then you'd better do it."

He drove us to one of the warehouse buildings I owned in town and where we'd set up a makeshift field office. I needed all hands on deck for this one.

"Gracie doesn't want a Christmas-loving potential husband," I reminded them. "She wants a bad boy with a dangerous streak."

"Thankfully, you're a grade-A-certified asshole," Jake said as Anderson parked by the loading dock door.

Inside the field office, several large monitors were set up on tables. The stale smell of coffee hung in the air. Lawrence and Talbot, the third and fourth youngest, stood in front of a large TV where drone footage played.

Elsa, our little sister, was up in Harrogate with our aunt and uncle, helping them with the Christmas rush at their lodge.

This job should have been a straightforward corporate espionage contract. Robert O'Brien's company was a family office, and there was no HR, no IT, and no corporate structure. The whole thing was held together by a shoestring. It should have been like shooting fish in a barrel.

Except that Gracie's cousins hadn't had anything on the laptops my men had managed to gain access to, Gracie kept blocking access to the office, and all of my team's attempts at using phishing to gain access to the EnerCheck computer system hadn't worked.

I had a sinking suspicion that Gracie, with her soft, pretty mouth, big innocent eyes, and curvy body was not, in fact, a dumb, coddled daddy's girl like I'd originally thought.

No matter. I'd taken down men ten times what Gracie was. I'd deliver her and her family wrapped in a bow before Christmas.

"The O'Briens are having some sort of big family gathering," Lawrence said, showing me live drone feed from outside of Gracie's house.

We watched as Gracie entered the frame, lugging a heavy rolling grocery sack behind her up the icy walkway.

"Wait. She has a baby?" Anderson asked in alarm. "There wasn't anything about a baby in the file."

I suppressed a growl as a familiar stunted black snout poked out from under her scarf.

"That's just her pug. She's overly attached to it."

I frowned as I watched Gracie haul the bags up to the porch. She pushed up her skirt and pulled up her tights then adjusted her bra.

Probably because she thinks no one is watching.

I scowled.

I don't feel guilty.

"Gracie and Hudson sitting in a tree …" Jake sang softly under his breath.

"Watch it," I snapped at him.

"K-I-S-S-I—"

"*Shut up,*" I growled at Jake.

"So what's the plan, chief?" Lawrence asked.

"Hudson has to wait for her to call him," Talbot said with a smirk. "Like a good little lapdog. Gracie's collecting quite the menagerie."

"Do not compare me to Pugnog," I growled.

Jake slapped the table, doubled over laughing. "Is its name really Pugnog?"

"Yes."

"Dude."

I worked my jaw.

"I am not letting this chance slip through my fingers." I grabbed my motorcycle helmet. "I'll be back later. I'm going to a Christmas party."

Chapter 6

GRACIE

"**N**o. No no no no."

I looked out of the upstairs bathroom window. I was quickly trying to shave my legs so that I could wear the dress I had planned on for tonight.

My mom's holiday party was in full swing.

"Gracie!" my mom shouted up the stairs. "Gracie, I need you to make sure the spinach turnovers aren't burning."

"Coming, Mom," I yelled as I desperately washed off the shaving cream.

Okay, so there were a couple stripes of dark hair I had missed, but I wasn't Kelly. I didn't have nothing to do all day except pamper myself, dream up ways to cheat, and destroy historic dresses.

"This was supposed to be a hallucination you made up," I muttered to myself as I raced downstairs.

"Gracie, the spinach puffs."

I ignored my mother and ran to the front door, catching Hudson as he was heading up the walkway, motorcycle helmet swinging in one hand, long shadow cast by the street-light darkening freshly fallen snow. Hudson's dark hair was trimmed short at the neck and fell in longer locks over his forehead.

"You," I hissed, "cannot be here."

Hudson dipped his head down. In the Christmas lights that decorated my parents' huge Victorian house, his eyes seemed almost luminous.

I shivered.

You made a deal with the devil.

Then the devil needed to remove himself.

Large hands encircled my waist, making me squeak.

"You didn't call me."

"I did not call you because I'm not ready for you to be here," I said through gritted teeth.

My second cousin and her new husband gawked at me and Hudson as they walked past us to the front door.

"You need to leave now."

Hudson tipped my chin up, the stiff leather of the motor-cycle glove rough on my chin.

"Where's the girl who was going to give me a hand job in a crowded bus? I don't want weak soldiers."

I glanced back at the house.

Through the large front-room windows, I could see everyone congratulating Kelly and James, gushing about the wedding, hinting at babies to come next Christmas.

Hudson narrowed his eyes.

"Shock and awe."

I nodded and straightened.

"I can't hear you," he said, voice softly mocking.

"Shock and awe."

"Good girl."

"Just give me a minute," I mumbled.

He let me hurry past him into the warm house.

"The spinach puffs are burning," my mom said when she saw me.

I am taking charge of my life.

"Sorry," I said. "A … uh … friend of mine stopped by unexpectedly."

"Was it Muriel?" my mother asked as I raced to the kitchen, feeling flighty and nervous about what I was about to do. There was no going back once I let Hudson inside.

I scooped the steaming pastries onto a platter decorated with scenes from the Grinch.

"No," I squeaked as I headed back to the living room. "It's a male friend."

"A male friend? What male?" my mother demanded.

"Holy St. Nick, Santa came early!" I heard my cousin Violet drunkenly whoop to shrieks of delight of my other cousins.

I raced into the foyer in time to see Hudson push his way into the house.

In his motorcycle gear, heavy boots, and black scarf that half obscured his mouth and nose, he clashed with the cheery Christmas décor—the garland winding up the stair banister, the vintage hand-carved Santa's reindeer, and the dancing Santa statue that greeted people on one side of the door with a Christmas tune.

My family, attracted to the drama, crowded around the doorways that led to the foyer. Hudson slowly unwound the scarf around his neck.

I cleared my throat. "There is someone I'd like for you all to meet."

Backbone. Show a backbone.

I straightened up, still clutching the heavy platter.

"Family, this is Hudson. I invited him to stop by the Christmas party tonight."

"Ooh la la!"

Several of my cousins were snapping photos of him and me.

"Thank you for coming, Hudson. Would you like a spinach puff?" I shoved the tray at him.

Those pale eyes flicked down to the platter then back up to my face.

"No." There was a scowl stamped on his mouth.

"I'll take one," my drunk uncles slurred, crowding around for a snack.

My family was on the shorter side, and Hudson towered over them as they crowded around him. Collar on his leather motorcycle jacket popped up, he surveyed the decorated room.

He only gave one-word answers or grunts when my family tried to talk to him. He didn't smile or act friendly or even offer his hand for a handshake like a normal man would do when he was meeting his girlfriend's family for the first time. Somehow his body language had shifted, making him give off even more of a fuck-you vibe.

"Um, so ... is that, like, your boyfriend?" Piper asked me.

"I don't do relationships," Hudson said, slamming the motorcycle helmet down on an antique side table. "I just hook up with her on the regular."

I clutched the platter of slightly too-brown spinach puffs.

Hudson flicked the nose of a Rudolph clock that was hanging on the wall.

"Disgustingly cute house. Got anything to drink?"

"Sure. I'll make you a drink." Ducking my head down, I hurried over to the wet bar, thinking that I'd made a terrible mistake.

Hudson followed me.

"Do you want an elftini or a candy-cane mojito?"

"I don't want any of your Christmas shit," he said loudly. "Just give me a scotch."

"Oh. Okay," I said, feeling frazzled.

The dark-brown liquor sloshed in the glass as I handed it to Hudson.

He downed it in one go and handed it back to me.

You wanted an asshole, I reminded myself.

Still.

My parents pushed their way through the crowd of my extended family, confusion and concern on their faces.

My inner neglected teenage self was thrilled to finally be the center of their attention.

"Gracie didn't tell us she was bringing a boyfriend," my dad said, blinking rapidly behind his glasses.

"He's a man friend," Granny Murray crowed from where she was emptying scotch into a mug that read Let Me Make Your Nose Glow Bright.

"I'm Rob, Gracie's father." My dad stuck out his hand. "Nice to meet you."

Hudson ignored his hand and focused on my mom.

"Guess Gracie gets her great tits from you."

My mother made an indignant noise while Granny Murray cackled.

"Those are fake, sonny. Gracie gets those milk duds from me." The elderly woman reached for her blouse buttons.

"Gran, please leave your shirt on," I said loudly.

I saw the briefest crack in Hudson's façade, and alarm peeked through.

He squashed it.

"Gracie, can we talk to you privately?" my parents said in hushed tones.

Though my original plan was to waft Hudson under Kelly's nose like a pan of fresh peppermint bark brownies, it turned out there was an added bonus for having him as my fake boyfriend. I was now the belle of the ball. Well, Christmas party.

I followed my parents into the kitchen.

"Grace O'Brien, what has gotten into you?" my mother declared. "I don't want you dating someone like Hudson."

"You don't want me dating anyone at all," I said snidely before I could stop the words.

My parents had forbidden me from dating until I was eighteen, not that guys were that interested in me. I liked to sit in my room and read or sew and listen to audio books. I had had exactly two boyfriends before James, and Kelly had slept with both of them. Before the cheating, they had been fairly bland, vanilla guys, picked because I knew my parents would approve of them and, I had thought, Kelly wouldn't be attracted to them.

"This Hudson is all wrong for you," my father insisted.

My mom nodded. "He rides a motorcycle, and he isn't wearing a button-down shirt to a holiday party."

"Does he even have a job?" my father demanded.

"He works odd labor jobs. He used to be in the military," I added.

"An officer?"

"I don't believe he went to college."

"You don't know anything about this man." My father shook his head.

"What will the neighbors say?" my mother wailed.

"They'll probably think Hudson is Kelly's boyfriend," Granny Murray said loudly, coming into the kitchen. "Need some ice for this scotch."

"Mom, this is a crisis," Bethany said to her mother.

"Why, because my granddaughter finally has a piece of ass worth writing home about?" Granny Murray demanded.

"I know you're still upset about losing James," my mom began, pressing her hands together.

"You mean James cheating on me?" I asked, raising an eyebrow.

"Gracie, watch your tone with your mother," my father begged.

"Rebound relationships are beneath you," my mother scolded. "You need to try harder for a boyfriend. A real boyfriend."

"Maybe I'll just steal James back," I snapped.

"Gracie, don't say that. I didn't raise a home-wrecker."

Oh, the irony!

I pulled a tray of mini quiches out of the oven.

"I need to refresh the appetizers," I said, heading back out into the dining room, just in time to see James and Hudson sizing each other up.

James, in his Christmas sweater vest that I had made him, was puffed up to his full height, which was no match for Hudson's six-five.

James was blustering. "We all care about Gracie very much …"

Liar.

"We just need to know what kind of man she's dating. So I'm not going to ask you again. Tell us about yourself."

Hudson's wintery gaze slid over my family.

For once, a family party was dead quiet as people waited to hear what Hudson had to say for himself.

"All you need to know about me is that Gracie doesn't have any complaints ... if you know what I mean."

"Then I guess you can leave." James put his hands on his waist.

Hudson stared up at the ceiling, then his eyes flicked to mine. His posture was insolent. Bored.

"What the hell were you on when you thought it was a good idea to waste your time with him?" James turned to chastise me.

"Probably could say the same about you," Hudson drawled.

All the stress, the needling comments from Hudson in the bus, were worth it just to see my ex-fiancé's face fall and his smug expression melt like a gingerbread house in front of the fire.

Hudson unzipped the heavy leather motorcycle jacket.

Kelly's attention was glued to Hudson. Her eyes, framed by oversized fake lashes, followed his hands as he slowly pulled the zipper down, down.

Kelly's tongue darted out to lick her lips.

Hudson mimicked the gesture.

James noticed it, too, and his eyes widened in alarm.

"At least tell us where you're from," James barked at Hudson.

Hudson didn't look at him, his gaze still locked on Kelly, who made a big show of adjusting her top and sticking her chest out.

"I'm from Maplewood Falls, but the Gulch side. I went to Nixon High."

"The *bad* high school," Kelly said it like it was the name of an exclusive club.

"Then you're really not good enough for Gracie." James was bombastic.

Hudson tipped his head back and rolled his shoulders.

"Gracie thinks I'm good enough to come all over her face."

What the—

The color drained from my father's cheeks.

"Gracie?"

His elderly mother gave me a scandalized look. "Robert, I thought you raised your daughters better than this."

My cousins were snickering. One of them was streaming the whole dumpster fire to the family group chat for those like Dakota who hadn't been able to get off of work in time for the party.

My face burned.

Hudson gave me a feral look. His teeth were sharp. He was going for the kill.

It was then I realized I had made a grievous error in hiring Hudson Wynter to be my fake boyfriend.

He had, in fact, been correct.

I couldn't handle it.

"Your daughter's a little porn star," Hudson said, deep voice carrying around the packed room.

I felt my throat constricting.

Stop, I mouthed.

"James, you must have been doing nothing but missionary with Gracie," Hudson said in that same insolent, bored tone. "When I first had her on her knees in the back of my truck, she would barely let me eat her out. But I need a little more excitement when I'm fucking some girl." His eyes locked with Kelly's. My sister was practically panting.

"I showed her some porn flicks, told her to act like that, you know, really make it interesting. I slapped her pussy when she put on a good performance. That got her in the Christmas spirit." He smirked. "I took her hard, doggy style in the back of my truck. And you should see her suck my cock. She's a greedy little slut." He turned those snow demon eyes on my ex.

"I broke her out of the bad habits you put in her, James."

My cousins were whispering to each other behind their hands, and my aunts were looking at me in horror.

The room was too hot, too stuffy. There were too many people.

I cannot do this.

I dumped the tray onto a nearby table and raced outside, gasping in the cold winter air, the tears freezing on my face.

"That was humiliating," I sobbed to myself, digging my fists in my eyes, trying to force the tears to stop.

I was never going to be able to show my face again. This was so much worse than when everyone saw James cheating on me. What had I done? It really was a deal with the devil.

The side door opened then slammed. Heavy boots crunched in the snow.

"Gracie."

"I hate you. Go away."

Hudson stepped around to face me, crowding my personal space.

I stepped back, but his large hand settled on my waist, trapping me against him.

"Don't pull away from me." His voice was laced with warning. "Your family is watching."

I sniffled.

He dipped his head forward to whisper in my ear.

"You promised you could handle this."

"I lied," I sobbed. "This is terrible."

"Wrong. It's going perfectly," he crooned.

"You're awful, and you said dirty things. You were mean to me; you humiliated me. Why is Kelly going to want a man who treats people like shit? You're not just an asshole, you're a dick."

"Are you kidding me?" He tilted my head up to look at him. "All women want a man who treats them like shit."

"No, they don't," I protested.

"You're dripping wet thinking about me holding you down, fucking you raw, and calling you a slut." His tone was almost clinical.

I was glad of the dark so he couldn't see the heat in my face.

"After that little performance, all your sister is going to be able to think about is me coming on her face," he said in the dark. "Trust me. I understand how people work."

He wiped the tears off my cheeks, the leather of the gloves rough.

"That's not how I work," I warbled out.

His eyes narrowed.

"This is war, Sugarplum. We die like men."

He released me then stalked back into the house.

I followed, feeling stunned.

My family, who had been watching the whole thing from the windows, pretended like they were just getting more hors d'oeuvres and asking my mother for the spinach puff recipe.

Hudson stomped through the house and grabbed the motorcycle helmet.

"Not staying for dinner?" Granny Murray asked him, waggling her eyebrows.

"I have to go to work."

"Let me guess. You're a custodian," James sneered.

Hudson narrowed his gaze. "Someone has to clean up the trash."

My fake boyfriend tucked the helmet under his arm, shifted his weight, and tilted his head up at Kelly.

"You might want to level up, James," he said, "or she might pull a Gracie and go find herself a real man."

James gave me a dirty look.

Hudson zipped up his jacket and headed to the door. Before he left, he bent down to whisper in my ear, "*Man the fuck up.*"

The front door slammed, making me jump.

"Where," Kelly drawled to me, "did you ever find Hudson?"

"Nowhere," I said, eyes downcast as I grabbed an empty tray.

I hurried past my family to hide in my safe space, the kitchen, and plot how to remove Hudson from my life completely.

Because otherwise? I wasn't going to survive this Christmas.

Chapter 7

HUDSON

The private plane was waiting for me when I arrived at the small regional airport that supported Maplewood Falls.

It was not a lie I'd told Gracie's family. I did have to go to work.

I nodded to the pilot and flight crew then took a seat.

No, this wasn't my plane. A kid from the Gulch didn't grow up to be the type of man who owned his own plane. However, he could grow up to be the type of man who had clients who owned their own jets. I settled back in my seat, opened up my laptop, and typed in my password for the encrypted message program.

Did I feel bad about what had transpired at the O'Brien holiday party?

Not at all.

I had an in with the inner sanctum of Gracie's family. Sure, Gracie might have been upset, but I had preyed on her insecurity about her sister. She wasn't just going to walk away now that she had seen firsthand that her sister would have dragged me up to her bedroom and had her way with me if she could have.

I would have stayed to see it play out, but one of my teams had had a big break on another contract. Svensson PharmaTech, a major pharmaceutical company, had hired us to find evidence that one of their employees was selling top secret corporate information to foreign nationals.

A car was waiting for me when the plane landed.

It was a quick drive to the warehouse where my employees had been sorting through the literal tons of trash we'd recovered from the dump. Gracie's family might sneer at a man who worked a labor job, but there was no better way of digging out someone's secrets than if you had access to their trash.

After commandeering his household trash from the last eighteen months, Layla, a woman I'd served with in the military and then hired because she was organized and competent, had finally found what we were looking for. She waved me to a laptop, where a USB drive was plugged in.

"We ran a recovery program and found evidence of contact between the person of interest and a member of the Chinese government. We have a name, and we just ID'd the recipient. We also," she said, leading me to another station, where several people were meticulously piecing together scraps of shredded documents, "found the remains of a receipt from a deposit made to an account at a local credit union. Forensic financial analysis has determined the account has been closed, but Skylar created a fake Tinder account, went on a long and boring date with a bank executive, and was able to access his system long enough to pull records of transactions in the account."

"Thank you for your sacrifice," I said to Skylar, Layla's girlfriend, who had the body of a supermodel and the mind and constitution of a Cold War spy.

"I told her she owes me a ring for Christmas," Skylar replied.

"Obviously, the client can't give that information to the authorities. However, between the USB and the receipt, this is enough information for our client to get a warrant to have an official paper trail," Layla said loudly.

"Why don't you call the client with me, and let's tell them the good news," I told Layla.

The Svensson PharmaTech rep thanked us profusely when we showed them the evidence. After assuring them that the physical evidence would be delivered by hand that night by Layla personally, they wired over the money.

"Nicely done," I said, shaking Layla's hand when the money cleared our account.

"That's a holiday wrap!" Skylar fist-bumped me.

"Do you need help on the EnerCheck Inc. contract?" Layla asked as she put on her coat.

"No."

Layla raised an eyebrow. "That's not a confident no."

"You have your holiday plans," I reminded her.

"I can cancel."

"She cannot," Skylar said loudly.

"It's just one girl," I told Layla.

"I think you mean grown woman who's been leading you and C-Team around by the nose while eating copious amounts of cheese." Layla smirked.

"It's just because all my best people were focused on the Svensson PharmaTech contract."

"Flattery doesn't close accounts." Layla put her hands on her hips.

"Go enjoy your ski trip. And if you see a certain banker there …"

"She's not supposed to be working!"

"Please." Layla snorted. "I know you and Demarcus have a bet to see if you or I get the banker's passwords off him first."

I shook my head. "Enjoy your Christmas."

"Let me know if I need to swoop in and save the day," she sang as she accepted the locked case from Demarcus.

I headed up to the rooftop to look out over the industrial park where I'd set up shop.

Most people thought of hacking as something you did in a fancy war room with lots of blinking lights and frantic typing. However, brute forcing your way into a system wasn't how it was done. Hacking was all social engineering, a scavenger hunt, a monthslong process of carefully advancing your way past layers of security to reach the treasure trove.

Well it was months long in cases like the Svenssons' PharmaTech contract. For the EnerCheck Inc. contract, I should have had what I needed weeks ago.

Dammit, Gracie.

Usually, I didn't get directly involved in the project, but I needed to close this account. Gracie must have the information I needed on her laptop. Once she was used to me being around, I would wait until I saw her type in her password, memorize it, then while she slept one night, I'd log into her laptop and copy over her data. Done. Mission accomplished, just in time to be home by Christmas.

Not that I celebrated.

I felt the air move before I saw him.

"I am starting to think this job isn't a priority for you." Grayson Richmond stepped up beside me at the rusted railing on the roof deck.

"I told you we're ramping up."

"It's December. I've had to listen to 'Have Yourself a Merry Little Christmas' five hundred times already, and I don't go shopping, don't listen to the radio, and don't have a Christmas-obsessed girlfriend. It's everywhere. You promised me in July that this was a slam dunk, that you could do it with your eyes closed."

"This job has actually turned into one of my trickier ones," I admitted. "EnerCheck is locked down."

"It's run by frat boys and some girl," Grayson countered. "Are you even sure there's anything there?"

"Family businesses always have exploitations and skeletons in the closet," I assured him.

"I need this deal closed by—"

"December twenty-third, yes, I know," I told him. "Have I ever failed you?"

"There's a first time for everything."

"I'm in with her now," I told him. "Give me a week."

"I've heard that one before."

There was a pause.

Grayson stared out over the dark industrial park. It was down on its luck, like the Gulch of Maplewood Falls. It was just how I liked it. Fewer potential witnesses that way.

I had met Grayson over fifteen years ago and kept in touch. He'd been my first client back when he was building his empire by any means necessary.

I appreciated Grayson's take-no-prisoners attitude, his single-minded dedication to success. That was how he had become a billionaire. I was cold-blooded, but Grayson was ruthless, though not without reason. If you did your job to his satisfaction, he was generous. Fail, and he'd end you.

I also appreciated how he wasn't emotional about jobs he hired me to complete.

Give me a corporate espionage contract any day over someone trying to find evidence that their mistress was cheating on them. Yes, you read that right.

"You're not falling for her, are you?" Grayson asked.

Are you fucking kidding me?

I didn't fall in love period, especially not with someone like Gracie O'Brien. I pulled out an envelope from my jacket and waved it at him. "Just for that, I'm not giving you this."

"What the hell is that?"

"I came across this on another job. Looks like the woman your brother is dating is a ticking time bomb. She's got a track record of unsavory and self-serving behavior." I handed him the envelope. "Maybe he does his due diligence and figures it out, maybe not, but best to cut these things off at the knees before it gets too far."

Grayson was wary.

"Hey, I have little brothers too," I told him softly.

He snorted and opened the envelope and pocketed the flash drive.

"I can never figure out your motives."

"The best way to get rich is to do a good turn for an even richer man and take your cut," I quipped.

"Uh-huh," Grayson said.

The unspoken words between us:

He was going to fuck me up if I didn't deliver.

Chapter 8

GRACIE

"**S**o what the hell was that?" Dakota asked when I answered the phone the next morning.

I was making biscuits, so many biscuits, enough to feed an army. I had, on a whim, asked Dakota if she could talk, but since this was the Christmas season of me making terrible decisions, I realized belatedly that I should have just chosen an audiobook.

"I take it that my assumptions were correct and Bella and Violet were, in fact, live streaming the holiday party," I said with a sigh.

"You mean live streaming the preamble to a porno."

"What the—"

"God!" Dakota fanned herself. "That was so fucking hot. Where did you even find him?"

I looked around furtively.

It was early in the morning. I didn't hear anyone else in the historic house. I almost typed in the words in the chat then remembered what Hudson had said.

Nothing in writing.

I lowered my voice, cupping my hand around the phone receiver.

"*I hired him.*"

"He's an actor?"

"I think he just needs the money. He works as a custodian."

"I didn't know they made custodians that hot."

"*Keep your voice down.*"

"Oh my god, his eyes as he talked about taming you." Dakota swooned.

I ground my teeth in annoyance.

"It wasn't hot. It was demeaning."

"I mean yeah, sure. But a guy like that you don't want to do missionary with. You want hair pulling and dirty talk and getting fucked in his truck. I practically squirted when he said that. Also," she snickered, "Kelly is so jelly!"

"I can't even … This is … Argh! He's so … so …"

"Alpha? Assertive. Cocky. Rough?" Dakota was practically drooling.

"*Male.*"

"That too," Dakota purred.

She motioned me closer to the screen and whispered, "Does this arrangement come with conjugal visits?"

"Gosh no."

"Boo."

The ancient house creaked as my family woke up.

"Got to go."

I hated Hudson and hated even more that apparently he was right. Women were falling all over themselves, panties raining from the sky, just because he had said he liked fucking a woman doggy style in the back of his pickup truck.

I angrily cut the ice-cold butter into the flour.

Not me. I did not like bad boys. I wanted a grown man with a dad bod and a 401(k). I didn't do adventurous sex, and I didn't do relationship drama. Finding James screwing my sister under the Christmas tree notwithstanding, the most drama I'd had in any relationship ever was this fake one with Hudson blowing in like a winter storm, riling everyone up, being all possessive alpha male and talking down to me and mansplaining what women actually want. Which apparently is being called a slut while a hot guy fucks their brains out.

I cursed as I realized I was overworking the biscuit dough. I hoped it would still rise. I put it in the fridge to chill it out.

I needed to chill out.

Hiring Hudson was a mistake. I should have told him right then and there when he had followed me outside last night that the deal was off, and he could kindly take his big dick energy, his motorcycle, and himself on out of my life.

"You always let yourself get bossed around," I scolded myself as I started forming the sausage patties. Now I was angry and out of sorts. Nat King Cole blared from the stereo. I flipped the station to punk rock.

"Honestly, Gracie. It's December. Let me have my Christmas carols," my mother insisted, coming into the kitchen and flipping the radio back. "First, that man that you scraped up out of the trash and brought home, and now rock music."

"Someone get the smelling salts." I set the cast-iron skillet on the stove.

"And that attitude."

I gritted my teeth as I stacked neat round sausage patties on a plate.

"All of Hudson's big dick energy is rubbing off on her," my cousin Bella said with a giggle, coming into the kitchen and pouring out the last of the coffee.

"Pot's empty, Gracie," she said.

"I'll make some more in a minute." Then added, "Or you could."

"I'll wait."

"We can talk about your new man," her sister Violet said, hopping up on a stool.

"Hubba-hubba!"

"I'm so jealous."

"He is literally sex on a stick."

"He's not good for her," my mother scolded her nieces. "I need you two to back me up here."

My cousins just giggled.

"I'm one hundred percent team Hudson."

Kelly was wearing a robe that had Bride embroidered on the back in pink and gold letters, made with toxic positivity by her only sister.

My mother had always insisted that a woman be fully dressed when not in her bedroom. I had always followed the rules. My sister had not. Therefore she got to run around in a robe while my mother still acted like the biggest scandal last Christmas was not that Kelly had been caught with my fiancé but that I had been downstairs in my pajamas.

Kelly scoffed. "I just can't believe that he's actually her boyfriend."

Violet giggled. "He did say they weren't dating. He was just f—" My mother gave her a dirty look.

"They were just getting it on."

"In the back of his truck," Belle added, and she and her sister erupted in more giggles.

"Gracie?" Kelly gave me an assessing look. "I don't believe it. I bet he's some street person you gave twenty bucks to, to try to get him to show up and ruin my big moment. Right, James?" she called to my ex, who was grabbing orange juice out of the fridge.

More of my cousins had wandered into the kitchen, unable to resist the siren call of drama.

"Do you want any help?" Connie asked sweetly.

Sure. I needed help three hours ago when I started cooking.

"Nah, I've got it."

"Hudson didn't smell like a street person," Bella said, wrinkling her nose.

"He smelled divine," Violet swooned.

You don't care that they're talking about him like he's a piece of fried chicken. You don't even like Hudson, I reminded myself as I heated up the big cast-iron skillet on the stove.

"Prove it," my sister demanded. "Prove that you actually are sleeping with him."

"What do you want her to do? Throw down a used condom?" Connie asked, rolling her eyes.

"Text him."

Just tell them you broke up.

If having Hudson tell everyone fake stories about having sex with me in his car was bad, if everyone in my family thought I had paid for a fake boyfriend to steal my sister's spotlight, I would really never live it down.

I wiped my hands on my apron and pulled out my phone.

Gracie: *Hey Hudson, my cousins don't believe the story about the truck.*

I waited, unsure if he was going to text back. This might be against the rules, or it could be counted as part of the scam.

A scam that you need to end.

I didn't have the stomach for it. It hadn't even been twenty-four hours, and I was spent.

Hudson: *I'm still cleaning the back seat. You squirted everywhere.*

"Oh my gawd!" Violet crowed.

"How do we know it's him?" Kelly said with a scowl.

"Even if it is him," James said, "Hudson could just be a liar. Where does he live, Gracie? Where does he work? What kind of car does he drive?"

"He drives a Ford F-150," I said because that was the only brand of manly car that I knew.

"What year?"

"I don't know."

"What does it look like?" James demanded.

"It's green."

"Hudson has a green car?" Connie said in disbelief.

"It's a dark forest green," I backtracked. "Almost gray."

I was sweating. Did they make trucks that color? Who knew?

"What does the front look like?" James insisted, drawing the attention of my uncles who had wandered into the kitchen, drawn by the smell of biscuits and sausage.

"Did it have a big grille like this?" Uncle Eddie asked, miming with his hand. "Was the center console sort of swoopy shaped?"

I nodded. "Sure."

"It's the limited edition 2018," he said confidently.

"Sounds right," I said weakly, feeling like I was digging a hole for myself that was also quickly filling with water.

My mom handed Uncle Eddie an apple and sent him on his way.

"Breakfast will be ready soon."

"I think she's making this whole thing up. Gracie could just be texting with a chatbot or something," my sister declared.

Gracie: *They want photographic evidence it's you.*
Hudson: …

My phone dinged with an incoming photo.

"Oh my lord," I said as the photo finished downloading. Wasn't it illegal to send photos like that?

It was … well it wasn't almost porn. It was literally porn.

The photo was of Hudson, nude. I mean, I assumed it was. I hadn't seen him naked, but there was what looked like a military tattoo of a sigil with Latin script on the right side of his washboard abs, partially covered by his hands that were grasping the biggest, thickest cock I had ever seen.

Not that I watched porn, but even if I had, I doubted anything on Pornhub would match that weapon in Hudson's hands.

And this is why I needed to call it off.

Connie grabbed the phone and immediately started screaming.

Was it too early for a drink? Didn't 1950s housewives start drinking at like nine in the morning?

"I see why you had to parade him around," Granny Murray said, taking the phone and making an appreciative noise. "If you need a sex pad, you just let me know, girlie. I'll clear out of the in-law suite."

Violet and Bella screeched, holding on to each other and jumping around.

"What in the world?" their mother said as she and my other aunts rushed into the kitchen.

The phone was passed around. Appreciative noises were made.

"Kelly, are you so envious?" Connie teased my sister.

She snatched the phone.

"Is James that big?" Aunt Sandy asked me.

My mom glared at her sister-in-law, who shrugged with a smirk.

"She's the only one who knows."

James gave me an ugly look.

This was out of control. Completely out of control.

"And to think Kelly was bragging about James's American Express Black Card." Violet snorted.

Did she mean the company card? That I'd been on the phone for months trying to get from him? Sure. Okay.

"Can you text this to me?" my cousin begged.

"No."

"Text it to *me*. I'm the one who just got rid of my cheating ball and chain," Granny Murray declared.

"If you keep phrasing it like that, people will think you killed that poor man," Granny Astelle harrumphed, her cane dragging on the floor as she stomped into the kitchen, which apparently was no longer my safe space.

"I wish I had," Granny Murray stated.

"Do you want to see it, Grandma Astelle?" Connie asked as the elderly woman, hair perfectly coifed, slowly made her way to a chair at the kitchen table.

Astelle stared down her nose at the phone.

Connie gulped and handed it back to me.

She stomped her cane on the tile floor.

"This is absurd. Where is my son? Bethany, you need to control your daughter. One expects this type of behavior from lesser members of society, not from my granddaughters. You're better than this, Gracie. And you wanted to wear my mother's dress. She's rolling over in her grave right now."

I felt sick and ashamed.

"I'm almost glad Kelly destroyed it, if it was going to someone who's receiving lewd photos from a man who refused to officially court her."

Grandma Astelle was right. I was better than this.

And it ended now.

Chapter 9

HUDSON

A lesser man might have felt some kind of way sending a photo like that, but it was all part of my plan.

I'd had those photos saved up, ready to fire off if I felt like my hold on Gracie was slipping and I needed to reel her in.

That was when I'd thought that I was going to have to woo her, make her think she was falling in love with me, that I was the bad boy she was going to mold into the perfect boyfriend.

Thank god for dysfunctional families. It made my job a lot easier if I could keep her off-balance, keep her focused on her sister, and not her feelings for me.

Still, the pictures had come in handy.

"Let's try to close this contract up by the end of this week," I told my brothers. The security company was flush with cash from the last payout. Plus Svensson PharmaTech had recommended us to several other companies, and now I had contracts lined up for the first half of the year. Though Christmas was my least favorite holiday, I couldn't deny that it was going to be a good one.

So long as I delivered on Gracie.

My phone chimed.

"Does she want another nudie pic?" Jake snickered.

I hit him lightly on the back of the head then swiped open Gracie's message and scowled.

Gracie: *We need to talk.*

I dialed her number.

"Are you alone?" I asked in a voice that promised mind-blowing sex, just in case her family was listening.

"Yes," she said.

I let my voice grow cold.

"Then don't text me. We went over the rules," I reprimanded, stalking away from my brothers.

"Sorry," she said. I could practically see her tugging self-consciously at her skirt like she was doing last night.

"We need to talk. Verbally."

"I am not your boyfriend, Sugarplum. I don't do those little mind games women like to play where they go, 'We need to talk' then let their boyfriend stew for hours wondering what it's about," I said in a mocking tone. "So you can tell me what you want to talk about, or you can get lost."

"Fine," she hissed through her teeth. "We need to talk about the fact that I'm firing you."

Fuck.

You pushed her too far.

"You are not firing me," I spat.

My brothers looked over in alarm.

Anderson mouthed, *What the fuck, Hudson?*

"I can pay you for your time spent thus far," she said like she was some corporate HR rep giving me my walking papers.

Double fuck.

"Where should I meet you?"

"Are you free now?" she asked.

"Where, Gracie?"

"The Nutmeg Café."

"Meet me there in ten minutes," I barked.

"Ooh, Hudson's getting fired." Lawrence drawled. "I'm shocked. You should have had me do this job."

"Fuck you."

"With a charming attitude like that, is it surprising his fake relationship lasted all of twenty-four hours?" Talbot deadpanned.

I could kill my brothers.

"Maybe you could be ever so slightly nicer," Anderson called after me as I stormed out to my motorcycle.

It had taken me months to get to this point. I finally had a lucky break, and now Gracie had cold feet. I wouldn't stand for it. She wasn't firing me; she wasn't backing out. We would proceed according to plan.

Gracie was sitting at a small table in a back corner of the café, Pugnog on her lap, nursing an oversized mug of coffee festooned with snowmen marshmallows, when I stalked in. She looked up at me, wide-eyed, as I slammed the motorcycle helmet on the table.

Maybe Anderson was right, and I had been a little bit too harsh with her.

But I was so close to my goal.

Stay calm.

"Cold feet?" I asked, pulling the chair out across from her.

I expected her to launch into a tirade against me, like many of my more emotional clients liked to do when they felt like things were out of their control and they didn't understand what was going on.

Instead Gracie laid her palms flat on the table.

"I think firing might have been too harsh of a word," she said carefully. "It's not you. It's me."

I raised an eyebrow.

"Sometimes clichés are useful," she said, making a face.

"Sometimes they're annoying."

She looked down at her coffee. "You were right," she admitted, "about a lot of things."

"Oh?" I leaned back in my chair and crossed my arms.

"Apparently all of the women in my family would happily spit on Susan B. Anthony's grave if it meant getting it on doggy style with you in the back of your truck," she grumbled.

"Imagine that." I let a sly grin form.

"Especially after that photo." She scowled. "Don't look so smug. Who took that photo anyway? Did you do a photo shoot?"

"My brother."

"And I thought my sister and I had a fucked-up relationship," she said, shaking her head.

I bit back a grin.

"Anyways, I think it's too much. I can't keep the lies straight," she said quickly, lowering her voice. "My sister thinks I hired you, James is on to me, my grandmother is going to disown me—"

"No way. Your grandmother loved me."

"That's Granny Murray, not Grandma Astelle. She is the daughter of my great-grandma Cecelia, whose dress my sister destroyed. Astelle is the youngest daughter. The middle sister got their mom's engagement ring and pawned it while Grandma Astelle got the dress and let Kelly destroy it and then throw away any scraps in the dumpster so that no one with sewing skills could save them. Her eldest sister got all the recipes, and those are still in the family, letting you know that if you want to save family heirlooms, give them to the eldest daughter. Not that I'm bitter or anything." She took a deep breath.

"Spoken like someone who needs a little revenge in her life," I said after a moment.

"I can't. I'm not a soldier, and I'm going to crack under the pressure," she pleaded.

I took her hands.

Be nice.

Well niceish.

"Sugarplum, James isn't on to you. James is trying to get in your head and destroy your self-esteem so that you'll take him back."

"No, he's not," she scoffed. "He doesn't even think I'm attractive."

"I'm going to tell you a secret about men. Now, I'm betraying the bro code to do this," I said smoothly, "so I hope you appreciate my sacrifice."

"Uh-huh."

"Women think that men are after a pretty face and nice tits. That's not true."

"Then why do they all want supermodels?" Gracie argued.

"You're looking at it backward. Men want the super-models because they think all the other guys do. It's all one big territorial dispute. Every monkey wants the high-status banana. James now perceives you as a higher-value item because he thinks a higher-status male stole what he thinks of as his woman."

"He slept with my sister," she countered.

"He did it because he thought he could get away with it. But you're not going to let that happen, are you? Shock and awe."

"I'm not like you," she said desperately. "I fall apart."

"You're not falling apart," I assured her. "You just forgot your motivation. Tell me about discovering the affair."

Gracie made a disgusted noise and looked away.

"It was so humiliating to find my fiancé and my little sister doing *that* in front of the Christmas tree. What was worse was that my parents insisted we still have Christmas morning."

"So you burned down the Christmas tree and salted the nativity scene with your rage?" I asked.

"No, I baked cinnamon rolls and opened up my usual gifts of socks and regifted knickknacks."

"Now you finally grew a backbone and want to burn the place down."

"No. I'm just trying to … I don't know." She looked down at her coffee.

"I can break up their marriage," I promised her. "That humiliation you felt? I can make them both feel it tenfold. I can make your parents despise them, make your family hate them, make it so they never show their faces at a holiday party again. And I can make you the most beloved member of your family."

Take the bait.

"That seems …" She played with the mug in her hands.

"Like justice?"

"More like nuclear revenge." She wrinkled her nose.

"What's the point of revenge if you're not going to leave a smoking crater when you're done?"

Gracie chewed on her lip.

"I think maybe I just wanted my family off my back. It gets old, you know—the snide comments about how I'm almost thirty and don't have a boyfriend, how I'm going to be so old when I ever do get married that I'll only have one kid."

"If you wanted to impress your family," I said, "then you could have hired a man in a suit and had him pretend to be a billionaire. But you wanted a bad boy."

"I just want …" She shrugged helplessly.

"You want revenge," I said quietly.

"Yeah. I do."

"I want that for you," I crooned.

"You don't even know me. We're not friends." She poked at a marshmallow with her tongue. It was endearing.

And almost made me want to kiss her.

Almost.

"Let's just say I get turned on by wielding justice."

And by girls who lick their lips like that.

"You're like a superhero."

"More like a supervillain for hire."

She took a gulp of her coffee.

"So am I still fired?" I asked.

She shook her head.

"But you still may want to quit."

"Never." I pressed a hand on my chest.

"There's one small wrinkle." She made a face. "You don't happen to have a custom dark-forest-green special edition 2018 Ford F-150, do you?"

The confusion was clear on my face before I could stop it.

"I kind of told my family that was the car where you—where we … uh …"

"Where I fucked you so hard you squirted on the roof of the car?" I pinched the bridge of my nose. "How in the hell am I going to get a car like that?"

Gracie winced.

"My god. You really are bad at this."

Chapter 10

GRACIE

"That didn't go well."

Only I would set out to fire someone then get talked into putting all my trust in a man who had literally called me a slut to my family the night before.

"You have no backbone."

I couldn't lie though. Part of me was thrilled at the prospect of grinding James and Kelly into dust.

After buying another gigantic coffee to go, Hudson had left to try to miracle a green truck, and I had gone back to my parents' house to—you guessed it—cook.

At least I was alone, and the Christmas season was looking a little brighter. Hudson, even though he was rude and antisocial, was in my corner. Sure, I was paying him to be there, but it took the edge off while I had to listen to my sister regale the rest of our family members with her big wedding plans.

Kelly swept into the kitchen. She had taken to only wearing white the last few months and was now in a flowing lacy white knee-length wrap dress.

"Gracie," my sister said haughtily. "Aunt Janet suggested, and I agree, that we should serve pistachio cookies at the cookie bar at my wedding."

"We already have twenty-five different types of cookies," I reminded her, trying to keep the panic out of my voice.

I had a baking schedule planned down to the minute. I couldn't whip up two hundred pistachio cookies. They sounded simple, but it was a multistep process. I had to roast the pistachios, bake shortbread, make chocolate ganache filling, make a different type of chocolate frosting and carefully draw a lattice pattern on each cookie and sprinkle it with crushed pistachios while the chocolate design was cool enough to not run everywhere yet hot enough to adhere to the pistachios. And, of course, do all of the above with no help from anyone.

"It's my wedding," Kelly snapped. "And Aunt Janet thinks it's a good idea. Everyone is expecting them now."

Just say no.

Except I couldn't.

"Okay," I said, feeling harried. "I'll make them."

My earlier festive mood, buoyed by Hudson of all people, had deflated.

A timer beeped, and I pulled the pans of olive cheese bread out of the oven then gave the spinach salad another toss.

"Is lunch ready yet?" my sister asked, inspecting her perfect manicure. "We're supposed to go pick out more

Christmas trees for my wedding welcome party. I don't want to go when it's dark."

"It's almost ready."

The back door to the kitchen that led out to the deck opened. A shadow was cast over the kitchen as a huge man filled the doorway.

Hudson stomped the snow off his boots then stepped inside.

"Hi—uh …" Honey? Babe? Sweetie? None of the pet names sounded right.

"Hi, Hudson," I stammered.

I was a terrible actor.

Hudson wasn't.

He crossed the kitchen in two long steps and slapped my ass, hard, making me yelp in surprise.

"You look cute in that Christmas apron. Wear it tonight. Nothing else."

Kelly sucked in a breath.

Hudson leaned down, his breath hot in my ear.

"You need to act like you're happy we're fucking when I manhandle you, Sugarplum."

He released me and headed for the fridge.

"Lunch is going to be ready soon," I squawked.

I was frazzled and out of sorts. The kitchen was supposed to be my safe space, but it felt claustrophobic and too hot with Hudson filling the room with his arrogance and his maleness.

He slammed the fridge door, beer in hand, and bit the bottle cap off with his teeth.

I watched in horror.

My sister watched in fascination.

I resisted the urge to scold Hudson and tell him to take care of his teeth. He wasn't a five-year-old. He was a grown man—one who wasn't my friend, who I didn't care about.

Hudson locked eyes with me and drained half the beer.

I handed him a dish towel before he could wipe his mouth on his sleeve then pulled the mini sliders out of the oven. I set the large pan on a wood trivet and turned to pull the next one out of the oven.

"Why didn't you kiss her if you two are so into each other?" Kelly demanded. "You barely even touched her."

I almost dropped the pan.

Hudson took another long draught of his beer.

I scuttled away from him, pretending like I needed to check on the tray of condiments and toppings for the sliders.

If he kissed me, I was going to scream, and this whole revenge plan was going to come crashing down like an alcoholic Santa busting through a chimney.

I stared at Hudson, mouth dry as he gave me a predatory gaze, his eyes slowly sweeping down to my kitchen clogs and back up to my sweaty bun.

"Gracie read me the riot act yesterday," Hudson drawled, "and doesn't want her father to watch me tongue fucking his daughter. I'm trying not to act like a wild animal."

He finished off the beer and set it down on the kitchen island.

"Besides, your panties would be ruined if you saw it, and I'm trying to spare you. Gracie tells me you've been wearing your special bridal lingerie, and I wouldn't want to be the one staining those."

"Someone's cocky," my sister said, hand on her hip.

Hudson smirked at her.

Kelly made a big show of fussing with her top. Hudson's eyes tracked the motion.

"Excuse me," I said too loudly. "I need to get lunch on the table."

Neither of them offered to help.

It's part of the plan, I reminded myself.

After all, to actually break up Kelly and James, Hudson was going to have to sleep with my sister.

I felt a little nauseous thinking about him with her.

You just drank too much coffee, I told myself firmly. *It's good if he sleeps with her. Then James can get a taste of his own medicine.*

James and my father were already seated at the long dining room table, pretending to discuss business.

"… think that we should plan on expanding our offerings next quarter," James was saying, "and maybe expand our client base."

"EnerCheck cannot expand our client base," I interjected as I set out the trays of sliders. "Roscoe Energy Solutions made us sign very stringent noncompete clauses. And before you ask, no, we are also not expanding any offerings because we do not have the manpower."

James shot me an ugly look. Normally, I tried to ignore when he made stupid suggestions and just log it in my Festivus book of grievances, but seriously, he was going to tank the company with his incompetence.

"Maybe we could cut off the gravy train and hire some actual employees, or at least make people come into work."

My ex's voice dripped with condescension. "While it's cute you're trying to look after the company, you don't know what you're talking about. So why don't you leave the big decisions to the—"

James let out a little scream, and I jumped as Hudson slammed his fist down on the table, making the dishes rattle.

"Don't talk to my woman like that," Hudson said, voice dangerously soft.

Violet fanned herself.

I hated to admit it, but I was starting to see the appeal of a bad boy.

"Hudson came for lunch," Kelly trilled, walking into the dining room, carrying the salad bowl.

"Oh, Kelly, thank you for making lunch." My father beamed at her as she handed me the salad bowl.

I set it down heavily on the buffet.

My father hurried over to me.

"I know you made lunch, but the therapist said that we need to give Kelly praise for any positive actions," he whispered furtively.

"Yes, that is what the therapist said, Dad," I hissed back. "*When she was ten.* She's a grown woman now."

My dad looked hurt.

I scurried back into the kitchen while my aunts made a big show of giving Hudson the best seat at the table.

My family was already loading their plates when I returned with the remaining trays of olive cheese bread. I'd barely set it down before my cousins were all over it.

I dished myself up two sliders and some spinach salad. Though I loved the olive cheese bread, it was a popular item in my family, so I liked to let everyone else have a piece first.

"Are there any more croutons?" my uncle asked me right as I was about to find a seat.

"I have some extra," I said. "Let me go grab them."

I raced back through the house—historic homes used to put the kitchen all the way in the back—grabbed the dish of extra croutons, and returned to the dining room.

Everyone had already started eating. My food was growing cold. I was used to eating lukewarm food though. I had been raised to be a good hostess, putting the needs of my guests first. It felt good to know that I had at least this one part of my life under control, to be the master of my own universe even if it was just lunch.

"Gracie, is there any more ginger ale?" Aunt Giana called, right as I picked up my plate of food from the buffet. "The punch needs freshening up."

I set the plate down.

"Sure thing. Anyone else need anything from the kitchen?"

"Honey mustard?" my brother asked hopefully.

I came back with the condiments and soda a few minutes later, along with more beers and some chips that I knew my younger cousins were going to request.

Hudson was almost done eating, I noticed. He didn't eat like a refined gentleman. He ate like a soldier, hunched over his food, wolfing it down in large bites.

Before I sat down, I dished him up two more sliders. I even gave him the last slice of olive cheese toast.

"You look hungry," I chirped then gulped as those Ghost of Christmas Past eyes locked on mine.

"Gracie," one of my younger cousins asked, "are there more caramelized onions?"

"I have a few left. Let me …"

"*No.*"

Hudson's deep voice cut through my family's chatter.

"But I—"

"Sit down," he ordered me. The chair next to Hudson scraped as he pushed it out.

"Get the onions yourself," he told my cousin.

My face was hot, and I knew I was red under winter-pale skin. I should have taken Dakota up on her offer to go to that spray tan place, I thought as I sat down, feeling everyone's eyes on me.

"I don't mind," I said softly to him.

"I do. I don't want you up and down in the kitchen. Sit next to me and eat." He put the piece of olive cheese bread on my plate.

"Gracie knows where they are," my cousin started to protest then snapped his mouth closed after one glare from Hudson.

"The onions are in the cast-iron skillet, and he might scrape it," I protested.

Hudson's eyes bored into my teenaged cousin's.

"You scrape that pan, and I'll bash it over your head."

"Yes ... sir," my cousin added for good measure and practically sprinted out of the dining room.

Hudson turned back to his food.

I perched on the far side of my seat, trying to get as far away from my fake boyfriend as possible without it looking like I was terrified to be that close to so much testosterone.

Your family is supposed to think you're in a relationship.

Hudson set me on edge.

There was no way I'd ever be in a relationship with a man like him. I couldn't take the heat.

Hudson was a flaming shot of whisky in a dive bar. I was more of a hot-cocoa-and-marshmallows-on-a-West-Elm-couch type of girl.

I stiffly stabbed a piece of the crisp romaine lettuce with my fork. It was Granny Murray's old Christmas silverware from the fifties. After Granny Murray had finalized her divorce, she'd dumped it all on my mom's doorstep when I got engaged to James. It was supposed to have been my wedding present.

My cousin raced back into the room with the onions in a little glass bowl. He stuck his phone in front of Hudson to show him a photo.

"See? I didn't scrape the pan. "

Hudson grunted.

My father and mother exchanged a concerned look.

"So, Hudson," my mother said in a too-cheery tone. "Where did you two meet?"

"Um ... we ... um ..." I stammered.

Hudson and I hadn't discussed our origin story.

He kicked me under the table before I could launch into a half-baked story about him helping me carry my groceries up to my apartment, which would have been a really good meet-cute except that I lived in a ground-floor unit.

"Gracie and I met in a gas station restroom."

The dining room was so quiet you could hear elf footsteps.

Hudson took a sip of his beer.

I scrunched down in my seat. I had a sinking feeling this was not going to be a wholesome story about how he'd caught me when I slipped on a spilled slushie.

"We hooked up," Hudson said, wiping his mouth with his sleeve. "I didn't know her name."

I handed him a napkin.

"Somehow Gracie tracked me down a few months later. She was convinced she was pregnant."

I inhaled an olive and started coughing.

"Oh my god. Did you all hear that?" Bella said to the live stream that was being broadcast to the rest of my gossip-hungry family that hadn't been able to make the lunch.

"I thought Gracie got fat this summer," Aunt Giana said loudly.

"Obviously, she wasn't pregnant, but"—he possessively grabbed the back of my neck, running his thumb along the vein on the side of my throat—"you know how hysterical women can be."

"Ain't that right!" Uncle Albert said and caught a dirty look from his wife.

"Anyone want some more wine?" my uncle asked meekly.

"I remembered what a good fuck your Gracie was, so we started hooking up again," Hudson finished.

"Just in time for Christmas," I added desperately.

My mother had her hand over her mouth and was staring at a spot on the wall above my head. "Where did I go wrong?"

"I have a list," Granny Astelle said acerbically.

"She just wishes she was young and voluptuous like us," Granny Murray whispered, elbowing me in the side.

My father gave me a pained smile. "So is this what the kids are doing these days?"

"It's just a rebound," Kelly snapped.

"Exactly," James told my father in his I-know-better-than-you-because-I'm-a-man-who-went-to-Princeton voice. "Gracie is throwing a tantrum because her younger sister is getting married before her, and when she realizes she's not getting a rise out of anyone, she'll drop Hudson because he obviously doesn't have anything to offer."

"I hear he has a real nice truck," one of my second cousins remarked.

"We can only hope," my mother said faintly.

"I think it's the bee's knees that Gracie has a rebound hookup," Granny Murray declared. "I'm trying to find myself a hobosexual too."

I spilled my water all down my chin.

Beside me, Hudson made a strangled noise.

"I beg your pardon, a what?" Grandma Astelle said in horror.

"You know. A hot guy who travels from woman to woman, trading sex and masculine energy for food and a warm bed."

"Gracie, you and I are going to have another conversation about this later. I can't have Linda knowing you have a homeless person living with you," my mom said, lowering her voice.

"Don't get your panties all in a bunch, Bethany," Granny Murray stated. "God doesn't give with both hands. A man's not going to have a giant dick, a hot body, and a big bank account. You have to pick one. You read too many of those dirty billionaire romance novels. I should have divorced your father earlier. God help me, but you married someone just like him."

My dad's mouth fell open, and Granny Astelle harrumphed loudly.

"Pro tip," Granny Murray barreled on, "and I know Annedull—"

"It's Astelle."

"—didn't know this, because someone with that bad of an attitude clearly wasn't getting some on the regular, but you should mix the Viagra in his eggs. The protein makes it slow release. Keeps him hard for hours."

"It's a wonder you didn't kill your poor husband."

"Trust me, I thought about it, but someone needed to set the example for these children, and I couldn't do that from jail."

I wanted to crawl under the table and die.

"Do you have any single brothers?" Granny Murray asked Hudson loudly.

He shook his head, looking a little stunned.

He's not your real boyfriend, he's not your real boyfriend, I chanted to myself.

It didn't matter that this lunch was utter humiliation because it wasn't as if a wedding, babies, and a happily ever after was on the line. Hudson wasn't ever going to date, let alone marry me.

We are in our villain season.

"I do not want to talk about this anymore," my mother declared. "This is Christmas. It's about family and making memories. Now, Hudson, it was nice of you to stop by uninvited, but we have Christmas-tree cutting planned, and that doesn't seem like your style."

Thank god. I could lose myself in finding the perfect Christmas trees and take a much-needed breather from Hudson and his stories about what a sexual minx I was.

"Mom, in the spirit of Christmas," Kelly said, voice syrupy sweet, "I think we should invite the less fortunate. Hudson could use some Christmas cheer."

Chapter 11

HUDSON

"**W**here's this famous truck?" James asked snidely as we all headed out the front door.

Gracie opened her mouth.

I grabbed her hand.

"I lent it to a friend," I lied smoothly, before Gracie could dig this hole any deeper. She was killing me. The truck thing was a disaster.

"Dude, what the fuck?" Grayson had said when I gave him my request as soon as Gracie had left the café earlier that day, loaded down with enough coffee to send a giraffe into cardiac arrest.

"This does not sound like someone who has the situation under control."

"I could just buy a similar pickup truck and paint it."

"I don't want to leave anything to chance. I have no problem paying for quality. You cannot fuck this up. I'll have my secretary work on it."

James gave me a smarmy little smirk.

It rankled.

I hated guys like James, soft guys who had never suffered, never worked a day in their life, and thought their fancy college degree made them better than the rest of us.

"I can't wait to see this fancy truck."

Dammit. Usually I wasn't one to wish I was a billionaire. The little I spent around Grayson and other billionaire clients, it seemed like more money, more problems. However, there were times when I wished I had enough money to wave a magic wand and make anything I desired appear. Because what I wanted most in the world at that moment was to have that mythical green truck, just to wipe the knowing smirks off the faces of James and Gracie's other family members.

They don't believe her, and they don't believe me.

"F-150s are expensive," Gracie's uncle said, rocking on his heels. "Maybe it's a different truck and Gracie was mistaken."

"No, she was correct. You know us Marines," I said, leveling my gaze at him. "We make terrible financial decisions when it comes to cars."

"You and Hudson can ride with your father and me in the minivan," Bethany said to her daughter.

"It will give us a chance to get to know each other better," Rob said jovially, punching me lightly on the bicep then scurrying back when he realized what he'd done.

James gave me another greasy smile and circled his arm around Kelly, who snuggled against him.

If Gracie didn't seem like she was about to jump out of her own skin, I would have staked my claim over her in front of her ex.

As it was, she was fidgeting nervously with the ties on her dark-red coat. Pugnog was picking up on her anxiety, and he whined at her feet.

She scooped up the dog. He was wearing a ridiculous red-and-green sweater with a stoned-looking reindeer knitted on it.

"Aw. You and Hudson will be just like teenagers, Gracie," Kelly said as James pushed a button on his key ring. A white Range Rover flashed its lights.

"You can sit in the back with me, Hudson," Granny Murray stated. "Gracie gets carsick, so she needs to sit in front."

There is money at the end of this rainbow of shit, I reminded myself.

As I was about to climb into the minivan after Gracie's brother, a horn blared, and a dark-green pickup truck barreled down the road.

"Whoa!" one of Gracie's younger cousins yelled as the pickup screeched to a halt in front of the mailbox.

A man I'd never seen before parked in front of Gracie's parents' house and saluted me as he exited from the cab.

"Thanks for letting me borrow your truck, Hudson," he said, loping over, keys in his outstretched palm.

"No problem, man," I said, easily falling into the lie. "Any time."

"Your chainsaw's in the back. I gassed it up," he added, taking my hand and slapping me on the back.

"Grayson says Merry Christmas, asshole," he whispered in my ear as he crushed my hand. "And stop fucking up."

I practically dragged Gracie out of the front seat of the minivan.

"We'll meet you guys at the Christmas tree farm," I told her parents.

Gracie was grinning ear to ear as I ushered her to the truck. Pugnog wagged his curled tail happily.

"Stop smiling. You look like you're having an aneurysm," I hissed in her ear.

"Nice truck." Her uncles whistled appreciatively.

James looked like he was going to spit blood. "It's all scratched up," he said.

"Yeah," I told him, "because I actually use it to haul shit."

"Now we're hauling Christmas trees," Gracie's mom said brightly.

I opened the truck door for Gracie.

"I mean it about the smiling," I warned her.

But she was still grinning when I climbed into the truck next to her.

"I'm just so impressed you found this." She beamed at me. "You're happy this truck is here."

"No, I'm not. I knew it was going to get here. I called in a favor from a friend."

"You opened the door for me," she said, pleased. "You were so happy about getting the truck that you forgot to be an asshole. I think it's adorable. You're like a kid on Christmas."

"You know what your problem is?" I told her as I started the car. "You have low standards."

"And your problem is that you are not in touch with your emotions." She fiddled with the radio, and Christmas tunes blared out from the speakers. Gracie sang along as we drove into the snowy countryside.

"You're not singing."

"I hate Christmas music."

"Do you hate Christmas snacks? You sound hungry." She pulled a container of peppermint bark out of her purse. "I have Christmas trail mix, too, and dog treats, of course," she cooed to Pugnog.

I waved away her offer of food.

"I'm trying to steel myself for the coming trial."

"You're so dramatic. It's Christmas-tree cutting."

"I'd rather be tortured," I retorted as I pulled up next to James's white Range Rover at the Christmas tree farm.

My heart skipped as a memory surfaced: my mother, drunk as usual, taking us to find our Christmas tree while her latest boyfriend yelled at us that he was leaving in exactly twenty minutes, and anyone who wasn't in the car wasn't making it home.

This isn't your family, I reminded myself as I slammed the car door.

Pugnog was racing around in circles in the snow while Gracie gazed around, enchanted by the winter wonderland surrounding us.

I grabbed the chainsaw out of the back of my truck and lifted it on my shoulder.

"We like to cut down our trees by hand," James called to me, holding up a dull hacksaw. "It's more fun that way." He waved the saw at me. "You get to do the honors."

I took it with a disgusted noise.

Gracie pulled an overstuffed white notebook out of her bag and walked around, inspecting the Christmas trees carefully like she was a fancy art curator, not some girl looking for a Christmas tree.

Elsa would like her, I thought then killed it. Gracie wasn't my girlfriend. She wasn't meeting my family.

It's one tree. Cut it down and get the fuck out of there.

"Which tree do you want?" I asked her as she wandered dreamily through the neat rows of snow-covered Christmas trees.

If I wasn't there to ruin her family's life, I would have called the scene romantic.

"This one's beautiful, I think," she breathed, looking up in wonder at the huge fir.

I knelt down beside the tree.

"And this one," she said, spreading her arms in front of another large tree.

I stood up and hefted the handsaw.

"Let's take this one," Gracie said, flitting to yet another tree.

"Just pick one," I barked.

Gracie popped her head around a tree. "No, we need all of them."

"What the—"

"They're for Kelly's engagement party and wedding at the Canning Factory. It's that old historic warehouse that was converted into a wedding venue," she explained. "Do you know it? The space is huge, so I need a lot of trees."

Knew it? I owned it.

Like I said, I couldn't seem to quit Maplewood Falls.

"I'm not cutting down all these trees by hand," I forced out.

"But it's part of the experience," Gracie protested. "We always cut trees by hand, and everyone takes a turn."

I ignored her and thrust the handsaw at James.

"I'll cut it by hand," he promised Gracie. "I like doing things the traditional way."

"Whatever." I jump-started the chainsaw, and it came to life with a roar. "Point to the ones you want," I yelled at Gracie over the noise.

I made quick work of the trees as she pointed them out to me while keeping Pugnog out of the way as the Christmas trees came crashing down one by one.

By the time twenty huge firs were lying on the ground, James was still working the dull saw through the first tree Gracie had asked for.

"Move," I ordered.

"I almost got it." James was red-faced and sweating.

The saw was stuck in the pinesap and barely moving.

"Just give up, James," Kelly said to him. She fluttered her eyelashes at me. "Let the man work."

"Give me the chainsaw then," James demanded.

"Fuck no."

I kicked away the stuck handsaw with my steel-toed boot then let the chainsaw chew through the trunk. I killed the power on the chainsaw and hefted the Christmas tree over my shoulder, cutting a path through the trees back to my truck.

"You don't have to have such a bad attitude," Gracie said to me, finally showing some backbone, though I wished it would be about anything other than those fucking Christmas trees.

"There are other families here, and they don't want the sound of a chainsaw ruining their Christmas tree hunting."

I unhooked the back panel of the pickup truck so I could toss the tree and the chainsaw in the truck bed. Then I grabbed Gracie by the upper arm.

"What part," I snarled softly, "of 'I am not your boyfriend' don't you understand? I'm not here to be another little stuffed dog in your collection. I'm here to fuck your sister, blow up her wedding, and move on."

Gracie reacted like I'd slapped her.

"You're delusional if you think that I'm ever going to develop real feelings for you. I will never care about you enough to hand cut twenty fucking Christmas trees."

"I have a feeling," she said, eyes flashing, "that even if you had a real girlfriend, you'd still treat her like shit."

"Damn right." I grabbed her hand, her smaller one clenched in mine as I tugged her back to the rows of trees.

"Act like you like me," I ordered her, pulling her closer to my body.

"I don't. I can't stand you."

"Trust me, the feeling is mutual."

Bethany was tut-tutting as James and Rob struggled to drag one of the Christmas trees to the Range Rover.

I hope he gets sap all over the finish of the car, I thought savagely as I hefted two Christmas trees, one over each shoulder, and made my way back to the truck.

I remembered how my mom had complained bitterly the very last time we'd had a Christmas tree that the sap had ruined the carpet. Never mind that she was forever dropping cigarettes on it and burning black holes in the expensive wool.

As I threw the last of the Christmas trees on the large pile in the bed of the pickup, I noticed James struggling to single-handedly carry a smaller tree to his Range Rover.

I wordlessly grabbed it from him.

"I have it."

"No, you don't."

Kelly giggled. I winked at her.

Gracie was trying to get her father to drink some water from where he was leaning on the side of the minivan. She glanced up.

"James, just let Hudson help. You'll ruin your back."

Bitter acid burned the back of my throat.

She can't still care about him.

So what if she did? I didn't want Gracie to care about me. Some insipid Christmas-loving woman who runs back to her cheating ex at a moment's notice is not the type of person a man should desire.

Chapter 12

GRACIE

"We should have made popcorn for this."

Dakota and I were sitting on the boxes of decorations, watching Hudson carry in Christmas tree after Christmas tree.

"It's all my fantasies come to life." Dakota fanned herself. "If I'd known there were going to be hot guys chopping down Christmas trees with a chainsaw, I would have made sure I got into town earlier."

Hudson's leather jacket was off, and his tight gray T-shirt rode up slightly, exposing the edge of a tattoo on his hip as he swung one of the large Christmas trees off his shoulder before setting it carefully on the stand.

My cousins, who'd come to "help decorate," were really using it as an excuse to make lecherous comments about Hudson and drink wine.

"Tell him to take off his shirt," Dakota whispered to me.

"No," I hissed back, scooting off the box I was sitting on, and opened it, just for something to do that didn't include fantasizing about Hudson.

Not that I would, since he was, you know, not my type.

I pulled out a pitcher and hurried to the catering kitchen to fill it up.

"He works for you. You can just order him to take off his shirt."

"He doesn't work for me like that," I said to Dakota, letting the sound of the water disguise the words. "Besides, he doesn't think I'm attractive."

"Bullshit. You have great tits."

"Hudson doesn't look at me the way he looks at Kelly," I said, shutting off the water, hating how insecure I felt. "Not to mention, he's getting a front-row seat to our family. No man in his right mind would want anything to do with the O'Brien disaster."

"You don't have to date him, just sleep with him."

"No way. He hates Christmas."

"How can you hate Christmas?" Dakota asked. "It's literally the best time of the year."

"Because Hudson is a grinch," I said in a low voice as I approached one of the freshly cut trees propped in its stand.

I poured water into the red pan then stood up and fluffed out the branches, closing my eyes and inhaling the smell of Christmas. I just wanted to wrap it around me like a warm blanket, let it keep me safe, whisk me away to a magical land where it was always the holidays.

A large hand slid under my skirt, and I jumped. Hudson's slightly stubbly chin rested against my shoulder briefly.

The peanut gallery of cousins yodeled like horny cats.

"Get your money's worth," Dakota whispered to me.

Hudson's head snapped up.

"It's okay. Dakota knows." I patted him awkwardly on one bulging bicep.

"What the fuck?" Hudson dragged me back in the catering kitchen while my cousins whooped.

Contrary to what my cousins believed, my fake boyfriend wasn't taking me there for an afternoon quickie.

He picked up a bucket from under the sink, set it in the basin, and turned the water on full blast.

"Are you out of your mind?" he snarled, shaking me.

I braced my hands against his muscular chest.

"Dakota's fine."

"Three people can keep a secret if two of them are dead," Hudson said, clearly aggravated.

"Dakota's my alter ego. She won't say a word," I promised.

Hudson shoved me away from him.

"You know, I did two combat tours in Iraq, and somehow being your fake boyfriend is way more of a clusterfuck," he said, pacing in front of me. He picked up another empty bucket from under a nearby storage cabinet and slammed it under the rushing faucet.

Then he turned on me, his silver eyes dark.

I scuttled backward, my hip banging into a nearby table as he advanced on me.

"And stop," he continued, crowding my personal space, "jumping when I touch you. You're supposed to not be able to keep your hands off of me."

I was leaning back as far as someone who did zero stretching or exercise could, my face turned away from him, needing to escape all that raw masculine energy. It was making me feel lightheaded.

"Touch me," Hudson ordered.

I slid my hands as far away from him as I could.

"Do it, Gracie. You want to win, don't you?"

No, I wanted to put on my favorite pajamas and curl up in my bed and watch Hallmark movies while I knitted.

"No one's going to believe that you're the good girl gone bad if you act like I'm trying to kidnap you and throw you in my van every time I grab your ass."

I made a strangled noise as I felt his belt buckle dig into my belly.

"Touch me. Touch me like I did to you." His words were like a curse.

I closed my eyes, imagining myself grabbing the firm behind underneath the heavy canvas work pants, sliding my hands up the muscular thighs, pressing my face in the crook of his neck to inhale the scent of him.

"I can't," I said, eyes still squeezed shut.

I felt Hudson close a large rough hand over my wrist.

My heart hammered in my chest as I wondered if he was going to make me touch him *there*, with just a thin layer of fabric between my hand and that huge throbbing cock from the photo, and if I was thrilled or freaked out by the prospect.

Instead, Hudson brought my hand up to his face, his palm briefly lingering against the back of my hand as he guided me to cup his cheek.

I opened my eyes.

"See?" he said softly. "It's not that scary."

I swallowed heavily.

"Touch me like you want me," he whispered.

I let my hand drift up the slightly scratchy cheek to his hairline, running my fingernails along his scalp through the thick soft black hair, making him shiver slightly, the tremors sending zings of electricity through me.

"Not so difficult," he said, his voice rumbling through my chest. "You can manhandle me too."

"I don't want to touch your man handle," I blurted out.

He bit back a laugh.

I wiggled out from under him and shut off the water.

Hudson reached around me, the air puffing against my flushed skin as he picked up the heavy buckets.

"This one's looking a little dry," Dakota called when she saw me.

"No, she's not," Hudson said in a low voice.

Was he talking about me? Was he trying to make me wet? My heart pounded. Maybe Hudson did think I was attractive.

Or wait, no. My sister was marching over to us.

"Where were you?" Kelly's voice was shrill.

Hudson was immediately behind me. I could just reach back and grab his man handle.

"Just, *you know*," I said, trying to put some emphasis on the words so she would think Hudson and I were getting in the holiday spirit back there.

Except you were, technically, I thought hysterically.

Hudson had been practically between my legs.

I'd made a joke about his man handle.

It was hardly an innocent conversation between two people who had entered into a fake relationship contract.

Kelly scoffed. "Like you're going to have sex in public with him. I don't believe it."

I didn't believe it either.

"I just need to finish giving these trees water," I croaked.

"You better. I thought you already left to go to the gingerbread house decorating."

My face fell.

"They started without me?" I cried.

Kelly shrugged. "I guess. Violet has some sort of Instagram live stream going. Anyway, gingerbread houses are for kids. I don't know why you like it so much."

I looked around at all the trees in the venue that needed to be cared for.

"It won't take that long if we all work together," Dakota assured me.

Kelly scoffed. "I'm the bride. I'm not helping. Also I just had my nails done."

"Just go. I can give the trees water," Hudson offered gruffly.

Dakota was giving me a maniacal smile.

My heart was flip-flopping.

He's right. You do have low standards. One guy offers to do something nice for you, and you fall head over heels.

"You don't have to," I said to Hudson. "Anyway, I also need to straighten everything up. We can't just leave it like this. The venue owner will be mad."

"No, he won't," Hudson said. "I know him," he added when he saw my confused look. "It will be fine." He set down one of the heavy buckets.

Wrong. Hudson being nice to me wasn't fine. I needed him to go back to being an asshole, because I was afraid if I didn't hate him, I might start to fall for him.

Chapter 13

HUDSON

"You're making gingerbread houses with her?" Anderson asked, walking into the venue as I poured water into the last of the Christmas tree stands.

"Someone's getting into the Christmas spirit," Lawrence joked.

"Fa la la la la! We should get a Christmas tree for the office," Jake said, grinning.

"No Christmas decorations." I wiped my hands on my pants.

Something about Gracie was triggering some sort of weird protective instinct in me.

It's because she's completely useless.

"Glad to see you took my advice to be nice," Anderson remarked.

"I'm not nice. It was a strategic change." I picked up the empty buckets.

"You better go before you miss your big gingerbread house moment."

My brothers were smirking.

"Remember, slow and steady with the icing," Jake said cheerfully. "Use your pinky as a balance when doing intricate details."

The front door was unlocked when I arrived at Gracie's parents' house.

I dropped my bag on the floor with a thud.

Christmas carols played softly in the background as the Norman Rockwell scene played out.

Multiple generations gathered around an impeccably decorated dining room, garland over the doors, wreaths in the windows, a fire burning merrily in the hearth. It was warm and cozy.

It was also quite a bit different from the drafty house I'd grown up in that was crumbling from neglect around me and my siblings.

My heart clenched. Gracie looked up at me, delight on her face, like she was happy to see me.

"You made it."

I strode over to her.

The expected thing to do would be to tip her head back and kiss her. A part of me desperately wanted to, wanted to feel her cave to her desire for me.

However, I also didn't want her to freak out at me.

You're going to have to kiss her eventually.

Maybe, or maybe I would find what I needed before it advanced to that point.

The Christmas carols were streaming from a laptop that was perched on one of the side tables. I gazed at it hungrily.

There it was, what I'd come here for.

"Do you have anything other than Christmas carols?" I asked Gracie.

I let my fingers trail over the touchpad of the laptop, pretending like I was looking for new songs when really all I wanted to do was search for evidence that would end this mission and let me escape the heavy blanket of Christmas.

Unfortunately, she was still watching me with those big soft eyes.

"Don't you want to make a gingerbread house?" she asked hopefully.

I came up behind her, tipping her head back, some of the icing in the piper squirting all over her fingers.

The ghostly memory of the touch of her hand on my zipper chose that moment to conspire against me and make me wonder what it would be like to watch her lick my cum off her fingers.

Stay the fuck on mission.

"You sure you don't want to ditch the gingerbread and come upstairs and let me lick frosting off of your pussy?" The words were soft enough not to freak out Grandma Astelle but loud enough that Kelly heard.

I did allow myself to hold up her hand and lick the sweet frosting on it before sitting down beside her.

Her hand was shaking slightly.

"Do you want gumdrops on the chimney?" she asked. On the floor by her feet, Pugnog, wearing yet another Christmas sweater, begged and drooled for food.

Impulsively, I reached out and broke off a piece of the gingerbread house chimney then tossed it to Pugnog, who noisily gobbled it up.

"You—" Gracie's mouth opened and closed; her eyes looked at me in horror.

I suddenly felt like absolute shit.

"Oh no, poor Hudson," Kelly cooed at me. "Is Gracie making you help her with that stupid little gingerbread house? Gracie, he doesn't want to make a gingerbread house."

"It's funny watching her tongue stick out while she paints with the icing," I said as Gracie turned back to the house and tried to fix the chimney I'd broken.

"Just stick some gumdrops there," I said, tossing a handful on the table in front of her.

Gracie gave me a dirty look.

You're not actually trying to make Gracie fall in love with you, I reminded myself as I took a seat next to Gracie. *Remember? The plan changed.*

Kelly perched on the table beside me, one of her bare feet resting on my thigh.

"Gracie gets so anal about all her little Christmas traditions." Kelly laughed as Gracie hunched over the gingerbread house, trying to fix the chimney.

You're a fucking asshole, Hudson.

"I mean who wants to sit there decorating a cookie house when you could instead put that frosting to good use and let a hot guy with a big Christmas package lick it off of you?"

Kelly's bare foot crept up my thigh.

I grabbed it before she could dig her toes into my crotch.

That's how James found us, me with my hand on his fiancée's ankle.

He looked between Kelly and me.

She slowly withdrew her foot.

"What's for dinner, Gracie?" James demanded.

"Hudson," Kelly said, with a smirk in my direction.

"Let's just go out for dinner, Kelly," James said, taking her hand.

"Do you want to come with us, Hudson?" Kelly asked, running her hand through my hair. "You'll have to clean up a little bit though first."

"We're having a date night," James protested. "He can't come."

"She's trying to rescue me from gingerbread house purgatory," I drawled, leaning back in my chair, ignoring the guilt I felt for hurting Gracie.

"Gingerbread houses can be fun," Granny Murray said from where she was drawing snowmen with huge erections all over her gingerbread house.

"Mom!" Bethany scolded and tried to smear icing all over the Christmas porno. "Gracie, give me more gingerbread and throw these away."

"That's my masterpiece. I didn't even get to take a picture," Granny Murray complained as Gracie swept the plate away.

"Hudson, can you come help me with something?" Gracie said.

I stood up, hand on my belt, and followed her into the large butler's pantry.

Grace slammed the plate with the gingerbread on the counter and grabbed the side of my leather jacket, eyes flashing.

"I don't care," she hissed, "that you hate Christmas or that you're not my real boyfriend. Decorating a gingerbread house is the height of the holiday season, and you will not ruin it for me. So get back in there and help me make a gingerbread house."

I glanced down at the penis-covered house on the sideboard.

"Not that kind," she warned.

I gave her a lazy salute.

"Yes, ma'am." I followed her back into the dining room and accepted the bag of gumdrops without comment.

"You can hand me red and green ones."

"Isn't this adorable?" her grandmother said—the fun one, not the one that was silently sending me death wishes from across the room.

"Smile for the Gran Gram! Not you, Hudson. Give me a sexy scowl. Flex those biceps! Yeah, baby, that's the ticket! Hudson is getting me lots of likes. Way better than my ex-husband. Fuck that guy. Lazy bastard. You know, I bet I'm still on his life insurance." She tapped her chin. "Hey, Hudson, you ever kill anyone for money?"

"Gran, that's rude. And also you can't post photos of him online. You didn't get his consent." Gracie was exasperated.

Dakota snickered. "Granny Murray posted a video of him on her Instagram stories."

Gracie looked at me in horror. "I am so sorry."

"This is why I tell you kids not to sext," Gracie's dad said.

Kelly rolled her eyes. "People who look like me and Hudson don't care if people see our photos."

"Right." I smirked. "Did it get a lot of hits?"

"Are you kidding?" Granny Murray whooped. "I had all sorts of companies wanting to do sponsorship deals. You should quit being a maintenance man and start doing porn. There's quite a market for cougar content, if you know what I mean."

"Don't worry," Gracie assured me. "I won't let her take photos of you in your sleep."

"Of course not," her mother said in a too-bright tone. "Hudson's not sleeping here, and my mother is hardly going to sneak into whatever crack den he lives in."

I handed Gracie a red gumdrop.

"I'm staying here tonight."

Gracie dropped the candy, and it broke several of her carefully applied icing icicles.

"You are? Where?"

I raised an eyebrow.

"Unfortunately," Bethany said loudly, "we're old-fashioned in this house. We have rules about opposite-gender guests staying the night."

"Amen," Gracie's mean grandmother stated.

"We ask that our children be engaged or married before we allow overnight guests," Bethany continued brightly.

"You didn't with Kelly," Granny Murray insisted.

"To be fair," Gracie's brother said with a snicker, "James was already engaged when he started spending the night with Kelly. Just not to her."

"Dipwad!" Kelly shrieked at Logan.

"Piper and Logan aren't engaged either," Dakota added.

"Well, uh ..." Rob stammered. "It's a little different. Piper is from out of town. We can't make her pay for a hotel."

"Hudson lives in town," Bethany said firmly, "so it's perfectly fine if he goes home by curfew."

"You're kicking out a grown woman's boyfriend at nine thirty, Bethany?" Gracie's aunt Giana raised an eyebrow.

"Hookup," Kelly corrected.

"Kelly's had boyfriends here overnight before, and that was when she was in high school. Gracie is a grown woman in her late thirties," her aunt continued.

"I'm only twenty-nine."

"You act like you're fifty," Kelly snapped at Gracie.

"So," I said slowly, turning to Kelly, "what I'm hearing is that if you were riding my cock that I'd get to stay here free and clear?"

"The dinner reservations." James tugged on Kelly's arm.

"Uh, well ..." Rob squirmed in his seat. "I guess when you put it like that, maybe we can relax the rules."

He patted his forehead with a red-and-green towel embroidered with Christmas trees.

"Gracie can give you a rundown of the house rules."

"Hard pass. I don't do rules."

Chapter 14

GRACIE

"This is a disaster," I hissed at Dakota as we hid in the pantry.

My cozy gingerbread house evening had turned into a flaming dumpster fire. Hudson had been flirting with Kelly—correction, practically having sex with her at the dining room table—all evening. He'd broken off part of my gingerbread house, and I'd been too distracted by having him that close to me, our hands inadvertently touching every time I added a sugary decoration to the gingerbread house, to even finish the thing.

At the end of the evening, I felt so raw that I just wanted to chuck the whole thing in the fire.

"I cannot have a man in my bed."

"You slept in the same bed as James," Dakota reminded me.

"Yeah, but that's James. James wears long underwear and listens to entrepreneurship podcasts on his headphones. He's not a man like Hudson is a man. Hudson scares me," I admitted.

"Like he threatens you?" Dakota demanded. Unlike me, she had taken to the rough-and-tumble New York City life and had no problem charging after pickpockets and screaming at catcallers.

Dakota hefted a heavy mixing bowl.

"Put that down," I hissed. "It's not that. He just … he's always there, in my space, whispering in my ear, his hands all over me."

I chewed on my lip.

I couldn't explain to Dakota how Hudson made me feel supercharged, like I was about to burst out of my own skin.

"You're attracted to him," my cousin said knowingly.

"No!" I waved my hands. "I mean is he attractive? Sure. Did he help carry all my Christmas trees? Yes. But guys like him? They don't want girls like me," I said, blinking rapidly to keep the tears from welling up as I admitted my real insecurities.

"I'm too boring, too doughy, too uptight. He's going to lie next to me in the dark the entire night wishing he was anywhere else. Just like James did."

"So what if he does?" Dakota cajoled. "You're not trying to marry the man. This is part of your epic revenge plan. I'm so glad you're finally standing up for yourself. I'm here for the karmic destruction. And if you have to share a bed with a hot guy, then that's worth the sacrifice." She winked.

My stomach flip-flopped. I should not have eaten all that candy.

Picking up my laptop on the way, I crept back toward the living room, where Hudson was regaling my family with hilarious stories of his time in the military.

My sister, who was back from her romantic dinner with James, hung on to his every word. She also practically hung all over him—sliding her hands up his arms, periodically running her fingers through his hair, doing everything Hudson had told me to do to make my family believe he and I were sleeping together.

I had always envied my sister, how she was able to just claim men, run her thumb over their bottom lip, watch as they turned to putty in her hands.

Hudson and Kelly looked good together.

Maybe they'd fall in love and I could … well, I could get back together with James.

Hudson must have had a sixth sense for being watched, because he turned suddenly, eyes narrowing as he noticed me lingering in the shadow of the doorway.

"You heading up to bed?"

"Yes," I forced out. "Just looking for Pugnog." The small dog was lying on his back, snoring loudly in front of the fire. I decided to let him be.

Maybe you could book a hotel. There have to be some nearby that take dogs.

"I'll come with you." Hudson stood up.

"Are you sure it's okay?" I asked my parents.

My mom poured herself more wine.

"You're both adults."

Dammit. The one time I needed my parents to treat me and my siblings unfairly, and they flaked out.

Hudson followed me through the dim hallways, the only light coming from the electric candles in the windows. It was a touch I always insisted on because it really made the house feel warm like a cozy home pictured on a Victorian postcard.

Hudson picked up his black bag in the foyer, hefting it easily. The weight of it didn't put him off-balance at all. He strode through the house after me, footfalls rhythmic, purposeful, like he was heading into battle.

Normally, before I went to bed, I made a midnight snack and had a glass of wine to calm my nerves from the day. I didn't know how Hudson would feel about that. I didn't want him judging me any more than he already did.

I gave the kitchen a longing look.

Hudson paused behind me.

"We can take the back stairway," I said, leading him up the twisting stairs. I'd always loved them as a child. It felt like I was in a whimsical Victorian dollhouse, like the one Grandma Astelle had given me.

Crap.

I froze on the stair. Hudson paused a hairsbreadth before running into me.

"What?"

The word was cool on the back of my neck.

I was a girl who had never outgrown her toys. I still had all of my stuffed animals, my dollhouse, and the obscenely large collection of anthropomorphic mice decorating my room. I loved fairy tales and music boxes, and none of those were the types of décor a man like Hudson would respect.

"I might need to clean up a little bit before you come in," I said, picking at my nails.

Hudson snorted and pushed past me.

"I have four brothers and was in the Marines. It's fine."

I sprinted after him as he headed down the narrow hallway to my room.

"It's really not. It's—"

Hudson stood in the center of the hexagonal room and dropped his bag on the pink rug with its subtle flower pattern.

"Do you have sex with all these mice watching?" He reached for one.

I snatched Mrs. Cheese Crumpet out of his hands and placed her carefully back on the shelf.

"I saved all my toys for my future children," I told him defensively.

"Did you."

Crossing my arms, I stood protectively near the over-sized dollhouse while Hudson slowly made his way around my room, trailing his fingers along the shelves, opening a music box, listening to it play for a moment, taking in the floral wallpaper, the gauzy curtains, the canopy bed with pink drapes, the antique chandelier, and the small makeup table with its matching frilly stool against one of the six walls.

He prowled back to me then knelt down in front of the dollhouse.

"Did you decorate this dollhouse for Christmas?"

"It's always decorated for Christmas," I said, using my sleeve to clean a bit of dust off a miniature window.

The mice in their Victorian finery stared back with black bead eyes as his gaze swept over them.

He thinks it's childish. He thinks I'm childish. Now he sees why James didn't want to marry me, why he wanted Kelly.

"No asshole comments?" I snapped at him, unable to take waiting for his derision.

Hudson took a step toward me, then past me.

"When we're alone, I don't need to play up the sexual tension," he said simply, reaching for the door.

"What the hell?" he muttered, looking around the door-frame, where there were three hinges but no door.

He blinked at me.

"What the fuck? Where is your door?"

I looked down at the floor, hunching up my shoulders.

"The oldest child is the guinea pig," I said in a rush, "and my parents wanted to raise respectful children. They didn't want their kids to run wild like other teenagers. I had brought a miniature waffle iron to school for a history diorama, and my friend had taken it home and forgotten to give it back to me. My parents wouldn't take me over to her house to pick it up, so I took my bike to get it without telling them. They told me they were very disappointed with me. I argued with them, and they took the door as punishment."

All those years later, and it still stung. It had been my first and only act of rebellion in my life. Well—I looked at Hudson—not my only.

"Meanwhile my sister ran wild and was given a new phone."

"Okay," Hudson said slowly, "but where is your door now?"

"I'm not sure," I admitted. "They never gave it back, and I never asked."

"Huh." He sat down on the frilly little stool, looking like a giant in a fairy castle as he removed the heavy boots.

"And I thought my family was fucked up," he said as he pulled off his socks.

Having Hudson standing there barefoot in my child-hood bedroom, it was too intimate. It was too much. He set the boots by the doorless door.

"The bathroom is down the hall," I directed, fluttering around the room, trying to do anything to take my mind off the fact that Hudson, with his head almost touching the sloped ceiling, was in there taking up all the space and leaving those ginormous boots next to my reading nook.

"I'll grab you some clean towels from the linen closet."

"Thanks," he said, reaching behind his head to grab the collar of his T-shirt and pull it over his head.

"Oh my gosh!" I clapped my hands over my mouth.

Hudson didn't seem to notice I was having conniptions as he flexed his shoulders and twisted his torso, stretching. He was covered in tattoos—they trailed up his back and curled around his huge biceps. There was a bald eagle carrying a bomb on his pec and Latin sayings crisscrossed under his navel.

Wintery eyes caught mine. "You can touch if you want to."

I shook my head, crossing my arms over myself so he wouldn't see the effect he was having on me.

Hudson caught me as I walked past him, grabbing my face, tilting it up to his.

He's going to kiss me! I shrieked internally.

The kiss didn't come.

Instead Hudson inspected me coldly.

"You need to get with the plan, because pretty soon you're going to have to suck my cock in your mom's living room under the Christmas tree if you want people to believe we're together."

There wasn't a shred of desire in his eyes, just cold, calculating professionalism.

"Otherwise, eventually, your sister's going to think something's up." He released me, and his hands went to his belt.

I immediately clapped my hands over my eyes.

"You are so bad at this."

I could hear the humor in his words.

"I'm going to go find you a towel," I said, heading for the door but instead banging my hip into the side of a bookcase. "Ow!"

Hudson's hand was steadying on my shoulder.

"I think I can manage."

I waited for his footfalls to leave the room then peeked through my fingers.

Blessedly alone.

I turned around one dowager mouse with a large black hat, who was glaring at me disapprovingly, to face the bookshelf wall.

If only Hudson hadn't just gone to shower but instead left. Then I could watch a Christmas movie on my laptop and write in my Festivus journal to try to calm down.

My fake boyfriend was going to be back any second.

I left my laptop closed on my desk and quickly unbuttoned my blouse. I had showered after returning home from setting up the Christmas trees. Since Hudson was currently in the shower and wasn't going to pop out of the floor, cock erect, I used the opportunity to change out of my clothes.

I loved Christmas, and that extended to Christmas PJs. The ones I put on were decorated in happy bear families sledding, exchanging presents, and making cookies.

I grabbed the covers to climb into bed … my childhood bed … a bed not made for two grown adults, one of whom was a six-foot-five man built like a tank.

The bay window on one wall of the room had a small reading nook. I'd added oversized pillows to make it comfy. Sure, I wasn't ten years old anymore, but I would survive a cricked neck if it meant I didn't have to sleep next to Hudson.

"What are you doing?" His deep voice echoed around the room, making me shiver.

"Just ... uh ..."

Hudson was standing there in the doorway in nothing but dark-green silky shorts that ended right below his crotch.

Think the offer to touch is still on the table?

"You're supposed to be tempting Kelly, not me," I croaked out.

He raised an eyebrow.

"Sugarplum, we're going to have to have sex, otherwise your grand revenge plan won't fly."

"What if I don't want to?"

"I'll make sure you do."

"Are we going to have sex tonight? I don't think I can handle it," I babbled. "I'm already in my jammies."

He looked me up and down, taking in the flannel PJs.

"Is that what you wear to bed?"

"These are warm and cozy."

"You're a disaster."

"No. I'm a good hostess. You can have the bed. I'm just going to knit on the window seat." I held up my overstuffed knitting basket.

His eyes slid over the laptop to the reading nook. Then he advanced on me, grabbed me by the arm, and dragged me over to the bed.

"Since you have no door, we have a greater chance of someone looking in," he said in a low voice. "It has to look real. Get in bed."

"Right. Yeah, that makes sense. Not a problem. We can split the blankets. You can have the top sheet," I said, pulling back the comforter, "and I'll use this fleece throw, and then we can put the comforter on top."

"Yeah, fuck that," Hudson said and flopped face down on the mattress, one tattooed arm sprawled above his head.

Was he already asleep? I'd heard those military men could sleep anywhere. I looked longingly to my knitting basket.

"In bed now, Gracie." His deep voice was slightly muffled by the pillow.

Dammit.

The stuffed animals glared at me reproachfully.

I'm making these sacrifices for all of us.

I gingerly slid onto the mattress and pulled the comforter up to my chin.

The top sheet was half-tangled by Hudson's feet. I could pull it up, but that would mean I'd have to put my hands dangerously close to his half-naked body.

My ex-fiancé had always slept fully clothed, compared to Hudson, who slept in barely anything.

His body heat radiated from under the covers, making me sweat in the flannel PJs. But I would rather baste than remove a stitch of clothing.

It was my armor.

I was normally a side sleeper. I liked to lie facing the dollhouse and imagine I lived there with my perfect husband and wonderful children while I drifted off to sleep.

I couldn't tonight; that would put me face-to-face with Hudson.

I peeked over.

His eyes were closed, black lashes fluttering on his cheekbones.

The clock hands on his wristwatch glowed softly in the dark.

I could feel his breath ever so slightly on my hand.

I turned over gingerly, trying not to wake him up, and I huddled as close to the edge of the bed as I could, listening to his steady breathing next to me.

How could that man sleep at a time like this?

Especially after he had just told me we were going to have to have sex.

Chapter 15

HUDSON

My eyes opened at 5:45. It was pitch-black and snowing outside.

I raised myself slowly off the mattress. Gracie was sound asleep. Her laptop was sitting on the bookshelf.

I hadn't meant to fall asleep, but I hadn't slept the night before as I was dealing with our other contract, and Gracie's bed was so comfortable, the sheets so soft, the slightly sweet cinnamon smell of her hair so intoxicating, it had knocked me out.

I didn't need much time though. I just needed a good look at the laptop to see what I was dealing with, what kind of password protection she had on it.

As I'd walked around the room yesterday, I'd memorized where the creaks were in the ancient floorboards, and

I sidestepped them as I navigated my way silently through the room to her computer.

Right as I reached for it, robotic elven voices shrieked Christmas carols from the alarm clock by her bed.

Gracie murmured and banged the top of it with her palm.

"Sorry, Hudson," she mumbled, sitting up. Her pajamas, decorated with saccharine-sweet scenes of bears enjoying Christmas, had come undone while she'd slept, revealing a swell of her breast from the deep V of the opened flannel. Her curly hair was snarled in her face, and she yawned then yelped when she noticed me standing there in front of her.

Foiled again.

"Sorry. Did I wake you up?" Gracie asked.

"I was going for a run," I said, supplying the ready excuse.

"In the cold?" she asked, confused.

"You want to come?"

"I'm making breakfast."

I shrugged off the silkies, the ubiquitous shorts worn in the Marines during physical training, knowing it would make her shriek to see me naked in her bedroom.

Gracie pulled the covers over her head with a squawk.

I toyed with using the opportunity to open her laptop—it had been thirty-six hours since I'd made contact with her, and I had nothing to show for it.

Who wakes up at six in the morning to bake? I seethed as I tossed the shorts on her bed and pulled out my running clothes from my bag.

"Are you decent?" Gracie asked as I zipped up the hoodie.

"No, I'm a terrible person," I replied.

She lowered the covers to just above the tip of her nose.

Something about the gesture was almost adorable. It tugged on something in my chest. It couldn't be my heart. I kept that thing encased in ice.

If we were a normal couple, I'd give her a kiss, letting her feel the rough stubble on my chin.

I slid the black skullcap on my head.

"Be careful. It's icy out there," she called as I headed for the door.

I paused.

No one ever told me to be careful or worried about me when I left.

There didn't seem to be any ulterior motives in her soft brown eyes.

"Do you have any breakfast requests?" she asked.

What was this? Why was she being nice to me? I'd told her last night I was going to make her suck my cock. Yet she was waiting expectantly for my answer.

"Just protein," I said finally.

"Coming right up!"

"It was all that sleep," I told myself as I jogged lightly down the stairs.

Pugnog was snorting awake in his basket in the living room when I passed by to the front door, suddenly craving the numbing cold.

The pug stumbled out of the dog bed, stretching out his stubby legs.

"You're not a real dog," I whispered to him. "Real dogs are Belgian Malinois and German shepherds. They root terrorists out of caves. You wouldn't last a day with them."

Pugnog's tongue flopped out of his mouth. He looked like he needed to go out.

I didn't hear Gracie following me down the stairs.

Pugnog whined uncomfortably.

"Fine," I snapped at him.

Dog tucked under my arm like a football, I unlocked the front door and slipped out into the cold dark.

"Hurry up," I ordered Pugnog.

I tried not to think about that time when I was little and had asked my father for a dog for Christmas and he'd actually bought one. My father had already been wasted by the time we were opening presents, and he had this dopey, drunk smile on his face when the puppy had popped out of the box, a huge bow on its neck.

My mother had been so mad. They'd gotten into a screaming fight. She'd thrown a glass at him, and the puppy had cowered behind me as she'd threatened to skin it.

By New Year's, the dog was gone. I hoped he'd found a good home.

Pugnog couldn't decide which leafless bush he wanted to do his business on.

"That one," I pointed to a bush, "is a particularly good vintage, 1998, a great year."

"Are you being good for Hudson?" Gracie asked Pugnog in a baby voice. She stepped out onto the front porch, closing the heavy door behind her.

It felt oddly domestic, her standing there in a knitted sweater, tying an apron around her waist, the dog meandering in the snow.

"That was sweet of you to take him out." Grace beamed at me. "You can go on your run though. I'll watch Pugnog. He might be a while. He's like you. He can be pretty particular."

"I'm very low-maintenance," I countered. "Unlike you, with all your Christmas decorations just so." I winced. "I'll make you a new gingerbread house. I'm sorry."

"Don't worry about it. I wasn't in the right headspace for it." She sighed. "It wasn't going to be my best gingerbread house anyway. There's always next year."

There she was, making herself smaller to serve the people around her. This time I couldn't blame her family or James—it was my fault.

The pug had finally found a suitable bush and was whining to go back inside for his breakfast.

"You don't want to get some exercise with Hudson?" she cooed at the pug who barked at her.

"With his nose all smushed up like that, he probably can't breathe," I said, not sure why I hadn't just fucking left already.

Gracie looked guilty.

"I know that pugs are really inbred," she said defensively, "but I didn't buy him, if that's what you're thinking. My sister wanted a pug for Christmas, and of course my parents bought one for her. He peed in her Birkin bag, and she decided she didn't want him anymore and refused to take care of him. So I took him in."

Gracie gave a sad laugh. "Maybe Kelly will have a kid, and I'll take care of them too. It'll probably be the only way I get a family." Her eyes flicked up to mine. "Never mind."

Gracie rested her hand on the door.

I wanted to leave, run until I couldn't breathe, and also stay there and bask in the warmth of her forever.

"See you in a bit," she said cheerfully as she ushered the pug back inside the warm house.

The snow that blanketed the upscale neighborhood muffled the sounds. It was like being in a cocoon.

"Don't think about Gracie. Think about how you're going to get access to the laptop," I told myself.

Yet all I could think about was her soft warmth next to me in bed, her standing there, framed by garland in the doorway, the way she said *be careful* like she cared about me.

The kitchen was warm and smelled like sugar and spice when I slipped in after the brutal run I'd pushed myself through.

"They played this song twice already, didn't they?" Gracie was saying to the pug as she fiddled with the radio. "Why can't they play anything other than the same ten Christmas carols? Hi, Hudson!"

She beamed at me. "Did you have fun on your run?"

Gracie poured me a glass of water from a pitcher and handed it to me.

"Pugnog and I are going to listen to some vintage Christmas carols, aren't we?"

Fuck, I thought, fist clenched on the glass, as I watched her log into the computer.

Most people just used a simple pin to access their computer, or a password.

Not Gracie.

There was a long password that I memorized as I watched her type it in. That wasn't the problem.

No, she had a four-factor authentication.

What the hell was she, some government spy? What the fuck?

All my hopes for an easy, quick mission-complete went up in a fiery explosion to the sound of the Nutcracker's

Russian dance as I watched her swipe her finger, use the laptop camera to authenticate her face, and then enter in a code that had been sent to an app on her phone.

"I know it's a little overkill but I've been burned before," Gracie said quickly when she noticed me staring. "My sister was dating this bad boy—he wasn't like you, he was a really bad person—and he stole all my stuff. He used my computer to steal my identity, so now I keep it all locked down. Fool me once …" She laughed sadly.

I tried not to scowl. There was no way I was getting access to that computer without her knowing.

You have to. You have to try. Grayson Richmond does not tolerate failure.

Gracie navigated to a music-playing program on the computer.

"You might want to leave the room," she said as she reauthenticated her identity, because apparently she had her computer set up so that anything more than sending an email required a password and facial recognition. "Don't want you to melt from too much Christmas."

Fuck.

I drained the glass of water.

"I'll take a shower."

There has to be another way, I decided as I headed upstairs.

The O'Briens had a family office in town, I thought, desperately running through my mental file of the EnerCheck Inc. account.

Maybe there was something there.

My men had accessed the office, but Gracie hadn't been logged in on any computers there at the time. If I hung around with her, maybe she'd go to the office and log in on a desktop. Then I would have access to her company account.

Or maybe I wouldn't, and Grayson Richmond would have me drawn and quartered by Rudolph and his friends on Christmas Eve.

"Stick to the plan," I whispered to myself in the bathroom mirror.

The plan needed to change though. I needed to escalate. It wasn't enough to just hang around in the hopes that I would get a free moment alone with the laptop. I needed to get Gracie so wrapped up that I would be able to keep her off-balance enough to both leave the laptop logged in and unattended.

It was going to take time, more time than I thought. More time than I had.

Though I had joked to her about us needing to have sex, now it was true. Soon we were going to have to deliver, or her family would think something was up.

Would it be such a bad thing to kiss her, run my hands over the curves of her breasts, to bury myself in the softness of her?

You're just looking for an excuse to sleep with her.

If I could convince her to log into the company computer, then I would have what I needed.

I was not sleeping with her. I had done a lot of bad shit, but this was a line I shouldn't cross.

I pulled my military dog tags out of my pocket. I hated wearing them, hated thinking about that time, but it was part of the ensemble.

Combing my fingers through my damp hair, I headed through the chilly house to the warm kitchen, feeling like I was about to enter a war zone I was ill prepared for.

Chapter 16

GRACIE

The rest of my family was awake when Hudson came back downstairs.

"Make sure there is a vegan option for the eggnog at the wedding welcome party," my sister was telling me haughtily. "Miranda doesn't eat dairy."

"Why can't you just buy some from the store," I argued with my sister. "I don't know how to make eggnog with nut sludge."

"You promised you'd plan my wedding," Kelly snapped at me.

"I just think your guests might prefer store-bought. You know, Ina Garten says store-bought is perfectly fine," I told her as I flipped the bacon sizzling in the pan.

Hudson sauntered into the kitchen.

The buckle of his belt dug into my lower back as he wrapped his arms around me, peppering freshly shaven kisses on my neck. Sure, he was aggressive and cocky and oh-so male, but I was starting to get used to him. He had a soft side—I was sure of it. A real asshole would have just ignored Pugnog this morning.

"You hungry?" I asked him.

He kissed me under the jaw. "For you? Always."

One large hand slid under my sweater to briefly caress my stomach, making it flip-flop.

This isn't real, this isn't real.

But in that moment, I desperately wished it was.

He grabbed my ass, kneading it, then slapped it lightly.

He was more aggressively sexual than he'd been earlier this morning.

Because we have an audience, I reminded myself viciously.

I couldn't help but stare at him.

Hudson was shirtless and barefoot, his pants slung low on his narrow hips, the tattoos that traced his muscles twisted on his skin as he poured himself a glass of orange juice.

"Where is your shirt?" I asked. "It's cold."

He shrugged a tattooed shoulder.

"Maybe you can come back upstairs and warm me up."

I suddenly wondered what it would be like to kiss him.

Stop acting like a teenager.

"Someone has a tramp stamp." Kelly giggled, trailing her nails along Hudson's lower back where a *Semper Fi* tattoo was peeking just barely above his waistband.

My sister tugged at his pants, pulling them down as far as she could without removing his belt. The tattoo rested right above the curve of his ass. I could feel my face flaming as I remembered him stripping off his shorts in the dark earlier this morning.

I wasn't paying attention to the bacon, and a spatter of grease landed on my hand. I bit back a yelp of pain then stuck my hand under cold water.

"Since I got to see yours, it's only fair I show you mine," Kelly said with a flirty laugh.

"It's only fair," Hudson agreed.

My sister arched her back, sliding her white pants down to show the crack of her ass.

Hudson hooked his finger in the strap of her pink thong.

"Juicy girl. Is that what you are?" he asked, reading her tattoo.

I checked on the cheese-and-leek tater tots crisping in the oven, trying my best to ignore my sister and my fake boyfriend. I was scared of needles, and the thought of getting so much as a tiny heart tattoo made me feel faint.

"I can be with the right motivation," Kelly purred.

Hudson snorted. "Did you just get that tattoo so guys would ask you how wet you are or how sweet you taste? The tattoo is a lure to get guys back to your bed."

I bit back a scoff as I flipped the last of the waffles in the waffle maker.

I didn't know why I ever thought Hudson was attractive. He was disgusting.

"No," I said, before I could stop myself, "that's what the nipple piercings are for."

"You have nipple piercings?" Hudson looked aggravatingly interested in that fact.

His eyes were glued to her tits.

"You gonna show me?"

"You don't get to see the nipple piercings on the first date," Kelly said, making a big show of covering her boobs with her hands.

"Not even," Hudson said, dipping his head down to her, "if I ask nicely and say please?"

"I like to make men work for it. I'm not like Gracie, giving it away in a gas station bathroom."

Hudson's eyes slid over me.

I pretended to be very interested in the cheese grits in the big pot on the stove.

"It just goes to show you I can make a woman do anything I want," he rumbled.

"Hardly difficult," my sister scoffed. "All you have to do is give Gracie a compliment, and you'll have a little friend for life. You won't be able to get rid of her. I'm surprised she's exciting enough to keep a man like you interested."

"I could say the same about you," Hudson said inclining his chin slightly at James, who had entered the kitchen.

"When I'm on a first date, I like to test and see if a guy is gonna be a man in bed by telling him I want him to let me ride him while he uses a chain latched to the nipple rings like reins." She let out a musical laugh. "This Boy Scout got so freaked out he tipped over his water."

"That must have been disappointing. Go to all that trouble to make your tits extra special and he doesn't even appreciate them," Hudson said in that rough, deep voice that any woman would want to have saying dirty things to her in bed.

"It's not all a waste. One guy said he wanted to chain them up on his bedpost and ride me."

"Oh yeah?"

God, they were flirting, like really flirting, not the polite professionalism Hudson had shown me.

There was more heat in that *Oh yeah?* than there was when Hudson had told me I was going to have to suck his cock in front of the Christmas tree. Last night, he'd sounded like he was asking me a question about how to fill out his taxes.

Now?

He and Kelly were so into each other—the way his eyes flicked to her nose, her mouth, down to her ample cleavage (talk about store-bought).

I would never be able to enthrall a man like Hudson the way my sister did. My stomach sank with the truth of it.

"You got any other tattoos?" Kelly asked, running her fingers around the waistband of his jeans.

"Just a few. Maybe one day you'll see."

"I'll have to surprise you in the shower."

I stuck the hot pan under the faucet. The grease burst up in a cloud of steam.

Coughing, I waved my hand in front of my face.

Like a demented genie, James appeared. He grabbed my wrist before I almost inadvertently hit him in the face.

"I'm trying to cook."

James released me but still had me cornered by the sink.

"This is pathetic, Gracie. I can't believe how desperate you are."

I desperately wished Hudson would come rescue me even if it was just to pretend to be the possessive boyfriend, but he was too enamored with Kelly to see what was going on.

"You orchestrated all of this to get me back," he continued.

"As if." I sprinkled grated cheese on the pan of eggs.

"Of course you did. And it got out of hand because you don't know what you're doing. Now we all have to watch, embarrassed, as your 'boyfriend'"—James used air quotes—"stands there and flirts with Kelly. He's so out of your league. It's obvious to everyone. Just admit it—you're trying to use Hudson to make me jealous."

"I am not. I don't care about you at all." I stirred the eggs in the hot pan.

"Liar. You're still in love with me."

I hated the look that slithered over James's face, like he was looking at a turtle flipped on its back.

"You really would have taken me back, wouldn't you, if I hadn't proposed to Kelly?"

"No," I said, lying.

The truth?

Yeah, I probably would have. James also wouldn't have needed to grovel or buy me a nice present.

The timer went off.

"Breakfast is ready," I said loudly, breaking up the flirt-fest that Hudson and Kelly were having. "Hudson, can you please put on a shirt?"

"Gracie is such a nag," Kelly said, trailing her fingers down his washboard abs.

My sister helped carry out a platter of freshly made waffles to cheers and applause from my family while I struggled to carry the precariously balanced trays of food into the dining room.

"Did you make sausage?" one of my cousins asked.

"I don't see any," his brother said.

"Gracie," my cousin complained, "you know I like sausage not bacon."

"I know. Hold on. It's in the kitchen," I said, quickly setting out the food and hurrying back to get the rest. I almost collided with Hudson, who was carrying out several more platters, all balanced on his arms like a fancy waiter.

"Sorry." I sidestepped him.

Hudson efficiently slid the platters of food on the antique buffet.

"Thanks for your help," I said as he fixed a plate then handed it to me. "Don't you want more bacon?"

"That's for you," he stated, picking up another plate. "Sit down."

A moment later, Hudson sat next to me at the table.

No one asked me to get them more bacon, extra orange juice, or to make them more eggs.

It sure is nice to eat hot food.

He wiped his mouth after wolfing down his breakfast.

"I have to run," he said to me, reaching to tug one of the curls on my head, making me jump.

James looked smug.

My mom looked pleased.

"That's why you can't hang your hat on a man like that," she told me after Hudson had slammed the front door behind him.

I watched him through the window as he sprang into the cab of the dark-green pickup truck. I wished he would have taken me with him.

Piper gave me a doe-eyed look.

"Kelly says you're going to make some vegan eggnog, and we're having a tasting tonight."

"We are?"

"The wedding welcome party is tomorrow," my mom reminded me.

I felt the panic well up. I had to decorate the venue, finish cooking, and now make vegan eggnog, which I'd never made before?

"When you go to the store, Gracie," my mother said, "can you make sure you pick up some more flour?"

"Why do we keep going through flour?"

"Because your aunt keeps taking it to make playdough for your cousins."

"That's organic flour and very expensive," I said, trying to stay calm.

"They're family," my dad said reproachfully.

"Fine. I need to go to the yarn store anyway."

"You already have so much yarn," my mother reminded me.

"They're doing a drop for special-edition holiday yarn."

"You making everyone scarves again for Christmas?" Logan asked me.

"I'm sick of getting scarves," one of my cousins complained.

I shrank in my seat.

"No, I'm not," I said quietly.

"All she does is make outfits for the dogs now." Kelly rolled her eyes. "That's why I told you to stop worrying about her and Hudson, Mom. A man like him is not going to put up with a girl who knits dog sweaters. He's probably already tired of her."

The food roiled in my stomach. My mom was talking about me with my sister? As if my sister was in any way qualified to give advice about my life.

"Maybe you could start selling the dog clothes and make a little extra money," my dad said encouragingly.

Or maybe you could pay me what I'm worth.

Another entry in the Festivus journal.

James snorted. "That's what Gracie was thinking she would do after we had children—be a stay-at-home mom and knit. In this economy! I told her she was delusional."

Kelly let out peals of laughter.

"Kelly's not going to work either when she has kids," Dakota said, jumping to my defense.

"Yes, I am," Kelly shot back.

"Kelly is an influencer. That's different. She gets brand deals."

"I'm going to be a momfluencer." Kelly tossed her hair.

"An influencer?" Granny Murray scoffed. "So you're just flashing your nipple rings on OnlyFans, then. Got it."

"Mom, are you drinking?"

"Gracie made mimosas."

"No, I didn't."

"Fine." Granny Murray shrugged. "I made my own mimosa."

"We're meeting at the venue this afternoon to decorate, so don't be late. There's a lot to do," my mom reminded me as the rest of the family left the table.

"Is everyone going to be there or just me?" I asked as I stood up.

I was going to the yarn store before I went to decorate, St. Nick help me. So what if I was going to make another dog sweater? Dogs looked cute in sweaters.

"I'll be there after we finish dress shopping," my cousins swore up and down.

Translation: they were never going to show up to help.

"Mom, we're going to miss the flower shop appointment," my sister complained.

"I think the bacon was a little overdone," James told me, handing me the plate.

"Dakota, put that down," her mother scolded as my friend tried to pick up plates. "I told you I have a mother-daughter spa day booked, and so help me god, we will be spending quality time together."

Alone, I slowly picked up all the empty plates.

"You can go get a coffee too," I promised myself.

It took forever to do the washing up. I checked the time as I threw on my coat and wrestled Pugnog into his.

When I got outside, none of the cars were there.

"How am I supposed to buy gallons of nut milk, not to mention all this other stuff, and carry it home?"

I raced to grab the handcart and half jogged into town.

"Everything will be fine with yarn," I told Pugnog, who was trotting along next to me.

The yarn shop was a cute pink-and-white store on Main Street that had been decorated for Christmas with garland wreaths and ornaments made entirely out of yarn.

The shop owner gave me a sympathetic look when I stumbled in, out of breath and sweating under my knitted cap.

"I hope you're not here for the holiday drop," she said. "We just sold out of the last ball."

"You did?" I said, deflating.

"We'll get another order in soon," the shop owner promised. "And we'll let everyone know on Instagram."

"That's okay. I have a lot of yarn anyways," I said, trying to keep the disappointment out of my voice.

The bell over the door tinkled as I went back outside.

I felt like crying.

It was stupid. I knew it was stupid, because the shop was getting more yarn. But I wanted *that* yarn.

"You have a lot of yarn," I told myself. "Now you can go to the store. Just sit down and figure out what you need to make vegan eggnog."

Tears prickled my eyes as I tried to read through the recipes online.

"Where am I supposed to get thirty pounds of macadamia nuts?" I gasped, skimming one recipe.

The panic welled up in me as all the to-do lists raced through my brain. I knew that everyone in my family was going to flake tonight and I was going to have to be up in the wee hours decorating for Kelly's wedding welcome party. Not to mention Hudson was going to be there flirting with her because he liked my sister more than me, just like every other man in the world.

"It's just not fair."

Giving in, I buried my head in my hands and started sobbing right there on the bench.

Pugnog put his paws on my leg while I tried to calm down. I heard him whine, and then large hands cupped my face.

"Gracie, what happened? What's wrong?"

Chapter 17

HUDSON

"**G**racie, tell me what happened," I demanded, cupping her tear-stained face in my hands.

"Nothing. I—" she stammered.

"Did someone hurt you? Was it James?"

Maybe it was me.

It wasn't lost on me how hurt Gracie had seemed when her sister had her hands all over me.

She needs to just get over it. This was what she hired me to do.

Yet here she was crying on a bench.

I should have just ignored her, gone back to the field office to strategize after my meeting with one of my property managers, like I'd intended, but I couldn't just leave her. Everything in me had been screaming to go to her.

If Gracie was actually my girlfriend, I would have kissed the tears off of her face. But seeing as how she'd jerked away from me earlier, I was surprised she was even allowing me to stroke her face.

"Nothing happened," Gracie sobbed.

"Gracie—"

"It's stupid." She sniffled then picked up Pugnog. "You're going to think I'm stupid."

"I won't. I promise."

"I wanted this special yarn," she finally admitted, "and they ran out. See? It's dumb. You think I'm childish."

"You're allowed to like things," I told her carefully. "Can you buy some different yarn? What are you making?"

"I don't need you to solve my problems," she said, blowing her nose.

"To be fair, you did literally hire me to do that, so …"

"Fine." She rolled her eyes. "It's a special Christmas-themed yarn. I'm just complaining. I'll get over it."

"You don't have to pretend like things don't bother you with me," I told her. "I'm not your family."

"They're not like that," she said quickly. "They mean well. They're just stressed."

"Uh-huh."

Gracie fiddled with her mittens. I wondered if she'd made them herself. Probably.

"I don't know anything about knitting," I said, sitting down beside her on the bench, "but isn't it a little late to start making Christmas presents?"

"It's just a dog sweater. It won't take that long."

I looked down at Pugnog, who was wearing yet another Christmas sweater, this one different from the one he'd worn yesterday.

"Not for him. My cousin has a new foster Chihuahua, and I don't want him to feel left out."

"Your family really goes all out for Christmas, huh?" I said.

"It's the happiest time of the year."

"And that's why you're crying on a bench outside of a yarn store," I said to her.

"I'm under a lot of stress. Wedding planning is stressful," she protested.

"Especially when it's someone else's that you're not getting paid for," I added.

Grace crossed her arms and watched the cars, many with Christmas trees attached to their roofs, drive past.

"I see you're making progress though," she said. "The CIA should hire you to be a spy. Just flash that tramp stamp around, and people will be falling all over themselves to give you sensitive information."

I snorted a laugh.

"I always complete the mission."

I tried not to think about her laptop.

"I hope this mission isn't taking you away from your family," she said after another moment of watching cars. "Helping me, I mean."

"Nah," I assured her. "I don't do Christmas."

"Like, you're Jewish?"

"Like I told you, I can't stand the holiday."

"But surely you must do something for the holidays."

"You mean aside from getting shit-faced drunk on Christmas Eve and getting in fights with my brothers?"

I kept my tone flippant, but Christmas Eve before last, Anderson and I had gotten into a drop-down, drag-out fight and spent Christmas in the hospital drinking Pedialyte through a straw. Our little sister, Elsa, had sworn after that she was never spending Christmas with us again.

"How can you not like Christmas?" she argued. "The music, the decorations, the lights, the snow that makes the town look like a movie set. There's special holiday food and Santa and carolers. There has to be some part of Christmas you enjoy."

"Absolutely nothing," I told her. "I just try to get through the holiday as quickly as possible. Nevertheless, it keeps starting earlier and earlier every year."

"Christmas begins right after Halloween."

"It literally does not." I crossed my arms.

"Yeah, it does. That's why they made *The Nightmare Before Christmas*."

"That's not—"

She was smiling.

"Stop fucking with me." I tugged one of the curls creeping out from under her red wool hat.

"I'm going to help you find the true meaning of Christmas," Gracie said, standing up and dusting the falling snow off her skirt.

She grabbed my hand.

"There's a pop-up café that has snowman croissants," she said as she tugged me down the sidewalk. "And the best spiced nutmeg latte you've ever had. That reminds me, don't let me forget to buy macadamia nuts at the store, and if you can muster up a manifestation of a Christmas miracle, I could use one to make this vegan eggnog."

"Vegan eggnog?"

"Oh, sorry," Gracie said shyly, turning back to me, her feet sliding slightly on the icy sidewalk. "Of course you don't have to, if you have other things to do. This isn't a family event or anything, so I guess there's no reason for you to hang out with me."

After working ninety hours a week for the last several months, I had no desire to sit in a dark room scrolling through the illegal shit people did online when they thought no one was looking. All I wanted to do was bask in her enthusiasm and warmth, even it if was directed at Christmas.

"My shift got canceled," I lied.

"Oh yeah?" she asked, her mittened hand still in my gloved one. "Where do you work?"

"The country club."

"Fancy!" She giggled. "I bet you're a hit with all the neglected wives and girlfriends."

"Something like that."

"This is my favorite store," she said as we stopped in front of a display window filled with miniature trains chugging through a forest landscape toward a small village decorated for Christmas. Gracie leaned forward, immersed in the tiny world.

"A toy store?" I said mildly.

"Let's go in. Can we?"

Everything in my life, any menial job, any hobbies, was all a careful calculus of where I would be able to pull information on people for my clients. I didn't do things "just for fun."

Yet I was window-shopping with Gracie like I was a normal person out with his girlfriend. It felt like it had been years since I'd ever done something so mundanely human.

Except you aren't, are you? It's all another trick.

"Sure."

"Don't sound so enthusiastic," she teased as I allowed her to tug me inside. "It's Christmas. Find your inner child."

Pugnog was eyeing a basket of teddy bears under a Christmas tree festooned with ornaments. I scooped the dog up before he could eat anything.

Gracie was totally absorbed in the miniature scenes of domesticity displayed around the store.

"I always feel like a giant when I come in here," she whispered to me excitedly. "None of my family likes this store. They complain it's too expensive, and why does a miniature coffee pot cost more than an actual one."

She sighed and put it back.

"You don't want it?" I asked. Part of me just wanted to buy it for her, even though it might look suspicious for a down-on-his-luck bad boy to be shelling out serious cash for a tiny coffee pot.

"I don't really have the room," she said.

I smirked. "Really?"

She giggled.

"In my dream home, I was supposed to have a room just for miniatures. If I'd gotten married … Well, James and I were supposed to buy a big Victorian house."

"Guess that's never happening."

"Oh, he bought it. Just not for me." She trailed her fingers along a miniature piano.

"Screw James," I told her. "You don't need a man to own a house. It's the twenty-first century."

"It just seems silly for one person to have all that house." She sighed. "Besides I can't afford it. I've been trying to save up my money, but New York City is expensive, and you really need two incomes to buy a house, even in this town. Anyway, I can get my miniature fixes other ways. Every year, I go to Chicago for a miniatures conference. Did you know you can buy miniature working nacho machines?"

"What?"

"I'll have to take you sometime," she said, picking up a miniature knitting basket with balls of yarn.

"What do you think?" she asked, holding it up on the palm of her hand. "Look. The knitting needles work. If you had tiny hands, you could knit a tiny sweater."

"Is that going with the mouse in the kitchen who's stewing in resentment at her ungrateful children, or the mouse lying in bed in the attic sleeping off all that Christmas brandy?" I asked, referencing the elaborate dollhouse in Gracie's bedroom.

"Neither," Gracie said, sticking her tongue out. "You actually secretly like miniatures. You're making up whole stories for the people that live in the miniature house," she said, poking me lightly in the abs. "This is for my cousin. She's interested in miniatures."

"You're not making her a scarf or a hat?"

"I made beer koozies," she said, sounding slightly guilty, "but it's fun to give kids toys on Christmas. And pets," she added.

Pugnog's tongue flopped out of his mouth.

"Oh, look," Gracie cooed at a tiny painting of a pug in a tuxedo. "I can't not buy that." She put the miniature carefully in the small basket. "I just love this store. Did you see this lamp? It even lights up."

"That doesn't seem very Victorian," I said, inspecting the miniature lamp that had a more contemporary aesthetic.

"I know, but maybe one day I'll have a modernist doll-house, and then I'll need this lamp."

A rug, a tiny credenza, and a tiny teddy bear with movable arms also went into her basket.

"I'm buying local," she said defensively.

"I didn't say anything."

I shifted Pugnog to my other arm as we slowly made our way to the cashier's counter, where an ancient man greeted her like a long-lost daughter and rang up her purchase on an ancient cash register with physical painted buttons.

I wondered if there was a way I could convince Gracie to take me to her family's office as we headed back out into the cold. Unlike on the Gulch side of Maplewood Falls, here the shops were bustling, the sidewalks clean, and the people didn't clutch their purses close to their chests.

Not that the Gulch was as bad as it had been when I'd been a kid. But still. There weren't shops dedicated to high-end dog treats or cupcakes.

"This is Pugnog's favorite shop," Gracie pleaded as we walked past a small pet boutique decorated to look like a 1920s Paris café.

The dog was greeted like a celebrity when I opened the door for Gracie and the pug. Several middle-aged women rushed over to him, cooing excitedly while I stood there looking around at all the over-the-top dog accessories.

Gracie let Pugnog off his leash, and he ran around the store sniffing other dogs, stubby curled tail wagging.

"Is this him?" one of the women asked Gracie in a stage whisper.

"He can hear you, you know," her friend hissed back.

"I used to date a man from the other side of town," one of the woman said, eyeing me up and down.

I raised my eyebrow.

She sighed. "He had a motorcycle and got in bar fights. My father hated him."

"Did you run off with him anyways?" Gracie asked her.

"Oh, no. My father paid him $1,000 to never speak to me, and I married a banker. I was sad, of course, but it was for the best. Men like that are fun when you're young, not so great when you're older," she said with a laugh and elbowed me, like it was a joke that I should be in on.

Why do you care? I asked myself as the bitter bile rose up.

Because ...

Because ...

Because that wasn't who I was. Sure, I rode a motorcycle and got in bar fights, but technically, I could trace my family tree back to the Mayflower. My family had been one of the elite names in New England, along with the Rockefellers, the Van de Bergs, and the Rhodes.

All of that wealth and influence had been squandered in the last century.

My family had built the old resort area along the canal that used to be one of the hot spots in Victorian New England. That was before the hot springs had dried up and the highway had been routed through. The family's crumbling summer mansion had been partitioned for apartments in the '80s. When it burned down, it was the final elegy to what was once a great family.

These women, though, all they saw was some kid from poverty who had nothing to offer a girl like Gracie.

You don't, I reminded myself forcefully. *Remember? Gracie is a means to an end. So what if her family thinks you're trash. That's the whole point.*

The piece of me that I thought I had killed off was wounded.

Fuck you.

Some part of me wanted Gracie to defend me, to say that of course I would be a good husband, was someone she'd want to build her fantasy life with and live with in a historic Victorian house with a room dedicated to miniatures.

Instead she just laughed. "It is taking a walk on the wild side."

Bitch.

"You certainly are doing your best to domesticate him," one of the women chortled.

"He's being a trooper." Gracie patted my arm.

"She'll make it up to you later," one of the women assured me.

Yeah. She would as soon as I got my hands on that laptop.

"I need some stocking stuffers for the dogs," she said excitedly, handing me a basket and immediately filling it with dog treats. "I was going to bake some," she said as she stuck an oversized rawhide bone shaped like a candy cane with a red stripe into the basket. "But my sister wants pistachio cookies for her wedding."

"Why is the maid of honor cosplaying as the caterer?" I asked as she perused the selection of dog outfits.

"I'm not the maid of honor."

"Wait. What?"

Gracie gave me another guilty look.

"I'm just a bridesmaid. Well, an understudy bridesmaid, in case one of my sister's friends can't make it on Christmas."

I was suddenly sick of the whole thing. This was why I'd been trying to transition into more of a behind-the-scenes role. For some reason, my line of work never included spending time with mentally stable people.

"Do you see anything for guinea pigs?" Gracie asked me as she meandered through the store, filling up the basket.

"How many pets do you have?" I finally asked, unable to contain it any longer.

"Pugnog has thirty dog cousins and twenty-two cat cousins, not to mention my cousin Ari has a guinea pig that just became a mother of five."

"And they all need gifts," I said dryly.

"Of course! It's Christmas," she said determinedly.

A guinea pig outfit that made a rodent look like a reindeer was put in the overflowing basket.

"It's good to spend money in the community."

She and the woman at the cash register chatted about dog grooming as Gracie checked out.

You are getting paid to be here, I chanted to myself.

Except that was false. I was getting paid to snoop on Gracie's laptop or at the EnerCheck office.

I glanced at my watch when we stepped back out on the sidewalk, Pugnog hyped from being in a store just for him.

It was probably too much to hope that Gracie would suggest we head over to the office.

I rolled my shoulders.

"You can leave if you want," Gracie said in a rush. "You don't have to hang out with me while I shop."

I worked my jaw. If I left, she'd go to the office, and it would be just my luck to miss the opportunity.

"It's fine. Besides, the more pressure the townspeople put on your parents about you dating someone unsavory, the better."

Gracie winced.

"I don't think you're unsavory. Just ignore what those women were saying. They can be judgmental to people they don't understand. They don't know you."

"You don't have to lie to me, Sugarplum," I drawled. "I'm not really your boyfriend, remember?"

"No, but you are a good basket carrier," she said with a small smile and headed to yet another store.

"What happened to getting coffee and a snack?" I asked, trying not to sound desperate as I followed her in to the high-end home goods store.

Grace giggled behind her hand.

"I promise I'll give you a really tasty, yummy snack. You'll love the bakery down the street," she promised as ornaments, candles, and bags of potpourri went into the large basket I was carrying.

"I should have brought my rucksack."

I looked down at the pug. His tongue flopped out of his inset jaw.

Gracie had him tucked under her arm since I had been relegated to pack mule. For someone who claimed she wasn't planning on buying anything today, this woman could shop.

She led me through the store to the back wall where the store was selling novelty oversized porcelain drink dispensers with Christmas scenes on them.

"What in god's name do you need that for?" I snarled at her.

She gave me that wide-eyed look.

"I told you Kelly's wedding welcome party is holiday themed, and we're having a variety of eggnogs. This one is for the vegan eggnog."

"No wonder you can't buy a house."

"Okay boomer," she scoffed. "You live in a tent."

I gave her an odd look. "Actually, I live in a semi-nice apartment building."

"Oh." She seemed taken aback.

Yet another reason why you're an idiot for starting to feel anything for her.

"Unexpected for a boy from the wrong side of the tracks, huh," I said, acid in my voice.

"I, well … I just … I guess I wasn't thinking," she said. "I'm sorry."

She turned around abruptly to stare at the drink dispensers.

"This one is the only one big enough, but do you think vegans will be offended that there are animals eating mince-meat pie on it?"

"I'm not a vegan, and I'm offended by this whole shit show." I flipped over the price tag. "They want how much for this?"

"This is for family, and it's Christmas."

"That's your justification for everything," I said, scooting her out of the way so I could pick up the unwieldy beverage dispenser.

She hovered next to me as I carried it up to the checkout counter.

"Oh, isn't this snowman sweet?" Gracie squealed, holding up a smiling handmade snowman mug.

"No comment."

"You can't run your poor boyfriend ragged," the woman at the checkout counter said to her as she rang up the excessive amount of candles. I mean seriously, how many candles did one person need in their life?

"You push a man to the edge, and he'll walk off the job."

Gracie squeezed my arm and beamed up at me.

"I'm going to get him a cupcake," Gracie said earnestly.

"You need to give him a steak and a blow job," the cashier said as she typed in the price of the beverage dispenser with a stylus.

"I like the sound of that." I grinned.

Gracie chewed on her lip.

"Guess you know what to put in his stocking." The cashier winked at her, and Gracie handed over her credit card.

"Oh my gosh," she said, when we were back on the sidewalk. "I forgot I'm supposed to go over to the venue."

If I was going to be committed to spending the day with her, I did not want to spend it decorating for her sister's wedding.

I couldn't understand the contradiction of Gracie O'Brien. How could she have the wherewithal to give me and my men the runaround while simultaneously be unable to say no to providing free wedding planning, decorating, and catering to the sister that had cheated on her with her fiancé the day before her own wedding?

"You promised me a cupcake."

"I thought it was upgraded to steak and a blow job," she said and stuck her tongue out at me.

"If that will get you to commit to this fake relationship, I'll even make sure I shave for you," I promised her, adjusting my grip on the oversized beverage dispenser.

Gracie looked at me in horror. "What do you mean, shave?" she blurted out. "Do you mean it's normally covered in hair like a sea cucumber?"

"What the hell?" I stopped short.

Pugnog crashed into the back of my legs. Gracie's eyes were big and round in her head.

"Holy shit," I said as the only logical conclusion dawned on me.

"It was just a joke," Gracie said in a rush.

I narrowed my eyes.

"When your grandmother suggested you and I make out, you looked like you were about to puke. And you act like a scared bunny rabbit anytime I touch you."

"No, I don't." Gracie reddened.

"You're not a virgin, are you?" I demanded.

"Virginity is a social construct," she said weakly.

"Fuck," I swore.

My job had just gotten a thousand times harder.

Chapter 18

GRACIE

"I think you're overreacting," I said desperately as Hudson looked like he was about to have an aneurysm there under the mistletoe.

"Why did I not know this?" he was muttering to himself.

I shifted my weight on my feet.

"I think we need some baked goods," I said, urging him to the Jingle Beans café.

The café was feminine with delicate metal chairs and small round tables.

"Hi, a Christmas Spirit, a Rudolph tea cake, and a White-Chocolate Winter Wonderland, please," I asked the server when she came by for our order.

"Look," I told Hudson when we were alone, leaning over the table and lowering my voice. "There is no need to panic. Man up, right?"

Hudson sat there for a good, long few minutes in silence, just staring at me.

"You knit," he said flatly, "and you wear flannel pajamas that your own grandmother wouldn't even be caught dead in."

I winced. "Now, see, that's just—"

"You collect stuffed mice. You like to shop for toys."

"Those were not for me. Well, not all of them," I protested.

"You're a child," he said, "and I'm going to hell."

The server brought over our drinks and dessert.

"Feast on the spirit of Christmas!" She set the food down with a flourish.

"I hate this town," Hudson said when she left. He looked suspiciously at his drink.

"I think you're being a tad dramatic."

"I'm being dramatic?" he snarled, leaning over the tiny table so close to me I could kiss him on the nose. Though with the state he was in, that might put him over the edge.

"All I'm saying is we don't have to have sex," I whispered.

"Half your family wants me strung up on the North Pole, and the other half thinks I'm a homeless drifter whom you hired to be your fake boyfriend."

"Homeless drifters don't know how to use whom properly," I said, "so I highly doubt that."

Something akin to apprehension seemed to flash in his face.

Probably related to his sudden obsession with my virginity.

"Fine. But we could fake it, right? We could pretend?"

"They're going to know we didn't actually do it," he countered. "Fuck. We got lucky that they didn't ask prying questions before. I mean, fuck, you think a penis is covered in hair."

"They could be." I felt sick.

"No," he said, shaking his head. "No, they are not."

"You think that just because I made a choice that works for me that it means there's something wrong with me," I cried. "I mean, I know there's something wrong with me. James said so. He said he was going to tell everyone. That's why I didn't make a big stink about him and Kelly."

Hudson blew out a breath, cursed, closed his eyes, mumbled something about killing James, opened them, and laid his palms flat on the table.

"Look, Sugarplum," he said carefully. "I don't care if you wanted to wait to ride a cock until the dinosaurs came back. Your life isn't that important to me. But you have put me in a shitty position."

I winced.

"That's why I think we could just, you know, stage something," I said awkwardly. "Like jump up and down on the bed and make loud noises."

Those silver-gray eyes bored into me.

"Sure, but first tell me, what's your favorite way of getting fucked?"

"Um, I—" I stammered, reaching for my coffee to give me something to do. "Doggy style?" I said weakly.

"I'm not convinced."

"It's an awkward question."

"Tough shit, Sugarplum, because that's going to be a question your grandmother or one of the other thousand female sex-obsessed family members you have is going to ask."

"We can watch some porn together," I said, reaching for a solution, "and we can get our stories straight on our favorite sex positions."

"God help me."

He rested his elbows on the table, his hands sliding over his mouth.

"We are going to have to have sex, right?" It sounded like the question was directed to himself more so than me.

"Do we really have to?" I croaked. "I was sort of saving myself for marriage."

"I need to quit," Hudson said.

I pushed over the spiked hot chocolate to him.

He took a deep swig.

"Can they put more alcohol in it?"

"Eat this. You need some sugar." I handed him the fork.

He cut off a chunk of Rudolph's ear then swore loudly as red currant custard oozed out.

"This is a very popular item on TikTok," I told him, stabbing the booze-soaked cherry that made up the reindeer's nose.

He pushed the plate towards me.

"I'm pretty sure I can fake an orgasm," I said determinedly.

"You've never"—he gestured at me—"made yourself come with a snowman-shaped vibrator?"

"Look, mister, I don't need your judgment," I said hotly.

I took a big swallow of my coffee and licked the whipped cream off my mouth.

"I was trying to be not like my sister," I said, cutting off a big hunk of Rudolph's head and shoving it in my mouth, the whipped cream, currant custard, and chocolate cake doing very little to calm my frayed nerves. "Kelly started having sex when she was thirteen. Convinced one of the teacher's pets to do it with her in an empty classroom. His parents flipped out and showed up at the house. Kelly lapped up the attention and made everyone think she was pregnant. My mom and dad sat me down and read me the riot act about how sex can ruin your life and that I needed to wait until marriage. They begged me to have some self-control because they couldn't have two children going off the rails. I was just trying to be a good daughter."

The server came back over.

Hudson was still staring at me, horrified, through his fingers.

"Could I have a Candy Cane Crunch Frappuccino?" I asked the waitress.

"Can I have another Christmas Spirit?" Hudson asked the server. "But without the Christmas part? Just the spirit part."

"No," she said, shaking her head. "You can't just have the alcohol by itself. We do have a rum-spiked eggnog cheesecake. I can put extra rum on it for you."

"I'll take it," Hudson said.

"Look, Sugarplum," he began when the server was safely out of earshot.

"Please don't quit," I begged.

"I wish I could quit," he muttered then straightened up. "Part of the rules you agreed to were that you did what I say."

I drained the rest of my coffee.

"I agreed to those terms before I knew what I was agreeing to," I rasped out.

His silver eyes narrowed.

"Why can't you just try harder to break up my sister and James?" I wheedled. "I saw the way she was all over you this morning."

"Kelly wants the hunt," he said simply. "If I sleep with her now, she'll just whine and cry to your parents and James that it was a mistake, that the bad boy seduced her. I bet she turns it around and blames you somehow. No, we need to make it spectacular, irrefutable, then we hack the AV system and play the video of her cheating on James at the wedding ceremony."

My eyes bugged out like Pugnog's.

"After the big explosion, you and I will get engaged at your sister's reception. Maximum pain."

"You're evil," I said after a moment.

"You in or out?"

"Does being in mean I have to ... you know?" I was sweating. My tank top under my sweater was drenched.

Hudson's face softened ever so slightly.

"I really don't want to be the person to take your virginity. I've done a lot of bad things but ... shit. I'll figure something else out."

"I'm pretty sure I can give you a hand job," I offered. "I'm not totally inexperienced. One time James asked me to dress up in lingerie and humped my leg."

Hudson growled low in his throat. "I'm going to fucking murder him."

The server came by with the next round, winked at Hudson, and handed him a scotch.

"I think it's only fair, considering all the community service you do."

"Right," I said faintly. "Are there veteran's discounts here or something?"

"Not that. The photo." The server winked at him again.
I slid down in my seat.

Hudson blinked and took in a deep, long breath.

"I am so sorry, Hudson," I said my chin barely above the edge of the table. "I swear I didn't send that photo to anyone."

Hudson twisted his neck, cracking it.

"Gosh, I'm a terrible person," I babbled. "I shouldn't have shown anyone. I am so sorry."

"That was the point of the photo," he said, voice tense. "To prove to your family that we were the real deal."

"It was still wrong of me. I should have kept better control."

I pulled out my phone. "I bet Violet freaking forwarded it to herself. She is getting coal in her Christmas stocking," I promised. "Oh fuck."

He gave me a questioning look.

"Fuck, fuck," I said as I scrolled through the phone. I had a thousand missed calls and messages.

"I'm hours late for decorating. Everyone is so mad at me. Oh my gosh. What am I going to do?" I wailed, wishing I could just go home and hide except …

"I forgot about the vegan eggnog." I stuffed a big forkful of Hudson's cheesecake in my mouth.

"What the—"

"You don't like desserts," I said hysterically. "And I need this cheesecake."

Chapter 19

HUDSON

"**S**top panicking," I ordered. "You need a plan."

"I had a plan," she said pulling out an over-stuffed white notebook covered in feathers from her large bag.

"That's not a plan. That's an abomination."

What I needed to do was not get involved in her family's wedding drama, but everything in me was screaming out for something, anything to distract me from the fact that Gracie was a goddamn virgin. She was almost thirty, for fuck's sake.

"What are your goals?" I asked, taking the glitter pen from her and opening a blank page in the overstuffed notebook.

"I need to make that eggnog."

"Wrong. Eggnog simply needs to be at the venue to taste test. We're going to stop at the store and buy some. Next."

"But Kelly said—"

"I don't care what she said. You lie," I ordered, enunciating the words, "and tell her what she wants to hear."

"They're going to know," Grace said nervously.

"People are never as perceptive as they think they are," I told her. "Trust me."

Or actually, don't.

"Next goal."

Gracie reached over for another bite of the cheesecake. I finally just pushed it over to her.

"Kelly wants a winter wonderland theme for the welcome party. Everything has a specific place. I have a diagram. Oh gosh, it's going to take me all night to decorate."

"I supposed it's too much to ask if your family is going to help," I said dryly.

"I mean maybe?"

"Yeah, and maybe I'll win the lottery," I said. "Kelly just needs a nicely decorated party. Turn the lights down low, serve lots of booze, and no one will know the difference."

"But if it's not exactly like she wants—"

I sat back in my chair. "Who planned the wedding?"

"Me," she admitted.

"Just you or you and Kelly together?"

"Kelly told me what she wanted, and I showed her sketches. She was so nitpicky."

"Were her requests random and contradictory?" I pressed.

"My sister can be flighty."

"Kelly didn't actually have an opinion," I said confidently. "She was just trying to fuck with you. She's not going to know that the inflatable Frosty the Snowman was supposed to go in the corner with the Christmas trees or by the front door."

"This party will not feature an inflatable Frosty."

"I feel like you sold me a bill of goods on your love of Christmas, Sugarplum."

We were on the back side of the Canning Factory venue, and I was emptying jugs of almond milk eggnog into the drink dispenser. I wasn't a chef, but the mixture seemed a little gritty.

"This doesn't look anything like eggnog."

I dumped in cinnamon, nutmeg, and, of course, half a bottle of rum.

"Now it does."

"I can't handle this," Gracie fretted. "You know I'm terrible at lying."

"Oh, I know," I said, picking up the beverage dispenser off the bed of the forest-green pickup, then headed through the service entry into the venue where Kelly's party was being held.

You would think with thirty people already at the venue that more would have gotten done on the decorating front, I thought when I carried in the tureen. There were tangled strings of lights lying near the stairs up to the mezzanine, a tipped-over glass of eggnog was drying on the floor, and I was no decorator, but the way the tinsel had been dumped all over one of the trees was not—I was pretty confident— what Gracie had imagined for a winter wonderland.

The whole place smelled like boozy eggnog, and the wedding party was lounging on several overstuffed red velvet couches.

"Where's the rest of it? The tasting is supposed to happen after decorating," Gracie cried as she saw the empty jugs of eggnog on a nearby table.

"You weren't here," Kelly snapped at her. "You abandoned me, and Miranda didn't get any eggnog."

I set the heavy drink dispenser on the table.

"Vegan eggnog for her pleasure."

The drunk bridesmaids let out wolf whistles.

"There rum in that nut sludge, sonny?" Granny Murray slurred.

"I'm sorry, Kelly," Gracie apologized. "I lost track of time."

"If I had a man like that at my beck and call," Granny Murray hooted, "I'd lose track of time too. Shit. I wouldn't have even shown up, and let him come down my chimney all night long."

"Funny," Dakota said, loud enough for all of us to hear. "I'm pretty sure that's how Kelly got engaged." As apparently the only person who could actually do anything, Dakota was stringing up a garland on the balcony up above.

"Aunt Babs," Kelly raged.

"Girls, why don't we all go eat dinner at the country club tonight," Gracie's mother said. "They have cilantro soup, Kelly, for your wedding diet. Also, Mitsy said that the chef created a new caviar dish that we absolutely must try. Gracie can finish up the decorating. The party is tomorrow, and we're under the gun."

I tried hard to resist the urge to yell, *What the fuck* at her family, but Dakota beat me to it.

"You all suck," she said, pointing at the bridesmaids, who were knocking back shots of vegan eggnog.

"We've been here all afternoon. We need a break," her cousins complained as Bethany herded Kelly and the bridesmaids to the door.

"They only decorated half a tree, for chrissake!" Dakota hollered.

"It's fine," Gracie pleaded. "They're too drunk to be useful anyway."

"I'm going down with the ship," Granny Murray called after them then saluted Gracie, almost falling over.

"How much eggnog have you had?" Gracie wrinkled her nose.

Granny Murray elbowed me.

"The question is how much rum did I have with my eggnog." She poured herself some vegan eggnog, took a swig, and smacked her lips. "That hippie nut sludge shit is pretty good."

She offered me the cup.

"What the hell." I took a sip. "It just tastes like rum."

"Damn right."

There was beeping outside and a crunching noise. It sounded expensive.

I'd invested a fair amount of my military reenlistment bonus into fixing up this former canning factory, and at the rate this mission was going, I wasn't going to have extra money to devote to fixing whatever the hell had just been broken.

Gracie hurried after me as I jogged outside. She skidded to a halt beside me as a dump truck was emptying out a dumpster's worth of round logs in front of the venue, all over the dormant flowerbeds.

"Hey, man, what the hell? You can't dump this here," I shouted at the driver. "You need to take all this back to whatever construction site you hauled it off of."

The driver sighed and made a big show of pulling out the shipping manifest.

"This is a delivery, man."

"Who orders unsplit cut-up tree trunks?" I growled.

"This is Ms. Gracie O'Brien's order."

He tipped his hat to Gracie, standing behind me.

"Would that be you, miss?"

"I didn't want all of this," she cried. "We just needed a cord of firewood. It's supposed to be for atmosphere."

She waved the overstuffed white notebook at him.

"I have the order here," she said and flipped through the notebook.

"Ma'am, we ran out of seasoned firewood. This is all we got. We understand that it's for a wedding and didn't want to let the bride down." He pressed a button on the truck, and the dump-truck bed swung back into place.

"No, you can't leave," Gracie begged, pushing her way around me. "Take this wood back. This is not my order. What am I going to do with it?"

"Well," the driver said, pulling out an axe with a bow on it. "Since it's Christmas and you've been a wonderful customer, here's your Christmas present." He handed it to her. "Maybe you can convince the groomsmen to show off some muscles."

He put the truck into gear and rumbled off, turning onto the industrial road that led to the interstate.

Gracie picked up the axe and dragged it over to the nearest log.

"Gracie," I said as she swung the axe down on a log. It hit it unevenly and bounced off, flying back up.

She raised her arms to strike the log again.

"Gracie, stop. You're going to cut your foot off. Put the axe down."

Her eyes were watering, and her chin was trembling.

"This party is going to be a disaster."

"Hey," I said, taking the axe away from her, "remember what I said? It doesn't have to be perfect. It just has to be done."

"But all this wood …"

It was a lot of wood.

I shrugged off my jacket and dumped it on a nearby log.

"I'll take care of it," I promised her.

What are you doing? You are way too enmeshed with her.

With practiced ease, I swung the axe, bringing it down parallel with the wood grain. The log split easily in two.

I turned it and split it again, tossed the firewood into a pile, and moved to the next log.

"Where do you want all of this?" I asked, hefting the axe again.

"We can just artfully pile it around the venue," she said. "I'll have to figure out where. Gosh, this is such a disaster. Maybe Dakota is right and I should just buy a plane ticket and spend Christmas in Aspen."

And have all the work I'd done, the bus ride, the shopping trip, the dealing with her overbearing family, go to waste? No fucking way.

I dropped the axe and stepped up to her.

"What did I say?" I told her. "Man the fuck up. No prisoners. You want to get back at your sister? Or do you want to be here two years from now when she's cheated on James and everyone is simultaneously telling you to plan her second wedding, take care of her kid for free, and go back to being James's little hand-job robot, while you stand there and take it? Stop being weak."

Grace swallowed.

"Are you going to collapse on me?" I asked her.

"No."

"Good girl. Now get decorating. We want done, not perfect."

Gracie hurried back to the venue then paused and glanced back at me over her shoulder.

"You're pretty good at motivational speeches."

"Your tax dollars at work," I said dryly.

Through the large factory windows, I watched Gracie determinedly decorate for her sister's holiday wedding.

The sky was quickly darkening—the sun went down early this far north—and I moved the logs into the cone of light from a nearby light pole. I could chop wood in my sleep. When I was a teenager, I basically had. It got cold in New England. The wood-burning fireplace in the ancient mansion was our only source of warmth. We'd had to sleep like puppies to keep from freezing, and I'd always had to set alarms to make sure to feed the fire.

"That's not you anymore," I reminded myself.

Yeah, because one Christmas Eve the fucking house had burned down.

I brought the axe down hard on the log, splitting the cold air with a sharp *crack*.

I shouldn't be thinking about it. I should just get over it.

That day had been the last time I'd seen my mother. She had been screaming, throwing things at me as the firemen had milled around, spraying the giant hose on the flames.

I hadn't known what to do. She kept telling the police I'd burned the house down on purpose, that I was a murderer.

"You are a bad person," I reminded myself as the axe fell on the half-moon of log, covered by a light dusting of snow.

"You're going to take some innocent girl's virginity."

You don't have to.

But I did.

The thing with blending in was maintaining expected patterns. If walking into an office, pretend like you belong, wear an orange vest, a button-down shirt with a name patch, and carry a clipboard and a ladder.

People expected maintenance men to be around and were trained to ignore them, even if they seemed slightly confused, because, well, that's normal. If, by contrast, you showed up in a suit at a banking office and started wandering around then, people were going to notice and home their attention on you, ask you who you were, if you're there for a meeting. Scrutiny ruined missions.

If Gracie's family thought we weren't sleeping together, if they never saw me kiss her or saw us with our hands all over each other, then we would be going against the expected pattern of a bad boy and good girl gone wrong.

It was clear I wasn't going to get in her laptop anytime soon. I had to escalate in order to not blow my cover.

"Gracie is not a girl. She's a grown woman," I reminded myself.

Yeah, a full-grown woman with huge tits and soft thighs.

If she doesn't lose it with you, I tried to rationalize, *she might with James. She's so desperate for a husband and family, she's got blinders on.*

Snow crunched behind me, and I jumped out of my skin.

I strangled a curse and whirled around, furious that I'd allowed myself to be so consumed with thoughts of Gracie that I hadn't noticed someone sneaking up on me.

"I don't have the fucking patience," I snarled.

Gracie skittered backward, almost falling down.

I grabbed her before she could trip over a nearby piece of firewood.

"I just wanted to see if you were hungry. I can see if Uber Eats delivers out here."

"They won't." I stated, swinging the axe and splitting another log. "There's a great Philly cheesesteak place near here," I told her, trying to keep my tone even. "They serve the few factory workers left in the area, plus they stay open late after servers get off the restaurant shifts. It's likely the only place open. It's not a fancy new caviar dish, but they have pretty good fries. They're not going to deliver for just anyone, but Gio and I go way back."

Gracie reached up on her toes and wrapped her arms around my neck.

"Thank you. That sounds wonderful."

I had a sudden awful desire to kiss her right there in the swirls of snow.

I pushed her off.

She seemed slightly hurt.

"There's no audience," I said, my tone harsh to my ears. "So don't pretend to be my girlfriend."

"Right," she said. "Well, thanks for the food."

"I'll bill you your half." I turned back to the wood.

"Oh, of course."

You are such an asshole.

Chapter 20

GRACIE

I shouldn't have been so taken aback that Hudson would want me to pay for my share of dinner. He'd just heard my mom talk about eating caviar at the country club, not to mention he was telling me about a cheesesteak place only people who worked minimum wage jobs knew about. This was all after I'd spent way too much money on dog treats.

"Hudson thinks I'm a spoiled princess," I said miserably.

"You can't seriously be falling for this guy," Dakota said. "He is not at all your type. He must really have a magical D."

The dull thudding sound of Hudson chopping wood outside in the cold sounded through the windows.

I sat down on a bench and looked around the venue. We'd made progress, just not enough.

"I'm going to tell my mom to make everyone come back," Dakota told me.

"It won't help. I'm going to have to chase after everyone to make sure they're doing it right then have to redo it myself anyway," I said dejectedly.

Thud.

Outside, the axe continued to fall.

"Just peace the fuck out," Dakota insisted. "We can steal Hudson's truck and just drive. Shoot, we could go back to the city, give Kelly a taste of her own medicine."

We both looked out the window to where Hudson was in his T-shirt, chopping wood.

"I feel like he's just showing off," Dakota mused as we watched him, body twisting like a dancer's as he split the heavy logs.

"He's had a stressful day," I said, wincing as the log split with a *crack*. "He probably needs to blow off the steam. Or maybe having him chop several cords of wood is the thing that is going to send him over the edge. Who knows?"

"Aw, so you weren't losing the V-card. Or wait—did you, and that's why he's stressed out?"

"Shhh," I hissed at Dakota. "No one can know."

Though I had promised my parents to not give it away like my sister did, I assumed that they and the rest of my family thought that I had lost my V-card eventually.

Little did they know that I carried that bit of repressed toxicity with me. Now I was coming up on thirty, and I was sure they would like to believe I'd already lost it because otherwise it was a pretty big red flag on my part. Yet here I was, all alone at my sister's wedding venue, lusting after a man who I had paid to be my fake boyfriend.

"Does he know?" Dakota asked, eyes wide.

"Yes," I admitted, "and I think he hates me for it."

"You hired him, so what does he care?"

"I don't know," I whimpered, remembering the coldness in his eyes.

Gran was thankfully asleep, the eggnog and rum doing their job.

"I don't want to sleep with him. At all. Like you said, Hudson is not my type. I do not find him attractive, and, unlike the rest of the women in this town, I don't stare at a photo of his naked penis."

Dakota snickered.

"You said penis."

"Two master's degrees, and she's an eight-year-old boy at heart." I stood up and grabbed a nearby box of Christmas lights.

Dakota sighed and climbed back on the ladder.

"You slept next to his naked body. I cannot believe you didn't cop a feel. If you're going to go to the trouble of paying a hot guy to be your sexy motorcycle-leather-wearing daddy, then you should get your money's worth."

"It would be completely unethical and immoral to sleep with Hudson," I told her in a low voice as we strung up the Christmas lights in even loops along the brick walls. "He works for me."

"Weren't you telling me how he seems very insistent that you two needed to do the nasty?"

"That was before I told him … you know."

My cousin shook her head. "You seriously need to keep that information under wraps. You cannot keep telling your boyfriends you're an inexperienced virgin."

"Hudson is an employee of sorts. He needed to know."

"James didn't."

"I had to have a reason I wasn't putting out," I hissed.

"Or you could have taken it as a sign that the two of you were not meant to be together."

"He thought it was exciting that he was going to deflower me on our wedding night."

"Gross. Big waving bright-red flag, Gracie," Dakota warned. "If you had told me that last year, I would have run over him with my car."

The door to the venue opened, letting in the winter chill.

Hudson stalked over to me, large paper sack in hand.

"Dinner's here." He set the bag on the table and opened it.

My mouth watered at the smell of french fries, fried beef, Cheez Whiz, and fried onions filling the air.

"I got everyone a Coke," he added.

"A Coke," Dakota said dreamily beside me.

"Is there any more rum?" Granny Murray sat up from one of the velvet couches.

"Gran, come have some french fries," I urged the elderly woman as, bones creaking, she slowly stood up.

"I ordered her a cheesesteak," Hudson told me, still cold and distant, not like how he was earlier that afternoon, where if you squinted, he almost felt like a boyfriend.

Not your type. Bad boys are not your type, I repeated, moving the garland off of one of the tables, spreading out a table runner, and making a quick centerpiece from sprigs of garland and a few candles. "Where's the cigarette lighter?"

Hudson pulled a metal one out of his pocket. "This is unnecessary."

"Just because it's cheesesteak doesn't mean we can't be civilized," I argued.

He snorted and pulled out a cheesesteak, unwrapped it, and took a huge bite.

"But where's the rum?" Granny Murray mumbled, sitting down at the table.

"She masturbates to *Pirates of the Caribbean*," I told Hudson, handing out the Christmas plates and cloth napkins. "Just ignore her."

Hudson inhaled the bite of cheesesteak.

I whacked him on the back while he coughed.

"That's why you need to sit down and eat."

He pulled out a chair next to Granny Murray.

I gave each person a helping of fries.

"Damn, these are better than sex in the back of a pickup," Granny Murray said, stuffing several in her mouth.

"Gran, this is a nice dinner," I warned.

"Damn right. I love cheesesteaks," Granny Murray said happily as I handed her a sandwich and sat down, spreading the cloth napkin over my lap. "My ex-husband, that bastard, hated them. I think they're great because I don't need my teeth in to eat them."

She popped her false teeth out of her mouth and set them in a snowman candy dish.

Hudson stoically ate his food. He was unlike the soft, refined young men I'd gone to private school with who used fish knives and got mad if their wine was the incorrect vintage.

I gave him more fries, and he wolfed them down like someone was going to take them from him.

"Does he eat pussy like that?" Granny Murray stage-whispered to me.

"This is the worst Christmas ever," I said to the ceiling.

Hudson wiped his mouth with the back of his sleeve, took a long swig of Coke from the paper cup, then stood up.

I had barely made it through a third of my cheesesteak.

"Heading back to work already? Don't you want me to give you a back massage first?" Granny Murray offered, pouring the rest of the bottle of rum Hudson had brought into her Coke cup.

"I'll have to finish up," he said, "to keep up with Gracie. Did you secretly blackmail Santa's elves to come help you?" He inclined his head to the decorations.

"Oh!" I said brightly. "We still have a lot to do, but do you think it looks nice?"

"Nicer than your sister deserves," Granny Murray said loudly.

That earned her a small smile from Hudson.

"It wasn't too difficult to get all the bones in," I said. "This was how I decorated for my wedding around this time last year."

Hudson's face was cold.

He didn't have to say it; I could practically hear him thinking it:

Pathetic.

Chapter 21

HUDSON

"It is the great irony of our time that you are making more progress on the fake job as opposed to the one I am paying you real money for."

Grayson sounded, not angry, but just a knife's edge away from it, which was somehow more unnerving.

I knew who his father was: I made a point of knowing all my clients before taking their money, and the ability to do terrible things to people was hard-coded into his DNA.

"It's part of the plan."

"Jake tells me that you went shopping with her yesterday and spent all night decorating. Are you having a midlife crisis?"

"I'm not middle-aged."

"In your line of work you are."

"My brothers aren't supposed to be interfacing with you," I said tersely, trying to keep the anger out of my voice.

Even though Jake was technically a grown man, he was always going to be my little brother, and no one fucked with my little brothers. I didn't care how much money they had.

"Relax," Grayson said. "Whatever you think of me, I'm not coming after your brothers. However, I want you to deliver me EnerCheck with a stake through its heart."

While Grayson might sneer at decorating a wedding venue, after seeing her interact with her family then pull magazine-worthy décor out of thin air, it was more clear to me than ever that I was on the right track, and Gracie was the key to taking down her family. The rest of them were completely useless.

She'd have to go into her family's office eventually. They couldn't resist making her do free work. If I hung around her, with a little bit of a nudge, she'd invite me along too. Then I'd grab all the evidence and send Grayson a bill for a seven-figure amount.

Merry Christmas to me.

Speaking of Christmas ...

"What are you going to wear?"

"Get off of my bed," I yelled at Talbot as I toweled my hair.

"You're not wearing a suit?" Anderson asked as I threw a pair of black jeans on the bed.

"I don't know why you all are here. Do you not have anything to do?"

"It's Christmas, Mr. Scrooge," Jake said in a terrible British accent.

Lawrence stuffed a handful of condoms in the jacket pocket. "I am not ready to be an uncle yet."

I sighed and pulled them back out before shrugging on the jacket, letting it settle around my shoulders like armor. I'd gone to a high-society party before, real Manhattan high-society parties, not Maplewood Falls high society. Still this was my hometown, and old childhood hurts never seemed to heal.

They were going to look down their noses at me.

That's the point. The best disguise is other people's prejudices.

"Not the hat, please. Have some class," Talbot said as I reached for the black ski hat.

"I'm working, not going on a date."

"We know how irresistible you are to women," he said as I tied up my boots.

"Besides, you've been on edge lately. It could be a win-win. You could hurry this job along and blow off some steam."

Hook up with Gracie?

No, that wasn't what virgins did, right? She would be expecting me to, I don't know, make love to her, tell her how precious she was to me, make her feel safe and cared for.

That was not the kind of sex I had.

It was not the first time I'd done sexual stuff in the pursuit of a security contract. It might be the first time I felt bad about it.

"I don't think so."

"Come on. That's what your target is expecting. She hired you for your looks. She's clearly attracted to you," Lawrence said with a smirk. "I bet you could convince her to spread her legs for you in the back of your truck."

I punched him in the stomach, and he doubled over, sinking to the floor.

"Fuck you," I enunciated and zipped up my jacket.

"Don't drink too much eggnog! Be home by ten," Anderson called as I stalked to the front door.

"Go to hell."

Chapter 22

GRACIE

"What a lovely party," my great-aunt Myrtle was gushing at the top of her voice. Every so often, her hearing aids gave a loud, long beep.

"Where is the man of the hour?" her sister asked.

Good question. Where was James? Maybe he had found someone to cheat on Kelly with, and I could politely tell Hudson that his services were no longer needed.

"Kelly likes to make a big entrance," I reminded my aunts. "She probably has James backstage with her."

"That sentient lump of dried whale sperm? No, I meant *him*." She lowered her voice to what I'm sure she thought was a whisper. "The one from the photo that you had sex with in a gas station dumpster."

"Good news and misinformation sure do travel fast in our family."

"I haven't seen a member that big since they banned *Playgirl*," her sister, Lottie, said to me. Both elderly women fanned themselves. "My sugar went sky-high when I saw that photo."

"Aunt Myrtle!" Dakota kissed her on the cheek. "Don't call it a member."

"We started charging because so many of our neighbors at the retirement community wanted to see it," Aunt Myrtle said.

Oh no. Hudson was going to kill me.

"Bertha thinks it might be a scam. We promised her we'd see for ourselves. So where is he?"

"Hudson might have to work," I said desperately.

I'd been at the venue all afternoon, putting up the finishing touches. I had half expected Hudson to show up, my dark knight in blackened armor.

Maybe he skipped town. Maybe he decided that $5,000 wasn't worth it to deal with my family.

I tugged at the hem of my cocktail dress.

Squeezed into the strappy heels, my feet felt numb. I wished he would have told me he wasn't coming. I would have worn flats.

One of my dad's cousins, Emily, came into the venue, her two teenage daughters sulking behind her.

They perked up when they saw me.

"Where's the famous boyfriend?" one of the teens asked me, twirling a strand of her hair, which was done up in bows and clips and was reminiscent of how I had tried and failed to wear my hair in middle school.

Everything was just one big redux. Even weddings.

"Kelly probably knows," her sister said snidely.

Man, teenage girls really know how to find your weak spots and dig the knife in.

"Gracie is having a mental health crisis," their mom scolded them. "Don't make fun of her."

"Actually, I'm fine," I said.

Emily gave me a blandly sympathetic smile.

"Good for you for keeping a positive attitude. If it had been me, I would have married the asshole, done the whole marriage song and dance for a few months, then divorced him and cleaned him out and bought a nice cottage on a lake."

"That's why Holbrook Enterprises pays you the big bucks." I gave her a pained smile.

"Where's the gift table, dear? My husband has your sister's present. And really, you didn't need to send back the stand mixer I bought you for your wedding. You could have kept it."

"I rent a tiny New York City apartment. I don't have room for a stand mixer."

"I told you, you could have come stayed with me. Kenny has an extra bed. Kenny, watch out," Emily snapped as an eight-year-old boy on a scooter slammed into me.

"Say 'sorry, Gracie,'" his father scolded, running up to him.

"I told you I wanted McDonald's," Kenny screamed while I rubbed the back of my legs.

"The scooter is an outside toy," his father said over the screaming.

"I need to go make sure my daughters don't get into the holiday punch," Emily told me.

"Is it the same punch as at your wedding last year? That was really good. And the spicy cheese straws were …" Emily's husband trailed off as his wife glared at him.

"We have a spiked and nonspiked punch option," I told them weakly. "Enjoy the party."

I could feel a bruise forming on my leg.

I went to the drink table and grabbed a Christmas Cosmo, sipping the syrupy red drink.

The venue was crowded with family and friends, and everyone was talking about me. They were either whispering to each other or, in the case of several elderly family members, talking at the top of their lungs about how it was quite the shock last year when the wedding was abruptly canceled, and isn't it nice that Grace is finally getting back out there, and where is that young man anyway?

I huddled behind a column as I tried to tune out one of my aunts talking to a family friend who was saying that this engagement party was so much better than the last one, and wasn't it just fantastic they used a different wedding planner.

Gulping my drink, I wondered if I should make a break for it and grab some cheese straws. What if my teenage cousins were right and Hudson was with Kelly? They could be hooking up right at that moment. He was probably telling her that she was perfect and secretly glad that he didn't have to have sex with boring, inexperienced me.

Yeah, I was definitely going to need those cheese straws and another drink. Head bent down, hoping no one would notice me, I held my breath and ducked back into the crowded engagement party.

"Gracie." My mother grabbed my arm. "Where is Kelly? She's supposed to make her big entrance soon. Can you go find her and make sure she doesn't need anything?"

"Sure, Mom," I said, flashing back to my big entrance at my wedding welcome party exactly a year ago.

As I headed through the crowd, the chatter of voices at the party slowly morphed into gasps of surprise. All the people in their holiday finery parted, and there was Hudson.

He wasn't wearing his skullcap, and his black hair was swept off his forehead and parted severely on the right. The collar of his leather jacket was turned up. In black jeans and heavy boots, he was even more underdressed than the valets.

"You made it," I said feeling slightly out of breath. I really needed to actually stick to my New Year's resolution to be healthy. Clearly things were getting dire.

Was this dress too small for me?

Yes.

Was it impossible to breathe?

Also yes.

Had I skipped breakfast and was now seeing beef Wellington and Christmas cookies blowing kisses and winking suggestively at me in the corner of my eye?

Yep, but it was worth it to see Hudson's eyes slide from the top of my head with the messy updo my cousins had tamed my curls into, to the subtle swell of cleavage in my black bolero cocktail dress, down my curves that had been Spanxed into submission, to the high-heeled shoes and back up again.

See? Just because I was a virgin didn't mean I was a little girl.

Hudson reached out, hooked two fingers in the top of the dress bodice, and pulled me to him.

"I can't wait to take that dress off you tonight," he said, leaning in to kiss my neck, where my pulse jumped.

He's not interested in you. Don't throw yourself at him.

It was going to be like that time in eighth grade when Claire stole my notebook and saw me making up wedding monograms for me and Franklin Prescott the Fourth and told everyone I was a delusional stalker.

It was too late. Hudson smelled amazing, and I relished the feel of his hard muscles as I looped my arm through his. I could definitely see why my sister constantly chased bad boys.

You're not thinking rationally. Those Christmas Cosmos were strong, and you didn't eat all day.

"She's obviously with him for one reason," one of my mom's friends joked.

"Certainly an upgrade from James," another woman said.

"I just got divorced. Maybe I'll take a walk on the wild side," Mitsy joked.

"Please. He's with her for her money. They'll have a fast marriage, then six months from now we'll hear about all the messy details on a true crime podcast," Claire's mom said.

Under my fingertips, I could feel Hudson tense up.

Somehow it was easier to defend other people from mean comments than myself.

I turned to Claire's mom.

"Actually," I said loudly, "I'll have you know he's not with me for my money. Because I don't have any. My dad hasn't given me a dime since I finished college. He wanted us kids to be independent. He's even underpaying me at the job I work."

"Wait. I thought Kelly said he paid her credit card," Claire said in a slightly nasally tone.

I clenched my jaw. "Shockingly, the rules are different for my younger sister. Come on, Hudson. Let's get you a drink. You got here a little late, and I saw all my senior relatives pilfering the hard liquor, so you might have to survive on wine."

"Psst!" Granny Murray waved us over. "Hey, handsome!" She lifted up her skirt.

Hudson sucked in a breath.

"Gran, please. This is a nice party," I begged.

My grandmother pulled out a bottle of whisky from a thigh holster and a glass out of her bra.

"Someone has to take care of this poor man, Gracie," she said, handing Hudson a glass and filling it up.

"Don't!" I tried to snatch it from her. "We need to wash that."

"What? It's not like I was hiding it up my snatch."

Hudson knocked the drink back.

"He really knows how to bring the heat," Granny Murray said appreciatively as Hudson handed her the glass back.

"I need some cheese straws and another drink." I massaged my temples.

"Good fucking luck with these lushes here. You put out free food and alcohol, and family members you haven't seen in a decade show up."

"Up yours! I'm here for the drama!" yelled one older woman with pink hair and a dress that was more see-through than I would be comfortable in, but more power to her.

It wasn't even eight thirty, and the elderly relatives were wasted.

"I bet you're loving this then," Granny Murray shouted at her. "This is your fantasy come to life, Mildred, considering you were the mistress, but our father had the good sense to threaten to disown my brother if he married you."

"Mistletoe!" one of my elderly great-aunts drunkenly screamed, pointing up above my head.

"Kiss the girl!" Granny Murray hollered.

What? A kiss? Here? Now? With *him*?

"I, um—" I stammered.

Around me, all my relatives tapped their silverware on their goblets and cocktail glasses like we were the soon-to-be-married couple they were all here to celebrate. No, we weren't going to be using disposables at my sister's engagement party—cheating whore or not, some of us had standards.

Hudson's arm came around my waist.

I pressed my hand against his chest, under the thin T-shirt fabric, below the plates of muscle, his heartbeat under my fingertips.

Was I cut from the same unwholesome cloth as my sister? Probably. Because all I wanted to do in that moment was kiss my fake boyfriend.

DO IT! Dakota mouthed off to the side.

Hudson wasn't waiting for me to finish having an existential crisis.

"We don't—" I managed to squeak out, right before he grabbed me by the back of the neck, pulled me to him, and crushed our mouths together.

I had never been kissed like that before. It was like jumping out of a plane into the middle of a blizzard.

Though the hand against the back of my neck was hard, unyielding, holding me in place so he could claim my mouth, his lips were soft. He tasted like freshly fallen snow, pure and exhilarating.

I clung to him, my fingers digging into his shirt as his tongue swept in my mouth, stealing my breath, tossing me every which way in a storm of desire.

He withdrew, the kiss gradually subsiding, his mouth lingering on mine as I gasped for breath.

"That—that was—"

It was like being kissed by a man is what that was.

Hudson nuzzled my neck softly then whispered in my ear.

"You look like you just got dragged by a snowplow. Smile, Sugarplum."

I wasn't sure if my sister thought she was missing her cue or if she had a sixth sense for someone else being the center of attention, but the DJ suddenly blared "All I Want for Christmas," and Kelly sashayed out onto the low stage.

"I know what I want for Christmas," Hudson said, ignoring my father, who was trying to get everyone's attention.

Then Hudson started some sort of club dancing that I was neither coordinated nor popular enough to know how to do. It involved a lot of his hands on my ass though.

"Partay!" Granny Murray whooped, holding up the flask of whisky.

"If you could all please turn your attention to the bride," the DJ practically yelled out over the loudspeaker.

"Why do you taste so sweet?" Hudson murmured, cupping my chin and kissing me again as he spun me around.

His hands were sliding under my dress, right as my sister screamed, "Gracie, stop acting like a teenager. This is someone's wedding kickoff party. It's pathetic."

I tugged my dress down, feeling guilty. I also didn't want Hudson to know I had two layers of spandex on under this dress. That would be the opposite of the raw sexual power of that kiss.

Kelly didn't wear Spanx. Actually, Kelly liked to brag that she never wore anything under her dresses.

My elderly relatives and, let's be fair, a good handful of my nonelderly relatives were going wild.

"Take off your shirt!" someone in the audience hollered.

"Oh, stop it," Kelly said, pretending to be offended. "This is a nice party."

"Not you. I'm a plastic surgeon," the man slurred. "I already know what fake tits look like. I meant him. Uh—"

"Uncle Kirk?" I said as the crowd shuffled to look at him.

He shrugged helplessly.

"Surprise, everyone. I'm bi."

"Aw. Is this a coming-out party?"

His sister started crying and gave him a big hug. "I always knew you could live your truth."

"Adorable," I said and started to get teary-eyed.

"Mazel tov!" Granny Murray yelled while Granny Astelle had conniptions, her hand fluttering to her throat. "Shots all around!"

"This is not his coming-out party. This is my wedding," my sister screamed. Her eyes, surrounded by thick eye makeup, bugged out in fury.

"Best get back in the closet, Kirk," one uncle muttered. His wife hit him with her clutch.

James took the microphone from Kelly.

Hudson wrapped his arm possessively around my waist. Now that we'd seemingly broken the kiss-me-like-you-want-to-fuck-me barrier, he had put the car into overdrive and was rubbing his hands all over me.

It was doing *things* to me and probably ruining my Spanx. I shifted in my heels, trying to ease the ache between my legs.

I didn't know what I was going to do if we did start having sex. I already felt like I was going to pass out just from having Hudson's fingers trailing slowly up and down my dress, giving me the barest fluttering sensation.

"I just want to thank everyone for coming," James said over the noise of people talking, either engaging in postgame analysis of The Kiss, yelling at the kids, or asking Uncle Kirk about his journey of self-discovery, and oh, by the way, could he also hook up a very supportive family member with some fillers?

"As you know," James soldiered on, "this has been a big year for Kelly and me. Obviously, we didn't have the most traditional start, but we are looking forward to taking the next step in growing our little family."

"As a gynecologist," one of my aunts interjected, "I would like to remind you that anal doesn't make a baby. Just felt the need to clear that up. I know that's your preferred method, based on what we all witnessed last Christmas. What?" she said as my mom yelled at her. "This week alone, I had two infertile couples who were just shocked—*shocked*, I tell you—at this information. This is a public service announcement. Be blessed!"

Hudson leaned down to whisper in my ear, "Can you do me a favor and hit me over the head with the Christmas punch bowl to put me out of my misery?"

I elbowed him, and he grinned against my hair.

"Just keep going, James," my mom said.

"We're so thrilled to celebrate with all our friends and family," James added, taking Kelly's hand.

"Someone control that boy," Grandma Astelle scolded as Emily's son zipped by on his scooter. Astelle swiped at him with her cane.

Kenny yelled and swerved around her, taking out a nearby Christmas tree. The tree went one way, ornaments flying, while the scooter went the other, right into a large pipe running up the wall.

"I am so sorry," Emily said, stalking over to retrieve her son as she drained the rest of her glass of wine. "Forget what Abigail says. Just do anal. Your life will be a lot better. Get up," she snapped at her son. "Stop embarrassing me."

There was a loud hissing noise, and then water started gushing out of the pipe.

I raced over to it. All the food, the decorations, everything I had worked so hard on was going to be ruined.

"Someone get some duct tape!" I yelled.

No one was listening. My dress, my hair, and my makeup were quickly ruined by the spray of water.

"Your little brat is destroying my wedding," Kelly was shrieking while Granny Murray yelled at everyone to save the liquor.

"I've got the cheese straws," my brother called.

"You're going to pay for this! You're going to pay for all of this!" Kelly yelled.

"Fuck," Emily cursed, grabbing one of the bottles of wine. "There goes my Christmas bonus."

"At least give me a napkin?" I pleaded, trying to use my hands to hold back the water.

James approached me, holding a tablecloth over his head and wincing as a bit of the spray landed on his shoes.

"I think we need to call a plumber."

"No shit, James."

"I don't know if any is going to come out here," he added. "It's late."

"Not helpful," I snapped.

Suddenly Hudson was beside me, shirtless, because what more did the night need to really push it over the edge?

"You're just going to make it worse," James said as Hudson picked up a huge mallet and started whacking at the pipe.

"Is everyone completely insane?" I shrieked.

Suddenly the spray of water stopped. Hudson continued to hit the pipe, which actually was a valve next to the pipe.

"It gets sticky," he explained, setting the hammer down and leaning the handle against the wall. "Sometimes you just have to bang it hard."

Chapter 23

HUDSON

Gracie's big brown eyes were glued to mine.

Thanks to the soaking-wet dress, I could see the outline of her nipples through the fabric.

She stepped up to me.

I watched her swallow, the pulse jumping in her neck.

Her hands slid up my chest, sliding easily on my wet skin.

She reached up on her toes in those high heels, leaning forward, catching her weight on me, then hesitated, her breath warm against my mouth.

"Thank you. You're my hero," she whispered then, softly like the first snowflake of winter, brushed her lips to mine. It was chaste, sweet.

I closed my eyes, savoring the purity of it.

Wrong fucking word, asshole.

I allowed my hands to rest briefly on her waist, resisting the urge to slide them up and cup her breasts, feel how hard her nipples were, to whisper in her ear that she should let me fuck her in the back of the truck and show her how wet she could really get.

"You saved Christmas." She really was gazing at me like I was her knight in shining armor, her Nutcracker Prince. That shy desire was intoxicating. All I wanted to do was wrap my arms around her, kiss her, bask in her adoration.

"It was nothing," I said after a moment, forcing myself to step away.

"For the man of the hour," Granny Murray announced, coming by with a tray of shots.

I knocked back the drink, then another, then a third. I normally never drank that much on a job. Sure, it might look like I did, but I would tip the drink out or leave the glass on a random table and go to the bar and grab another. I needed to be stone-cold sober to work. But now all I wanted to do was drink enough alcohol to wash away all thoughts of Gracie.

I grabbed a mop from the supply closet and tackled the water all over the floor.

It would be a lot easier if she would just go away. Anywhere. But Gracie kept trying to help me. Even though I had rolled my shirt back on after drying off, she was still in her wet clothes. She was practically steaming whenever she got close to me, trying to take the mop or roll the bucket closer.

The sweet cinnamon sugar scent of her, like Christmas morning, wafted up.

You don't even like cookies.

I bet I would like hers though.

"Seems he actually is a maintenance man," Gracie's ex said loudly. "Thanks for cleaning up that little spill there, Hudson." He tipped his glass to me.

"Anything for Gracie," I said, trying to keep my tone even.

I'd had good training in schooling my expression when I worked at the country club, cleaning up after the rich fat cats and their soft sons, picking up golf balls in the middle of the night and clearing tables.

Working in a country club will really make you hate humanity. I made good tips though.

"I'm going to call your boss and tell him what an upstanding employee you are," James continued.

I clenched the mop handle.

You don't care. You do not care. You just used these minimum wage jobs to be invisible, to have access. You are not a broke teenager anymore.

Between Gracie and the alcohol, I felt like I was starting to spiral.

"Shut up, James," Gracie snapped. "Go bother someone else."

After cleaning up the rest of the water, I ordered some new parts to fix the pipe.

While her family partied, Gracie kept bringing me snacks and drinks.

I both craved and hated the way I felt when she looked up at me like I was her hero, like she was in love with me. Usually the women I dealt with were spoiled princesses; it was easy to dismiss them.

"Did you not bring a change of clothes?" I growled when she came over with more food and another drink.

Her curly hair had been blown out of her fancy updo and was tangled around her face.

"Of course I did, but my cousin spilled wine on her shirt, so I lent her the dress," she explained, picking up the drink off the tray and handing it to me.

Against my better judgment, I downed it.

"You trying to get me drunk to take advantage of me?" I rasped.

"What? Of course not," she cried. "I feel bad."

She leaned in toward me, and I kissed her because I could, because we had an audience, and wasn't that part of the plan?

Gracie melted like hot chocolate against me.

I am fucking addicted.

Then,

I think I drank too much.

Which I hadn't done since I was a fucking teenager, and wasn't that just great? Gracie was standing between me and a big payday and undoing a decade's worth of self-improvement.

"I know cleaning up after my family is very much not in your job description," she whispered to me.

I kissed her again and slid my hands down her damp clothes that clung to her curves.

"I'm trying to be nice," she whispered against my mouth. "Also if you don't eat anything now, I can't promise there will be leftovers. My family attacked the food and drinks like a pack of locusts."

"Really?" I said, peering at her. "Because you're not drinking. Seems suspect."

"Gracie is our designated driver," her dad chirped from behind her. "Speaking of, I'm beat, Gracie. Do you think you could drop me and your mom off then come back here and clean up? We don't want to get fined."

I clumsily put my arm around her shoulder, drawing her to my chest.

"Designated driver, huh?" I said, squeezing her tight, loving the way her soft body fitted against mine. "Sounds like you're driving me home."

"Well, actually we—"

I ignored her parents and grabbed my jacket, herding Gracie out into the wintery evening.

"Where's your car?" I asked.

"I don't have a car," she said, digging in my jacket pocket.

"Fuck, you really do want me to fuck you." I kissed her again. She tasted like candy apple and was pliant in my arms. I suddenly wanted all of her.

I dipped my head down, brushing my mouth to the soft underside of her neck to her collarbone and down to the swell of her breasts.

This time I gave in and cupped her huge tits in my hands. Her nipples were hard, pebbled under my fingers.

Gracie was gasping, and I was sure if I slid my fingers between her legs, she'd be soaked, and not from the burst pipe.

"Are you wet for me?" I whispered against her mouth, claiming it again. "Tell me how much you want my cock."

"Get a room you two!" One of her great-aunts cackled as her nephew helped her to a waiting cab.

It broke the spell I had over Gracie.

"Where is your truck?" she asked, jingling the keys at me.

She was shivering in her damp clothes. The cold air was starting to sober me up too.

"Go back inside," I ordered her. "I'll walk."

"I'm not letting you walk home like this," she protested. "You're drunk."

"Bad boy, remember?" I said, reaching for the keys.

She skipped back, putting me off-balance.

"Yikes. Yeah, you're going to fall in a snowdrift and no one will find you 'til spring," she said. She was visibly shivering.

I took off my jacket and wrapped it around her.

She pressed the button on the key fob. A truck nearby beeped.

"Score!"

"You don't know how to drive this car," I said, following her through the dark. "I can call …" *My brothers.* "A friend."

"You have friends?" She stuck her tongue out at me.

"Aren't we friends?" I teased.

Of course we were not. Even though she had taken me shopping with her and I'd helped decorate the venue and chopped wood, we were not friends.

"Vroom!" Gracie said, sliding into the driver's seat.

"Your feet barely touch the pedals," I told her, leaning back against the frosty window and crossing my arms.

"I got this," she insisted as the truck roared to life.

Gracie was a horrible driver.

"Can you please watch the fucking road?" I bellowed as she careened down the empty, icy street back into town.

"I am."

"You're watching the radio."

"I don't understand why they can't put real buttons in a car anymore," she said as she peered at the touchpad while roaring down the street.

"For god's sake, woman, keep your eyes on the road."

"Fine. You look for a Christmas station, then."

"Can you go ten minutes without Christmas music?" I snarled at her as I turned the radio off, or tried to. It connected with her phone Bluetooth, and "Jingle Bell Rock" blasted out of the stereo.

"Put on the vintage playlist," she said, reaching for her phone.

"Fuck, Gracie," I shouted as she creamed an inflatable Santa Claus. "That's it. Pull over. I'm walking."

"Don't be so dramatic. It's just one little mishap. I'm not used to driving is all," she said, trying to put the truck into gear as we headed up a hill. "I've been living in New York City the past few years."

The truck lurched and made a grinding noise. Grayson was going to kill me.

"Oops. That doesn't sound good," Gracie said, both feet working the pedals like it was a fucking organ.

"At least I know how I'm going to die. That's one of life's great uncertainties solved," I said then hung on for dear life as she took a hard left turn at an intersection.

"Sorry," she called, watching the GPS, the phone still in her hand. "Oh, shoot. It was that building, wasn't it?"

"Just stop here," I begged, reaching for the handle.

"We provide door side service here at Gracie's taxi company," she insisted, making a hard U-turn in the middle of the road.

There was a horrible crunching noise as the side of the tire scraped against the sidewalk curb.

"Cut that one a little close," she said with a laugh and screeched to a halt in front of my building.

I let out a breath.

"You," I said, "are never, ever driving any vehicle I am in ever again."

"It wasn't that bad."

"It was. I'm stone-cold sober now. I've been in firefights in Afghanistan that were less stressful than driving with you."

Gracie unbuckled her seatbelt.

Did she want to come upstairs with me?

My cock was very intrigued by the prospect. Too bad I had sobered up enough to not give in.

Gracie was pulling off my jacket.

"Keep it. I'll grab it tomorrow," I told her then held out my hand.

She blinked at me.

"The keys," I said to her confused look. "I called you an Uber," I lied.

I had not, in fact, called her an Uber. I had called an employee of mine to drive her back to the venue and to text me immediately when she got there and to follow her as she drove her parents' home.

"Thanks, Hudson."

"It's because I don't want you tearing up my car," I said, opening the car door.

The driver's side door slammed, then Gracie was standing in front of me on the sidewalk, inspecting the car.

"Not too bad, right?" She winced. "Guess you're never letting me borrow the truck," she said, spontaneously grabbing my hand, like it was the most natural thing in the world.

"I'm baking cookies tomorrow," she continued, her smaller hand still warm in mine. "You should come." She was gazing at me with that shy desire again, then she started doing that hesitating lean thing, like she was silently asking me to kiss her.

All I wanted to do was fuck her.

Her body was pressed closer to mine now; my head dipped down.

Stop this.

"Don't touch me," I said harshly and pushed her away. "Don't get too cozy. This is a fake relationship, remember. I work for you. Don't be one of those girls that falls for every guy she sleeps with—it's not cute."

"Right," she said softly, shaking her head. "Sorry about that."

A black car pulled up with a fake Uber sign in the window. I recognized one of my employees.

Gracie reached for the door handle and hesitated.

"I guess I'll—"

I ignored her and turned to head to my apartment building. In the reflection in the window, I watched as she got in the car and it drove away.

"I am not falling for her," I said to my reflection as I unlocked the door to the building. "And I do not feel guilty that I yelled at her."

Chapter 24

GRACIE

"What are we going to do, Pugnog?" I said early the next morning as I stood in the doorway of the Canning Factory venue, gazing out over the remains of the wedding kickoff party from last night.

Hudson had not shown up for breakfast. I couldn't decide if that was a good thing or not.

I wished he had shown up, if for nothing else so that he would kiss me again. That first kiss with him had been single-handedly the most amazing kiss I had ever had in my life, ever. And if he made love like he kissed ... well, I didn't have any anxiety about losing my virginity to him.

"You're perverted," I whispered to myself harshly. "He's not attracted to you. He didn't kiss you good night, and he certainly didn't invite you upstairs to continue what he started."

I pulled on my rubber gloves. I wished my parents had just hired a cleaning company, but Kelly and James wanted to save money to help start them on the right path for married life.

At least being alone gave me the perfect opportunity to replay every single awkward interaction I'd had with Hudson last night.

"You're a terrible kisser," I berated myself as I stuffed used linen napkins into a garbage sack to take home and wash. "He probably went home and called some woman to come over who was actually good at sex, who he was actually attracted to."

I tied off the top of the bag.

I hadn't made a dent in the cleaning. I had been hoping to reuse some of the decorations for the wedding. The wedding that was still on. I chewed my lip and wondered if Hudson was going to bill me soon. I'd better scrounge up some cash.

I slumped in a chair.

In the morning sunlight, the broken pipe looked even worse. And even though Hudson had cleaned up the water last night, I was sure the venue was going to have a fit and charge a ton of money. The form I had signed when renting the venue meant I had assumed liability for any damages. Yes, I had signed the form against my better judgment, because Kelly was too busy not working to actually rent her own party venue. The Canning Factory had my credit card info; they were going to charge me an insane amount.

Which, I realized when I checked my credit card account, would be a real freaking problem for me, seeing as how the card was close to maxed out. The venue owner was going to take me to court. I would have a record. I could go to jail.

"You have a shopping problem," I told myself. "This New Year you're going to get healthy and stop spending so much money."

Gracie: *Can you ask Emily if she can contribute some money for the pipe repair? The venue is going to charge me.*
Dad: *Don't worry. She left some cash! *smiley face emoji**

I breathed out a sigh of relief. Emily, a high-powered attorney, was not the easiest to deal with.

My dad sent me a photo of three $100 bills on a tabletop.

Gracie: *I think it's going to cost more than that…*
Dad: *Really? Can you just pay the venue, sweetheart, and James will reimburse you?*

"Argh!"

Pugnog dragged himself up from where he was napping on a pile of garland I had spread out to dry.

I sat down in the middle of the mess, feeling hopeless. At this point, James and my sister owed me thousands for the wedding. I had a sinking feeling I was never going to see any of that money. At least with the decorations I could repurpose them for other uses or donate them to a local retirement home or hospice.

But this pipe? It was going to be a huge expense. One I couldn't afford.

I felt my chest tighten with panic.

Maybe if Dakota had been here she could have helped talk me off the ledge, but her parents had insisted on having breakfast with her because, *We never see you ever since you abandoned us for New York City.*

Guilt tripping is an art form in my family.

The lump was forming in my throat, and I felt tears prickle at my eyes.

"It's going to be fine," I told myself. "James and Kelly haven't paid you back for the other wedding decorations because they're busy. Planning a wedding is stressful, and you get tunnel vision. That's probably why you had no idea James and Kelly were having an affair last year."

I balled my fists up. Pugnog licked me on the ankle in concern.

"I am not crying over that," I whispered to myself angrily. "It's been a year, and I am over it. I even have a grand revenge plan. I am a woman in charge of my own life."

Unfortunately, my life was pretty lackluster, I realized, my stomach in a knot of anxiety and existential dread. My credit card was maxed out. I was going to spend Christmas in jail. Hudson thought I was gross, my sister was marrying my ex, and my job was low paying and sucked.

"Just focus," I told myself as I hyperventilated. "Clean up the venue then go home and bake cookies and listen to Christmas music."

I leaned over, feeling lightheaded. Pugnog barked in concern.

Faintly, I heard a man's boots on the old wood floor.

"Gracie. *Gracie.*" Hudson shook me roughly. "What happened?"

"I'm going to jail," I squeaked. "Also I think I'm going to pass out."

I fanned myself and leaned over to rest on the bag of dirty linen napkins and closed my eyes. Maybe I would just live here. I could tell the venue I could be the live-in care-taker like Quasimodo.

"I don't understand." Hudson patted my face in concern, almost like a worried boyfriend.

He is not your boyfriend, and that's good, because he's not your type.

Even if he was a panty-droppingly good kisser.

Maybe it was because he was a familiar face or maybe I ate too much bacon at breakfast, but all I wanted was for him to wrap me in his arms and hug me and tell me everything was going to be okay.

You're an adult. Yes, a virgin, and yes, you are currently sleeping in your childhood bedroom surrounded by all your toys, but you are still technically an adult, and you need to act like one.

"I'm sorry," I told Hudson. "This isn't your problem. I know you're not really my boyfriend, and you don't even like me."

His face darkened for a moment.

I sighed and forced myself to sit up and gestured help-lessly to the broken pipe.

"The venue is going to charge my card, and it's already almost maxed out, so I won't be able to pay, and they're going to send me to jail for the damage," I explained, almost succeeding in keeping my voice from warbling though my chin trembled there at the end.

"Gracie," Hudson said gently, taking my hand. "The venue isn't going to send you to jail. I promise."

"You don't know that," I argued, already accepting my fate of spending Christmas in prison. I was crafty and was sure I could repurpose Styrofoam food trays to snowflake decorations.

"This is a huge expensive pipe, and I signed a form promising I'd pay for damages. Honestly, I'd rather go to jail than beg James for money to reimburse me. He's so awful. Did you know he never paid a dime for his last wedding?" I said, feeling even more low. "I spent tens of thousands of dollars and *poof!* It's all gone. James acted like I was asking for his kidney whenever I would try to get him to pay for it. Now this. I don't want to spend Christmas in jail." I let out a sob and tried to control myself.

"It will be okay, Gracie."

"It won't."

Hudson rubbed his jaw.

He hesitated a second then said, "I know everything will be fine because I own this building."

"You what? How? It's huge. I thought you were a janitor."

"I used my military bonus," he said with a shrug. "Got a good deal. No one wants to invest in the Gulch."

I looked around at the cavernous space.

Hudson owned all of this?

"I think I severely miscalculated you," I said to him after a moment.

"Stop it," he said brusquely.

"What?"

"Stop looking at me like that."

"Like what?"

"Like I'm...like I'm some sort of catch, like I'd be a good husband. I'm not."

"I know. You made that pretty clear already."

He scowled.

Whatever. Screw him.

"I'll fix the pipe and bill James directly," he stated.

"I can't ask you to do that," I said stubbornly. "You're not my boyfriend, and you don't need to do favors for me. You're running a business. You should treat me like any other patron who ruined your property."

Hudson sighed, annoyed. "This is just a side thing."

"Don't undervalue yourself," I lectured. "Property management is no joke."

"I don't need you giving me lectures on how to run a business."

"I'm giving you a lecture on knowing your worth. Now put me on a payment plan," I insisted.

"Sugarplum, you are going to be the death of me."

"How much do I owe you?"

"Just let people do nice things for you."

"Your nice things come with strings attached."

He gave me a sly grin.

"Do they?"

He easily swung me to my feet.

"You've spent the last three days here cooped up decorating," he stated. "It's Christmas. Go do something fun. I'll have my team clean."

The lure of spending Christmas out in my small town as opposed to cleaning was strong.

"I do like spreading Christmas cheer, but I really shouldn't leave the venue like this. Are you sure?"

He winked at me. "I'll put it on your tab."

"At least take one of these Christmas trees home for your apartment," I told him. "Kelly doesn't deserve all this holiday cheer."

Chapter 25

HUDSON

There was no reason for me to offer to help Gracie pick up the venue. Doing something nice for her? What the hell was that? That was something one of those romance novel dream boyfriends would do, not me.

In the military, I'd seen guys implode their whole lives trapped in a toxic relationship, and all relationships eventually became toxic, no matter how well they started off.

I didn't do girlfriends or date. Yet here I was, trying to make Gracie's life easier, and I still wasn't any closer to completing the mission.

"This frees her up to spend time at the office," I tried to convince myself.

This would be perfectly logical if not for the fact that I hadn't offered to spread Christmas cheer with Gracie and steer her in the direction of the EnerCheck office. I had just let her loose in the small town of Maplewood Falls to Christmas it up.

"Get it together," I told myself after directing my cleaning crew on the mess and offering bonuses. "You need to go find her." Christmas was around the corner, and Grayson was no Santa Claus.

The thought of being around her, in a small space with her, felt unbearable. All I wanted was my hands on her body, my mouth on those pebble-hard pink nipples that I'd suck on until she was moaning and begging me to fuck her.

"Fuck. She's the target, not some girl you're trying to pick up at a bar."

It had been a while since I'd been laid, that was all, I decided as I headed to the truck, one of the Christmas trees tossed over my shoulder. I needed to blow off some steam then find her and convince her to go to the EnerCheck office.

I needed to be focused around Gracie. Her inno-cent-virgin woe-is-me shtick was lulling me into a false sense of complacency. I needed to remember that she was intelligent and observant.

I never should have told her I owned the Canning Factory. I berated myself as I drove across town.

It had been a little eerie to watch her make connections, reevaluate me, throw away all of her preconceived notions, and reclassify me.

It reminded me of something I would do.

You don't go home and bake elaborately decorated Christmas cookies.

"Does Grayson know you're playing games while the clock is ticking?" Lawrence asked me as I clomped on my skates over to the ice.

"Fuck you," I said and took off the blade guards.

"Touchy, touchy," my brother said, removing his own guards as I stepped on the ice.

Anderson was already on the ice. He bodychecked Talbot, who was going for the puck.

This is what I need, I told myself, rolling my neck, trying to loosen my shoulders. *Just some good ol' fashioned violence.*

I skated over to my younger brothers, snatched the puck from Talbot, and shot it neatly into a goal.

"Don't be so full of yourself," Jake called. "No one's playing goalie."

"Because you refused."

"Damn right. The last time I was goalie, you hit me with a hockey stick," Jake argued.

"Only because you almost broke my leg diving for a puck," Anderson yelled at him.

I loved hockey. In the winter, when my brothers and I were little, we'd flood a nearby low spot and create a make-shift ice rink in the patch of dirt that doubled as a backyard.

Before I knew any better, I'd dreamed of becoming a hockey player—traveling around with the NHL, being treated like I mattered, the camaraderie, the glory. Too bad you needed to shell out big bucks to be on one of the elite travel teams that fed the pro league, cash my family didn't have.

Now you lie to people for money and have sex with virgins in order to steal things.

Though it would kill me, I was going to have to sleep with her, wasn't I? Things weren't going in my favor, and I couldn't keep putting it off.

I hated to admit it, but a sick part of me was going to enjoy it.

You're going straight to hell.

"Fuck this shit." I scooped up the puck and sent it flying.

"What the fuck, man!" Anderson yelled as the puck flew past his head.

"He's salty he can't manage to get one little girl to do what he wants," Lawrence said with a smirk. "Christmas bells, are you listening? Grayson's going to make you miserable."

I grabbed my brother by the collar and shoved him against the Plexiglas barrier. Not hard—all his protective padding absorbed the impact, and my little brother just laughed at me.

"That doesn't even rhyme." I released him.

"Maybe you should try a different tactic," Talbot said in a low voice.

"Do you have any brilliant ideas?" I asked sharply.

He rocked in his skates.

"You could try to actually be her boyfriend and really love bomb her."

"He would have needed to start that six weeks ago," Lawrence argued. "Gracie will be suspicious if he flips the script now."

We are all horrible people, I suddenly realized. *We are all as bad as our father.*

"Can we play hockey?" I said. "Or are we going to stand around and gossip like middle-school girls?"

"Gossip! Gossip!" Jake and Lawrence shouted.

"You two …"

Jake focused on something behind me, grin slowly spreading on his face.

"Nice," my brother drawled, jerking his chin to what looked like a stripper in an elf costume meandering around by the check-in desk.

The woman was practically poured into the tight clothes—knee-high red boots, green miniskirt with white trim, and a red lace-up crop-top vest that pushed her huge tits up almost to her chin.

"Duty calls, boys," Jake said, pulling off his helmet and skating over to the desk area.

"If you hurry, you can beat Jake to it," Anderson whispered to me. "You know, blow off some steam? You seem like you need it."

I ground my teeth.

"I'm fine."

A dog let out a wheezing bark.

The hell?

"Hi! Do you work here?" a familiar voice asked.

Fuck. It was Gracie.

I sprinted across the ice and jumped off quickly, grabbing my skate guards.

Jake was flirting heavily with her when I rushed over, eyes locked on hers as he took a slow bite of a Christmas dessert bar that smelled like cranberries.

"Don't feed him sugar."

I knocked the treat out of his hands. Pugnog jumped on the treat, scarfing it down noisily and drooling all over the floor.

"Gracie brought these for the rink manager, who is out, as I explained to her," Jake said. "And I offered to take these desserts off her hands."

"I was just coming by as a preventative measure," she explained in a rush. "My family's annual Christmas hockey game is in a few days, and things get crazy."

"Crazy like blood all over the ice, or crazy like people in sexy elf costumes getting drunk and flashing unsuspecting bystanders?" Jake waggled his eyebrows.

I saw red.

"I swear to fucking god, Jake," I screamed at him, shoving him into the nearby desk hard. His breath came out in a loud whoosh.

I let him drop to the floor.

"When you stop wheezing, you can apologize for that comment," I told him.

Pugnog wandered over to sniff Jake and lick his face.

I turned back to Gracie.

She was apprehensive and clutched the box of desserts to her chest.

"I'm not offended. This isn't a sexy elf outfit," she babbled. "I'm out passing out holiday cheer." She held up the box. "You know, visiting the local nursing homes, hospices, things like that. People like an elf outfit. It's fun."

I cracked my knuckles.

"Don't worry about Jake. He's just my little brother. Honestly? If you'd just decked your sister last Christmas, you'd be a lot happier."

"Baking is a much healthier way to work out your anger issues."

"Most people say sex is the best way," Jake wheezed from the floor.

"That doesn't sound like an apology," I growled.

My little brother hauled himself up.

"My apologies, Gracie. Hudson told me all about your shitty ex. If you need to have a threesome on your sister's wedding dress, I'm happy to fall on that sword."

"That's thoughtful of you … Wait …" Gracie frowned.

I resisted the urge to run my thumb over her eyebrows. Instead, I grabbed my little brother and shook him.

"What the fuck is wrong with you?" I hissed.

"I'm giving us another path to success," he whispered back. "Bring it in, man." He raised his voice. "I love you, brother."

He slapped me on the back.

"I'm telling fart jokes at your funeral after Grayson kills you," he whispered. "See, Gracie, no hard feelings. We're family. We love each other."

"Did you say you had food?" The rest of my brothers were wandering over.

"Wow!" Gracie's eyes lit up. "There are more of you."

"This is not a family affair," I told my brothers.

"I don't know. Jake's offering some sort of life-changing incest situation on my sister's wedding dress, sooo …"

Anderson doubled over laughing. Lawrence chuckled and slapped her on the shoulder.

Gracie grinned.

I scowled.

"Do you play?" Anderson asked her, holding up his hockey stick.

She shook her head. "I'm not that coordinated. Did some figure skating, but I was never very good."

"You certainly have the outfit for it," Lawrence said then yelped when I turned on him.

"They definitely need more revealing uniforms for hockey players." She winked at Talbot, whose eyes widened.

"You mean you don't like the oversized pajamas accessorized by chipped teeth?" Anderson drawled.

"My sister seemed to, except that Kelly actually played hockey. Mainly so she could sleep with the players." Gracie made a face.

"No judgment," Jake said with a laugh. "Everyone loves a puck bunny."

"Especially one with desserts," Lawrence added reaching for the box.

"Er, that's not quite what I …"

"All of you leave," I barked at my brothers.

"He's mad we're flirting with you," Lawrence stage-whispered.

"I'm not. Any of you touch her, you're dead," I said flatly. "Not just dead to me but dead, buried in the yard dead."

"Look at Mr. Moneybags here with his own yard," Gracie quipped.

My brothers howled in laughter.

"She's amazing." Lawrence wiped away a tear.

"You're not," I shot at him.

"Be nice to your brothers. Your mom must be proud to have such big, strong handsome sons. I'm baking cookies this afternoon, Hudson. If you come, you can make some to take to her."

"Unless it comes in a bottle and you need an ID to buy it, our mom won't touch it," I said before I could stop myself.

Those big brown eyes went soft. "I'm so sorry to hear that. I didn't mean …"

I didn't need her pity.

"Are you going to the office later?"

"The office?" she said in confusion. "Why would I go there?"

Fuck. Why are you so clumsy?

"You said you were passing out holiday cheer." I gestured to the box.

She opened it and offered treats to my brothers.

"There's no one working there right now. Well"—she rolled her eyes—"there's never anyone working there ever."

"Sounds like Dad's office," Talbot said around his cranberry chocolate bar. "Our dad was a serial entrepreneur, liked the trappings of business but not the actual work."

"Sounds familiar," she said acerbically. "Did he also have his kids working for free?"

Where was this Gracie normally, I wondered, the one who wore a skimpy elf outfit and made dirty jokes and complained about her family? Why couldn't she stand up for herself around them?

She was like a different person. I really liked this Gracie.

You sure you don't just want to slowly undo the lacing on the bodice and see her tits fall down?

"He had you working as a child?" I asked.

She shrugged. "Bookkeeping, scheduling, admin work, accounting."

"Our dad was never that organized. He didn't get much further than the fundraising-slash-scamming-people stage," Jake told her.

Gracie grimaced. "Mine did a little of that too."

Now this—this I could use. This was gold. Give me three days, and it would be mission accomplished. That data was somewhere in the EnerCheck office. It had to be.

"Sounds stressful," I said, hoping I sounded sympathetic.

"I think that's how a lot of early startups are run. Things aren't as aboveboard as they should be, but you find your groove." She adjusted her top. "I'll let you boys finish your hockey game. I have a thousand cookies to make."

"You know what, Sugarplum?" I said, reaching down to unlace my skates, feeling happier than I'd had in months, "I think I will take you up on that cookie offer."

Jake wolf whistled.

"Cookie baking is serious business," she told him authoritatively. "It's not fun and games. I have an assembly line. Grown men cry during a Christmas cookie marathon."

"Damn."

"You up for a cookie marathon, Hudson?" Anderson drawled.

"Was that a double entendre? I think your brothers are making dirty jokes," she teased me as I grabbed her arm to haul her away.

"We're leaving now."

"An after-game snack," Grace said, handing Jake the box. "Share these. Merry Christmas!"

"Merry Christmas," Jake said in that voice that would have every woman in a bar in a three-mile radius crawling to get him.

Gracie was not immune, I noticed, feeling the scowl settle on my face.

"I'll meet you over there," I told her.

"My sister needed the car and so she dropped me off at the assisted living center," she admitted as she followed me, taking mincing steps in the high-heeled boots, her tits bouncing. "Do you think you could give me a ride to my parents'?"

I opened the car door for her. She struggled to get up in the tight clothes while I waited.

"I'm trying not to flash you," she finally admitted.

The thought of seeing her panties under that miniskirt was too much.

I picked her up by the waist and sat her on the seat, kicking myself for reinforcing the no-touching-without-an-audience rule because I really wanted to kiss her, undress her, then fuck in that truck.

Chapter 26

GRACIE

As soon as we pulled up in front of my parents' house, Hudson was on me, pushing off the elf hat, large hand tangled in my hair as he tipped my head back so he could kiss me, claim me.

The whiplash was disorienting.

He had drawn a hard boundary about no kissing. Now this?

Hudson tugged at the strings on the bodice of the elf costume while his tongue tangled with mine.

"Oh my god," I moaned as he cupped my tits through the wool fabric then slipped his hand into the bodice, his large hands warm against my skin.

"I thought you—this is—" I tried to form coherent words, but it was hard with him teasing my nipples.

He nipped my bottom lip.

"You like it when I grab your tits, don't you?" he crooned.

"Yeah," I panted, "but ... um ..."

His mouth was on mine again.

"I've never wanted to fuck anyone as much as you," he whispered against my mouth. "I want to come all over your face."

"Mhmh." The strangled noise was lost against him.

Suddenly, I very much wanted Hudson's hot cum all over my mouth. I had a sudden image of me on my knees in front of him, running my tongue along his cock, my hand between my widespread legs, doing something that I'd never done before.

The ribbons on the bodice had been worked free, and my tits spilled out.

Hudson dipped his head, finally letting me breathe.

I felt hot as he trailed kisses down my chest.

"St. Nick, fuck, that feels good," I moaned as he sucked on my breasts, rolling the nipple with his tongue, nipping with his teeth.

His large hands were on my thighs, and I spread them as wide as I could in the elf skirt.

I wanted his fingers to go higher, to give me ... something.

This was way further along than I had ever gotten with anyone. My panties were soaked as he teased my nipples, sucking on my tits while his fingers made little circles on my inner thigh.

I didn't even recognize the sounds I was making— panting, gasping needy noises. I grabbed his hair, pushing him down.

"Knock knock!"

I screamed and pushed Hudson off as a face appeared in the foggy car window.

"Do you want me to take the dough out of the freezer?" Granny Murray yelled through the glass.

I hastily pulled at my top.

"Um, sure. Yeah," I said. "Please."

The elderly woman flashed me a thumbs-up. "Carry on. Don't forget to put your tits away before you come back inside. Astelle is in a state."

"I should ... um ..."

Hudson kissed me one more time.

"You want my tongue on your clit, don't you?"

Geez. When he put it that way ... Yes. Yes, in fact, I did.

"I think you probably made your point," I said, hastily stuffing my boobs back in the top and trying to neaten my hair. "There's no audience anymore."

"Your family is watching from the window," he said.

There was a hungry look in his eyes.

I wasn't sure if Hudson was still just acting or ...

Or what? You think he's actually attracted to you in your homemade elf costume that is, let's just say, not quite your size?

"Time to make cookies," I croaked, opening the car door.

"Don't pretend to be wholesome," Hudson said, joining me on the snowy sidewalk. "You liked having my mouth on your tits."

"I'm making sugar cookies and chocolate," I said loudly, praying that the cold air would cool the redness in my face. It was hard, considering Hudson's hand was cupping my ass.

"Gracie was a tiger," Granny Murray was saying when I walked into the kitchen. "Anyone who doubted the sex in the pickup truck story, eat your words, haters!"

"This is shameful behavior from your daughter, Bethany." Grandma Astelle was shouting over Granny Murray. "Now we know why Kelly makes such terrible life choices—her older sister was a bad role model."

Granny Murray put up her hands like a boxer. "Don't you talk shit about my granddaughter. Good for her for finding her bliss."

Grandma Astelle picked up her cane.

"Fight fight fight!" my cousins hollered and banged on the table.

"It's Christmas!" my mother shrieked. "Rob, do something with your mother."

"Are those two old women really going to fight?" Hudson whispered to me in alarm.

"Ooh yeah. I'm shocked they lasted this long."

"Granny Murray is going to kill that old woman."

"Don't count out Grandma Astelle. She has a sword in that cane."

"My god."

"My bad. Didn't mean to cockblock you, Hudson," Granny Murray called. "I'm going to kick this ho's ass, then we're going to make Christmas cookies."

"Or we could make cookies right now," I said, grabbing an apron.

"Boo!" Dakota called.

I whistled sharply, making my family clap their hands over their ears.

"Christmas cookie production is no joke," I yelled at the gaggle of family members in the kitchen. "I need everyone focused. Baking is a precision art. I have everyone sorted into stations. Directions and diagrams have been provided for reference."

"Gracie, is this really necessary?" My mother sighed.

"Do you want cookies to give to your friends and neighbors?" I asked her. "Or not?"

Hudson leaned against the counter.

I handed him an apron.

"Put that on. You're going to get flour all over those sexy black clothes."

It was an hour into Christmas cookie baking, and I had a rhythm going. Hudson, because he could lift the heavy sacks of flour and really work a rolling pin, was helping my mom and Granny Murray make the dough and roll it out. Dakota was on decorating duty with Grandma Astelle. The littler kids had gotten bored of cutting out shapes, and I'd set them up making their own cookies to give to classmates, away from my operation.

"Kelly and James, that's too many stars. Please keep track of your production numbers."

James rolled his eyes.

"You see what I have to deal with in the office every day?"

"She sounds like CEO material," Hudson drawled. "Maybe you all need a shake-up at the office."

"Gracie cannot be a CEO. Look at her. She bakes in an elf costume. This is the best she'll ever do," James scoffed.

Hudson smirked. "She is with me, so yeah, that tracks."

James scowled and threw down the cookie cutters. "I'm going to watch the game."

"You are making fun family memories," I reminded myself.

Three hours into the cookie making marathon, and the children had already tired of it and had wandered off to go watch *Elf*.

Kelly was spending more time making videos for social media than actually cutting out cookies. Yes, friends, she was indeed pretending like she had baked these cookies. Never believe anything you see on Instagram. Granny Murray was spending more time drinking than baking. Dakota had taken over the cookie-cutter station.

"This is why you shouldn't let just anyone make Christmas cookies," Astelle sniffed. Say what you would about her, but the old woman knew how to decorate a cookie. She had towers of perfectly frosted Christmas trees, snowmen, and reindeer in front of her.

Thank god for Hudson, who had multiple timers going on his phone and was watching the cookies in the oven like a hawk.

Bless people who are self-sufficient.

He must have felt me staring at him because he turned his head.

I made a heart shape with my hands and beamed at him. He shook his head.

We had now been baking for seven hours straight. "White Christmas" had played on my playlist at least fifty times if you counted all the variations. It was dark outside, and the kids were on their second movie. Takeout had been ordered and eaten. Dakota had left to meet up with some friends from school who were in town. Unlike me, who liked to pretend that high school had never happened and I had just appeared one day a fully formed adult, she still kept in touch with high school acquaintances.

Still we soldiered on.

"How you doing there, Hudson?" Granny Murray asked him, hustling back into the kitchen. "I see Astelle gave up."

The elderly woman had decorated hundreds of cookies then made my father drive her home.

I had taken up her post with the royal icing. Hudson seemed to have the mixing, rolling, and baking under control, which was good, considering my mother had thrown in the towel.

Weaklings.

On a nearby chalkboard, he was neatly keeping track of the cookie shape counts.

"That's a man who's digging deep into his military training to survive," Uncle Bic joked, wandering into the kitchen for more ice for the wet bar. "He must really like you, Gracie!"

"Yeah, I mean, you know," I said with a helpless shrug as Hudson took another tray of cookies out of the oven.

Uncle Bic reached for one.

"You touch one of those cookies," Hudson said in a low warning voice, "and I'm breaking your hand."

My uncle cursed and scurried out of the kitchen.

Granny Murray cackled as she grabbed yet another bottle of wine from the wine fridge.

"Looks like Gracie's met her baking match."

I smiled at Hudson after she left.

"Normally, at this point in the evening, everyone has given up," I said as I quickly, using white and black icing that I had squeezed in both hands, made eyes on twenty smiling Rudolphs.

"Isn't your family going to give away these cookies to their friends?" he asked, frowning.

"Not all of them. I'll give some away to the EnerCheck employees," I said with a sigh. "Besides, it's Christmas, and making Christmas cookies is tradition."

"Even if you do it all by yourself?" He slid another tray into the oven.

"Usually Dakota stays," I said defensively.

Hudson thinks you're pathetic. If you were someone with a life, you'd be at a holiday party or something right now, not baking cookies in your mom's house.

Shoot. I liked baking Christmas cookies. I liked the colors and the frosting designs and the smell of freshly baked sugar cookies.

"I'm going to grab more flour," Hudson said, untying the apron. "Then I'm going to find whatever homicidal maniac thought it would be a good idea to combine Chipmunk singing and Christmas carols and strangle them."

I smiled to myself.

Then froze, suddenly having a horrible vision of Hudson grabbing the bread or biscuit flour and ruining dozens of cookies.

"I just want to make sure you got the right flour," I said, rushing into the pantry.

Hudson put back the bag of flour.

"No, that was the right one."

He didn't pick up the bag.

"Take off that apron," he said, voice deep, commanding.

"Why? Is there icing on it?" I asked, untying the apron and slipping it over my head.

"No, because I want to fuck you in that costume," he said and crushed our mouths together.

He was rough as he pushed me against the pantry wall, the glass jars of flour, sugar, and spices rattling. His hands were everywhere, pulling at my clothes, under my skirt.

I bucked against his hand as he pressed it between my legs.

"I want to come in that tight little cunt of yours." The deep baritone was hot in my ear.

"Right now?" I squeaked.

He pulled at the ribbons on the hastily tied bodice; my tits spilled out. His mouth was on them, reminding me of why sex in his truck was sounding like a totally amazing idea. Except this time, his hands didn't just stay on my thighs.

I bit back a moan as he stroked me through my soaked panties.

"You like that, don't you?" he whispered harshly. "Are you going to come for me?"

His hand slipped under my panties, and I let out a loud gasp as he stroked me.

"That feels—"

"I could make you come just like this. I don't even need my cock."

"I want—"

"You want me to fuck that tight little cunt of yours, hmm?"

He kissed me. My legs were trembling. Only his weight crushing me against the wall held me upright. Two of his fingers dipped in my opening, making me wish it was his cock instead.

His mouth was back on my nipple, sucking it while his fingers played in my pussy. Then he was back in my ear, whispering dark and dirty things to me.

"I want to bend you over on your bed, spread your legs, really spread them, make sure you're dripping wet. I want your juices running down your thigh."

I panted against his cheek, imagining it, imagining me bent over for him.

His hands on my clit was not enough.

"I want you to hold your pussy open for me so I can ram my thick cock into your tight little cunt, give you every thick inch, pound into you until you're screaming my name, make you understand what it's like to be fucked by a real man."

Santa, that is all I want for Christmas.

He was stroking me harder now.

"Take me back to your apartment and fuck me right now."

He chuckled; it vibrated in my chest.

"I am a bad influence on you."

"I don't care if I get coal for Christmas," I choked out, clinging to him, my nails digging into his biceps, "if it means I have your cock."

I nipped his mouth like he'd done to me. In response, he stroked my clit hard, and I moaned, my teeth scraping down the stubble on his chin.

"*What the fuck are you doing?*"

"Oh my god!" I screamed. "James?" I tried to push Hudson off me while simultaneously covering my bare chest.

Hudson didn't jump back or curse or act like a normal person would when getting caught in a compromising position. Instead, he dipped his head down to kiss my neck. His fingers still working between my legs.

"Relax. He's never seen you come before," Hudson said, voice rough as he continued to stroke me, his fingers swirling around my clit.

"This is ... um—" He kissed me hard, swallowing my protest.

My eyes flicked to James.

He was furious. The vein in his forehead popped out, and his nose was red.

"Don't look at him. You're mine." Hudson's fingers were rough in my pussy. "That's right," he breathed against my mouth while James yelled at him, *Get off her,* and *What the fuck is wrong with you, Gracie?*

Hudson kept up the pace with his fingers, one hand on my neck holding me in place while he stroked me, flying me higher and higher. I couldn't stop my breath from coming out in high-pitched gasps, couldn't stop myself from careening to the edge.

"That feels good doesn't it? You like what I'm doing to your clit, don't you?"

I whimpered.

"You don't want me to stop, do you, Gracie?" he crooned as I moaned again and bucked against his hand while he stroked me.

"Say my name when you come," Hudson ordered as he gave me one last hard stroke.

Then I was crashing over the edge.

"Hudson, oh my god, Hudson!" His name came out in a squeal.

I clung to him, my heart yammering in my head.

That was better than Christmas morning, cookies, and decorating a Christmas tree.

"Shoot." I sagged against him.

Hudson chuckled and tugged his hand out from under my skirt, still holding my head in place. He smeared his wet hand all over my mouth then licked it off.

"Delicious."

"You're perverted," my ex choked out.

"It's only perverted," Hudson said coolly, "if the guy looks like you. With someone like me? It's just hot."

He kissed me again, long and slow, his tongue lazily drifting in my mouth. Then he broke the kiss, holding me by the jaw.

"I can't believe you let this one go, James," he said to my ex. "She's a damn good fuck."

"*What in the world?*"

Crap. That was my mom.

"Gracie, what are you doing?" My mother was appalled.

"They were having sex in the pantry," James yelped.

Next Christmas I was staying in a hotel.

"This is obscene," James was practically spitting. "No decorum."

"Too bad Astelle isn't here," Granny Murray said. "She'd have a heart attack and die, and wouldn't that be a great Christmas present."

"I can't believe you turned into a slut," James screamed at me.

A cold hand of fear chased off the lingering echoes of pleasure. I was afraid James was about to tell everyone my secret.

Hudson just smirked.

"Best damn fuck on the East Coast. Maybe you just suck at sex, if you're so surprised to see her come."

James sucked in a breath. "No, she—"

"Considering I walked in on you fucking my sister, I think fair's fair," I said loudly, not wanting this incident to become an even more embarrassing core memory and having everyone in my family question why an almost thirty-year-old was still a virgin.

"Gracie, I thought you let that go. What has gotten into you?" my dad begged.

"She's jealous," Kelly said haughtily while my cousins filmed the whole thing.

"Sorry I flaked on the cookies," Dakota hollered, sprinting into the kitchen. "That dinner took longer than— Oh my god."

"You're the one who's jealous, Kelly," I screamed at my sister while Dakota silently mouthed, *What the fuck?*

"You know, I was at this sexual wellness retreat," Piper was saying over the din, "and they really taught me to get in touch with my inner sexual being. You should try sunning your vagina."

"I sun my vagina," Granny Murray said, "but not in the winter. You'll freeze your taint off."

"She's just trying to take all the attention away from me, Dad," Kelly insisted.

"… and after sex you need to put a bulb of garlic—" Piper was saying.

"Ooh, you don't want to put anything that can sprout up there. One of the ladies in my book club—" Granny Murray interjected.

"I feel sorry for you, Kelly," Hudson said. "Maybe one day someone will show you what a real man looks like."

My sister looked like she'd like that very much.

Hudson's phone started ringing in his jacket pocket. He slipped away from me and grabbed it.

"Anyway," Granny Murray continued loudly while Kelly and I screamed insults at each other and my mom begged us to calm down.

"I have to go," Hudson said, heading to the door.

James sneered. "Oh, to your minimum-wage job?"

I hastily put some cookies in a box and ran out the door.

"Take some cookies for your coworkers," I said, thrusting the bag at him.

He tilted his head down. "Not your boyfriend, remember. But the grand plan is in progress."

"Oh, right. The plan. That's why you stayed to make cookies." I nodded. "Yeah. That makes sense."

He leaned in to kiss me.

I closed my eyes, savoring the memory of the pleasure he'd given me.

"Are these enough cookies for your coworkers?" I asked.

"I'm not going to work, Sugarplum. I'm going to get laid."

"Oh. Oh!"

Right.

I stood there shivering, watching him leave.

Of course, your fake boyfriend wants to go have sex with an actual experienced woman. He probably has a whole contact list full of them.

It felt shitty though, that Hudson would rather go find some other girl to sleep with instead of me. Especially after he'd just had his hands where no man had ever been.

I shivered, wrapping my arms around my chest, watching as Hudson's truck's headlights disappeared down the dark road.

"Your sister is right. You are delusional," I scolded myself as I forced myself back inside.

Suddenly, the prospect of making Christmas cookies didn't seem as much fun if I had to think about Hudson out with another woman.

"He's allowed to live his life," I reminded myself.

Granny Murray was filling Dakota in on the happenings when I went back to the kitchen.

I pulled a tray out of the oven. The cookies were burnt. I dumped the whole pan in the sink then started packing up the finished cookies.

"Life is not in the kitchen," Granny Murray said magnanimously. "Get in your club gear, girls. We're going to hit the town. It's Grandma's secret medicine."

Chapter 27

HUDSON

"I don't need you to fucking micromanage me."

"You reek of Christmas," Grayson replied in greeting.

I scowled at him.

He gestured with his beer to the seat across from him in the dank motorcycle bar in the bad part of the Gulch, the part that hadn't been gentrified yet.

I slid into the sticky booth.

Grayson handed me one of the beers sitting in front of him.

"You have frosting in your hair."

I brushed my fingers through it, feeling slightly self-conscious.

"I'm assuming that it's all part of your grand plan."

"We're making progress," I said. "Gracie's sister clearly has it bad for me. It's only a matter of time before I have her in a compromising position. Then there will be a big video reveal at the ceremony, and I propose to Gracie, and James has a fit. Her family finally treats her with the respect she deserves."

"What," Grayson said slowly, "the fuck. How is that in any way related to the information I'm paying you to find?"

Good fucking question, Hudson.

"I have to stay around her and give her a reason to trust me," I said rapidly, trying to recover. "It's working. I got a good lead today. Gracie admitted that her father did some shady shit early in the business. We're delivering cookies to the family office tomorrow. She'll log into a computer system, and *bam*, we're in. Mission accomplished."

"I could build another skyscraper if I had a dollar for every time you've told me that."

I tried not to seem concerned. Grayson didn't tolerate woolgathering. He paid for excellence. I had to make sure he was confident I would deliver.

"It's under control."

"And add a helicopter pad to my new skyscraper," he said acerbically. "I have my next year's companywide business plan riding on this. There is a European contract I'm going to be the only contender in the running for once I'm able to bring down Roscoe Energy. There are hundreds of billions of dollars at stake here, Hudson."

"I'll deliver. I always deliver," I promised. "Gracie's smart, competent, decisive, and she has a knack for sniffing out when something's out of alignment. She actually would have done great in military intelligence. She has the mind for it. Only problem is when it comes to her relationships. It's a blind spot for her. She thinks men don't like her as much as her sister, but she's wrong. She's very alluring. She just doesn't realize it. I'm staying solidly in that blind spot though, hence the cookies, the car, and the engagement ring. She's going to hand me the information you need on a silver platter."

Hopefully while wearing that elf outfit.

Grayson took a sip of his beer. He was a man who preferred $50,000 scotch, but he came from nothing, even more nothing than me, because at least I had my family. And he didn't mind drinking cheap beer in a smelly bar.

He set the bottle down on the tabletop.

"You like this woman."

"What? No, I don't," I said, forcing myself not to sound defensive.

I took a swig of the beer. It was worse than the homemade shit we used to drink in the military.

"Gracie's not my type. She's mousy and meek."

"And yet she's given you and your team the runaround." The corners of Grayson's mouth turned down slightly.

"It's like she's wearing the world's best disguise. She lulls you into thinking she's this precious object that needs to be protected at all costs, then *bam!* she knifes you. You wouldn't know it, but she's sharp, observant, and has a filthy sense of humor."

And filthy other stuff.

"She's efficient, she wakes up early, she's organized, she plans, and she takes care of her family, but," I added, "she's no match for me. I'm making progress."

Grayson leaned back and crossed his arms.

"Uh-huh. So what kind of ring do you need for your fake engagement?"

"I'll just buy one."

"Like I told you with the car, I'm leaving nothing to chance."

"I'll get you your information before I have to propose. If not, I'll have Jake pick up something that looks expensive."

"If Gracie is the knife-you-when-you're-not-suspecting type," Grayson said, "then I don't want you to just get a ring. Follow through with what you were planning with her. I don't want her to scuttle my plans at the last minute because you weren't detail oriented enough to keep from making her suspicious."

I pulled up the file on Gracie through an encrypted app on my phone and navigated to the photo of her great-grandmother.

The smiling young woman looked a bit like Gracie; they had the same eyes. In her arms she cradled a pug, a historic one, not the one whose eyes looked like they were going to fall of its head, like Pugnog.

Prominent in the photo was a sparkling diamond ring on her left hand.

"I'd get her something like that," I suggested.

Grayson peered at the image.

"Send that to me."

I texted it to him and finished off the beer while he sent a note to his assistant.

"I'll have my secretary find it. Lately she's been on a roll for delivering difficult-to-procure items. Thank you for the information about my brother, by the way. He removed that woman from his life. Eventually. He ignored it at first, so I sent the information anonymously to my other brother Aaron, who made it very clear she needed to go."

"Fucking little brothers, man."

That earned me a small smile.

"Fucking little brothers," Grayson agreed and downed the rest of the beer.

"One more round before you go back to the land of caviar and champagne?" I offered.

"Sure. Why not? It's—"

"You fucking bitch!" a man yelled out over the din in the bar.

Grayson and I both stood up.

"Don't insult my grandmother, asshole!"

"Fucking hell, is that Gracie?"

Chapter 28

GRACIE

"I thought we were going to a bar. This looks like a place where you lose a kidney," Dakota said.

"This is the happening spot. Mildred told me that she found two guys for a threesome here. Nothing like cheap alcohol and daddies in leather." Granny Murray licked her lips.

Dakota and I shot each other looks of horror then ran after Granny Murray as she power-walked up to the door of the dilapidated-looking bar.

My cousin and I had dressed for going to one of the nice but low-key spots on Main Street. We were way overdressed for the Broken Bottle. Some person had hung up Christmas decorations that looked like they'd been in use since the '80s. The string of tattered Santas hanging from the bar were begging for release from this mortal realm.

I ducked my head down, trying not to make eye contact with anyone as Granny Murray led us to a corner booth.

"I'll grab us a pitcher," she said, pulling a fistful of cash out of her wallet. "They don't take credit cards here."

Dakota huddled down in the booth across from me.

"I'm going to take a wild guess and say that they don't serve cute holiday-themed cocktails here either."

"I think you'd be hard-pressed to find so much as a craft beer," I said.

"I'm surprised you weren't finishing the pantry sex," Dakota said with a giggle. "This seems like a downgrade from riding Hudson's sleigh."

I chewed on my lip, wishing I had a drink, any drink.

"I don't think I was quite up to his standards," I admitted, feeling sick.

"What? You have tits, and you don't have a yeast infection. What's not to love? What more does a man need?"

"I don't know, but whatever it is, I don't have it. You should have seen his eyes," I whispered to Dakota. "Hudson was so cold. He looked at me like I was nothing, like I didn't even matter. Then he just said, 'I'm going to get laid.'"

"Well, fuck him."

"We're not dating," I reminded her and myself. "Hudson doesn't owe me exclusivity or kindness. He's fulfilling a contract. He just did it with me in the pantry because …" The hot wave of humiliation was going to drown me.

"Because he knew James was going to walk in and see. It was a power play."

"I don't believe he didn't find it a little bit hot," Dakota argued.

I squirmed in my seat.

"Did you feel any poking action?"

I hadn't felt anything except for his hands giving me the most amazing pleasure I'd ever felt, his tongue on my nipple, and his mouth whispering in my ear all the dirty things he wanted to do to me.

"I didn't notice."

"After you get your epic revenge on Kelly and James, you should start trying to date again. The company that made the Meat Market app has a new dating app out for divorced people looking for a second chance."

Could I go back to dad bods and men who liked missionary sex then watching an episode of *Masterpiece Theatre* after I had experienced Hudson with his tattoos, his hands, and his male arrogance?

"Maybe I need to give up and lean into my season of spinster auntdom."

"You're breaking up Kelly's marriage, so no auntdom on the horizon."

"There's always Piper and my brother."

"Your brother's going to get another look-alike VSCO girl in three months, rinse, and repeat until he's in his forties and has an existential crisis," Dakota said.

"Fine. I'll adopt a cat."

"Not while we're still living together."

"Why is my life so horrible?" I groaned.

"Smile, honey. You're too pretty to look so sad."

Dakota sucked in a breath to berate the man who had catcalled us.

"Look what I found," Granny Murray crowed as she and the catcaller, holding a pitcher of beer, headed over to our table.

"These guys want to party."

"Gran!" I exclaimed, horrified.

I felt dirty as the catcaller and his minions leered at me.

The beer sloshed on the table as the catcaller set it down along with several dirty-looking glasses.

One sour-smelling man scooted into the booth with me.

"She's going senile," Dakota whispered to me. "This is the early stages of dementia."

"Girls, be nice," Granny Murray chided. "Bertie and his friends just want to have a good time."

"I have a boyfriend," I said automatically.

"He's not your boyfriend. He's a standing hookup," Granny Murray corrected.

Had Bertie drugged her drink, or was this what Gran got up to now that she was a free-range woman, as she put it?

"Bertie bought drinks for us. Isn't that gentlemanly of him?"

Bertie smiled at me. He was missing several teeth.

"Yeah. I'm not drinking that," Dakota muttered.

"What the hell did you say, you stuck-up cunt?"

"Fuck you," Dakota enunciated. "I'm not drinking your cheap roofied beer. Let's go, Gran."

"You owe us," Bertie bellowed.

"I don't owe you shit," Dakota snapped.

The five men boxed us in at the booth.

I'm never going out with Gran anywhere again.

"Show us your tits, and we'll let you leave," one of Bertie's minions demanded.

"Okay," Granny Murray said and lifted her shirt.

There were hisses of horror. One heavyset man looked like he was going to faint.

"What the fuck, you crazy old bat? Not you. I want to see her perky nipples." He pointed at me.

Gross gross gross.

"What's wrong with my tits?" Granny Murray demanded.

"Everything!"

"Don't insult my grandmother, asshole!" Dakota shouted.

"We need to leave, Gran," I said, clutching my purse. "Thank you for the drinks."

Another balding minion grabbed my jacket.

"We didn't say you could go. We're going to have a drink."

His breath smelled sour as he jerked me to him.

I picked up the beer and dumped it over his head.

"Here's your drink."

"You fucking—" He wound back a punch.

I closed my eyes and turned my head reflexively. But the punch never came.

"Don't fucking touch her."

"Hudson?" I opened my eyes.

"I thought you said you didn't have a boyfriend!" The minion howled in pain as Hudson twisted his arm behind his back and slammed his head into the table.

"It's complicated," I said to the red-faced man.

"This isn't your business," one of the smelly minions yelled as a chair crashed down on Hudson's back and neck.

I screamed as blood ran down his face.

"We're in a bar fight!" Granny Murray whooped.

The man reared back for another hit. The chair crashed against Hudson's back again, and the leg hit me on the arm. Not hard. Hudson seemed to take the brunt of it.

The balding man used the opportunity to scrabble out from under Hudson.

Hudson kicked him hard in the ribs, and I heard something crunch. His fellow minion took another shot with the chair.

Unfortunately, Hudson wasn't able to effectively fight them because he kept trying to block anything from hitting me with his body.

You need to do something! I internally shrieked. *You're going to lose him.*

I couldn't lose him.

I grabbed the spilled pitcher of beer and threw the plastic container at the nearest minion, wishing I'd taken a page out of Dakota's book and bought a Taser.

Bertie was trying to drag Dakota out of the booth while Granny Murray hit him with the plastic pitcher.

Dakota got him right between the eyes with her Taser, but he was built like a beer-soaked ox and was only momentarily stunned.

His friend lunged at Dakota.

"Bitch."

Before he could touch her, another man—tall, broad shouldered, built like Hudson—came flying in, grabbed Dakota's attacker around the neck in a chokehold, and pulled him back.

The minion wheezed and flopped around like a fish then went limp.

Was that Hudson's brother?

His face was partially obscured by a scarf and the turned-up collar on his winter jacket.

Though he moved like Hudson and his brothers—strong, athletic, easily ducking under a flying chair and punching the catcaller in the stomach—he had green eyes, not wintery gray.

He has expensive boots, too, I noticed as one of those boots came down hard on the minion's knee.

More people in the bar were rushing to join the melee. Hudson jumped up on the table then leapt off, joining the green-eyed man in the brawl.

They both moved like they'd been in a bar fight together before, aware of each other's movements.

Hudson ducked the punch thrown by a minion and knocked him out with an undercut while the green- eyed man finished off the catcaller by hooking his leg under him and sending him crashing to the ground.

Granny Murray was fending off two men with a broken pitcher and a plastic fork.

She stabbed one in the arm, making him wail.

Hudson grabbed the man by the back of the collar and slammed his head into the edge of the table, sending teeth flying, while the green-eyed man tackled the third attacker. He did some sort of ninja roll thing and sent the bald man flying into the bar.

The minion lay there in a heap.

The bar patrons who didn't really have a bone to pick backed away warily as the two men stared them down.

Mumbling excuses, the patrons returned to their beers.

I threw my arms around Hudson's neck.

"You saved us," I exclaimed.

My heart was still hammering, and I felt shaky and unsteady. I kissed his bruised mouth gently then released him.

"You saved my cousin. Thank you," I said to the green-eyed man, wrapping my arms around his neck and kissing his cheek. "Your poor hand." I reached for it.

"It's fine," he said in a deep voice.

"He has an expensive watch too," I chattered, not really sure why I was still talking. "What's a guy like you doing in a place like this?"

Gracie, shut up.

It was the shock.

He and Hudson exchanged a look.

The green-eyed man adjusted his jacket and headed over to the bar.

"We need to get out of here." Hudson took my arm.

"I didn't get a drink," Granny Murray complained as Hudson herded us out into the cold.

Hudson grabbed my shoulder.

"What the hell were you three doing here?"

"Picking up men and getting wasted!" Granny Murray hollered.

"All of you?" Hudson raised an eyebrow. "I'd be offended, except you're so far out of your depth right now, Sugarplum." He paused as two men passed us, walking up to the entrance.

"You boys looking for some action?" Granny Murray yelled to them. "I've been in a bar fight and flashed my tits, but it really seems like you have to put on a whole dog and pony show around here to get laid." She headed in their direction as Dakota raced after her.

Hudson's eyes flicked up to the night sky as he tried to center himself.

Through the window I watched the green-eyed man hand a stack of bills to a bartender, who stuffed them under the counter. The green-eyed man turned his head, briefly making eye contact with me.

"Who was that?" I asked Hudson, pointing.

"He's just ... he's—" Hudson worked his jaw.

"I thought you were going to get laid. Er … wait. Is that your uh, lay?" I asked weakly. My mouth was dry. "I'm so sorry. I didn't know. I mean, I'm not sorry. That's great. He seems nice. And handsome. You two are cute together."

There was a slow grin on Hudson's bruised face.

"Sugarplum, all I can think about is putting my mouth on your sweet, juicy cunt, but I'm glad to see you're an ally."

I gulped. "Let me take you home. I need to put some ice on your face."

"I think that's my line." He tugged one of my curls that had escaped from my ponytail.

"That guy," he said, nodding to the green-eyed man who was walking quickly out of the bar, hands in his pockets, "is just a friend from work."

I perked up. "A friend from work? Hi! Merry Christmas!" I called loudly to the green-eyed man, who froze. "Did you like the cookies?"

He seemed confused.

"Hudson, did you give him the cookies?" I demanded.

"I left them at my apartment."

"Which job is he at? I'm going to bring you some more cookies as a thank-you!" I yelled after the man, who gave me a half-hearted wave. "Hudson helped bake them. He's a really good baker."

"Gracie."

"Is he shy?" I asked Hudson as his friend practically ran to his car.

"I got both their numbers," Granny Murray crowed as Dakota led her back to me and Hudson. "The one guy has a very nice grandson. Dakota and I are going to double-date."

"We are not."

"Where's your car?" Hudson asked, pressing his fingers to his nose and wincing.

"You're drunk, and you got hit with a chair. I can drive. You look like you're in pain," I said, reaching for his keys.

"Absolutely not."

Chapter 29

HUDSON

"I see what you mean about her," Grayson remarked on the phone that evening when I was lying in the bathtub packed in bags of ice.

"You see what I mean about her," I repeated tensely.

He sees what? That Gracie was pretty, that it was bliss when she wrapped her arms around you and kissed you and looked up at you like you were her hero? How you could get lost in her eyes, how soft and warm she felt in your arms?

I'd watched her and Grayson, how she couldn't keep her eyes or her hands off of him.

The Hallmark movie practically wrote itself. Big city billionaire tries to ruin pretty small-town girl's company with the help of his obnoxious sidekick. Billionaire saves girl in a fight. Girl teaches billionaire the true meaning of Christmas. They fall in love and move to the small town and live happily ever after with lots of money while the sidekick gets thrown in a lake or kicked by a donkey in the Christmas pageant or something.

I couldn't compete with Grayson; he was every woman's dream man.

"You're such a liar," Grayson said conversationally. "You do have it bad for her."

"Gracie is nothing to me."

"All those bruises on your face say otherwise, but sure, wallow in your self-deception. As long as you give me what I want, I don't care."

"Uh-huh."

"No, I see what you mean about her being observant. It was like she was cataloging everything she saw about me. And the cookies? She's not going to show up somewhere and start asking questions, is she? She could become a real problem."

"I'll keep Gracie distracted," I promised.

"We should take some cookies to your friend after we drop these by the EnerCheck office." It was late morning in the O'Brien house. Grace was piling dirty dishes by the sink.

I shrugged off my jacket, wincing slightly, turned on the water in the sink, and filled it up so I could help her wash up.

"You don't have to. Here. Sit down. I made you a plate," Gracie said.

She had saved me food. Of course she had.

"It's okay," I said gruffly. "I can eat after."

Gracie beamed at me.

It was like being drowned in warm caramel.

I let my hands settle on her waist and leaned in to kiss her.

I wanted her.

Soon.

"Where does your friend live? We can stop by his house."

"Richard's already left," I said, the lie and fake name spilling off my tongue. "He went to go see his brother's kids. I'll save him some cookies though."

"Do you have any other friends? We should take some to your brothers and maybe a few more to the nursing home," she said, stacking boxes neatly wrapped with green-and-red paper on the kitchen table.

"You can't spend all day delivering cookies," Kelly complained, waltzing into the kitchen. "Mom said you were going to come by and decorate James's house for the company Christmas party."

"It's going to be your house soon, Kelly," Gracie said desperately. "Don't you want to decorate?"

"Mom said you would do it. I have my hands full with this wedding. Besides, I don't work at EnerCheck; you do. So you should decorate for your company party."

She flounced off, not before pausing in front of me.

"Poor Hudson. Your face. Were you in a fight? Naughty boy." Kelly slapped me lightly on the ass.

"I thought you had another wedding dress fitting," Gracie said through her teeth.

"Someone has to take care of poor Hudson," Kelly said, grabbing an ice pack out of the freezer and dabbing it on my face. "Making him do dishes when he's injured. You're such a bad girlfriend, Gracie. Here. I'll kiss it and make it better."

Gracie's sister reached up and pressed lips like plastic to my forehead.

"Are you coming to the party, Hudson?" she asked me.

"Depends. Is it one of those crazy Christmas parties where people get drunk and have sex on the copy machine?"

Kelly twirled her hair. "It could be."

Gracie seemed quiet as she sat next to me in the truck, box of cookies on her lap.

"I don't know why I'm bringing cookies to the office," she sighed.

"Because then everyone will know they're from you," I reminded her. "Otherwise, your sister or mom will take credit."

"No one's going to even be in the office."

"Even better because then you can send out an email." I glanced over at her.

"You need to let everyone know when you did the work because otherwise someone else is going to put their name on your effort, and you won't get the credit," I told her as we drove through town to the EnerCheck office.

I was trying to keep it casual, light, that this was just another instance of me hanging out with her, just keeping the fake boyfriend revenge plan in motion, and not letting her sense the tension and excitement. I was close to completing the mission. I could feel it.

The EnerCheck Inc. office was in a restored old factory that had been converted into office space.

They were at the far end of the complex. I parked the truck in one of the empty spaces then took the boxes from Gracie.

I'd snuck people into this office before with the same maintenance scam. However, they'd been unable to find anything useful on the accounts they'd been able to access. We hadn't tried Gracie's company account yet.

"Man, you weren't kidding by no one being here," I remarked as we headed through the empty office. "Guess everyone's pregaming for the company holiday party."

"There's never anyone here." Gracie rolled her eyes.

"Which one is your desk?" I asked her.

"There."

"Someone put Sugarplum in a corner."

"James said it was because I worked out of the New York City office," she said, lips thinning. "Except that even so, I'm in the office more than most of my cousins who live in Maplewood Falls."

I sat down in her chair and pulled her on my lap.

The desktop computer was dark.

"They still have you guys on desktops?" I asked, silently sending her the thought to turn on the computer.

"This office is still stuck in the early two thousands," she said as I slowly ran my hand up and down her leg. "The server system is a mess, and people store files on their personal computers. I don't even store certain files on the server because someone will inadvertently delete it. Shoot. I'm the only person making backups."

"I'm just a humble janitor," I drawled, "but that doesn't sound like a way to run a business."

"Tell me about it," she muttered as she stood up to remove her coat.

Turn on the computer, turn on the computer.

I could tell Gracie that I wanted to look up something? Maybe I could tell her I wanted to buy the engagement ring. But that was clumsy. And I would pull it out only as a last resort. I was hoping force of habit would make her turn on the computer.

Luck was on my side today.

"I guess I'll tell people cookies are here. It will probably be the first time in months some of them will come into the office." She reached down to turn on the desktop.

The flash drive with the Trojan horse program that was going to allow my company to remote access into the computer and scrape off the data was burning a hole in my pocket.

Gracie sat on my lap as she wrote a companywide email and attached a photo of the cookies.

I settled her back against me, letting her feel the hard bulge in my crotch.

When she went to go put them in the break room kitchen, I slipped the flash drive into the back USB port of the desktop and quickly stood back up. The program flashed up on the screen for a second then minimized.

The computer needed to stay on while the program ran. If Gracie started poking around in the computer, she would see it running. Fortunately, I knew a few ways to keep her distracted.

I caught her in my arms when she came back to the desk. My hand slid under her skirt to stroke her through the tights.

She squeaked as I pulled them down.

"Someone could see."

"The danger makes it fun," I whispered in her ear, stroking her hot, wet pussy. "Undo your top. Let me see your tits."

Gracie looked around furtively, breath coming out in needy gasps. It was driving me crazy.

I nipped her ear.

"But there's no audience," she panted.

"You really want an audience for your first time, Sugarplum?"

"Here? Now?" she stammered. "That seems awfully fast. Don't we want to, I don't know, talk about it fir—*Ohhh*." She let out a low moan as I found her clit.

I kissed her hard and plunged two of my fingers in her opening.

Her eyelids fluttered, and her fingers reached for the buttons on her blouse.

I grabbed one of her huge tits in my hand, rubbed her juices all over the pink nipple, then sucked it.

"You want to talk about it?" I bit her nipple, making her gasp, then rolled it with my tongue. I kissed her hard, still rubbing her tit.

"You want to talk about me spreading your legs? You want to talk about how you'll whimper and moan and beg for my cock? You want to talk about the first time you feel a cock in your tight little pussy?"

Her hips were bucking against mine; my pants were tight, my cock hard.

"You want to talk about how I'll stretch you, fill you, spread your legs and your pussy lips wide and ram you with my thick cock?"

"How big is it going to be?" she asked in a faint whisper.

"Feel it," I breathed, guiding her hand to my pants.

I undid the belt, slipped her smaller hand under the waistband, and hissed as her fingers grasped the thick length.

"I don't know if that can fit," she whimpered.

The sound went straight to my cock.

"You sure do know how to make a man hard." I ground against her hand. "But don't worry. I'm going to make sure you're dripping and ready for me, Sugarplum."

I kissed her, my tongue claiming her mouth.

"You're going to be on your knees, begging for my cock."

I pulled her tights down further, giving me better access to her wet pussy, then I spread the folds, stroking her, driving her into a frenzy.

"Please," she whimpered.

"Please what?"

"Please make me feel *that* again."

"Sugarplum, you can't tell me that was the first time you ever came." I leaned back to look at her.

Face flushed, eyes glazed, she nodded.

"Well, don't I feel special."

"Prick."

I kissed her hard and bit her lip.

"You have a filthy pretty mouth. I want to come in it."

She made a strangled sound then cried out as I twisted my fingers around the hard nub of her clit.

The bell over the door jingled.

"Yoo-hoo! Gracie, is that you? I could only find my sunglasses, and I can't see in here."

"Shit." Gracie hastily pulled up her clothes and hid behind the desk, in full view of the desktop monitor.

Fuck.

I practically dove behind the desk. Fortunately, she had turned away from the monitor to fix her clothes.

"I wanted to get some of those delicious cookies," the older woman was saying to Gracie as she headed back through the open office. "Did you and your mom make those?"

"They're just in the break room. Help yourself," Gracie called, shoving her arms in her jacket. "Hudson and I were just leaving. I have to go decorate. I'll see you at the party."

"I'm so looking forward to the Christmas party," the older woman chattered. "And look at these delicious cookies. How sweet."

"We need to go," Gracie whispered to me.

I ignored her, cupped her face, kissed her.

"Too bad. I want to finish what we started."

"We almost got caught," she hissed, reaching around me to turn off the computer.

The program was designed to make it look like the computer was turning off, but only turn off the monitor.

Sure, if you looked closely, anyone with half a brain would see the computer was still running, but I was going to make sure that more than half of Gracie's brain was focused on me.

I pulled Gracie in for one more kiss. The computer fan was still whirring as the data copied over back to my office. I could feel her attention slide over as her brain tried to process what was wrong with the computer and if she should do a hard shutoff or investigate.

Neither of those options worked for me.

I cupped her face and locked eyes with her.

"I want you to go home," I told her, "and shave your sweet little pussy, because I'm taking your virginity tonight."

Chapter 30

GRACIE

"*Tonight*," I whisper-shrieked to Dakota.

We were in James's house, the big Victorian home that he and I were supposed to be living in if the wedding had actually happened.

"Good thing you're all waxed and ready to go," my cousin teased as she helped me measure out the yards of garland.

I made a face.

"Gran's friend did a great job," Dakota said. "I've booked an appointment with her."

I felt like getting a full Brazilian bikini wax in the living room of an elderly woman with poor eyesight was not one of my better moments.

"She has muscle memory. Also she was so cheap." Dakota picked up a box of candles and headed into the living room. "You can't waste the pain. You need to do the deed with Hudson."

"I can't have sex with him tonight."

"Why not?"

"I'm not ready."

"Don't be scared," my cousin said. "It's not that big of a deal."

"It feels like a big deal. Being a virgin was something I was proud of. It meant I had self-control, that I was a better person than my sister because I was saving myself for marriage. If I lose it to Hudson, that's bad. We're not in a committed relationship. We don't even like each other. Hudson's not even attracted to me."

"First of all, let go of the toxic patriarchy. You are still valuable even if you're not a virgin. Don't believe any of that used-gum bullshit," Dakota lectured. "Second, a guy doesn't tell a woman he wants to come all over her cunt if he doesn't think she's at least mildly attractive."

"If he thought I was someone worthy of him, he wouldn't use that kind of language," I said as I smoothed out a table runner.

"He's just trying to get your engine revving, make sure you're loosey-goosey enough to fit that weapon he's hiding in his pants."

"This is too much for me," I said, pulling an emergency stash of Christmas cookies out of my purse. They were the bad ones, where the icing looked a little wonky or they were a little too crispy. But a cookie was a cookie, and I needed a cookie.

"I don't know what to do, where to put my arms. What if I make weird noises?" I stuffed a sad-looking Santa in my mouth. "This is a terrible idea. Hudson is going to laugh at me."

"You always jump to the worst-case scenario."

"Because the worst-case scenario always happens," I wailed. "I'm not meant to be in a relationship. It always ends in disaster and heartbreak."

"You only had two and a half real relationships," Dakota reminded me. "That's hardly enough to be statistically significant."

I reached for another cookie. "Oh my god, where did all these cookies go? Pugnog, did you eat them?"

The dog whined.

Dakota gave me a pointed look.

"I think we need some wine," she said. "Let's see what James is hiding in his wine cellar, Pugnog."

I chewed on my hair as I climbed up the ladder to hang garland and glass ornaments on the oversized antique chandelier in the living room. I remembered picking out this chandelier, imagining the Christmas mornings it would preside over. Now I was just the hired help. No, not even that. I wasn't getting paid for any of this.

James and Kelly were going to have a beautifully decorated home. Everyone was going to congratulate them on it and tell Kelly what a wonderful job she had done with the party, and I was going to stand all alone in the corner. Just like when I was a teenager and Kelly had always been the center of attention. She was the pretty daughter; I was the good daughter, the one who everyone could ignore because they knew I'd always do whatever was asked of me.

The ladder wobbled as I climbed up to the next step, not quite tall enough to drape the garland nicely to the chain where it hung from the plaster ceiling.

Maybe I wouldn't quite be alone at the party. Hudson would be there, right?

Who was I kidding? He was going to flirt with Kelly the whole time, just like all the guys. Then he was going to take my virginity, realize that he might as well fuck a dead fish, then go back to Kelly. Shoot, I bet he would break up her marriage then decide that he wanted her to himself after all and whisk her away in a romance-movie-worthy ending while I was left sad and alone to pack up another failed wedding.

I sniffed as I reached, trying to hook the garland on a bronze arm.

"Gracie, get down from there," a deep voice cut through my self-pity session.

I screamed, and the ladder wobbled dangerously then steadied. I peeked down to see Hudson holding the ladder in place.

"Gracie, what in God's name are you doing? You could get hurt."

"I'm a pro at decorating."

"I don't care. Get down. I'll do it," he said flatly.

I sighed loudly and climbed down.

Hudson grabbed me around the waist and set me down on the floor then took the rest of the garland and ornaments from me.

"I came to make sure you didn't chicken out," he said in a low voice when he'd finished decorating the chandelier.

"No. You came to decorate," I said stubbornly.

Gray eyes narrowed.

"I wasted hours in the living room of a seventy-year-old woman with a collection of reborn dolls, getting waxed in places no one should ever be waxed, just for you. Then I had to recover from said Brazilian wax, and now I'm behind schedule. So you're going to help."

"Bossy." He smirked. "But I'm glad to see you're following orders."

He easily picked up the heavy box of Christmas knick-knacks. I trotted after him into the dining room.

"Yes, let's talk about that. I don't need you ordering me around like that anymore. You can't just tell me what to do with my body," I snapped at him, nerves frazzled. "Get the other side of this table. I need it moved closer to the wall."

Hudson pushed me out of the way and easily picked up the table to move it where I wanted.

"The fact that you were practically coming on my hand earlier, in your dad's office, with your tits hanging out makes me think that I can tell you to do whatever I want."

"Asshole."

"You hired me for all my positive qualities," he said, setting the table down.

I spread a white tablecloth out on it and fished in the box for holiday figurines.

"You can't just tell a woman to shave *down there* because you like it."

"You'll like it too," he countered. "I can't wait to run my tongue in your slick pussy. From the way you're panting, your tits practically popping out of your shirt, you can't wait either."

"Are you serious about tonight?" I lowered my voice. It trembled slightly.

Something flickered in his eyes.

"I could soothe you and pet you and tell you of course not, that you can have sex when you're ready to, that I'll be gentle and go at your speed," he said in a mocking tone, "but I'm doing you a favor. Besides"—he dipped his head down to press a kiss to my neck—"once I have you on your knees, legs spread, pussy dripping, all your little insecurities are going to fly away along with your clothes. You'll be begging for my cock. Don't worry about it, Sugarplum. Just let me take control."

"You are such a piece of shit," I whispered to him.

"That's why you're sexually attracted to me," he said against my mouth.

Hudson grabbed my ass, pressing me against the bulge in his pants.

"Disrespectful, narcissistic," I said.

"Look at those multisyllabic words. Someone went to private school," he said.

"Rude." My hands splayed over his chest.

"Sheltered," he retorted, his hands sliding up to my waist.

"Uncultured."

"Spoiled." A smile played around his mouth.

"Aggressive."

He grabbed the back of my neck and kissed me.

"Damn right."

A wheezing bark sounded in the large wood-paneled room.

"Pugnog!" I untangled myself from Hudson as the dog trotted in, wagging his stubby tail at me.

The pug rushed to Hudson, who bent down so the little brown-and-black dog could snuggle in his arms.

"I checked all his wine labels online, and this one is the most expensive one, so let's drink up," Dakota called. "Or were you about to …" My cousin waggled her eyebrows.

"Ew, no," I said as Hudson smirked at her meaning.

He held out a fist, and Dakota fist-bumped him.

"Nice."

"I heard she told you about her condition," Dakota said as she opened the bottle of wine.

"A terrible affliction for a young woman from a lovely family to suffer from," he said solemnly.

"Now who's using SAT words," I clapped back at him.

His eyes narrowed slightly.

Dakota handed him a Santa Claus mug.

"It seems especially disrespectful to drink James's $800 bottle of wine out of Target Santa cups," she said cheerfully.

"He doesn't get a drink," I said, grabbing the mug from Hudson. "He's here to decorate."

"It is nice to have a big, strong man to help you, isn't it?" Granny Murray said gleefully a few hours later.

The house looked beautiful all dressed up for Christmas. I sighed wistfully.

Hudson came up from the basement, where I told him to store the empty boxes.

"Looks nice," he concurred.

"Yeah," I said, feeling sad. "That's why I told James to buy this house. I knew it would look amazing for Christmas. Anyway."

I shook off the sadness. After all, I was getting my revenge, right? I couldn't be sad. I picked up the bag Granny Murray had brought me. I needed to change for the party.

"Take me to this wine cellar," Granny Murray told Dakota.

"James is going to be so angry when he realizes we drank all his wine," I said.

"He's going to be even angrier," Hudson said conversationally as he followed me upstairs, "when he finds out I fucked you on his bed."

"You what? But it's not tonight," I babbled. "I thought you meant tonight like after the party."

"Shock and awe," he told me.

"It seems a little bit wrong to do it on James and Kelly's marriage bed," I whispered as he pushed me down the hall into the master suite.

"Not as perverted as doing your fiancée's sister under the Christmas tree on Christmas Eve with Santa's milk and cookies three feet away," he replied, reaching for my clothes.

Large hands pushed under my skirt.

"Thank god you're not wearing those fucking tights."

"Seemed like a recipe for disaster after the waxing," I said nervously as the skirt pooled around my feet on the floor. "I didn't wear nice underwear. I thought this was happening tonight."

Hudson snapped the waistband of the full-coverage black cotton underwear.

"These make your ass look great."

"So, like, how does this go?" I squawked as he unbuttoned my shirt, kissing the skin as he revealed it. "I might need to read a Wikipedia article first."

Hudson mouthed my tits through the bra then unhooked it, letting my breasts swing free. He pulled off his shirt over his head and flung it on James's bed.

My mouth watered at the sight of his chest.

Fuck, Hudson was ripped.

I clutched my shirt to my chest, suddenly feeling very self-conscious next to this perfect man who clearly spent hours working out and didn't stress eat cookies. Shoot. I'd been with him all day, every day practically the last week, and I'd never seen him eat anything as sweet as a piece of fruit. It was all protein and vegetables.

"Get your head in the game," Hudson hissed. "I know you're not thinking about getting fucked."

"I'm just thinking about cooking," I admitted.

"Focus, Sugarplum."

"It's just a lot for me," I gasped.

His fingers were between my legs, and he was kissing me, and it was hard to form coherent thoughts.

"I just want to say something."

"If it's not something along the lines of, 'I want your hot cum in my pussy,'" he warned, "I don't want to hear it."

"I just ..." I stammered, still holding my shirt to my body, "this wasn't part of the deal. Sex wasn't part of our arrangement. This is wrong."

He scowled.

"You shouldn't have to have sex with someone you don't like," I said in a rush.

"You don't like me," he enunciated.

"No. I mean, you're a selfish jerk, but like, you're obviously really hot, and I do intellectually see the appeal now of why women set fire to their whole lives just to bang a bad boy. I meant more for you," I said hastily. "I'm taking advantage of you. You don't even like me. You don't think I'm pretty," I said helplessly. "I'm taking advantage of you."

His mouth was slightly parted.

"I told you, Sugarplum. This is war. We need to make it seem like you really are in love with the bad boy. Don't worry about me. You have the nicest tits I've ever seen, a tight little pussy, and a mouth I get hard thinking about coming in. After I help you get over your hang-ups about sex, I'm going to make sure you take full advantage of me."

He winked.

It was hot.

Maybe he was slightly attracted to me. My hopes rose.

"Sit in that chair," he ordered.

"It's right in front of the door," I protested.

"Good. You can be the lookout."

Gingerly, I sat on the edge of the white stuffed chair.

"Not like that. Sit back. Spread your legs. Wider. Let me see your pussy. Now touch your tits."

"I can't do this," I gasped.

His eyes were glazed dark; he stalked over to me.

He put one hand on either side of my head on the back of the chair, leaned in, and kissed me, jostling me. My head bounced back as he took my mouth.

"I need you to commit to this fake relationship, Sugarplum."

His large hands grabbed my thighs. His fingers dug into my legs as he spread them wider.

"Fuck yeah, that's what I wanted to see," he whispered. "You're dripping wet for me."

He spread my pussy; I felt the wetness dripping down onto the white chair cushion.

"Are you going to fuck me?" I stammered as he spread me even wider using his finger.

"No, Sugarplum, I'm going to eat you out 'til you scream."

Then he went down on me.

His mouth felt a thousand times better than his fingers. My head lolled back as he licked me, his tongue dipping in my opening, sweeping up my pussy to lap at my clit.

I bit my lip, stifling the groan.

Hudson paused. One large hand grasped my neck.

"No, I want to hear you. Let me hear how good it feels. Lose control."

I moaned as he leaned his head in to nuzzle my breast, sucking on one nipple, then the other.

"Louder," he ordered, raising his head.

I let out a loud cry of pleasure as his mouth made contact with my clit.

"*Fuuuck*, Hudson," I cursed, tangling my fingers in his hair.

His tongue worked my slit; two of his fingers slipped in my opening, stroking me.

"I want your cock," I begged. "I want you to fuck me with that huge cock, Hudson."

He added another finger as his tongue gave me those long, slow licks.

Downstairs, guests were starting to arrive.

In this old house, for sure, someone was hearing me having my pussy eaten.

"Fuck, Hudson," I moaned, eyes closed, legs spread, my head tipped back as I raked my nails over his tattooed back.

His tongue was going faster now, the pleasure intense as he finger fucked me while he lapped at my pussy, swirling his tongue around my clit.

"Make me come, Hudson," I begged, my voice echoing around the large room. "I need you to make me—"

I came with a loud cry as his tongue milked the orgasm.

Hudson pulled back and regarded me sprawled there in a heap on the chair.

"That was—"

"Just an appetizer," he stated.

"I don't know if I'm ready for the full meal yet."

"I told you," he growled. "I'm taking your virginity tonight."

He unbuckled his pants.

I stared wide-eyed.

"Where is your underwear?"

"I came prepared."

He was better than the photo. My mouth watered as he stroked his huge cock.

"Get on your hands and knees on the bed," he demanded. "Now that I have you good and wet, everyone in the party is going to know that you like getting fucked by your bad-boy boyfriend."

"Yeah?" I squeaked, lightheaded from the orgasm and the huge cock.

This was about to happen.

I leaned forward to touch it, running the nail of my thumb along the length.

That was going to be inside of me.

"I'm going to put my huge cock in your pussy," he growled. "Make you feel what it's like to have a real man claim you. Now be a good girl, and spread your legs for me."

The postorgasm clarity was closing in. I wasn't sure if I could go through with it.

"It is a very nice cock," I began.

"Gracie? Gracie!" my mom called. "Are you up there?"

"Crap." I struggled out from under him. "Sorry. Holiday duties call."

He grabbed my wrist briefly before letting me go.

"You can't keep running from me forever."

Chapter 31

HUDSON

Gracie had changed into her party outfit, another one of those tight cocktail dresses that made her look like she was wrapped up like a Christmas present. I tugged at the bow on the back of the cocktail dress that rested right above her ass.

Across the room, James was giving me a dirty look.

I locked eye contact with him, draped an arm around Gracie's shoulder, then stuck my hand down the bodice of her dress, squeezing her breast.

I smirked at James.

Though I was projecting confidence, a part of me was relieved that Gracie had chickened out.

Did I want to fuck her?

Yes.

Did I want to watch her come around a cock for the first time in her life?

Fuck yeah.

However, just because I was getting reeled into Gracie's life didn't mean I could forget what my real purpose was. It was one big nested lie.

Hudson: *Any movement on the data.*
Talbot: *It just now finished copying hundreds of gigabytes worth of data.*
Anderson: *We should get something good on here.*
Hudson: *I need people working all night on it.*
Talbot: *It's going to be at least twenty-four hours before all the data is analyzed.*
Hudson: *I'll come by after the party to help sift through the data.*

Soon I would have what I needed, and I would do it without actually crossing that line, without actually sleeping with Gracie.

Really? Having your tongue on her clit, her naked and sweaty and moaning around you while you finger fuck her wasn't a line?

Yes, it was a line but not *the* line. I still hadn't crossed the point of no return.

"The house looks amazing!" Gracie's coworkers—I recognized them from the file my team had put together—congratulated Kelly, who basked in the praise.

Beside me, Gracie angrily sipped her wine.

"Stop letting Kelly get the credit," I hissed at her. "Say something."

Gracie made an unhappy noise.

"It's no use. They'll just act like I'm the one being rude and ungracious," she said, tipping back the wineglass.

"Besides," Gracie added wistfully, "this is the only chance I'll get to decorate my own historic Victorian home for Christmas. It's as close to living my dream as I'll ever get."

Suddenly, all I wanted to do in the world was buy Gracie that Victorian house and help her decorate it, just to see her happy.

Kelly and James were walking around like they were politicians or royalty while the employees of EnerCheck Inc. fawned over them.

I suddenly couldn't stand it.

Spoiled lazy country-club kids.

"I'm going to get you another drink." I kissed Gracie softly on the mouth.

Now that my real mission was close to being done, I was going to fucking finish this other one.

"I just love the garland on the chandelier," gushed one middle-aged woman in the group of James's relatives gaggled around Kelly.

Gracie's sister preened.

"I only do real garland," she said. "That fake plastic stuff just doesn't have that traditional feel, does it?"

"You must have had a crane to get it up there," the woman joked.

"No, she had me," I said, inserting myself into the conversation.

James scowled at me.

Kelly's eyes widened.

"Kelly's a little too short to reach," I told the woman. "I mean look at her." I picked up Kelly, lifting her over my head while she shrieked.

Across the room, Gracie was watching. She looked almost sad.

She'll be happy once Kelly and James's relationship is a smoking crater, I told myself. *Stop feeling guilty.*

"Show off." Kelly, still cradled in my arms, swatted me playfully on the shoulder.

"I was going to tell her to sit on my shoulders," I said to the crowd, "but she got wise to what I was doing when I tried to have her sit facing me."

"Oh, my word." James's cousins gasped from behind their hands.

"You are so bad, Hudson," Kelly said with a nasally laugh and shook me by the chin. "He's from the Gulch," she told the crowd.

"Put her down," James snapped at me.

I set Kelly on her sparkly red stilettos.

"You better be careful, James," his aunt joked. "He looks like the type of man who will steal your girlfriend away on the back of his motorcycle."

"Probably more like fuck your girlfriend on the back of his motorcycle, right?" Kelly said, trailing her fingers along the collar of my leather jacket.

I gave her my best sexy and dangerous smile.

She lapped it up.

"I'm being a bad hostess, Hudson. You need a drink." She grabbed my hand and led me over to the wet bar. "Do you want Sex in Santa's Workshop or a Naughty Girl martini?"

"Can I just have straight sex without all the sugar?"

Her eyes widened.

"I meant a scotch," I said after a beat.

"Coming right up." Kelly made a big show of arching her back as she reached for the bottle.

She handed me the glass of scotch.

Across the room, Gracie and Dakota were sharing a plate of snacks while pretending not to watch Kelly and me.

"Poor little Gracie. Is she still being a boring old wallflower?" Kelly asked while one of James's family members asked him loudly about the history of the house.

"You have no fucking idea," I said, making a big show about knocking back the glass of scotch. "At first, her innocent little-girl act was a huge turn-on. I liked pushing her boundaries, making her let me do shit to her that she wasn't all that enthusiastic about. But now it's just a buzzkill."

Kelly poured me more scotch.

"I really just need the type of girl who will let me come in her ass under the Christmas tree without a lot of back talk."

I let my gaze slide down Kelly's chest.

"That's not really Gracie's style," Kelly said, putting her hand on her hip. "She's pretty boring and vanilla. It's weird that we're even sisters. We're the exact opposite."

Trap baited.

"Gracie isn't completely boring," I said, lowering my voice and draping my arm over her shoulders conspiratorially. "I did convince her to let me eat her out on that white chair in your master bedroom."

"It's not really my bedroom," Kelly said.

I could make out the outline of her nipples under the thin fabric of the cocktail dress. It was one of those ones with lots of cutouts that a woman couldn't wear undergarments under.

"Huh," I said. "That's too bad, because the whole time I kept wishing it was you gushing all over that white chair."

Trap set.

"I'm engaged, Hudson," Kelly purred.

"I don't mind fucking engaged women. It gets me pretty fucking hard knowing that I'm stealing some idiot's fiancée away from him because he didn't fucking know how to take care of her, give her what she needs."

Kelly's eyes lit up.

"You really are a bad boy."

Trap sprung.

Chapter 32

GRACIE

"That asshole." I paced around Dakota's room. "Did you see him with Kelly?"

"Isn't that what you wanted him to do? Flirt with her?"

"That wasn't just flirting," I declared, hoisting up my bottle of wine. "They were practically fucking right there in the living room."

I took a swig from the bottle. It was another of the expensive ones Dakota had pilfered from James's wine cellar. I needed alcohol after watching Hudson with Kelly, him all over her, whispering to her. I knew he was talking shit about me. That triumphant smirk on my sister's face confirmed it.

Before I could burst into tears in front of everyone at the party, Dakota had grabbed me and loaded up a box of food and stolen wine. Now here we were.

I'd run away like a child, again.

"Hudson is mad that I didn't sleep with him," I said dejectedly. "Now he's letting Kelly stroke his ego, among other things."

"If he's that kind of guy," Dakota said, "so what if he doesn't like you?"

"Part of me, the inner romantic who believed that every girl would find her Prince Charming, the part who crushes hard on unavailable guys, she secretly thought Hudson might be falling for her," I admitted. "I guess I thought he was maybe warming up to me, that maybe he did like me. Hudson saved me in a bar fight, he baked cookies with me, he helped me decorate, he chopped all that wood, and he went shopping with me."

Dakota sighed and poured herself more wine.

"Here's the deal, Gracie. You know I love you, and that I'm your biggest fan and supporter."

"You don't have to say it," I said miserably. "I know he's out of my league."

"Hell no! You're out of his!" My cousin slammed her mug of wine on the nightstand.

"You practically run EnerCheck, you can cook for a hundred people like it's nothing, you can bake, decorate, plan a major wedding, and you volunteer. Hudson is a dumpster fire compared to you. He's sex obsessed, doesn't have a career, has a bad attitude, lies, and thinks sleeping with Kelly is a fantastic way to blow off steam. He and Kelly are made for each other—bad boy and bad girl."

"He's not all bad," I said weakly. "There's a good man in there. I just know it."

"It's a myth," Dakota said flatly. "That's how bad boys lure nice girls in so they can use them for free food and a place to stay. You heard Gran. Hudson is a hobosexual.

Good girls don't tame bad boys. Bad boys just drag good girls down to their level, use them, then leave them and move on to the next mark."

"I could change him."

"Your skills at rationalizing your own delusions are legendary."

"I'm just supposed to watch Kelly steal another of my boyfriends?" I cried.

"*Fake boyfriend.* Let's take, like, three steps back." Dakota made a rolling motion with her hands. "Hudson's here to break up her marriage."

"I think he's falling for her for real," I said miserably. "Kelly has that effect on men."

"So what? Even if he does fall for her, it's not going to last."

"Everyone is going to talk about it," I wailed. "I'll be planning her wedding again this time next year."

"Let's be honest: a man like Hudson does not marry. At worst, he'll get her preggo," Dakota said confidently.

"Oh my god. He's going to get her pregnant." I collapsed on Dakota's bed.

"Maybe. But he won't stick around, and neither will she. Their baby will be super cute though."

"Why is my life such a disaster?" I moaned. "Why can't men like me?"

"There are lots of nice guys out there." Dakota patted me on the back. "We're going to kick your love life into gear next year. New Year's resolution."

"I already have a lot of resolutions pending that I have no hope of keeping," I admitted.

I ate a cheese straw.

"I just wanted him to want me—not fall in love with me. I'm not that delusional. I know I wouldn't want to be married to him for the rest of my life."

"If that's really all you want, you have to play the game," Dakota lectured as she poured us more wine. "Have sex in a public place. Show him you can be as sexy and exciting as Kelly."

"I'll get arrested."

Dakota looked at me and slurped her wine. "Hopefully, you can convince Kelly not to name that poor baby something dumb like Aspyn with a Y."

"Kill me," I groaned.

I am a nervous baker. When I'm anxious or stressed, which recently has been all the freaking time, I bake elaborate desserts. Today, though, I couldn't make a pavlova. I was baking miniature yule logs for Kelly's wedding.

With the frosting and the jelly, they would keep a bit better than some of the cookies I was going to make for the wedding. Therefore they were first on the dessert schedule.

The plan Dakota and I had come up with last night to make me more appealing than Kelly had seemed like a fantastic idea after drinking two bottles of very expensive wine.

Now in the cold, sober, and slightly hungover light of day, it seemed like a terrible decision.

My parents' house was unusually quiet. The men were at an afternoon hockey game for the local minor league team. My mom, sister, and cousins were off for final fittings for the bridesmaids' dresses and Kelly's wedding dress.

I jumped when the back door opened. Pugnog sniffed in his sleep but just rolled over.

"Some guard dog," I told Pugnog as Hudson stamped his boots on the mat outside then stepped into the warm kitchen.

He narrowed his eyes when he saw me.

"You need to keep this back door locked."

"Why, because dangerous men could sneak inside and have their way with me?"

"Exactly." The scowl deepened. "That walking, drooling creampuff is not any protection."

"I don't know. Sometimes his eye pops out of his head. That is quite the deterrent," I quipped, using a pair of tweezers to place a sugar mushroom on the miniature Yule log.

"What the fuck?"

If Hudson were really my boyfriend, he would have swept me in his arms and kissed me. Instead, he shrugged off his jacket, still keeping the kitchen island between us.

I wiped my hands on my apron.

The rational part of me reminded myself that Hudson was not going to go for my plan, that there was no audience, and had we already forgotten how humiliating it was the last time he rejected me when I tried to kiss him? And what I was proposing was way more than a kiss.

"What are you baking?" Hudson asked.

"Just more desserts," I said, straightening up and untying my apron.

"I'll let you get back to it then," he said after a moment. *Now or never.*

"I want you to come on my tits."

His eyebrows shot up, and his jaw dropped.

It was almost cartoonish.

"Gracie," he said warily.

"Fair's fair," I said, trying to sound calm and in control and not like someone who twenty-four hours ago was still scared of losing her virginity even though she was almost thirty. "Yes, I know the rules are there needs to be an audience, but you seem to think that having people overhear or walk in on us having sex is good for the mission. People will be back soon because you can't ever get any alone time in the house."

Hudson rubbed the back of his neck.

"I actually—"

I started unbuttoning my shirt.

"Now that he's the one who has to come for an audience, the bad boy is suddenly shy. Guess he can dish it but not take it."

He crossed the kitchen in three long steps and crushed our mouths together and kissed me hot and heavy. He pulled his T-shirt over his head as he kissed me. The table where I had the miniature Yule logs rattled.

I dragged his head back by his hair.

"I have been up since 4 a.m. working on these. They will not be ruined. In the living room."

Hudson picked me up, wrapping my legs around his waist as he carried me like I weighed nothing into the living room, where the Christmas tree sparkled and stockings were hung on the fireplace.

"You really want to suck my cock, huh, you little slut?" he growled and nipped my mouth.

"Yeah," I breathed, undoing his belt. "And I want your cum all over my face and tits."

He tore at my shirt. The fabric fluttered to the ground, followed by my bra.

His tongue tangled with mine. His hands were all over my tits, squeezing, pinching the nipple. His hands moved down to slide under my skirt. Stroking me through the fabric of my panties, nice ones this time.

"Gracie, I could fuck you like this," he groaned, as I palmed his hard cock through his pants.

"You're really playing with fire here with no boxers and that zipper," I said to him, tugging his hard cock out of his pants.

"You should try it," he said in a strangled tone, "then I could play in your pussy under the table and bend you over and fuck you at the kitchen sink without having to fuck with those tights you always wear. *Fuck*, I want to fuck your tight little cunt right now."

I slapped his chest. "I'm driving."

"The fuck you are. You already ran over one inflatable Santa," Hudson growled.

I bit his chin.

"You really want to suck my cock, Sugarplum?"

I was satisfied to hear how ragged his breathing was. "Give me your hot cum."

Hudson grabbed my ponytail and forced me down on my knees in front of him.

"That's right, Sugarplum, take it," he snarled as he buried his thick cock in my mouth. "I can't wait 'til I'm buried in your hot pussy."

His hips jerked in my mouth. His fingers tangled in my hair, rubbing little circles on my scalp, guiding my head while I sucked his cock. It was really fucking hot.

"Shit." He hissed out a curse as I flicked my tongue against the head of his cock.

Thrilled, I thought, "I'm doing this to him. Take that, Kelly!"

I hummed and sucked around his cock, flitting my tongue against the slit then taking his cock deep in my throat.

"Touch yourself, Sugarplum," he ordered.

I let my hands roam on my breasts, squeezing and playing with them. Then I pulled my head back, felt it strain against his fingers, and he released me.

"Can't take it?" he asked, eyes dark, voice ragged with pleasure.

"Sit on the couch," I ordered him. "I told you I want you to come on my face."

"Yeah?" Hudson sat back on the couch.

I raked my nails down his chest, along the tattoos.

His hand moved to my hair. I grabbed his wrist.

"Nuh-uh. I told you I'm driving. Buckle up, asshole."

He hesitated then put his hands behind his head.

"You're better than the photo, bad boy."

I tugged at his cock, running my hand on it, feeling how thick it was. I bobbed my head down over his thick cock, then back up, letting him feel a little teeth. That's what the lady on TikTok who gave blow job advice said to do anyways.

"You ready for me to make you come?" I crooned, slipping off my panties. I straddled him.

His eyes were dilated as he looked up at me.

I am a sex goddess!

I lifted up my skirt, making sure he could see what I was doing as I used the wetness of my pussy to lube up his cock.

Hudson cursed as I ran the length of his cock along my dripping wet slit, then shimmied back down to my knees on the floor. His glistening cock jutted up in front of me. I took my tits and squeezed them around his cock.

His hips thrust up, fucking my tits.

"Come on me," I moaned. "I want your cum on my tits, and then I want you to come in my pussy. Can you do that, bad boy? Can you fuck my tight little pussy?"

"Fuck, Gracie." His hands were digging into the couch, still obeying my no-touching rule.

I squeezed my tits tighter around his cock, half-gone myself.

"Oh my god," I said, breathless as he fucked my tits. "You're making me so wet right now."

"Gracie, what the fuck is wrong with you?" Kelly exploded. "How dare you?"

"Shit," Hudson swore as he came all over my face and tits.

My sister picked up a fistful of Christmas chocolates out of a nearby candy dish and threw them at me. I winced as they bounced off my face and Hudson's bare chest.

"Put a shirt on," Kelly screamed.

I crossed my arms.

My sister's eyes were flitting from Hudson, to Hudson's cock, to his washboard abs, then back to me.

"You … you slut," she screamed.

"Stop acting like you don't wish it was you sucking his cock," I said as I threw a cushion featuring a smiling Rudolph on Hudson's lap.

"He's way bigger than James. I can barely fit it all in my mouth. It's so sad that you're giving all this up," I continued, gesturing to Hudson. "No more hot guys with big dicks who are good in bed. You'll forever be a despised wife, stuck with a husband with no ass, who doesn't help take care of the kids, while you waste the best years of your life and have to hump a washing machine just to come."

The words hung in the air while Kelly gaped at me.

"Damn," Hudson finally said, eyebrows raised.

Kelly pulled out her phone.

"You're going to pay for this. *Mom*," Kelly screamed into the phone. "No, it is an emergency. I need you to come home right now. It's Gracie. She is out of control." My sister sounded shrill, unhinged, angry, like she had just walked in on me fucking her boyfriend. She stomped outside.

"Where the hell did that come from?" Hudson asked me. He looked a little bit dazed.

Tossing the pillow away, I pushed him back down on the couch and kissed him. I grabbed his hand and guided it between my legs.

"Make me come."

I kissed his mouth and grabbed his jaw, pulling back to stare at that handsome face.

"Now who's the slut?"

I kissed him again then pushed his head to my breast.

He sucked my nipples as he stroked me, my hips rocking against his hand. Soon I was coming, his name on my lips, the waves of pleasure making me shudder on his hand.

"Damn," I breathed against his mouth. "You"—I kissed him noisily—"are a good fuck."

He traced a snowman in the cum on my chest.

"See?" I said to him, sliding off his lap. "I told you someone was going to show up. Just our luck it was Kelly."

Hudson zipped up his pants.

"It wasn't chance. I told her to meet me here so we could fuck."

What the hell?

Chapter 33

HUDSON

"I don't understand."

"The plan, Sugarplum," I reminded her, "to break up a wedding that's only a few days away? I figured it would make it more enticing to Kelly if she thought she and I were sneaking around behind your back."

"Right," Gracie said faintly.

"But this is fine too. You give a pretty good blow job for a virgin."

I kissed her.

"I have to get back to work. I only had so much time allotted for a quick fuck."

"You shouldn't have wasted your time coming back here," Talbot said. "We didn't find anything in the last few gigabytes of data."

318 • Alina Jacobs

"Fuck," I swore. I rubbed a hand over the back of my neck.

"Then it's on her laptop. What we need is on her laptop. And that means I am fucked."

I let out a breath.

My phone beeped, not the one with the number I'd given Gracie, the other one I used to communicate with Kelly.

My grand plan had been to wrap up the EnerCheck Inc. account, blow up James's wedding, and end the year on a high note.

Fuck me, right?

Kelly: *I cannot believe her.*
Kelly: *Does she know???*
Kelly: *About us???*
Hudson: *She ambushed me.*
Hudson: *Don't worry, you can suck my cock next time.*

"Damn." Jake read over my shoulder. "Both sisters, huh, man?"

Sleeping with Kelly *had* been the plan. The plan had been operating under the assumption my team was going to find the evidence I needed on the data from the desktop. I wouldn't have needed to take Gracie's virginity. Instead, I would have to sleep with Kelly and manufacture enough incriminating evidence to blow up her marriage.

Now?

With the way Gracie was acting today—territorial, like she actually was starting to believe I was her boyfriend—there was no way I could actually sleep with her sister.

Gracie would be heartbroken.

She cared about imaginary things too much—she named all her toys, she had that dollhouse. She couldn't *not* get emotionally attached to something, even a fake boyfriend.

If I slept with Gracie's sister before I got the data I needed, I was fucked.

New plan.

Somehow figure out a way to keep Gracie distracted enough that she lets me have unsecured access to her laptop.

Chapter 34

GRACIE

I huffed and puffed as I lugged the carts packed full of groceries for tomorrow's big lunch behind me.

I wished Hudson was there. Sure, he was hot and his cock was amazing, but he also had exclusive use of a pickup truck and was strong enough to easily carry multiple frozen turkeys inside.

I paused before the front porch. There were five icy steps up.

"Come on, you can do it."

I didn't want to ferry the food in multiple trips.

"These carts have wheels," I grunted as I dragged them up the steps. "Crap!"

I stumbled, and Pugnog yelped as I fell hard on the steps, the overstuffed grocery sacks tumbling open and spilling food everywhere.

"My life sucks," I said to the snowy sky. My Very Merry Berry latte had exploded all over the steps.

"Fucking great." I sighed.

I unstrapped the baby carrier and set it and Pugnog on the top step.

I'd gotten a lot of weird looks in the grocery store, but I couldn't put him in a purse because I needed my hands free to lug the carts, and besides, he liked having a nice view.

"Pugnog, no," I scolded him as he headed for the spilled drink.

I didn't hear my family inside or see anyone in the windows. Maybe they were at the park with the younger children?

I unloaded a fifteen-pound turkey, steadying it in my arm, and slowly made my way up the steps.

At the front door, I fumbled with my keys, Pugnog winding around my feet.

"Are you trying to make me and poor Mr. Turkey trip?" I asked to the dog as I pushed the door open.

I headed through the house to the kitchen. "You're going straight to the defrosting, Mr. Turkey. Yes, you are. Who's a big boy, such a big, beautiful turkey b—"

I strangled a scream as I walked into the living room.

A number of my family members, including my ex-fiancé, my parents, several aunts and uncles, and my sister were sitting there in silence, the chairs loosely assembled in a circle.

Pugnog flopped on the floor and wheezed.

"Sit down, Gracie," my father said solemnly.

I sat in the only empty chair. Not knowing what to do with the turkey, I set it on my lap.

"What happened?" I said in concern. "Is it Granny Murray?"

Granny Astelle thumped her cane on the floor. "If only the lord would be so gracious."

"Grace," a woman, who I didn't recognize, said in a kindly voice. "Your family has come to me to voice some concerns about your recent change in behavior. Please know that these concerns come from a place of love. They have letters prepared and would like to read them aloud to you. No one is judging you."

"But the foo—"

"Grace, please give space for your family's feelings."

I clamped my mouth shut.

"Thank you, Dr. Bergen. I'll go first." James stood up. "Gracie, when I first met you, you were a sweet girl, who loved cooking, family, and decorating. In the last few days, I've seen a woman I care very much about spiraling out of control. Your sex addiction—"

"*My what?*"

"Grace, this is a safe space," the therapist said serenely.

"Your sex addiction is ruining the holidays and my wedding," James said. "There have now been three separate occasions where you have clearly orchestrated a situation in order to get caught having sex. There was the pantry incident, the living room couch incident, and, of course, the time in my own bedroom."

My father shifted uncomfortably in his seat.

Papers rustled.

"Gracie, I love you, and I don't want this addiction to ruin your life. I understand that this is not you. It's not who you are. You fell in with the wrong crowd. We're all here today to ask you to see reason and remove Hudson from your life."

"Is this an intervention?" I hissed.

"Gracie," the therapist said, putting her hand on my shoulder, "your family is concerned by your behavior. There's nothing wrong with sex, but when you let it control your life in a negative manner, it's time to review your behavior. There are programs that can help."

"Programs?"

"Please." My mother dabbed her eyes and held up her letter. "Gracie, just listen." She took a shuddering breath. "When you were born, I held you in my arms, my sweet little baby girl …"

I sat there, the frozen turkey slowly defrosting on my lap, and listened to my mother as she cried and sobbed her way through the letter.

"You loved to play with dolls. She still has all her toys," she said to the therapist. My dad slowly rubbed circles on my mom's back.

"She's not a teenager; this isn't some rebellion. Gracie was a perfectly nice girl until she met that Hudson. Now it's not just the sex," my mother lowered her voice on the S-word, "but she's become mean, argumentative. She shows up late to decorate for the company Christmas party and her sister's wedding."

I sat there and fumed.

"Yes, late to do all the free work that you promised I would do," I snapped at my mother.

"Gracie," the therapist said in a soothing voice, "you will have your time to speak."

My mother cleared her throat.

"I wish to have," she read off, "my sweet baby girl back, the one who put others first and always had a smile on. Sometimes I see her in my—"

My mother started screaming. I whirled around, the frozen turkey almost falling off my lap, and gasped as Hudson walked into the room, silent as death, wearing a thick-plated vest over his shirt and carrying the biggest gun I'd ever seen.

James swore, and Astelle started praying.

Hudson wasn't the self-absorbed bad-boy or even the slightly annoyed aloof male who was pretending to be my fake boyfriend. This was something else, something dangerous.

He trained the rifle on my family.

My father's hands flew up.

"You see?" Granny Astelle said to the therapist. "She brought this animal into our family. Now he's here to murder us. Call the police."

Hudson lowered the huge gun. It wasn't a hunting rifle; this was a war rifle.

"They've already been called. There was food all over the sidewalk," Hudson said in a clipped tone. "What appeared to be blood all over the floor and cracks in the paint like someone had been thrown onto the ground. The door was ajar. I assumed the worst."

"It's okay, Hudson," I said quietly. "I'm fine. Just overzealous with how much I could carry."

His eyes swept over me, cataloguing me, seeing that I still had a venti latte's worth of blood in my body.

"You can't barge in here. We're having a family meeting," James blustered. He was sweating.

"I don't care." Hudson's voice was as cold as the gray of his eyes. "Gracie, get up."

"I ... um—" My hand fluttered. "They're reading letters."

"To fucking Santa?"

"Er ... no ..."

"Then let's go. Get your dog and your turkey and move."

"It's because he took her virginity that she's acting like this," James yelled. "That's right," he said to my family. "Gracie was a virgin until she fell in with him. She's inexperienced, and he's taking advantage of her naivety."

I felt like I was going to vomit as my family members gasped in surprise.

Hudson turned his cold gaze on James. My ex shrank like a micropenis in the cold morning air.

"I took it because you weren't man enough to do it. Guess that makes her mine now."

"Gracie, you were still a virgin?" my cousin asked, confused. "That's really weird. You're like ... *old*."

"Why is she even in this meeting?" I asked the therapist shrilly.

The gray-haired woman was frowning.

"This was supposed to be a cross section of people in your life who cared about you and were hurt by your behavior."

"What behavior?" I shrieked. "I always do everything they ask me to. I didn't even have a real relationship until I was in my twenties because I thought that was what was going to make my parents happy, make them proud of me."

Hudson stood next to me, a silent sentinel.

"You said that's what good girls did, that they were quiet and obedient and didn't have sex," I said accusingly to my parents.

Kelly scoffed.

"No wonder James was all over me. You weren't putting out."

"Because that's what Mom and Dad said!" I cried. "You always told me that I shouldn't be having sex, that it was going to ruin my life."

"Well …" My dad was embarrassed as the therapist gave him a scathing look. "We just meant in high school, not, well—not forever."

"Do you feel ashamed now, Gracie?" the therapist asked kindly.

"Why?" I yelled, clutching my frozen turkey. "Because I slept with my hot boyfriend? Fuck you. No, I don't."

"I bet she had the best sex of any virgin in the history of forever." Aunt Stacy winked at me. "I would have waited, too, if that meant I got to have him as my first. For the record," my aunt added, "I thought this whole thing was bullshit, but someone has to relay the gossip to everyone else." She shrugged. "You know how it is."

"My apologies, Gracie," the therapist said, standing up and closing her notebook. "It looks like you're the one who should really be hosting an intervention for your parents. Let me give you my card."

She looked Hudson up and down. "I do couples sessions too. Might be a nice Christmas present."

"She always gives everyone knitted socks, scarfs, or other accessories," Hudson said in a monotone.

"You cannot seriously be leaving," my father demanded. "James, you said this woman was going to convince Gracie to get rid of Hudson."

"Get rid of Hudson?" Several of my male cousins and uncles bounded into the room.

"Man, this is creepy," one of them said, looking around.

Uncle Bic clapped Hudson on the back, seemingly ignoring the gun.

"He's on our hockey team for the big family match tomorrow. What the fuck do you mean you're trying to get rid of him, Rob? Fuck that."

"He's bad for Gracie," James insisted.

"James doesn't even go to this family." My cousin Bobby booed behind his hand.

"How do you know he knows how to play hockey?" James demanded.

My cousins were appalled.

"Hudson grew up in Maplewood Falls. Of course, he knows how to play hockey."

"Of course, I know how to play hockey." Hudson was offended.

"He also knows how to fight," Granny Murray crowed, bustling in behind them, holding up an armful of kale. "You're not seriously feeding this to everyone, are you, Gracie?"

"It's a good pregame meal," I said faintly. "Lots of vitamins and minerals."

"Hell yeah! We're going to win!" my cousins whooped.

I sat in the kitchen with Hudson while Granny Murray bossed several of the male family members to ferry in all the spilled groceries.

The gun and vest had disappeared, but Hudson still seemed on edge.

He had given me a cup of tea and an ice pack for my shoulder then made me tell him what food needed to be prepared for dinner. Now he was washing ten pounds of kale in the sink while my cousins hovered around him talking hockey strategy.

"He has brothers," Uncle Bic declared. "Where's Dakota? She needs to date one of them so he's eligible to play too."

"Yes, please!" Dakota said, popping out from behind the fridge door, where she was rearranging the food to make room for all the milk.

"They're busy," Hudson said.

"Too busy for hockey?" my uncle demanded.

Hudson smirked. "All they do is waste time playing hockey."

Chapter 35

GRACIE

"**A**re you sure you're all right?" Hudson asked me later that evening after dinner had been served, eaten, and leftovers put away.

"Totally. I'm clumsy. That is not the first time I fell on the steps."

"No. With your family."

I snorted "The intervention? Sure," I lied. "I'm fine. Turns out I was worried about everyone finding out I was a virgin for no reason. Joke's on me." I gave a half-hearted laugh. The whole thing was still making me queasy.

"Uh-huh."

There was that assessing look.

"I did not need you to come in guns blazing. I can take care of myself."

"I was worried about you," he said, resting his forehead to mine. "I thought … I thought something bad had happened to you."

"I live in a nice neighborhood," I joked. "The worst that happens here is someone sabotaging someone else's Christmas lights."

Hudson wrapped me in his arms and kissed me softly.

I felt a thump in my chest.

"But thanks," I said to him. "That was nice of you to put yourself in danger for me."

"Oh, yeah. Your grandmother is terrifying."

"Don't worry. Grandma Murray won't let Grandma Astelle stab you."

I felt him smile against my hair.

"I still want to see that mystical sword."

"You hang around my family long enough, you'll see the fight."

He pulled back from me.

"I guess we really better take your virginity now, huh," he said with a smirk.

Suddenly all the fear and inhibitions were gone. There wasn't anything I wanted more than Hudson at that moment.

I grabbed the collar of his shirt and kissed him hard. "I guess we'd better. Lying puts people on the naughty list."

"And you don't want to be a naughty girl."

He picked me up, easily carrying me up the stairs then down the hall to my bedroom.

I clawed at his shirt when he set me down.

"Fuck, Gracie," he hissed. "I want to give you every inch of my cock 'til you scream." He pulled off the shirt, revealing washboard abs, rippling muscles, and those tattoos.

Goddamn, he was perfect.

"Are you wet for me?" he asked between kisses. "You ready for me to take you?" His hands were under my shirt, cupping my breasts.

"Yes," I gasped as his hands caressed my curves, awakening the pleasure that had been banked from the last time we shared each other's bodies.

The back of my neck prickled.

I moaned as he kissed me, his tongue slipping in my mouth, but I couldn't quite surrender to him.

"I want you to come on my cock," he murmured as he unbuttoned my top.

"Ignore it," I whispered to myself.

"What?" Hudson asked, nipping my earlobe.

Around me, the beady black eyes of several dozen stuffed mice glared reproachfully.

"You want my cock, Gracie? You want my thick cock in your tight little cunt?"

"Er ... yeah ... I just ..." I pushed him off.

Hudson waited, body tense.

"Wait right there. Give me one moment."

Hudson watched in confusion then bemusement as I raced around the room, turning around all the stuffed animals so they didn't have to have their innocence sullied. Then I threw a sheet over the dollhouse so that the little Victorian mice could preserve their prudishness.

"I just felt like they shouldn't see," I said and gulped. "Um, you know."

"I can't imagine why no man wanted to fuck you here," Hudson said, bottom lip catching on his teeth. "Under the judgment from all your stuffed animals."

"Okay," I said. "I'm ready. I think." I clapped my hands.

I felt more awkward than I had a few minutes ago. Maybe I should have told him that we should go to his place. But that would break the rules. That this was a fake relationship, not the start of our great love story. Going to his place made it some sort of intimate special moment for two people falling in love, which I would never do. Not ever.

There was a dull clunk as Hudson's belt buckle hit the floor. Then his heavy boots came off.

"We are really doing this, huh?" I said, starting to panic as he reached for his zipper.

"Don't worry, Sugarplum," he purred. "I told you: you're going to be begging me for my cock before I fuck you for the first time. Now, make sure you scream real loud. You need to wake up the whole house."

"Right." I clutched my shirt closed.

Hudson stalked me slowly, circling me in the hexagonal room.

Tall, dark-haired, with those eyes, he was like a swimsuit model. No, wait. Better. Swimsuit models didn't have that rugged maleness. Hudson was all alpha male.

My stomach was flip-flopping. Sure, we'd gotten handsy in my mom's pantry, and I'd sucked his cock in the living room, and of course, there was that time he had his tongue in my hoo-ha, but I had been so wrapped up in him that I didn't have time to think.

Now?

Hudson came closer, closer. In the soft glow of the lamp, his muscles rippled. With the tattoos, the dark hair that was cropped low on the back of his neck and fell rakishly over his forehead, black jeans undone, riding low on his hips, he was every inch the bad boy.

"Let me see those tits, Sugarplum." That deep voice sent shivers down my body.

I slowly inched the unbuttoned blouse off and let it fall to the floor.

I'd always imagined my first time as it being pitch-black, everyone under the covers, thirty seconds, then I'd get a snack and some wine, a check off my to-do list while I let the nameless, faceless guy sleep it off.

"We can turn off the lights," I squawked, unhooking my bra but still holding it together.

There was a lot of pressure here on me. I needed Hudson to release his inner Regency duke and have his way with me to consummate the marriage.

Instead he watched me, a big cat and its prey.

"Nah. I want to watch the juice run down your legs."

Wowza.

I let the bra fall.

"I want to see that pussy," he ordered.

I hesitated then reached for my skirt and pulled it down while he watched, eyes tracking the motion as the skirt joined my shirt on the floor.

"Now bend over that table." His voice was measured though I detected a tinge of tension in the baritone.

I knelt over the vanity, one knee balanced on the tiny fuzzy stool.

"Stick your ass out." He was closer to me. "Yeah, like that."

He was behind me now.

His large hands grabbed my ass, kneading it then spreading my thighs farther apart.

I whimpered as he buried his face between my legs and breathed, the air hot as he mouthed me through the soaking-wet panties.

"You taste divine."

"Not as good as your cum," I moaned.

His fingers hooked in the panties, and he slid them over my ass, down my thigh.

"Spread your legs."

I shimmied them apart.

"Further."

I was soaking wet.

"Reach behind," he said. "Now touch yourself."

I rubbed a circle in my swollen pussy, my hips rocking against my hand.

"Tell me what you want me to do," he said in that deep voice.

"I want." I swallowed.

"I want you to …" I said, grasping for some of the raunchier romance books my grandmother had gifted me on Kindle. I mean, yeah, sure, I read them—it would be rude not to read a book someone gave you, even if it did involve blue alien men with horns. "To tie my hands above my head. I want your tongue on my clit. I want you to eat me out until I beg for mercy, then I want you to spread my legs and fuck my pussy raw while I scream your name."

"Damn, Sugarplum."

Hudson leaned over to kiss me, the stubble on his chin rough against my cheek. He caressed my ass, his hand joining mine briefly.

"You're a kinky little slut for a virgin, aren't you? You want my cock that bad? You want me to fuck you raw?"

"Yeah," I breathed, rubbing myself harder thinking about him there.

"No. Don't touch your clit."

He pinched my nipple.

"And pat your head and jump in a circle," I joked.

He slapped my ass hard then squeezed it. He ran his tongue along my pussy, just on the edge of the slit, only teasing.

That got me really wet.

"I need you," I moaned, arching my back. "Fuck me with that thick cock."

"I'm not going to fuck you until you're dripping wet."

His voice was rough. He stepped behind me, his thick, hard cock pressed against my pussy.

I let out a loud moan. He tangled his fingers in my hair and pushed me forward, then ground slowly against me.

"Fuck me," I begged. "Fuck me, Hudson, please."

"I don't think you're wet enough."

He slid his cock against me again.

Gosh. That was going to be in me!

I craved it.

I ground back against him, needing his cock inside me.

I felt something drip down my thigh.

"Now she's good and wet."

Hudson turned me around, hoisted me up, and shoved me against the bookshelf.

Figurines and little feminine knickknacks I'd collected over my childhood rattled.

"You gonna give me that thick cock, bad boy?" I said against his mouth as he kissed me.

Hudson shoved me back against the bookcase again.

"You want to beg me for it?" he said, fingering me roughly.

My hips rolled as his cock rubbed against my clit.

He ground against me then hoisted me up higher. Three of the stuffed mice bounced off his back and to the floor as he ate me out, his tongue lapping me, dipping in my opening, sweeping up my swollen, hot pussy then teasing my clit.

I whimpered and moaned and begged for his cock, my arms wrapped around his head.

He only teased my clit briefly, his tongue staying down lower. He kept me like that, on the edge.

"Yeah, your pussy's nice and wet now." He gave me one more lick then tossed me on the bed.

I reclined back, one arm on a stuffed reindeer. The crocheted flowers on the pillows dug into my bare back as I watched him fish something out of his pants then come to me, muscular, tattoos everywhere, washboard abs leading to that magnificent cock jutting out.

My mouth watered, remembering how it had felt to have his hot cum all over my face and tits.

He ripped the silver packet with his teeth.

My hands came down to play with my tits.

"Hudson," I moaned. "Take me. I want you to fuck me. I'm so wet for you. I want your cock in me." One hand crept down between my legs, splayed on the flower comforter. I lifted one of my breasts up and licked the nipple.

Hudson made a strangled noise.

I did it again.

His cock throbbed.

"I'm just an innocent little virgin, and I've never had a man take me before. But I want to feel your hot cum inside me."

"Jesus fucking Christ," he swore. "Get up. No. I feel like I'm going to hell."

"It's the stuffed animals," I groaned, as he threw the flower comforter, the pillows, and the remaining stuffed animals on the floor.

Then he pushed me back on the bed.

I moaned loudly as he sucked on my tits.

His fingers were between my legs, stroking my aching slit.

"Beg me," he rasped.

"*Please*."

"Louder," he ordered.

"Please, Hudson, please," I begged as he licked me. "Please. I want your cock."

"I told you," he said, pulling back. "On your knees, begging me."

Legs shaking, I clambered off the bed and knelt in front of him.

I clasped my hands.

"Please," I said, sticking my lower lip out. "I'm begging you to fuck me, Hudson."

"Damn." His eyes were heavy lidded.

I leaned forward to run my tongue along the length of his cock, making him hiss.

"I want to fuck you so bad, Gracie."

He grabbed me up around the waist, shoving me back against the bed. He rubbed his cock in the wetness.

My hips made needy little circles. I arched back on the bed as his fingers stroked my pussy then spread it.

I widened my legs for him, urging him to take me.

He reached up and stuck two fingers in my mouth. I sucked on them as he pushed in me, slowly, just an inch.

My pussy flexed.

"Fuck, you're so tight, Gracie."

I moaned around his fingers. He withdrew them and went to my breasts, pinching them. He pushed in another inch. Now I could really feel how thick and hard his cock was. It was huge, filling me, stretching me.

He grabbed my legs, forcing them wider apart, centered himself, then slid in another few inches. I let out a loud cry, my pussy aching as I took him.

"Hudson," I panted.

"Tell me how much you like me in your pussy."

I moaned, "You're so big. Oh, you're so huge in my pussy." I didn't know what to do with my hands and ran them over his face, his chest.

His body vibrated.

He pushed in me another inch.

I cried out, my voice coming out in high-pitched gasps.

"You're so big. Oh god, that's so big, Hudson."

His jaw was tense with concentration as he pushed into me the rest of the way. Slowly.

I let out a loud moan of pleasure.

"Fuck. You took all of me, Gracie."

He leaned over to give me a hard kiss.

"Your pussy feels so tight."

He held us there, connected. Him in me, me clenched around him. Then he withdrew achingly slowly, as I panted and pleaded for him to fuck me.

I wrapped my legs around him as he pushed into me again.

"That feels sooo good," I moaned as he stretched me, filled me, fully, to the hilt.

"I want you to fuck me," I pleaded as he pulled out again.

He ignored me and eased in again, filling me. The pleasure was agonizing. I dug my nails into his arms.

"Hudson, make me come," I moaned loudly as he pulled out and snapped his hips, taking me again.

I tangled my fingers in his hair. He increased the pace. He rocked his hips, his cock thrusting in me. Then he was fucking me, jackhammering into me.

I had already been halfway gone on the bookcase, and the feel of his cock stretching me, taking me, was enough to send me over the edge.

Not Hudson though. He kept up the relentless pace, grinding his teeth then kissing me, his nose banging into mine as he fucked me while I screamed out my orgasm.

He grabbed my wrists, forcing them above my head as he rutted into me, taking his pleasure in my body while I pleaded and begged for him to make me come again.

His rhythm got more erratic.

"Come in me," I chanted. "I want to feel you come."

Then he was shuddering in me.

I cried out his name, grinding my hips up to meet his as I came too.

He kissed me, sloppily, as he pounded in me, drawing out the orgasm as I screamed in pleasure.

"I should have"—I gasped as he collapsed on me—"done this sooner. Oh my god. You've never made me come so hard."

I let him shower me with kisses. There were fireworks. Candy canes rained from the sky, applause …

Wait, applause?

Outside the bedroom non-door, there were definitely people applauding.

"Holy shit."

The applause was punctuated by people complaining about their sleep being interrupted.

"Why can't they close the goddamn door?" one of my cousins bellowed.

"Oh my gosh. This is humiliating." I buried my face in Hudson's bare chest as my family crowded in the doorway.

Hudson dipped his head to kiss me lightly, seemingly unconcerned that my family had a 4K view of his bare ass, though if I had a body like his, I'd probably show it off too.

However, I did not have a military-grade, chiseled-out-of-testosterone-and-American-granite body. I had a yes-you-earned-that-third-donut body.

Hudson laughed softly against my mouth.

I felt my heart flutter. I pushed it down.

"Your sister," he whispered and nipped my ear, "is stewing in jealousy right now, and I bet your ex is hard."

I scrabbled for the sheet as he arched his back then leapt off the bed gracefully.

Meanwhile, I grabbed the sheet to myself, tried to extricate myself from the bed, crashed to the floor, then hefted a Christmas-themed blanket and raced after him, clutching my sheet with one hand.

"You're not covered."

"That is a work of art. You don't throw a ratty blanket over Michelangelo's *David*," my aunt scolded me.

"This is a custom Rudolph blanket," I insisted.

"Rudolph looks like he had a stroke," Violet said flatly.

"I think he's cute," I said, throwing the blanket over Hudson.

"Somehow that makes him look more erotic," Dakota said.

"Not helping," I hissed to my friend.

She flashed me a big grin and a thumbs-up.

I winced, blinded by a flash as Granny Murray took my photo. "For the scrapbook."

"This is not a spectator sport."

"What a performance though." Granny Murray whistled and clapped. "Brought down the whole house, that did."

Hudson gave me a slow, lazy grin and winked.

I wanted to sink in the floor and die. All that fluttering in my chest was hopefully me having a heart attack so that I wouldn't have to face my family.

"All of you stop it this instant," my mother was shrieking.

"This is why we had the intervention," Kelly said snidely. "This is pure exhibitionist behavior."

"Maybe she ate a wild mushroom," Piper said.

"Someone call that therapist back," my mother begged. "My daughter is out of control. Gracie, what were you thinking?"

"She wasn't thinking, ma'am," Hudson drawled. "She could barely talk." Hudson smirked and sauntered out of the doorless doorway.

"I—Oh." My mother reddened as he walked by.

My cousin Connie literally fainted in Dakota's arms, and Kelly looked like she was doing a little melting of her own.

That's right. I had sex with him, and you didn't, I wanted to shout, but that would be rude, beneath me, petty, some might say.

"Thank god James never likes to walk around naked, huh, Kelly," I said as we both admired Hudson's backside.

My uncles came stomping up the stairs.

"Kelly wasn't stealing another of your boyfriends, was she?" Uncle Eddie joked.

"I wish I was in my twenties again," his brother remarked, raising his beer to Hudson.

"You never in your life looked like Hudson," his wife said tartly, eyes sweeping over my fake boyfriend's naked body.

"We are all way too close," I muttered, tugging the sheet more tightly around me.

"Better flush that condom, Hudson," my brother said as he and my cousin snickered. "Kelly might steal it and make a superbaby."

"Mom!" Kelly screamed.

"No way anyone's going to think my kid is James's," Hudson said with a snort and headed for the bathroom.

The shower ran.

"Can no one close a door?" My mother pinched the bridge of her nose.

"You took my door," I shrieked. "So I can't shut it. Play stupid games, win stupid prizes."

"I did?" My mother's hand fluttered to her chest.

"You took that poor girl's door?" Aunt Giana turned on my mother.

"She's a grown woman. Why did you take away her door?"

"We were—It was when she was a teenager," my mother stammered.

"Gracie never asked for it back," my dad said defensively. "If you'd asked for it back, we would have, of course, given it back."

"Do you even know where it is?" Aunt Janet asked.

"It doesn't matter because your husband doesn't know how to hang a door, Bethany," Granny Murray said. "Astelle spoiled that boy soft. That's what happens when you have a youngest son. Rob is just like your father, that lazy useless sack of sentient pot roast. I hope he chokes on a donut. Cheating bastard."

"I need a drink," my mother muttered.

"No, you need some of what Gracie has," Granny Murray insisted. "Now there's a man who can hang a door." She stuck her thumb out.

"Who takes a shower that quickly?" I yelped when I saw that Hudson had appeared, naked and decorated with water droplets, beside me.

He shrugged. "The military."

"Where is your towel?"

"In the bathroom."

Dakota took another photo.

"Put that on the group chat." Violet elbowed her.

"Smile for your fan club, Sugarplum," Hudson said, almost playful as he nudged me lightly with his shoulder.

I felt a fluttering in my chest gain, harder this time, a yearning.

It's heartburn or anxiety. You ate too late at night and aren't used to this much strenuous activity.

Or what if it was something else?

It was like that time in middle school when I had a crush on my science fair partner with his Justin Bieber haircut. Yeah, I was a real basic tween.

Hudson gave me that lazy, smoldering grin again.

Crap.

I had it bad for my fake boyfriend.

Chapter 36

GRACIE

M y family was in the dining room, hyping up for the hockey game as I served breakfast.

While my brother ate a slice of the monster ham-cheese-onion-and-spinach omelet, Piper was carefully painting a Rudolph on his cheek.

On the other side of the dining room, James, with team Frosty, was whining to Kelly that she hadn't washed his jersey.

"Don't be so hard on her," I said brightly, whisking away empty plates and topping off orange juice. "Kelly doesn't know how to use the washing machine. My mom does her laundry."

"Yes, I do! You didn't ask me," Kelly snapped at him.

"Hudson didn't have to ask me to wash his clothes last night," I said, barely able to contain my shit-eating grin. "I washed his things to be a good girlfriend."

Yes, friends, your girl was officially not a virgin. The world was brighter, happier, and I felt taller, more confident, if not a little bit sore.

Pugnog raced to the front door. Hudson came in from his run.

"You were out running? You need to save yourself for the big game," my uncles cried, hurrying over to him.

"It was only a few miles. It's just a little warm-up," Hudson said as he was draped in towels and handed a kale smoothie. The blender was the morning's hockey reveille.

Hudson smiled at me and wrapped his free arm around my waist for a sweaty kiss.

"Just a little warm-up," Uncle Eddie declared. "This guy is our ringer."

"He's got that big dick energy," Kelly called, earning an ugly look from James.

Hudson's mouth quirked.

"You want some pancakes?" I offered.

"No." My uncles booed. "No carbs. Protein only."

"You trying to sabotage the game, Gracie?" My brother Logan threw a fork at me.

Hudson was ushered to the place of honor.

"No one has even seen him play," James protested.

"I have," I said. "He's pretty good."

"Pretty good? That's not what you said last night," Granny Murray hollered.

That earned me another self-satisfied grin from Hudson.

"He needs to wear a shirt at the table," my mom scolded me.

"Nah," her younger brother said affectionately and started doing rapid karate chops on Hudson's massive shoulders. "Gotta loosen him up."

"I think Gracie got that covered last night too," Granny Murray whooped.

Hudson followed me into the kitchen and pulled me in for another hot kiss.

"Do you want to loosen me up in the locker room before the big match?"

"I don't usually go to the games," I said.

Hudson stared at me. "You're not going to the hockey game?"

"I have to make lunch."

"You have three coolers of food loaded in the back of my truck," he said flatly.

I squirmed. "I usually just stay home."

"That's a problem for me," he murmured, pulling me closer to him. "Because I want you there." He wrapped his bare arms around me. "So you need to be there."

"It's just a family holiday game." I wiggled against him.

"I know it's going to make you all hot and bothered to see me on the ice, and I like fucking after I play." He kissed my mouth.

"In that case."

If I actually cared about my revenge plan, I'd tell him that it was a perfect moment to get the fuel we needed for the nuclear-level explosion at Kelly and James's marriage.

But there was that fluttering in my chest again.

"Sure." I smiled up at him. "I'll go to the game."

"*Bloood!*" Granny Murray bellowed as Hudson and my uncle crashed into each other on the ice. "Slit his throat!"

"Gran. That's your son."

The elderly woman blew a raspberry. "I have three more sons just like him. Kill him, Hudson! Fight fight fight! We paid good money to be here. I need a viral TikTok video."

Hudson did some sort of jujitsu hockey move, then he was flying down the ice with the puck.

He passed it to my brother, who shot it back, then Hudson scored on the goal. My male relatives on his team went wild.

"That man is a machine," my aunt Stacy remarked, pouring everyone fresh rounds of the Christmas cranberry vodka cocktails I'd made.

"I hope he doesn't hurt someone," my mother fretted as Hudson stole the puck away from my dad, sending him reeling on the ice.

"If he didn't break Gracie apart," Granny Murray stated, "then Rob should be okay. Unfortunately."

It did look a little dicey. My family was on the shorter side. Hudson with his huge six-foot-five frame, dwarfed the other players.

He was careful, however. Even though he was focused on the game, he was still fully aware of what was going on around him and was gentle with my smaller, younger cousins, even tossing the puck to Dakota's littlest brother on occasion so he could take a shot at the goal.

"I see you," Dakota hissed in my ear, making me yelp in surprise.

"Hudson is not husband material."

My ovaries very much disagreed.

"Scooore!" Aunt Janet announced on the sound system.

"Logan got a goal!" Piper cheered.

"Hudson set him up to score," Kelly said, rolling her eyes.

"Team Rudolph is really wiping the floor with Team Frosty," Aunt Janet added.

"Good thing Hudson didn't let little things like the lack of a bedroom door scare him away from Gracie. He certainly is an upgrade from Gracie's last boyfriend. Speaking of, maybe the Frosty team coach wants to sub out James for a fresh player. Maybe Codie?"

Codie was my second cousin who had just turned four and had all the coordination on the ice of a newborn foal.

My brother and cousins on Team Rudolph jeered at Team Frosty, shit-talking them.

"You should have set up Kelly with one of the Wynter brothers."

"Put Codie in. Make it a fair game."

James shifted on his skates angrily while Team Rudolph ribbed him.

"I'll fight all of you," Uncle Albert yelled back.

"I'm not stitching anyone up," Kirk said. "I'm going to pretend like I don't know any of you."

"Can I play, Dad?" Codie called. "I wanna play."

"Sub him in," Hudson called, skating around in tight circles. "I need a challenge."

Codie squealed, "Yay!" and jumped on the ice, racing to the puck that Hudson had.

He smiled at the kid. It was the single most adorable thing I'd ever seen.

"Ahead there be dangerous waters," Dakota said.

"What?" I hissed to her. "I want a big family. He comes from a big family. What could go wrong?"

When I turned my attention back to Hudson, I noticed James barreling across the ice toward him.

Hudson had seen the movement before I did, because he'd already turned to block his body to protect Codie, who was twirling around on the ice, oblivious to my ex hurtling toward them.

"Hudson!" I yelled as James collided with him.

Hudson twisted his body, flipping both of them over Codie who stared, mouth open in awe as the two men sailed over him.

"I got the puck," Codie called.

No one was paying attention because James was swinging his hockey stick at Hudson, hitting him in the face under the brim of his helmet.

Hudson caught the next blow and wrenched the stick out of James's hand, shoving him in the stomach with the stick then throwing it aside.

James came back at him red-faced, arms swinging.

"You fucking piece of white trash," James screamed at Hudson, who blocked the punches.

"Fight!" Granny Murray bellowed. "*Fight!*"

Both teams raced over.

James might have gotten in an easy punch, but I'd seen Hudson fight, and my ex was no match for him. He got his arm around James as James's fist glanced off the side of his helmet.

I screamed as Hudson and James crashed into the Plexiglas protection screen right in front of where we were sitting.

Then both teams were pulling their players apart.

"It's fine. Relax."

Hudson shrugged off my brother who was unfastening Hudson's helmet so Kirk could inspect the blood running down his face. "James is just salty I took his ex's virginity."

James lunged at Hudson, and his fist collided with Hudson's nose. The larger man body-slammed him down into the ice; his knee dug into James's side as he pinned him down. Hudson's face was terrifying.

"Calm the fuck down," he growled.

"Fuck you," James spat. "Gracie, you see what kind of animal he is? He's beneath you. He's embarrassing."

"You started the fight," I screeched at James. "This is your fault. You almost killed Codie."

My dad and his brother ushered James off the ice.

On the center of the ice, Codie was wobbling impatiently on his skates.

"You guys, I'm about to score."

Hudson dragged the sleeve of his jersey across his face, smearing the blood on his cheek, then reattached his helmet and skated over.

The rest of the hockey players still seemed slightly stunned.

It was a little unnerving how quickly Hudson was able to just shake off the violence.

Meanwhile, I couldn't stop trembling.

Hudson scooped up his hockey stick and made a big dramatic show of trying to stop Codie.

The four-year-old giggled and skated around him then took a swing with his hockey stick.

"Nothing but net," Dakota whooped.

"Wrong sport," Granny Murray stated.

"And with that final tiebreaking goal, Team Rudolph is the winner," Aunt Janet declared.

In the last period of the game, the younger kids had opted to grab a snack and water in the stands with the rest of us nonathletes while the adults finished the game. Thankfully, James had disappeared.

All my cousins and, of course, my brother had grown up playing hockey competitively, and the game moved at a quick pace, the puck flying.

Logan and Hudson played easily off each other, but my uncles on Team Frosty were also no slouches. Most of them were in adult leagues, and my dad's cousin Nate had played goalie in college and then professionally for a couple years. That was Team Frosty's saving grace. Usually Rudolph never won because of Cousin Nate's wizardry in the goal, but Hudson had been able to get a few shots on him.

"Yes!" my brother and cousins screamed, swarming Hudson.

Nate took off his helmet.

"Man, if I was about ten years younger, you wouldn't have had me beat so bad." He grinned and slapped Hudson on the shoulder.

"Dude, are you kidding me?" Hudson said, shaking his hand. "I haven't had to work for a goal like that in years. I need to up my game. If I'd lost my focus for a minute, you would have crushed me."

It felt like my insides were gooey and made of marshmallows watching Hudson with my family, like he was meant to be here with me.

Dakota cleared her throat.

"See?" Violet said to Kelly. "You were chasing quantity when Gracie was chasing quality."

"Not too late to cancel that wedding and get an upgrade, Kelly," Aunt Janet said over the loud speaker.

My mom got up to yell at her sister.

"Dinner and a bonfire at Bethany's house," Janet hollered as I heard my mom and her little sister squabbling over the loudspeaker.

I ducked out of the seating area and headed down to where the players were changing out of their skates. I hovered as Hudson pulled off all the padding over his head.

Hudson's gray eyes were dancing when he noticed me. He seemed happy, relaxed. He picked me up, spun me around, then kissed me loudly.

"The man of the hour."

"My good luck charm."

"Your face," I said with a wince when he released me.

"It's fine."

"Another scar to add to your collection," Logan joked.

"What do you need me to load into the car, Gracie?" he said, draping his arm around my shoulder.

Hudson received congratulations and handshakes as he helped me ferry coolers and boxes to his truck.

"That's the last of it," I said to him as I opened the passenger's side door.

He was on me as soon as I got in the car. He smelled like sweat and adrenaline and male. He pulled off his T-shirt, his sweaty body against mine.

"Ooh my gosh," I gasped as he kissed me, my mouth, my neck.

He pulled at the zipper on my coat.

"Let me see your tits."

I panted.

The windows were starting to fog up. The heat was radiating off of him, his sweaty hair falling over his forehead.

I struggled, pinned by the jacket as he pushed it down my arms then slid my sweater up. His mouth was hot and hungry on my tits, sucking a nipple.

"What are we doing? This is a public parking lot," I squeaked.

"I told you I like sex after hockey."

"Here in your truck?"

"Yeah. I want to fuck that tight pussy."

My panties and my tights were drenched now.

"Maybe this isn't—oh my god," I groaned as his hands slipped under my panties to stroke me.

Hudson kissed me roughly.

"Now you want me to fuck you, don't you?"

"Um ... I—"

He stroked my clit hard.

"You're practically gushing against my hand, Sugarplum. Don't lie. You want me to fuck you with my thick, hard cock, don't you?"

"Yeah," I gasped and kissed him, sucking on his lower lip.

"You want to be my little puck bunny, Sugarplum?"

"Your what?"

"The hot piece of ass I fuck after winning a hockey game."

"Guess Santa doesn't need to bring you any self-esteem for Christmas."

"And he doesn't need to bring you a vibrator, Sugarplum," he said, pushing me between the center console to the back bench in the pickup. "Get on your hands and knees. I need to fuck your wet little cunt."

I heard his zipper rasp.

"You need to stop wearing these fucking tights," he said, pulling them and my panties down.

His tongue was in my pussy now, licking me, sucking on my clit.

I whimpered when he withdrew.

"Since you're not a virgin anymore," he said as I heard a condom packet rip, "I'm going to fuck you hard and fast."

His hand slipped briefly under my sweater to squeeze my breasts. Then he spread my legs. They strained against the thick tights around my knees.

"Yeah, I want to fuck that pussy," he said hoarsely, spreading me.

I felt the tip of his cock briefly at my opening.

Before I could beg for him, he was in me in one quick motion, buried to the hilt. I moaned loudly as he filled me.

"You like that, huh, Sugarplum," he said, one hand tangling in my hair, the other on my ass holding me still, keeping me from falling off the truck bench.

His hips snapped back, then he was buried in me again.

"Fuck, your pussy feels so good."

Then he fucked me for real. Last night had been a leisurely trip through the snowy woods. This was a fucking blizzard.

Hudson kept up the furious pace. I tried to stifle my cries, but it was no use.

Something about how the tights at my knees kept my pussy clenched tight around his cock was enough to bring me rapidly to the edge as he fucked me, quick and dirty doggy style in the back of his pickup truck.

The zipper of his pants scraped against my ass as his thick cock pounded in me.

"You like being fucked like this, don't you," he growled, his hand tight in my hair.

I gasped for breath as he pulled my head back, arching my back, his cock hitting some deep point of pleasure inside of me.

"Hudson, fuck me," I moaned. "Fuck me harder. Make me come."

Out of the corner of my eye, I thought I saw motion through the slightly foggy windshield. But I didn't want Hudson to stop. I needed him.

I panted and whimpered as he kept up the furious pace, driving me higher and higher until I was falling over the edge as he pounded away in me.

I heard him grunt, and he was pressing sloppy kisses on my neck, his cock spasming in me.

"Fuck," he said in my neck. "I really am a bad influence on you, huh?" he said, squeezing my ass one more time then tugging up my tights.

"You seem pretty proud of yourself."

"You can't tell me I'm not the best fuck you've ever had in your life."

He laughed at the joke, still high on the win and the fighting and the male sports stuff and, of course, the sex.

I turned my head to kiss him again.

"I just love fucking a good, tight pussy."

Hudson practically had to lift me into the passenger's seat, and I landed like a beached whale while he climbed over the console to the driver's seat with way more grace and agility than someone his size had any right to.

"Just for that," he said, grinning as he leaned over and kissed me, "I'll let you listen to Christmas carols. I might even sing along."

"If that's your reaction, I need to let you fuck me in the back of your truck more often," I joked.

"I'm pretty sure I almost made you pass out," he said, slipping on his sunglasses.

"Cocky asshole."

I reached over to wipe my mitten across the fogged-up windshield and screamed.

There were James and Kelly, whispering to themselves.

Hudson rolled down the driver's side window.

"What?" he barked.

James jumped. He still had tissue stuffed up his bruised nose.

"Gracie is my future sister-in-law," James said stubbornly. "She comes from a good family, and you need to stop treating her like the trailer trash where you come from."

I sucked in a breath.

Hudson just smirked then swung his head to me.

"Did you like getting fucked in the back of my truck, Sugarplum?"

My face felt hot.

He raised an eyebrow.

"Um … yeah," I stammered.

Hudson turned that feral grin back to James and slapped the side of his truck.

James winced.

"She liked getting fucked, so I think we're good, thanks. Unless you want me to break your jaw this time."

Chapter 37

HUDSON

had forgotten how much I liked playing hockey, to be able to focus on the game, not have to worry about fucking up a mission or losing a contract or wondering how in the world I was going to get into a laptop that was locked down like one of the princesses of England.

Not just that, but while my brothers and I liked to scrimmage sometimes, it was nothing like the big to-do Gracie's family organized.

Sure they were fucked up and held an intervention for her, but those were a small bucket of bad apples. The rest of her family—her cousins, her uncles, her brother—they weren't half bad. I actually kind of liked them.

"Hudson! Hudson! Hudson!" several of the guys on my team chanted as I followed Gracie outside into her parents' backyard.

It felt like I was just a normal man, and Gracie was my normal girlfriend, in a normal relationship, not wrapped in the layers of lies I had spun. I let myself believe for a moment, savoring the fantasy.

Someone wants to be a real boy for Christmas.

Fuck off, I told my subconscious.

One of Gracie's uncles sat me in a chair and handed me a beer and a burger.

I took a huge bite, suddenly starving.

"Eat this venison sausage," another uncle said, setting a fat sausage on the plate. "Mom, please don't make a filthy joke," he added to Grandma Murray, who had her mouth open.

"I mean, we were all thinking it," she said.

Gracie came over to me, bearing a tray with a bowl of soup, salad, and … toys?

"I don't need a stuffed animal," I said as she picked up a hand-knitted Rudolph.

"It's an ice pack, silly," she told me.

Her fingers were gentle as she pulled back my collar and pressed the ice pack against my bruised shoulder. Her hand was steady as she held it there. Then she picked up a penguin holding a Christmas wreath and dabbed it gently on my face.

"I already have a bandage," I said, finally moving her hand off my forehead.

"I can't believe James attacked you."

"It means it's working," I said, lowering my voice.

Gracie seemed a little apprehensive. Maybe the fight had freaked her out, though it wasn't much of a fight. James was a complete wuss.

Gracie fidgeted with the bowl of soup on the tray in her lap.

"Is that the clam chowder your aunt made?" I asked her as I took a huge bite of the broccoli salad.

"Aunt Babs has a supersecret recipe. She says she has it written in her will to be left to me because, quote, Dakota can't cook worth shit."

I smirked. "I'll have to go grab a bowl."

"This is for you," she said, sliding the tray over to me.

"Where's your dinner?" I asked her pointedly.

"I'll get some later," she said, still with that wide-eyed look.

I held out the burger. "Eat."

"I—"

"Eat," I ordered.

She leaned in and took a bite.

"Another."

As she chewed, she lost that freaked-out look.

I handed her my plate and took the chowder from her.

"Damn," I said, savoring it. "That is good. Can your aunt add me in her will too?"

Gracie smiled at me softly.

The ice on my heart was threatening to crack.

"You really went above and beyond today," she said softly. "I feel like that was more than—"

I silenced her with a kiss.

Her body was warm from the fire.

I had just meant to kiss her to keep anyone from over-hearing her mention a contract, but then I couldn't stop kissing her.

"As I said, I like playing hockey," I whispered against her mouth then kissed her again because I could, because she felt perfect and pure as freshly fallen snow.

Gracie sat next to me in the oversized chair barely big enough for two, her leg pressed against mine as we shared the dinner.

"Smile for the scrapbook," one of her cousins called and took our photo.

"I wasn't ready," Gracie mumbled around the bite of hamburger she'd just taken.

"To be fair," her cousin said as a Polaroid shot out of the camera, "everyone's going to be looking at this picture for Hudson."

"Marry him, Gracie," her brother called, walking by, holding aloft a plate loaded with venison sausage.

"I don't know why you're so gung-ho," joked one of the Team Frosty players. "Hudson's going to be on our team next year."

"You can't have both Nate and Hudson," Logan complained to his uncle.

"Don't screw it up, Gracie. You're the dream holiday team."

"Hudson wins hockey games, and Gracie cooks," her uncle concurred. "They're the whole Christmas package right here."

"Hey, I make cookies too," I said with a wry smile.

"And he's funny."

It felt nice, like a normal family.

Sure, Gracie called them dysfunctional, but compared to my family, it was Mister Rogers and his band of wholesome puppets in the O'Brien household.

Gracie had finished her dinner and was snuggled up against me. I wasn't sure she was even aware she was doing it.

I allowed my arm to rest around her shoulders and kissed the top of her head, feeling warm and sated by the heat of the fire. All I wanted to do was crawl in bed with her, make love to her, tell her how much I adored her.

The mission …

Fuck the mission.

Just for tonight anyway.

"Did you make spiked hot chocolate, Gracie?" her brother came by to ask.

"Sure. Just let me …"

"If she gets up because of you," I told him, eyes still half-closed, "I'm going to break your face."

"The god has spoken." Logan raised his arms.

A few moments later, Gracie's brother came back out, lugging the huge pot of hot chocolate while Pugnog and several other dogs roamed around, begging for scraps.

"You didn't bring the homemade marshmallows," Gracie protested.

"I have them!" Codie hoisted a tray above his head.

I peered at it. "That looks like it should be in a magazine."

"And he's probably going to drop it." Gracie sighed.

"No, I'm not!" Codie yelled as he zoomed after Logan.

I laughed deep in my chest and kissed her sweet mouth.

"Ugh. I'm a terrible hostess. I should—"

"No," I said, wrapping my arms around her, holding her in place against me. "You're perfect."

I want this forever.

"You would be a great mother. You always go above and beyond. I saw all those hockey-themed bento boxes you made. Don't act like you don't like to show off," I joked.

"That was nothing." She waved a hand.

"Please. My mom never did half this shit."

Gracie looked up at me, brown eyes sparking in the light of the bonfire.

"I can come by and decorate your apartment for Christmas," she offered. "Give you all the homey touches and make your house smell like cookies."

Ice-cold lake water washed over me.

And just like that, I had a plan.

This is why you can never be a normal person.

"Gracie," I murmured against her neck. "I'd love for you to come decorate my place for Christmas."

She beamed at me.

"But," I lowered my voice, "only if you wear that elf outfit."

Chapter 38

GRACIE

Hudson had left last night and hadn't stayed over like I'd wanted. Maybe he thought that the sex in the back of his pickup truck had been good enough for a day's work.

"Do you think he invited me over to, *you know*?"

"Have sex? You're a nonvirgin now. You can say it. The gods won't smite you down where you stand," Dakota said from where she was lounging on my bed, clipping the tags off underwear.

"I think we're supposed to wash this first." I chewed on my lip.

"There's a line for the washer after that hockey game," Dakota said. "Besides, Hudson's not going to leave you in them that long."

I picked at my nail polish. Last night, I had lain awake, trying to convince myself that it was a terrible idea for a person with no door to touch herself like that. With my luck, it was asking for trouble. So I just laid there, panties soaked, trying and failing not to think about how Hudson's cock had felt in me, the dirty things he'd said to me as he'd taken me in the back of his pickup truck.

"Hello? Earth to Gracie," Dakota waved at me.

"Sorry."

"You need to wear these." She held up a pair of very skimpy red lace thong panties.

"Maybe he just wants decorations. I think he might have just said he wanted me in the elf outfit just to, you know, sell the relationship," I worried. "What if I show up in sexy lingerie and it's super awkward?"

Dakota scoffed. "No man is going to get angry if a woman he is regularly sleeping with shows up in a sexy outfit."

I busied myself selecting which Christmas decorations I was going to take to Hudson. I'd hauled a number of old decorations out of the attic. They were a little dated—not good dated like vintage fifties décor, just dated like from the '80s. Still, I could make anything work.

"You cannot take those ornaments. It's not late enough in the twenty-first century for satin-covered ornaments to be back in style," Dakota said, grabbing the box from me.

"I think they're kind of cute."

"Barf."

I tossed them back in the box and added some glass ornaments to the bag of garland. I'd been making more fresh garland for Kelly's wedding venue décor, but Hudson deserved some, especially after James had attacked him.

Into the bag, I added an envelope of cash. I had stopped at the bank earlier to take out a cash advance from one of my credit cards. Of course, the payment from EnerCheck

Inc. was late. I marked it down in my Festivus book of grievances since it was useless to complain to my father.

"We put it in our book, and then it's the universe's problem to take care of," I said, dating the latest entry, and stuck the notebook back with all the others.

"Yet another of your maladaptive habits." Dakota shook her head.

"Do you think this is enough cash?" I lowered my voice. Despite the very loud, very sexy exhibition with Hudson the other night, I still had no door. When he was around, it was as if I was the princess of the family. When he was gone, I was just Cinderella again.

"It's too much," Dakota said flatly.

"Hudson did go all out yesterday at the hockey game. I can't stiff him on his money. Also he's having sex with me. I know he says he doesn't mind, but what if he's lying?"

Dakota threw the underwear at me.

"Stop overthinking. It's just sex. You always get too worked up over things. It's not like you're going over there to get proposed to."

Was it bad I almost wished I was?

"We've been friends since we were babies," Dakota said. "I know what you're thinking, and yes, it's a bad idea."

"I'm not," I lied. "I just think that this one's not festive enough." I picked it up and sat down at my sewing machine. "Why own an expensive sewing machine that makes custom embroidery if you're not going to sew snowflakes on your underwear as a nice surprise for your fake boyfriend?"

Hudson was shirtless, barefoot, his black jeans slung low on his hips, when he opened the door.

"I have the Christmas decorations," I said as I pushed past him into the warm apartment.

"You should have told me you were bringing all this stuff. I would have come picked you up," Hudson scolded, picking up one of the large duffel bags and carrying it to the stairs up to his unit.

"It's not my whole collection. Just a little something festive. I spared you from all the ceramic figurines. I think they have lead in them," I told him.

He hoisted me up by the waist, kissing me. I wrapped my arms around his neck, losing myself in the sensation of him.

He set me down, and I felt a little off-balance.

"Let me see you," he said, turning me around, sliding his hand along my bare midriff.

"She's such a good girl and didn't wear tights this time," he purred. His fingers trailed up my thighs.

"The other night," he said almost conversationally as he ran his hands down to my ass, fingers digging between my legs, making me inadvertently widen my stance, "I was about to jack off thinking about you in that ridiculous outfit."

"You were?"

"Yeah. You in those boots, riding my cock," he said. His voice seemed to drop an octave. "That bodice undone, your tits hanging out, you're playing with them while your tight little pussy rode my cock. Then I decided," he added, sliding his fingers under the band of the crop top, "I should just make her come over and fuck her in that outfit for real."

I licked my lips.

"Do that again," he ordered, eyes heavy-lidded.

I licked my lips again. "It's a nervous gesture."

"Really? Because all I can think about is you licking my cum off your face."

"So I see this is not going to be a wholesome, Christmas-filled evening."

"It can be, Sugarplum—you're dressed in an elf costume."

"What about the rules?" I croaked.

Sure, I wanted to believe that he was completely obsessed and in love with me, but sometimes I could be a little slow on the uptake. Like when my little siblings finally had to spoil the magic of Santa for me at the ripe age of fifteen. Yeah, late bloomer here. Very late.

"I'm a bad boy, remember? That's why you hired me."

He nuzzled my neck. His cheek was smooth against mine. He'd just shaved.

"Fuck the rules."

"I think," I told him, "that you're chickening out and scared to bring the magic of Christmas in your home."

He kissed me long and slow.

"I mean, clearly," he said, still kissing me. "I brought you over here to fuck."

I leaned back, placing my hands on his bare chest, and stared up at him.

"I still want to make your home festive," I told him. "Everyone deserves some Christmas cheer. Look at the poor Christmas tree. It's sad and naked."

"I want you naked," he murmured in my neck.

I batted away his hands.

"First," I said, feeling a little awkward. "I have something for you."

"It's not a sweater, is it?" he teased.

"I'll have you know, my sweaters are a hot commodity, sir," I said, rummaging around in one of the bags and pulling out the stuffed envelope.

"Your, uh, well, your payment." I stuck my hand out to him.

He looked down at the envelope.

"Thanks," he said slowly and frowned.

I rocked back on my heels.

"I know we said 5,000, but I prorated it since we're a few days from Christmas. I didn't want to keep you waiting. I pay my bills on time unlike some people," cough, "James. Payments and invoicing was one thing he insisted on doing in the company, and he can't even do it correctly."

Hudson ran a hand through his hair.

"Right." He set the money on the table.

"So," I said, whipping out my notepad. "Tell me about all your favorite things."

"Fucking your pussy."

"I can't decorate with that," I said, tapping my pen on the notebook. "Your family never did anything for Christmas? We can mine a little Christmas nostalgia."

"No." His expression was dark.

"Okay," I said brightly. "How about a little Christmas music?"

"I don't have any Christmas music," he said, shoulders tense.

Chapter 39

HUDSON

What if she didn't have the laptop?

She always has the laptop. Gracie's paranoid. She's not leaving it in her parents' house with her sister.

Stay calm.

It was a struggle to maintain my composure as Gracie poked around one of the boxes and bags she'd brought with her.

She beamed at me and pulled out her computer. "Don't worry. I came prepared."

I tried not to laugh from relief.

Thank fucking god she has the laptop.

"I have downloaded a list of heavy metal Christmas songs. Thought that might be more your jam," she said as she went through the excessive password unlock sequence.

The music app loaded on the screen, and hard rock Christmas carols blared through the speakers.

Step one down.

"Keep an open mind. You might discover you like Christmas after all," she teased.

"I think your outfit is doing the heavy lifting on that one."

I opened a bottle of wine and handed her a glass.

"Merry Christmas!" She toasted me.

I set my glass down and leaned in to taste the wine on her mouth, my hands slipping up her thighs.

"Merry Christmas to me," I replied as I trailed my fingertips up her bare thigh.

"You make it sound so dirty," she said, giggling into the wineglass.

After kissing me again, she went back to her bags and pulled out a box of Christmas-tree lights. She handed me the end of the strand, and I helped slowly wind it around the tree.

If I weren't about to steal the data off her laptop, it would almost be like we were a real couple.

"Now some ornaments," she said, grabbing a box. "Don't worry. We're not going all out. This will be a super-minimalist tree with just some glass ornaments."

She held the box out to me. "Come over here Mr. Tall Person. You can do the star."

I approached her as she sat under the tree, a perfect Christmas card, and accepted the ornaments.

Then I let out a heavy sigh as I stared down at them.

In a horrible twist of fate, they did look like the ones on the last Christmas tree my family ever had.

"I actually—we did use to celebrate Christmas, before it all went to shit," I remarked as I opened up the box. "Huh. Funny, I had forgotten about these."

"What were your holiday traditions?" she asked softly.

The memories resurfaced.

"My brothers and I would always wait up for Santa," I said, staring out the large industrial steel windows. "My dad loved Christmas—he liked to spend a bunch of money, buy us anything we wanted even though we couldn't afford it. He just loved the magic. Always went all out." Then he and my mom would fight, but Gracie didn't need to know that. "Anyway, we would use these ornaments. They were my mom's favorite."

"It's fate." Gracie was smiling, big and happy.

"Yeah. Fate."

I hung an ornament on the tree. It glittered in the low light.

"I actually," I said casually, like I'd just thought of it, "have some videos of me and my family from Christmas, if you wanted to see them. My brother's been dubbing over old home movies."

"I'd love to," she said softly.

The external hard drive was sitting on the kitchen counter waiting. Last night at the headquarters, I'd paced around while Talbot configured it and loaded the Trojan program on that would steal all of Gracie's data.

She took it from me and plugged it into her laptop.

I had spent hours carefully selecting a clip, the perfect thing to entice her to put her password in the computer so that the program could steal it and run the data scraper.

"Oh," I said as the message popped up that administrator permission needed to be granted. "Never mind. It doesn't like my hard drive. I think the video is a weird format. It was copied over from one of those old video recorders. Don't ask me how—my younger brother Talbot is the tech wiz in the family. I'll have him look at it later."

I saw her wavering, saw part of her thinking.

I picked up my wineglass, took a swallow.

Gracie mimicked the gesture.

I reached for the hard drive.

"I do want to see you as a kid," she relented.

Yes.

"Now I don't know if I want you to see it," I said wryly. I put my hand on the hard drive. "It was just some dumb video of me and my brothers when we were little. We're cutting a Christmas tree."

Gracie slapped at my hand.

"You're not going to keep me from seeing little Hudson!" She grinned as she typed the password.

ARE YOU SURE YOU WANT TO CONTINUE? the program asked.

She hit Yes then verified her identity, fingerprint, face recognition.

I could barely breathe as the video played, disguising the program in the background that was unpacking.

"Aww!" Gracie clasped her hands together as the video started.

There was my father and my mother, arm in arm, maybe the last time they were happy together.

It had been emotionally brutal, sifting through all the old home movies, remembering when things were good, and with the benefit of hindsight, finding clues of the oncoming disaster.

"Don't drop Elsa," my dad called as my brothers and I trooped through the rows of snow-covered Christmas trees.

"Sleigh bells ring …" my mother sang out.

Anderson's face appeared briefly in the camera.

"I want a dinosaur for Christmas," he said solemnly. "Hudson, what do you want Santa to bring you?"

"Hmm." The younger version of myself considered it.

"You're so serious," Gracie said softly, taking my hand.

"I think new hockey skates," younger me said.

"Elsa, what do you want?" Jake yelled, jumping around me as I held my baby sister.

She burbled.

"I think she wants a dinosaur too." Lawrence grinned at the camera.

"We need to get this tree," Talbot called, toddling over to a nearby fir.

"No," younger me said, pointing. "That one. That's the best tree."

"Bring 'er down, boys!" my dad whooped.

"They're little children." My mom swatted him playfully while my dad laughed and kissed her.

God, what happened to you two?

My mother took Elsa and the camera while my brothers and I took turns with a saw, bringing down the dark-green tree. All five of us had a go, though I finished it off.

"Say merry Christmas!" my mom called from behind the camera.

"Merry Christmas!" we all chorused.

"That was so sweet!" Gracie clapped her hands then kissed me. "We're going to find that Christmas spirit that's been hiding inside of you."

"You're all I want for Christmas," I said, grabbing her jaw and forcing her face to me so she wouldn't notice the scraping program running on her laptop.

Smoothly I plucked the wineglass out of her hand and pushed her back against the couch, turning her around so she was face down.

"Remember how," I said, sliding the short little green skirt up her bare thighs, "you told me when my tongue was on your clit that you wanted me to tie you up and fuck you raw?"

I heard her gasp a yes.

I mouthed her through the panties, a red lacy thong that was made slightly less sexy by the addition of smiling, fat, happy snowflakes.

"You have a Christmas addiction," I told her, raising my head.

"No." Her voice sounded slightly muffled. "I have a you addiction."

"I haven't even given you the holiday special."

"Someone's been holding back." She raised her head slightly up off of the couch pillows.

"I think your Grandmother Astelle would have a heart attack and die if she saw me doing to you what I want to do to you."

"Granny Murray's going to be sorry you wasted all that effort." She smirked then moaned as I mouthed her through the panties.

"So is that a yes?" I breathed.

"I'm not sure what I'm agreeing to."

I grabbed her ass in both hands, kneading it.

"I told you I'm going to tie you up and fuck you raw. Or is that not your fantasy?"

"Um … It's actually more of my grandmother's?"

I glanced over at the laptop. The status bar in the corner was at 5 percent.

Fuck.

"It was from a book she gave me. I actually really sanitized it for you."

"I don't want anything sanitized," I told her, sneaking my hands under the crop top to cup her breasts.

"So there was this alien with all these tentacles …"

"Christ help me."

She giggled.

"As long as you're not sprouting tentacles, I'm game."

"Famous last words."

Her eyes were dark with anticipation. "You know, I love a holiday exclusive."

I picked her up and carried her to the other side of the room.

I'd tested various vantage points, wanting to make sure there was no way Gracie could see what I was doing to her laptop.

Then I reached up and pulled down the handcuffs I'd already attached to the steel beam in the ceiling of the loft.

Gracie shivered under my hand.

"They're Christmas themed." I waved one of the handcuffs that had silk green-and-red-striped padding on it.

She seemed slightly apprehensive.

"Handcuffs?"

"Don't worry. I'll let you order me around after this if you let me make all of your fantasies come true. You just tell me when you're good and fucked, and I'll let you down. Swear on my honor."

I kissed her, my tongue slipping into her mouth, kissed her until she was breathless and half collapsed on me.

Then I stepped back.

Her eyes were glazed with desire.

Slowly, she held up her arms.

The handcuffs fastened around her wrists with a metallic click.

Chapter 40

HUDSON

With her hands above her head, her breasts rode high. The heeled boots she wore lifted her ass, putting her right at perfect fucking height.

I grabbed her hair. She moaned, the chains clinking softly as I kissed her, taking my time, savoring her. Her arms strained against the cuffs.

I undid the bodice of the crop top elf costume, unlacing her, letting her tits spill out. I took one in my mouth, feeling her nipple harden.

"I really want to touch you," she gasped.

"You're going to feel me in you soon enough, Sugarplum."

I knelt down in front of her.

"I thought you were going to fuck me raw," she panted as I lifted up her skirt, exposing the bright-red panties.

"Is that why you're so wet for me?"

Hooking my finger in the string of the thin fabric, I pulled the panties to the side, flicking my tongue against the slit of her glistening, wet pussy.

She twisted in the handcuffs.

Behind her, the program ran on the computer, copying the data to the hard drive.

I licked a stripe along her pussy. Lightly. I just wanted to give her a taste. As I licked her, I tugged on the fabric, using the panties as added friction in her pussy.

"I want you in me," she begged as I teased her. "Hudson, I need you."

I stood up as she moaned, and I undid my belt.

"I can't wait to bury my dick in you."

Her arms strained against the cuffs.

My pants dropped to the floor. I fisted my cock.

Her hips rolled toward me, and I teased her clit with the head of my cock while I kissed her, rubbing my thumb over her breast.

"Fuck me," she begged against my mouth. "Please, Hudson."

I grabbed a condom from the nearby floating shelf, let her watch me put it on, her panties soaking up the wetness.

I stepped behind her.

I didn't bother to take off her panties before I slammed into her. Her pussy clenched around my cock as I buried myself in her.

She was mewling and panting as I fucked her with wild abandon, like I'd wanted to do last night.

Unlike in my truck, here I had room to fuck her, spread her legs, let her feel the thick length of my cock in her tight little cunt.

"You feel so good in my pussy," she cried deep from her throat.

The dirty words were driving me crazy. I fucked her harder, pounding into her as my fingers worked her clit.

She rocked forward against my hand then back against my cock, her hips moving in needy circles as I fucked her.

She came with a loud cry.

I wasn't done.

I pulled out of her as she moaned. Then I stepped around in front of her and kissed her swollen mouth. Leaning down, I took one of her tits in my mouth then dug my hands into her hips, lifting her up.

In the thigh-high red boots, her legs wrapped around me. She cried out as I took her again, sucking and nipping her tits as I gave her my cock. I felt her teeth in my scalp, felt her body seize up, felt her come around me.

I gritted my teeth then pulled her off.

"How are you still hard?" she whimpered. "I want to feel you come in me."

I ignored her and ignored my aching cock.

This is going to be a long night, buddy, I told it.

Too bad all I wanted to do was fuck her, finish in her.

I gritted my teeth and slowly unwound the side lacing on the crop-top bodice. The ribbon fluttered to the floor as she gasped.

The bodice followed. I left on her bra. Strapless, sexy, it made her tits look like presents, just waiting for me.

I practically came there as I drank in the sight of her, arms above her head, huge tits on her chest, ass high in those boots and that little skirt.

Suddenly, I lost control.

Getting behind her, I slammed my cock into her as she gasped and pleaded for me to make her come.

"I'm going to fuck you raw," I snarled in her neck.

She whimpered as she took my cock, feeling every thick inch inside of her, begging me to claim her.

"You like that, don't you? You're a bad little elf."

"Punish me, Santa," she gasped.

I slapped her ass then pinched her tits, making her cry out.

"I'm in control here. You don't get to call the shots."

"Not even if I say, 'Santa, come in my ass'?" she gasped.

Just the thought of shooting my hot cum in her was enough to make me spill my load. Gracie came again as I pounded in her, erratic, milking the last of the orgasm.

"Just for that"—I nipped her shoulder—"I'm leaving you tied up here."

She giggled, sounding slightly drunk on the pleasure.

I quickly padded over to the laptop, tossing the condom on the way.

Only thirty-two percent.

I came back with her wine, held it up to her lips. Some of it spilled on her chin, and I lapped it up, tasting the sweet wine on her mouth.

Then I unzipped the side zipper of her skirt, and I knelt down in front of her. I brought the skirt down with me, and she stepped out of it, standing there only in the thong panties.

I mouthed her through them, making her jump.

I stood up, walked around her.

"Like what you see?" Her hair was sweaty, tangled over her face.

I unhooked her bra, let it fall to the floor. Took her huge tits in my mouth, kneading them, working the nipples with my tongue.

I snapped the band of the thong and caressed her ass.

Spreading her cheeks, I ground my bare cock against her, letting her feel me.

"Am I making you hard?" she whimpered.

"All I want to do is fuck you all night," I whispered against her neck as I ground against her, savoring her. Shit. I better—I had 68 percent to go.

I knelt down in front of her, pulling the soaking-wet fabric to the side as I mouthed her, tasting her sweet pussy. Her moans of pleasure made me so hard, I thought I was going to come right there. Her clit was swollen, her pussy hot and ready as I lapped at her, working my tongue in the slit.

She leaned forward, resting part of her body weight on me.

I held her upright, fingers digging in her hips as I licked her, teased her, brought her to another screaming crest of pleasure.

Don't bother checking it, I told myself. *It's not done yet.*

I stood back up in front of her, playing with her tits, letting her arch against me. I dipped my head down to take one in my mouth.

"You fucked yet?" I asked, scraping my teeth on her nipple then kissed her hard on her swollen mouth, letting her taste herself on me. "Hmm?"

"Uh …"

"You feel fucked?"

I reached down her, stroking her once.

"You want me to convince you?"

"Yeah. Convince me," she breathed.

My cock ached with need as I stepped behind her and finally slid those bright-red panties down to her ankles.

She lifted one booted foot then the other, then she was standing in front of me, sexy and beautiful, her inner thighs slick with a fine sheen of juice from her pussy.

"Damn, you're fucking sexy," I whispered, kissing her neck noisily and grinding against her. I turned her head so I could claim her mouth, letting her feel my hard cock against her ass.

"You want me to fuck you, or you want me to untie you and watch Christmas movies?" I asked, pressing kisses along her neck and jaw.

"Depends on the Christmas movie."

I slapped her lightly on the ass.

"How about I give you the sequel then you can decide," I offered, sinking down to my knees behind her. I spread her ass cheeks, mouthing her. First dipping my tongue in her pussy, then higher. She gave a loud gasp as she felt my mouth there.

"I um ... Oh my gosh. Why does that feel so good?"

"I can make you feel even better," I promised, mouthing her again, letting her feel my tongue poking at the tight pink opening.

I stood up and walked around her, grabbed her jaw.

"Or are you not feeling it?"

I picked up the lube from the floating shelf.

She watched me with huge eyes as I unscrewed the top.

"Well," she said, her voice high-pitched. "It was a full Brazilian wax, so it seems a shame to waste it. I hate throwing money down the drain."

I paused.

"You spent like a hundred dollars on dog treats."

"It's Christmas," she protested.

"I'm going to make a white Christmas in your ass."

"He does love the holidays." She winked at me.

I spread her ass cheeks again, having to pause and bite my lip to keep from coming as she gasped when she felt my lubed-up fingers against her. She was so tight as I eased in a finger, first one, feeling her whole body shudder with anticipation. Then another, stretching her as she accepted me.

"You're going to take all my virginity, aren't you?" The words were breathy.

My cock jumped.

I added a third finger, curling them into her as she moaned and ground back against my hand.

"I want you, Hudson," she groaned as I stroked inside of her, making sure she was good and ready for my huge cock. "I want to feel your hot cum in me."

I swallowed, trying to get a grip as I positioned myself behind her.

"Take me," she whimpered spreading her legs wider for me, coaxing me in.

I pushed the tip of my cock against her, more careful than when I'd taken her virginity.

"Tell me when," I breathed in her neck.

She was so tight as I pushed into her slowly, letting her feel every inch as I filled her, stretching her. She rippled around me.

With my hands on her hips, I eased out of her.

"Your cock feels sooo good in my ass," she slurred.

I pushed in her again, faster this time, trying to keep in control of the rhythm, keeping her steady, on the edge of pleasure.

"Faster," she moaned. "Fuck me faster. Harder. I want to feel your cum, Hudson," she begged. "Fill me with your hot cum."

Not completely losing myself, because I didn't want to hurt her, I increased the pace, letting her feel my hard cock as I took her, taking her again and again, her cries echoing in time to my thrusts. Her tits bounced as I fucked her.

"You're gonna make me—" She came with a cry that sent me over the edge.

"Feels so good, your cum feels so good," she whimpered as I spilled into her, sinking my teeth in her neck, breathing hard, hissing breaths, my cock spasming in her.

She moaned softly as I disentangled myself from her.

"Okay," she panted. "I think I'm fucked."

"Are you?" I murmured, grabbing her jaw and kissing her mouth again.

I headed back over to the laptop while I let her catch her breath and checked the computer: 88 percent.

Almost there.

I pulled out a vibrator from under the coffee table where Gracie had her laptop.

So sue me. I had no idea how much data she had hoarded on that laptop, and it was that or the off-market Viagra Jake was trying to peddle to me.

I came back over to Gracie and stood in front of her, kissed her nose, her chin.

"You fucked?" I asked her, showering her with little kisses. "Are you sure you're fucked?"

"Yeah," she gasped.

I turned on the vibrator.

"Extra extra sure?" I breathed in her ear.

As soon as the vibrator touched her clit, she was a whimpering, shuddering mess.

"Hudson," she cried, half leaning on me, her skin hot against my bare chest. "You gonna make me come again?"

"Well," I took away the vibrator. "You said you were fucked, so I guess not."

"Asshole."

There was that hungry desire in her eyes again.

I reached for the cuffs.

Her forehead tipped forward, banging into my nose as she kissed me, biting my lip.

"Make me come again."

"I guess I can extend a little charity," I told her, holding the vibrator back against her pussy, satisfied when she let out a soft cry. "It is Christmas, after all."

I felt myself grow hard again as I listened to her gasping, needy noises and watched her grind her hips against my hand and the vibrator.

You better pace yourself.

"You fucked yet?"

"*Nooo*," she slurred. Her hips rocked against the vibrator as she took her pleasure from it. Her hair, sweaty, was plastered to her forehead.

"You look pretty fucked to me," I told her, nipping her ear.

Using my fingers, I scissored them inside of her, using three fingers to fuck her, stretch her, send her over the edge. Her pussy gushed all over my hand as she came on the vibrator.

"Oh, Hudson!"

Her gasps were throaty, lusty.

"You fucked?" I asked, still holding the vibrator against her pussy.

"I need you," she pleaded.

Taking the vibrator away, I set it back on the table, checked the progress, then approached her. Seeing my cum dripping down her legs, her tits rising and falling, was enough to make me fully hard again.

I trailed my wet fingers over her mouth. She nipped the tips of my fingers then suckled them.

I couldn't help it. I slipped my cock between her legs, playing in her pussy.

"You gonna come for me again?" I asked her, kissing the bruises on her shoulder.

I grabbed her round ass, spreading her cheeks. She was still slick with my cum.

"Can I fuck your ass again, Sugarplum?"

Her answer was a shaking, "Y-yes."

"Yes, what?"

"Yes, I want to feel you come in my ass," she moaned.

That was all I needed.

I forced my hard cock in her as she let out a loud cry of pleasure.

I took her harder than I had the first time, knowing she could take me.

"Your cock feels so good." She strained against the handcuffs.

"You feel so tight, Gracie. God, you're such a good fuck." I cursed as I pounded in her, sinking my teeth into her shoulder. I felt her come around me.

"You're mine, Gracie. Don't ever forget it."

With one last thrust, I spasmed in her, filling her.

"I'm yours," she said breathlessly. "I'm yours."

There was a faint beep from the laptop.

I disguised it by nipping her ear and growling, "I've never fucked anyone like I have you."

I gave her another sloppy kiss, still inside of her, not wanting to let her go just yet.

I had to. The data was copied.

I slowly withdrew.

This was the last time I was going to have Gracie.

And I would do anything to keep her.

Chapter 41

GRACIE

"We're supposed to be decorating your apartment," I slurred as Hudson unlocked the handcuffs. My legs were cranberry jelly, and my arms were numb. Everything was sore in the best possible way.

He picked me up, cradling me in his arms as if I weighed nothing. Nuzzling my neck, he carried me back through the apartment, the old wood floors creaking slightly.

"I don't know why all the boys were chasing after your sister when you have the sweetest cunt in the Northeast."

"I'm not—"

"Don't play coy," he murmured, kissing me again. "You know you're sexier than your sister. I'd fuck you any day over her."

Even though I knew it was petty, I basked in the praise. Hudson wanted me!

Still cradling me in his arms, he took me into a spacious bathroom and turned on the tap. Steaming water rushed to fill a claw-foot tub.

He took off my boots, then I sat on the counter, draping my legs on either side of him, kissing him. Not in any anticipation of sex, because he'd completely sated me in every way possible, but just for the familiarity of him, the warm, comforting weight of his arms around me, the way his huge muscular body made me feel safe.

Hudson kissed me softly, taking his time, nuzzling me, whispering to me how much he adored me, how perfect I felt, how sexy I was.

I desperately wanted him to say he loved me. I felt it in my chest—I was falling head over high-heeled boots for him.

I kissed him, my tangled curls falling over his forehead.

"You're everything I've ever wanted, Gracie," he murmured then stood up, me still in his arms, and placed me gently in the water.

I lay back, sinking under the warmth, blowing bubbles under the water. When I surfaced, rubbing the water out of my eyes, I gazed at him. In the low light from the vanity sconce reflecting on the droplets of water on my eyelashes, Hudson seemed like a fairy prince surrounded by starlight.

"A prince of darkness."

His mouth quirked.

"Ignore me. I read too much YA fantasy as a teen. And young adult, let's be honest."

Hudson grinned, a relaxed happy smile that made him seem more like that little boy in the video.

I grabbed his hand, laced our fingers together.

He leaned in to kiss me.

"I can't ignore a girl with tits like those," he said, caressing my wet breasts.

"You can't keep distracting me. We didn't finish decorating for Christmas." I tapped his nose with my nail painted in a red-and-green checker pattern for the holidays.

"Bring the decorations in here," I ordered as I lounged in the claw-foot tub.

"What?" I said to his raised eyebrow. "You said I got to order you around if I let you chain me up. Not to mention I let you come down my chimney."

"Let me?" He snorted. "You were begging me for it."

I stuck my tongue out at him. "You can put on a little home decorating show for me."

He came back in with the bag, muscles bulging as he set it on the floor along with my laptop that still churned out holiday tunes.

"Put on the vintage playlist."

Various 1940s Christmas songs crooned as Hudson unpacked the decorations.

"Very sexy. Now put some candles on the vanity."

"All that glass is dangerous," he protested.

"We'll make sure to move them when we have sex in here," I assured him.

He splashed some of the warm water at me.

I cupped my hands and squeezed, sending a spray of water in his face. I giggled as he sputtered.

"What? I have siblings, too, you know. Though I wish I had a big family like yours. That's all I want for Christmas!" I sang, "A handsome husband. A whole pack of children. Okay, now put some of that garland on the mirror. Yes. Make me wet."

I wolf whistled as he arranged the garland neatly over the antique mirror.

"Did your little sister decorate in here?" I asked as he added some Santa figurines on a floating shelf.

"She did," he admitted as he lit the candles.

"Knew it! I like her already. Send her photos so she knows someone's making sure you're not wallowing in your own filth for Christmas."

He shook his head, smile playing around his mouth.

I patted the water. "Now that your hard work is done, you can come relax."

Hudson slid into the warm water behind me, wrapping strong arms around me, my hair plastered to his chest. I closed my eyes, the smell of the cinnamon-and-spiced-apple candle filling the bathroom, mingling with the steam and the masculine scent of Hudson. I relaxed, savoring the moment.

Turning my head, I pressed my mouth to his jaw.

"You're perfect," I murmured to him.

He kissed me softly. Almost as if in a trance, he said, "I think I'm falling for you."

"I already fell for you," I whispered to him.

We lay like that as the candle burned down.

Finally, Hudson roused.

"You cannot fall asleep in here. Your grandmothers will join forces and kill me if you drown in the tub right before Christmas."

I snorted and sputtered in the water.

Hudson lifted me out of the tub and wrapped me in a big warm fluffy towel.

"Okay," I said as he settled me on his bed.

I am in Hudson's bed! In his bedroom!

"I'm ready for my payback," I told him.

"You're what?" He frowned.

"You said I could have my way with you," I reminded him.

"Now? You were half asleep a moment ago. Don't you want to wait for a better time?" he asked.

"No. I failed the marshmallow test. If there is dessert in front of me, I eat all of it now. Even if I'm already full and it will make me sick."

He worked his jaw.

"Fine."

Gleeful, I clapped and flopped over on the bed, resting my chin on my hands.

Hudson leaned in.

I admired the long, muscular lines of his body, the broad shoulders, the scratched-up face, the washboard abs, that cock.

I beckoned him closer, took that cock in my mouth, and sucked it briefly, feeling the desire awaken in me.

Yeah. I could totally go again. Like I said, all the cookies, all the time, immediately.

I released him with a *pop*, feeling a heady power as he stared down at me with raw desire.

"Tell me what you want, Sugarplum."

"Hmm." I ran my fingernail along the length of his thick cock.

"What do I want for Christmas? First things first, there's a Santa hat in that bag. Go put it on."

He scowled.

I flicked him in the abs, making him hiss.

"Go on." I waved him to the door.

He turned, and I slapped his firm buttocks.

"Almost broke my hand there," I said cheerily.

He came back with the hat.

"Put it on," I coaxed.

He scowled, then he rested it on his dark hair.

"So sexy," I purred. "Mommy wants to kiss Santa Claus."

More scowling from Hudson.

I giggled.

"Tell me what you want," he said in that deliciously deep voice that would forever haunt my wet dreams. "Order me to do it."

"Like a good little Marine?"

Something glinted in his eye.

"Yeah."

I snapped my fingers at him. "Dance!"

"The fuck?"

"Go on, Marine."

"You're supposed to say, 'Suck my clit,'" he argued.

"You always suck my clit. This is a special moment."

Hudson tugged the Santa hat more firmly on his head then did a spin, perfectly balanced on one foot.

I screamed as he did a Magic Mike move, dropping low then thrusting back up.

He laughed at my reaction then took a bow as I applauded.

"Come here." I patted the bed. "I think you earned your Christmas present early. I'm going to suck your cock though, okay, because I don't know if I can come again. You really know how to give a girl a workout."

"Sure you can," he murmured.

I slapped his shoulder. He responded by kissing me, nipping my lower lip, grunting softly as I ran my nails over those muscles and tattoos.

"I want to give you my cock."

He rolled us so we were on our sides.

Propping one of my legs up to give him better access to my pussy, he stroked me as he nuzzled and kissed my neck.

I gasped as I felt myself grow wet from his touch.

"Fuck, Gracie," he groaned as his fingers stroked me, dipping in my opening. "I want to take your tight little cunt."

My breath hitched as he scissored them in me.

His hand cupped my breast, kneading it, pinching the nipple as he finger fucked me slowly, leisurely.

I heard him fumbling in the nightstand, then the ripping of a condom packet.

Then his cock was *there*, sliding into me in one strong motion. He pulled out as I let out a low, long moan, then he thrust into me again, taking me with strong, slow ease.

My fingers clutched the comforter as his hands moved down to stroke my clit, sensitive and raw from his cock and mouth earlier. I let out a long, low cry, my head falling forward as I gave myself up to him.

"I—"

I love you, Hudson.

"I'm going to come," I panted as the pleasure crashed over me.

"I'm not." The words were hot in my ear.

He twisted us so I was on my hands and knees. He grabbed my ass, then he was jackhammering in me, taking me for his pleasure while I cried and begged for him, in time to his thrusts.

"Fuck me. Take me, Hudson. I'm yours."

His pace was unrelenting, and I could feel my thighs tense up, needing release. I moaned loudly as he pounded into me. I knew him now, knew that he was close.

"Come for me, Hudson," I begged.

His fingers worked my clit, bringing me to the edge again. Then he was spilling into the condom with a loud curse as I came around him.

As he kissed my neck, I wished he had come for real in my pussy because then I could have a cute little gray-eyed baby under the tree this time next year.

And that's how you know you've completely fallen dangerously hard for a man.

Thunder clapped.

There was pounding on the metal roof of the old industrial building.

"Is it hailing?" I mumbled.

I sat up. The bed felt cold, and I patted around for Hudson.

"Hudson?" I called.

I padded through the apartment, drawing the blanket around me. Through the windows, I could see the hail coming down.

Maybe he went up to the roof to check if everything was okay?

I peeked out onto the balcony, but didn't see a sign of Hudson.

I shrugged on a pair of his boxers and one of his sweatshirts, wrapping the fabric around me. It smelled like him.

"Hudson?"

I waited around, thinking he might show. Turning on the lights, I busied myself with decorating the rest of his tree, arranging the other homey bits of Christmas décor, and making breakfast. Then I placed the present I'd carefully wrapped for him under his tree. He was going to be so surprised when he got back.

But when the sun started to rise, he still hadn't shown up.

He'd just disappeared.

Chapter 42

HUDSON

A car was waiting for me when the airplane landed on the pitch-dark runway of the small executive airport near the nondescript New Jersey industrial park.

I took the stairs down two at a time, the hard drive tucked safely in a hard case in my jacket. There was so much data, and we were under the gun, so I was having our New Jersey location process it.

Should I have waited until the morning, waited until Gracie had woken up, cooked me a leisurely breakfast, let me make love to her, so that she wouldn't think anything was wrong?

In an ideal world, yes.

Unfortunately, the clock was ticking. The deadline was two days away. We had to find enough incriminating evidence against EnerCheck so that Grayson Richmond would be satisfied. With almost four terabytes of data to sift through, we were cutting it dangerously close.

"Bro!"

"Elsa!" I wrapped my little sister in a hug when she greeted me in the lobby of the warehouse. "What are you doing here?"

"I missed you all, and I heard you were in the Hail Mary stage of your super-duper secret mission."

"I couldn't call Skylar and Layla back to help," Lawrence stated. "Layla would kill me. Literally dead."

"What about the lodge?" I asked my sister.

"Dear cousin Noelle is driving me batty," Elsa said as we walked into the bowels of the facility. "Harrogate is completely insane right now. Someone was caught cheating at *The Great Christmas Bake Off* and then took a rolling pin and smashed up everyone's plum pies. There was a riot."

"There was about to be a riot here if Hudson hadn't gotten that data," Anderson said.

"He always closes the deal." Lawrence slapped me on the back when I handed him the hard drive. "Let's see what this baby has to offer."

My brother carefully plugged in the hard drive, and the light blinked.

"Woof," Talbot said. "Four terabytes of data?"

"There has to be something on it," Jake said, taking a bite of one of the cookies Gracie had insisted I take home with me the other night.

"Score! She has her photos set to sync with the laptop," Lawrence crowed. "Everything we need should be on here."

"Ooh. Has someone been fighting?" Elsa asked, poking at the cut on my jaw while my brothers set up the protocol for the file review.

"His fake girlfriend's ex-fiancé hit him in the face with a hockey stick," Jake said with a laugh.

"Did you win?"

"The hockey game? Of course," I answered smugly.

"No, the fight."

I pushed her lightly. "Do you even have to ask?"

"I interrupt this family reunion to bring you four terabytes of data," Talbot announced, looking up from his computer.

"Clock starts now."

Talbot had created a program that could sort out folders and parcel them to my various employees. Simultaneously, he also ran another text search program to scan any note files or PDFs on the drive for certain keywords.

I poured myself some coffee, black, and settled at a desk to start sifting through files.

"Oh my god!" Elsa exclaimed.

I jumped up.

"Surely it can't be this easy," Anderson said, rushing over to her desk.

Elsa giggled.

"Look at this beautifully decorated apartment. Are you turning over a new Christmas-loving leaf, Hudson?"

I scowled at the photos of my apartment on Elsa's screen.

"His fake girlfriend decorated for him," Lawrence said with a shit-eating grin.

"Look at Hudson underneath the Christmas tree."

"Wait, what?"

"Oh, this girl has it bad for you, bro." Elsa cackled. "Oh my god, look at Hudson with the pug!"

"Pugnog's inbred, and supposedly his eye randomly pops out," I said flatly.

"His name is Pugnog? Adorable! And he's wearing a Christmas sweater!" my sister shrieked, which caused all the rest of my employees to rush over to see what she'd found.

Elsa pointed to the screen. There was a photo of me at Gracie's parents' table, Pugnog in my lap, his eyes going different directions, the dog drooling as I helped Gracie make her gingerbread house.

"She's cute." Elsa punched me hard in the chest.

"Ow!"

My sister knew how to hit. She grew up with five brothers and played hockey, sure, but she also spent time with our cousins in Harrogate and one cousin, Noelle, had, on multiple occasions, been involved in out-and-out brawls in the middle of Main Street.

"Aw, there's Hudson after winning his big game," Jake said with a smirk.

"We should make Gracie a little scrapbook of the two of you."

"This isn't real," I snapped too harshly.

Elsa didn't seem fazed. She just flipped to another photo. It was from earlier that evening—a selfie of me and Gracie in front of the glowing Christmas tree, her kissing my cheek.

"Go back to your desks," I growled. "This is not what any of you are being paid to do."

"I'm not being paid to be here at all," Elsa declared.

Six hours in and no one had had a hit on anything good, though Gracie sure took a lot of high-definition videos of her pug.

Elsa joined me at the coffee table when I went for a refill.

"You're seriously going to walk away from her after this?" Elsa asked. It was 3 a.m., and she was hyped up on caffeine.

"I—"

"Don't you see how much she adores you?" She waved her phone with the photos on it.

"You cannot have those." I tried to grab her phone.

"Too bad."

"It's better that I break Gracie's heart now," I told her viciously. "I'm not stupid. I can see it in her eyes, see how she's falling for me. Especially last night."

"So you just ran away in the middle of the night? Bawk bawk bawk!" Elsa flapped her arms. "Chicken! *Bawk*!"

"St. Nick help me."

Elsa doubled over in laughter as I swore.

"I spend too much time with Gracie."

"Hudson likes Gracie!"

"Elsa," I said grabbing her shoulders. "I can't. Even if I cared about her, which I don't, I can't be with her. That would be wrong. The whole relationship is based on a lie. I used her to get to her company. You don't understand. You don't know Gracie. She's like this pure, good person. She loves Christmas and sings along to the radio and still has all her stuffed animals, and she likes to decorate cookies and make specialty hot chocolate and wear flannel pajamas. I—I can't be with her. She deserves better than me."

"Oh, man." Elsa patted my head like she used to do when we were kids. "You really do have it bad for her."

"No. I'll get over it," I said gruffly. "We're going to make a lot of money on this job. I'll have enough to pay off that loft building I just renovated, and I can send some to our uncle for the lodge."

Maybe that would be enough to assuage my guilty conscience.

"You should at least give Gracie a Christmas present."

"Yeah," I said, suddenly feeling exhausted. "Yeah. I'll do that."

"Make something from the heart," my sister recommended.

"I'm not five. I'm not making her a macaroni necklace." I took a swallow of coffee. "I have to get back to work."

I stood at a desk next to my siblings as we sifted through Gracie's digital life—medical records, internet search history, text message strings.

I still felt sick about what I was doing to Gracie.

Should I give her a present? It seemed like a trite gesture after what I'd done. Not to mention, I didn't give Christmas presents. Maybe I could give her something, a token parting gift, something meaningful. It would be a gift to let her know, if she ever found out the truth—which she wouldn't—that it wasn't all a lie, that a part of me did really care about her.

But what?

The dress.

I went into my office and called the head of my waste disposal company that I used to gain access to people's trash.

"Boss! Merry Christmas!" Trevor yelled into the phone.

"Do you know anyone at the dump in Washington County, Rhode Island?" I asked him.

"My cousin works down there. We got another job?"

"Please bill this to me personally," I said, cupping my hand over the phone. "I need the trash from Gracie's address. I'm looking for antique lace scraps."

"You want all this at the warehouse?"

"We're a bit packed here. Did you already clear out the Quantum Cyber job up in Connecticut? Can you take it there?"

"You got it."

"Tell me your secrets," Elsa hissed at me. "Are you planning a Christmas surprise?"

"It's a long shot." I waited a beat. "Hey, you used to make shadow boxes, right. What would I hypothetically need?"

My sister grinned maniacally. She had had way too much caffeine.

"I'll do it for an unnamed favor to be specified at a later date, no questions asked. Or," she amended, "you can actually come up to the lodge and spend some time hanging out with your family."

"Fine."

"Leave it to me." She slurped her coffee. Her eye twitched.

"I need to go back to Maplewood Falls," I said, grabbing my keys. "Let me know the minute you find anything."

Chapter 43

GRACIE

"**Y**ou don't think it's weird?" I asked Dakota the next day when we were five hours deep into decorating for Kelly's wedding at the historic Canal Club on the water, where rich families of Manhattan used to host their families in the summer.

Yes, this was where I had been going to get married to James. The venue was beautiful—black-and-white marble floor, high plaster ceilings decorated with mythical creatures, huge brass-and-crystal chandeliers with real gas lights. The place had been dilapidated for years, crumbling and disintegrating, until some nameless developer had bought it, painstakingly renovated it, and turned it into one of the hottest wedding event venues in the area.

Too bad I hadn't gotten to have my wedding there. What stung more was, even if I did marry Hudson—which wasn't going to be likely since he had just ghosted me after that intense night where I thought we were having a connection—my family was just going to say I was copying Kelly's idea.

I looked around wistfully. I had kept the decorations more minimal than at the Canning Factory, so that the architecture of the space could really shine.

My phone buzzed, and I scrambled for it.

Hudson: *Sorry for running off. Something came up with work.*
Hudson: *I'll come by to see you.*
Gracie: *We're almost done for the day.*
Gracie: *See you for dinner?*

"Wow," I said, staring at my phone, the screen swimming in my vision as I tried not to cry. "It took him eight hours to respond to my message. What an asshole."

Dakota gave me a knowing look.

"I know," I said dejectedly. "I know you said not to fall for him." I wiped my nose.

"He's a bad boy. That's what they do," she said gently. "Look, you had a night of romance-book-worthy passion. Be appreciative of that, but be prepared to block him and move on with your life."

"I guess." I sighed. "It's just the whole thing feels a little off?"

"It's the postorgasm letdown. You're always worried about getting your next fix. That's why bad boys are dangerous," she said matter-of-factly. "They make you feel special, like you're the most important thing in their life, then they treat you like shit and expect you to take it. Don't play his game. Tell him not to come over unless he's going to fuck your sister."

I winced.

"You just gave that man $3,000." Dakota shook me. "Therefore I better see a marriage end in a fiery explosion in"—she checked her watch—"thirty-six hours."

My fingers hesitated over the text messaging app.

"Hudson does not love you," Dakota stated in a low voice. "He is incapable of loving you. He is an asshole, and that makes him attractive and fun for a hookup situation. That does not make him suitable for the type of life you want to build."

"Hudson said he was falling for me," I said desperately.

"He was lying. He is a bad boy. That's how they are, and Hudson seems like he'd be the worst of the bunch."

I knew what my friend and cousin said was true, and yet, if Hudson had shown up and whisked me away in his arms, I'd forgive him for everything.

Chapter 44

HUDSON

'm losing my edge, I decided as I stalked up the drive to Gracie's house.

I needed to back away. This wasn't going to end well. Gracie was a means to an end, not someone to fall for.

Yet I had the sense that it was already too late.

I'm falling for you.

I couldn't completely ghost her—that would be suspicious—but playing hot and cold with her would hopefully break her of the idea that she and I were truly meant to be.

What if the person I was most trying to convince was myself?

Except I wasn't.

I'm not made for love. My heart is ice.

I was just using her for her information and for sex.

Yeah, that was it.

"The man of the hour!" her uncle called from the den where he and a number of her male family members were watching a hockey game.

"Come watch the game. You want a beer?"

"Sure." I accepted the offered beverage. "Gracie around?"

"Nope. Off doing wedding stuff."

We watched the game, though I was too antsy to sit there for long.

All I could do was think about getting that data.

You'll just have to be patient.

On a whim, I headed down to the basement. On one side was a wine room, on the other more storage. In the back corner, I saw it—a door. It still had her name stenciled on in fading paint.

Gracie.

The hinges were still attached though one looked a little bent.

I carried it upstairs then went back out to the truck, where I'd stashed a toolbox. I headed back into the house and picked up the door, maneuvering it up the small staircase.

It only took me about a half an hour to get her door back on its frame. A little oil and a rubber mallet and it was like it never left.

While I was in her bedroom, I fixed the stiff hinge on the large round window on one of the hexagonal walls and replaced a burned-out light bulb in one of her lamps.

"Hudson?" Gracie said from the doorway as I was inspecting the bottom drawer of her dresser. It looked like it needed a new track. "You're home." She didn't smile.

"Yeah." I stood up, dusting off my hands, feeling almost like a teenager, unsure what to say to her.

"I wasn't sure if you were coming back."

"I told you I was," I said.

"Where did you go?" She set her bag down on the little makeup table.

"Had to work."

"In the middle of the night?"

She was waiting for an answer.

Instead, I pulled her inside the bedroom and shut the door.

"You fixed it."

"Somehow fucking you is better without an audience."

This is it. This is the last time, I thought as I kissed her, hungry, frenzied kisses, knowing I should savor it but wanting all of her.

I pulled at her clothes, needing to feel her all over me. Her shirt came off and fell to the floor along with my shirt and pants. "You're wearing underwear this time," she said, tugging at my boxers.

I tossed them on the floor.

Savor it.

I couldn't. My mouth was all over her. I needed all of her. I tried to memorize her body, the way she smelled, the little gasps that she made.

I didn't even wait to take off her bra and panties before I had my fingers in her pussy.

"I need you on my cock," I hissed, ripping a condom packet and rolling it on.

I pulled her onto the bed with me. I was on my back, her on my chest kissing me as I stroked her through the panties.

"I want to watch you ride my cock," I whispered to her.

She lifted herself up on her knees.

I pulled her panties to the side, lifted her higher, then impaled her on me.

Her head tipped back, and she let out a long, throaty moan as I thrust up into her. She reached behind her to unhook her bra, letting her breasts hang free. I reached up to play with them, feeling the velvety tightness of being inside her. I gazed up at her as she rode my cock, eyes closed in pleasure, like she knew what I wanted, like we were perfectly in sync, made for each other.

Her hips ground against me in needy circles as she lifted herself up and down on my cock, her pussy clenching around me.

I teased her clit, stroked her, felt her crash over the edge. She came with a cry.

I wasn't done.

As she panted in my ear, I tumbled us over on her back on the bed, so I could fuck her into the mattress.

"Fuck, Gracie," I cursed as I slammed into her. "Fuck, I love—"

You.

"—your tight little cunt. Damn. You like being fucked, don't you? You like it when I fuck you with my huge cock, don't you?"

She was making those high-pitched, panting cries as I fucked her hard, my hand clenched on the headboard while she clung to me, taking every inch of my cock.

"Goddamn, Gracie." I grunted as I came in her, the condom catching the load.

I rested my forehead against hers, stared in her eyes.

I would do anything to stay there with her.

Yet if I actually loved her, I would never see her again.

Even though I'd rather tear out my own fingernails than live without her.

Chapter 45

GRACIE

It was the day before the rehearsal dinner.

I was at the country club, walking through the evening's schedule with the manager.

In another blatant copy of my wedding, my sister had opted for having a day of Christmas festivities between the rehearsal dinner and the wedding.

Last year, I had planned to do that so people could party hard at the rehearsal dinner, to which the entire family was invited, and the wedding, which was going to be another big bash.

Any other bride would be at the venue with me, inspecting the final preparations. Of course, my sister had insisted she needed a spa day, a me-treat if you will, in order to recover from all the wedding planning she'd been doing.

Yes, please roll your eyes. I'll wait.

As we walked through the country club, I kept looking around furtively for him—Hudson. He'd disappeared again after we'd made love. He'd gotten a phone call and just vanished again.

It's not love. You don't love him. You hooked up after he fixed your door.

I wondered if the manager had seen him.

Don't ask him. Don't be that needy, weird girlfriend.

Too late.

"Um," I said, interrupting the manager. "I was—er, the bride was wondering if one of your employees would be working the rehearsal dinner—Hudson, Hudson Wynter?"

The manager frowned. "No, he wasn't scheduled for this week, but if you see him, let me know. I need extra hands."

At least Hudson was telling the truth about who he was. But why had he disappeared? Maybe he was just reverting back to his natural state of being a bad boy, like Dakota had said.

I picked at my nail polish then stuck my hands in my pockets, hearing my mother in my head criticizing me for damaging my nails.

After the walk-through with the manager, I gave in and tried to call Hudson again. It just went to a voice mailbox.

Crap.

I ran a hand through my hair then headed back to my parents' house, trying to ignore the sick feeling in the pit of my stomach.

"No word?" Dakota asked in concern when she joined me in the kitchen later to help with dinner.

"He'll show up," I said with more confidence than I felt.

"Hudson coming tonight?" Uncle Eddie asked as I dished out dinner that night.

"I don't think so."

"Did he know you were making meatloaf?" my uncle asked as he poured more gravy on his plate. "Your meatloaf is amazing. If Hudson had known you were making it, he absolutely would have shown up."

I scooped crab, cheddar, chive, and garlic twice-baked potato onto his plate. Yes, it was imitation crab, but if it ain't broke …

"I hope you're not thinking I'm going to start feeding you bacon-wrapped meatloaf smothered in brown sugar and ketchup," his wife said pointedly. "You're going to eat your grilled chicken breasts, and you're going to like it."

"I always made sure my husband knew what to expect for dinner," Grandma Astelle said, dabbing her napkin on her mouth. "Knowing he has something good waiting for dinner ensures your man comes home at night instead of wandering the neighborhood."

"Don't worry. Kelly was with me all day," Aunt Janet joked, "so we know Hudson wasn't with her."

I hunched my shoulders as my family laughed, and Kelly glared at me.

My uncle reached for another slice of meatloaf.

"Give him some salad, Gracie," my aunt told me.

"Sure. There's more in the kitchen," I said, glad for the excuse to escape.

Where was Hudson? Was he going to show up tomorrow? Would I ever see him again? Had I lost yet another boyfriend?

Fake boyfriend.

Yeah, tell that to my heart.

I had saved a piece of meatloaf and a twice-baked potato for myself in the oven. Leaning against the warm oven door, I scarfed down several bites, trying to fill the pit of anxiety.

Dakota hurried in the kitchen, and she grabbed the plate out of my hand.

"What is going on with Hudson? The rehearsal dinner is tomorrow. He knows that, right?"

"He knows. He's just working," I said weakly. "He'll be here tomorrow."

"Girl." She shook me. "You gave that motherfucker $3,000."

"*Shhh!*"

"He probably cut and run," she said in a low voice. "A truck like that is expensive. He has a lifestyle to maintain, and he does it by scamming innocent people."

I shook my head. "He said he owns the Canning Factory."

"I looked it up, and it's some random New York LLC."

I felt sick.

"Maybe he started a shell company so his name wasn't on the property."

"Or maybe he's been lying to you."

"Hudson would never," I insisted, not wanting to believe it. "He said he liked me, said that he was falling for me. I decorated his house for Christmas. He came back yesterday afternoon, and he'll be here for the rehearsal dinner. He has to be. He promised."

"Woman the fuck up," Dakota snapped at me. "You can't rely on flaky people. Stop seeing the good in everyone."

"I see the good in you."

"I ate all your Nutella and blamed the maintenance guys," she said flatly. "I am a bad person. Rely on yourself. Stand up for yourself. For once in your life."

"Hudson is going to propose to me," I said quietly.

Dakota sucked in a breath.

"A fake proposal," I added. "Right after he shows proof Kelly is a cheater."

"Has he actually slept with her?" Dakota asked pointedly.

I squirmed. "Not that I know of?"

"The wedding is in two days, yet there has been no cheating. He was never intending to help you. You picked him up on a bus, Gracie. Stop being so obtuse. Everyone is using you, especially Hudson. He is not showing up," she hissed. "You gave him cash. He is gone."

"He's not."

I refused to lose faith. I believed in Hudson like I believed in the magic of Christmas.

Or maybe it was more like how I believed in Santa Claus, and we all saw how that turned out.

I tried calling him again. This time the phone said the mailbox was full.

"Oh my god." I started to panic. "I think I'm going to puke." The rich meatloaf churned in my stomach. "Oh my god. I thought I was in love with him." I pressed a hand to my chest, fanning myself, trying to get some air. "He took my money, my virginity, and now I'm going to have to watch my sister get married to James. Oh my god."

Dakota shook me. "Snap out of it, Gracie. You can end this wedding. You don't need a man to ruin Kelly's relationship. What would Carrie Nation do?"

"Go after both of them with a hatchet?"

"Exactly. Well, actually no, please don't do that. You don't want to spend Christmas in jail."

"Right," I said faintly.

"Think!" Dakota urged. "You have to come up with a plan. You are the only one who can save you now. Well and me. And Pugnog is there for moral support."

"I'm having a panic attack. I can't do this." I gulped in air.

"Magic meatloaf." Dakota cut off a piece and stuffed it in my mouth.

I snatched the plate back from her and wolfed down several more big bites, the flavors of beef, bacon, and ketchup exploding in my mouth.

"I need a cookie and an eggnog latte. Then I think I may have an idea."

Chapter 46

HUDSON

t felt like a funeral as we watched Elsa scan through the last folder.

My nerves were shot. I hadn't slept since I'd dozed next to Gracie that night in my apartment.

"No," I said, shaking my head. "No."

"There's nothing here," Lawrence said quietly. "I think … Hudson, I think EnerCheck is clean."

"I've been in their office," I snarled at Lawrence, grabbing him. "I was there. It is a complete sham operation."

Anderson pulled me off of him. "Stop it."

"You said it yourself," Talbot said carefully. "That people underestimate Gracie. Maybe … maybe she has actually been running a legitimate company this whole time in the background."

I closed my eyes, trying to control my breathing.

"I cannot," I forced out, "tell Grayson fucking Richmond that we wasted over half a million fucking dollars on a wild-goose chase. Oh fuck." I sat down on a stool and buried my head in my hands.

"He is going to fucking kill us. There is big fucking money riding on this. Hundreds of billions of dollars. He's—he's going to—I don't know, he's going to fucking ruin us."

"We can check the files again," Jake offered.

"We already checked," Elsa said. "There's nothing on the disks. We've all been up for the last thirty-six hours with the team scouring it. There's lots of pug pictures, some work stuff, sure, but nothing incriminating."

I hurt her for nothing.

"Today is the day," I said, feeling like I was watching the scene from far outside my body. "We have until midnight, then Grayson is going to want an answer."

"Welp," Jake declared, grabbing his jacket. "I'm going to get on a plane and fly as far away from here as possible."

"The fuck you are," Elsa said. "We die together!"

"Hell no. I'm going to Vegas," Jake said.

I knew what I was going to do. If I only had a few more hours left on this earth—I was spending them with Gracie.

Chapter 47

GRACIE

"Such a lovely party! I can't believe she organized all of this while she was working, poor dear."

Was Great-aunt Mildred talking about yours truly?

Of course not. Kelly got all the credit. She would always get all the credit. My sister was going to have an amazing wedding, a perfect life, and beautiful children, and it was all because Hudson took my money and ran.

I hadn't wanted to believe it last night. I'd lain in the bed that still smelled faintly of him and wished with all my heart that he'd show up in the morning with the grand revenge plan ready to go.

Then I wouldn't have to use my backup. I could forget that Dakota and I had even planned it.

However, in the cold light of morning, when I finally had stumbled downstairs unable to sleep, there was no Hudson waiting in the kitchen for me.

He didn't show up while I was directing the caterers, he didn't show up when I was changing into my cocktail dress, and now at the party, when all the guests had arrived, he still wasn't there.

Hiding behind one of the large Christmas trees that decorated the space, I opened my clutch and looked at my phone, ignoring the backup plan in a baggie. No missed calls, no messages, no nothing.

Hudson was truly gone.

I wrapped my arms around myself.

"Eat." Dakota appeared in front of me with a plate of reindeer deviled eggs and cranberry brie bites.

"All you've had today were three eggnog lattes. You need your strength."

I scarfed down the food, barely tasting it.

"I can't believe he abandoned me," I said hoarsely. "I can't believe this is the rest of my life. How was I so stupid? I need to go lie down. I can't do this."

"Cut the negative self-talk. Don't you dare chicken out. There are moments in life that define who we are. This?" She tapped my clutch. "Is your moment. You regret the things you don't do, and trust me, you will regret not getting payback on your sister."

"Isn't the best revenge a life well lived?" I said faintly.

"That's for middle school bullies, not sisters who fuck your fiancé the night before your wedding. This calls for scorched earth."

I was hyperventilating. I felt nauseous. Why couldn't Hudson just show up?

"Maybe something bad happened to him," I whispered. "Maybe he wrecked his motorcycle. Maybe he's lying in a ditch somewhere freezing to death, wishing that I was there."

Dakota pulled a bottle of eggnog-flavored vodka out of her purse.

"Or maybe he's in Vegas getting wasted, spending all your money on strippers."

"Hudson's not that kind of man."

"You haven't even known him a month. In fact, you don't really know him at all," Dakota reminded me.

"I should go home. I don't feel well." I felt queasy thinking about that stack of cash I'd given Hudson. "Maybe it's a misunderstanding. Maybe—"

"Stop making excuses for him. Have some liquid courage," my cousin said, tipping the vodka to my mouth.

"That's nasty," I rasped after drinking a few swallows.

"Have some more."

I was starting to feel a little bit better, more floaty. My heart was still racing though. I should cut back on the caffeine in January, I decided as I followed Dakota back out into the party.

"Where's that boyfriend?" Kirk called out when he saw me.

I looked longingly to my hiding spot behind the Christmas tree.

"I think he might be working," I stammered.

"You think?" Violet butted in.

"Didn't you tell him how important tonight is?" Emily demanded. "You can't just let people walk all over you."

"He knows," I said helplessly, wishing I were anywhere else.

"Then he'll be here," Granny Murray assured me. "Drink?"

I waved it away.

"It's Christmas," Emily insisted. "You can't *not* drink on Christmas, Gracie."

"I'm, um, I'm good."

I wasn't.

On the small stage at the front of the ballroom, my sister appeared, a serene vision, glowing in white. James had his arm around her as he escorted her to the head table with the rest of the wedding party.

I felt like puking. This was supposed to be my moment. I had been planning to have a big family baby shower here. Now I was watching my sister get married. Alone.

Because Hudson was a freaking liar.

Or he's going to walk through the door ... now.

... Now?

Maybe now?

My mother took the microphone.

"Gracie, why don't you come up and say a few words?"

Is she freaking for real?

"Are you sure you don't want a drink?" Granny Murray asked out of the side of her mouth.

"I'm not drinking." I set down my clutch on a small table and slowly made my way to the front of the room.

My mother handed me the microphone.

I peered into the crowd. I felt hot and sweaty. Servers were passing out flutes of champagne. An antique silver champagne bucket was sitting on the bridal table, filled with ice.

I longed to grab a handful, just to settle my stomach.

"Thank you all," I began, "for coming tonight to celebrate my wonderful sister and her beloved fiancé. We've had our ups and downs, but family is the most important thing. You and James"—I felt the tears threatening to come—"are starting your journey and creating your family."

Which you thought you were going to have with Hudson except you're completely delusional, and he's not here, and this is going to be the rest of your life except that you'll be $3,000 poorer.

"I can't wait ..." I forced out the words.

"... to be ..."

Just finish.

"... an aunt—" I doubled over.

"Oh my god!"

"Gross!" came the cries of shock as I grabbed the champagne bucket and emptied the contents of my stomach in it.

"Shit," I groaned.

"Oh, Gracie," my mother scolded. "Look what you've done."

"She was looking a little queasy," one of my aunts said.

"You ruined my wedding!" my sister screamed.

I felt like I was going to faint from the nausea and the humiliation.

My cousins were recording the scene. Several people were taking photos, and everyone was pointing and whispering. My family was going to be talking about this for years.

"You just did this because Hudson dumped you," my sister screeched. "And you're jealous."

"He dumped her?" came the murmurs from the crowd.

"Praise god!" Grandma Astelle declared.

"Screw you, you old bat. Hudson was a catch," Granny Murray insisted.

"He was a bad influence," Grandma Astelle said, staring down her nose. "Gracie gets that from your side of the family."

"If you mean her ability to get top-tier dick, then yes, she does, and I'm proud of it," Granny Murray hollered. "And it skipped a generation, because my daughter married a complete loser with a small penis."

"You take that back. All the problems with my grandchildren are because your daughter is a terrible mother."

Granny Murray took a swing at Grandma Astelle, who blocked it with her cane then pulled out her sword.

It was a slow-moving fight as the two old women went at each other, Astelle using two hands to slash the sword at Granny Murray.

"My party is ruined, and it's all her fault, Daddy," Kelly was whining, pointing at me.

"Gracie, clean this mess up," my mom hissed, "and stop your grandmothers from fighting. We're going to end up on the evening news."

"You need to stop being so hard on a pregnant woman," Dakota yelled, hands cupped around her mouth.

Granny Murray dropped the chair that she was about to throw at Grandma Astelle.

The ballroom went dead quiet.

"Are you pregnant, Gracie?" my father asked in horror, the microphone picking up his voice.

I looked around at my grandmothers fighting, my family with their cameras out, my sister with her smug face, and the champagne bucket full of puked-up vodka.

We die like men.

"Yes," I said, holding my stomach. "Yes, I am pregnant."

"So that's why she was puking."

"Congratulations!"

"Who's the father?" Uncle Bic yelled out.

Everyone looked to me expectantly.

Granny Murray snorted. "It's not James's—clearly it's Hudson's."

"Hudson!" my uncles roared.

Guess they're excited ... wait ...

In the back of the ballroom was the man I'd been pining for over the last thirty-six hours and who couldn't have picked a worse time to show up.

"Congratulations!" My cousins and uncles were shaking his hand while Hudson looked confused.

Behind me, I didn't even have to look. I knew my sister was fuming.

"You don't announce your pregnancy at someone else's wedding," she was snipping to her bridesmaids.

I stood there awkwardly, hand still on my stomach.

One of my aunts took the puke bucket away while another one handed me a cup of ice chips.

"I could tell," Aunt Giana was saying as she petted my hair. "You were looking very round."

"That's why she wasn't drinking," Emily added, crowding around me with the rest of my excited family.

"Do you know if you're having a boy or a girl?"

"When's the wedding?"

Then Hudson was in front of me. He looked ragged, like he'd just survived a death march.

"Gracie."

"I um .... Hi. I didn't think you were coming. You ignored my calls."

"Sorry. Work."

"No worries!" I said, forcing my mouth into a smile. "So, surprise. Early Christmas present. I'm pregnant."

"*What?*" he snarled.

Come on, dude, I sent silent thought-waves to him. *Remember the revenge plan.*

Sure, it wasn't the full plan, but it was something. No, Kelly's wedding wasn't ruined, but we'd sure stolen the spotlight.

"You're not pregnant," Hudson said flatly.

"She is. Here's the test." Granny Murray stuck the pregnancy test Dakota had begged her friend from school to pee on since she was recently postpartum. The friend hated Kelly because Kelly had stolen her boyfriend and said she would do it for free, but those bribery cookies looked too good to pass up.

I smiled weakly at Hudson.

"You're going to be a dad."

"The hell?" He had a wild look in his eyes. "Gracie, you can't be pregnant."

"*Please*, Hudson," I hissed.

Unfortunately, he did not receive my silent messages.

He ran his hand through his dark hair.

"I mean, fuck, you can't think I'm the father, can you?"

The crowd let out a collective "*Oooh.*"

"Who else could it be?" James demanded.

Hudson stepped back shaking his head.

"It's not me. I can't—I'm not—that is not mine."

I felt the tears start. Days of no contact, running off with my money, and now Hudson shows up and acts like this? Who did my fake boyfriend think he was, not acting like the fake father of my fake baby?

"You asshole!"

I threw the cup of ice at him.

"Coward!" I screamed as he turned away from me.

Hudson didn't pause as he left the venue.

"Oh my god," my cousin Connie was saying. "Did you see that? How many men is she sleeping with that she doesn't even know the father?"

I wanted to crawl into bed, curl up under my covers, and not come out until spring.

How could Hudson just betray me like that?

My dad patted me awkwardly on the arm.

"Congratulations, sweetheart. Guess I'm going to be a grandfather."

"I bet it is Hudson's," Logan was saying confidently to our cousins. "Logically, who else could it be? Dakota, was she dating anyone else?"

"Nope."

"Hudson just got cold feet." My uncle slapped me on the shoulder. "Don't worry. It happens. When your aunt told me she was pregnant, I started driving then ran out of gas in Pennsylvania, and she had to come pick me up. Happily married thirty-five years," he said cheerfully.

"Poor Gracie." One of my aunts draped a blanket around my shoulders. "Don't cry. You just need to give Hudson a cooling-off period. He'll come around."

"I'm going to be a grandmother!" my mom was ecstatic as she told her sister.

At least someone was happy.

"They need to get married," my dad was muttering, walking around, his fist balled up. "They just have to get married, that's all there is to it."

"… met him in a gas station," Astelle was complaining loudly to anyone who would listen. "Gracie is having a gas-station baby. My granddaughter. The horror of it all."

"I like gas stations," Granny Murray argued.

Kelly took the microphone.

"I just want to say that normally a bride would be really upset that her sister would steal her thunder, but not me. I'm glad Gracie is having a baby because I have an announcement too. James and I are pregnant!"

"We are?" James was shocked.

"Surprise, baby! You're going to be a daddy."

Oh no. My sister did not just steal my fake pregnancy thunder.

There were cries of congratulations.

"And my man didn't run off," Kelly added as James kissed her.

Before I could stop him, James came over to me and kissed me on the cheek.

"Congratulations." He was so smug and self-righteous.

"Don't worry, Gracie, this is perfect. You can quit the company and watch both babies. I believe in charity for single mothers because, let's face it, no matter what anyone says, Hudson is not coming back for you."

Chapter 48

HUDSON

A father?

Gracie was pregnant?

My brain spun, trying to do the math. I hadn't been with her that long; it literally couldn't be mine, right? *Right?*

I pulled out my phone trying to keep it together enough to ignore all of Grayson's missed calls. He was too careful to leave a text message or voicemail, but I was sure I could feel his fury from two states away. In the background, I could hear the loudspeaker from Kelly's wedding.

He was going to fucking kill me, I thought as I googled how soon you can determine a pregnancy.

"Eight days, seven days," I counted backwards. "This website said five."

"Could be ... fuck." I sat down on the curb outside of the country club, getting strange looks from well-dressed wealthy people out to enjoy their holiday in splendor.

My boss came running after me.

"Where the hell are you going? Aren't you here to work? We're short-staffed. Go get your vest on."

I felt dazed.

"I'm not. I'm not on the schedule for today."

He blew out an angry breath. "Then you can't sit here."

"He's my guest!" a woman trilled. Kelly.

Why was she out here? Didn't she just say she was pregnant? Shouldn't she be with James?

"All right, ma'am," my boss said warily.

I knew I was going to hear about it at my next shift, if I survived that long.

Tick-tock.

Grayson called me again. I declined the call.

There was a reason people didn't fuck with billionaires. They were, in many ways, above the law. I knew several people I used to serve with in the military who Grayson could call and have me taken out. Shit. He had probably already called Crawford Svensson and had a hit out on me right now.

"You poor thing," Kelly said, stroking my back.

"I'm fine," I replied, pressing my fingers to my temples. Wrong.

I was panicking.

Do not panic. You're being hysterical. You haven't had any sleep. Panic is dangerous. You can fix this; you can fix anything.

Maybe there was something in her apartment I'd overlooked?

I knew though. There was nothing.

I'd tried every avenue, rifled through every potential source.

I'd failed.

Grayson was not going to take "sorry I screwed up" for an answer.

"Kelly," I said, glancing at her then away. "Just go back inside."

She ignored me.

"My awful sister did this to you." She gave me a sympathetic look. "You must be in shock."

Could there be a way to spin this to Grayson, ask for some sort of mercy, give him a credit on the next job?

Maybe. If the stakes hadn't been so high.

What if I could use the baby? Gracie was pregnant. I could beg Grayson for leniency because I was going to be a father.

Now there was an idea.

I needed to find Gracie.

"Gracie—she's always been the jealous type, not just of me, but of everyone," Kelly was saying as her fingers carded through my hair. "I wouldn't worry if I were you. I honestly don't think she's pregnant. She totally just made it up for attention."

"Made it up? Why would she …"

Of course.

You underestimate her.

She had played the damsel in distress on the bus, needing a big, strong bad boy to ruin her sister's wedding, but I'd flaked, left her in the dust, and she'd come up with another plan.

I let a hollow laugh escape my throat.

And yet …

"I wish she was pregnant."

"Why?" Kelly wrinkled her nose. "She's immature. She'd be a terrible mom. Do you know," Kelly scoffed, "she keeps a Festivus book?"

"A what?"

"A book of grievances," Kelly said in a mocking tone. "Anytime people don't listen to her or ignore her terrible advice, she just writes it all down in this little book. I found it in her room once. It has stickers all over it and everything. She has a whole bunch of them. Sometimes if I'm bored, I sneak in there and read them. She keeps them in this fake hidden drawer in her bookcase, like she's twelve or something."

Kelly tossed her hair, letting it flick in my face. She linked her arm with mine, leaning against me. "My sister is obsessed with James—she's constantly writing down things about him. Anytime she thinks he's mean to her at work or doesn't want to implement her stupid ideas, she just writes it all down. Can you believe it? She's crazy. Gracie is so not over James. He moved on to someone better, and it seems like you are too."

She ran her finger over my lower lip as I stared at her, her words locking into place.

"I could kiss you right now," I breathed.

"Can you?" She shimmied her shoulders.

I stood up.

"I have to go."

"You can't just say that to a girl then leave."

"I have something to take care of," I said brusquely. "I'll see you later."

I didn't dare to hope as I drove right under the speed limit over to Gracie's parents' house.

It was dark, the front door locked, but I picked it easily then crept past Pugnog sleeping in his basket up the stairs, up to the attic, up to where I'd made love to Gracie in her bed the other night.

I allowed myself a fleeting moment to breathe in her scent, remember her, then I searched the room for the secret drawer.

It was stupid. I should have found it earlier. I'd searched her apartment but never thoroughly searched her childhood bedroom. Because what twenty-nine-year-old woman keeps work-related paper journals hidden in her childhood bedroom?

Gracie, that's who.

They were right where Kelly had said they'd be.

Notebook after notebook—bless Gracie, each entry dated and time-stamped. It was all there—everything I had been searching for. She had logged every time James did something shady with accounting, every time her father farmed out some aspect of the coding to a Chinese firm against her advice, every time EnerCheck hired an illegal foreign student to work part-time. It was all there.

"Merry Christmas," I breathed.

My phone rang again. I pressed the green button.

"Where," Grayson said, cold anger laced in his voice, "are you? It is almost midnight, and I do not have what you promised, what I paid you to provide to me."

"You need to have a little faith in the magic of Christmas."

"You better not fuck with me."

"I just found it," I said in a rush, and I stuffed the notebooks in my messenger bag. "I have it here. I found it,

442 • Alina Jacobs

everything—there's enough to bury the whole company. I'm bringing it to you now."

There was a long pause.

"Huh," Grayson said. "Really?"

"Of course," I said, forcing my voice to steady. "I told you. I always deliver."

"So you do."

I hung up the phone and buckled the straps in my messenger bag, the seams practically bursting.

"Just get out, get to Manhattan, don't stop driving until you hand these off," I told myself.

My footfalls were light as I made my way down the stairs.

This had to be a dream. Maybe Grayson had already killed me and I was in purgatory.

I patted the messenger bag, feeling the books there, solid under my hand. No. This was real. I'd done it.

In the living room, there was the telltale sound of slobbering, snorting, and dog paws. Pugnog stumbled out into the foyer, whimpering.

"You need to go out?" I asked him.

Just leave.

But I couldn't just leave the dog like that.

"Okay, come here, buddy," I said, setting the messenger bag on the floor. "Come on." I picked up the dog. "I'm going to let you out, but this is not a tasting-menu situation. You need to take a piss where I tell you to."

Pugnog yipped as I unlatched the door.

"Oh, fuck!" I yelled as the dog peed all down my shirt, jacket, and pants.

"What the hell, Pugnog? God damn it."

I dumped the dog out in the bushes and tried to clean off the worst of it.

"I said when I tell you to, Pugnog."

The dog's eyes rolled in his head, and his tongue fell out of his mouth.

"Fine. Fuck it," I said, gingerly stripping off my clothes. I shivered slightly as the freezing-cold winter air hit my bare skin.

"Towel, towel," I muttered as I dumped the little dog back in the house, leaving the filthy clothes in a pile by the door. I hurried to the kitchen, opening drawers, grabbed a towel, and ran it under the faucet.

"There's my bad boy," Kelly purred.

This is a fucking horror movie.

"Kelly, I can't do this right now. God, where are your clothes?"

"Same place as yours," she said and tweaked the nipple rings on her boobs.

She stretched up against my bare chest, grabbed one of my hands, and forced it down her panties, grinding against it and moaning.

"I can't wait to have your huge cock inside me. You feel how wet I am for you, Hudson?"

"You're engaged," I hissed at her.

She licked her lips then bit me on the pec. "I know you like to fuck another man's woman. It makes you feel powerful." She grabbed my jaw and kissed me.

"Don't pretend like you don't want to come in my pussy. I could feel it as soon as we first locked eyes. Every time James stuck his puny little cock in and I had to pretend to enjoy it, I was thinking about you. I know you were putting on a show for me. You're so sick of my sister. I bet she's like a dead starfish."

"You're pregnant, Kelly," I snapped.

She let out a wild laugh.

"Right, 'pregnant,' and a few months from now, I'm having a miscarriage, and everyone will feel sorry for me. I'll get lots of presents."

"What about James?" I asked, trying to extricate myself from her.

"I just have to stay married to him for three years, then I get a big payout. I'm going to have a little fun before I'm shackled to that loser."

She was like a killer octopus, her limbs latched around me.

"I want to feel that big cock in my pussy, Hudson," she said and made a porn-star moan. "Come down my chimney, Santa. I'll be your good little reindeer and let you ride my sleigh all night long. You can hold the reins."

She rubbed the nipple rings along my chest.

There was a heartbroken cry, and the kitchen lights flicked on.

"Hudson?" Gracie said. Her brown eyes were horrified and filled with tears.

"Damn," one of her cousins said, taking a swig from a bottle of champagne. "Lost your man again on Christmas."

Chapter 49

GRACIE

Kelly kissed Hudson again. His hands were still down her panties, like I wasn't even there, like neither of them even cared that they were naked in the kitchen, having sex in front of me.

"Hudson, how could you?" I sobbed.

"This wasn't what was supposed to happen."

Yes, it was. Remember? This is literally what you paid him to do.

Maybe Hudson was doing the nasty with Kelly because he was sorry for flaking earlier, I told myself, and he was going to come back to me later like at the end of a Hallmark movie and sweep me up in his arms, saying that he really did love me and he wanted to be my real boyfriend.

Yes, that was absolutely what was happening.

Christmas delusions are back on the menu, boys!

"Hudson, I thought you loved me," I wailed, really giving my all for the performance. Yes, I'd played a donkey in the church nativity pageant when I was a kid, and it was quite the showstopper.

"I'm having your baby," I sobbed. "How could you sleep with my sister?"

"How could he not?" Kelly was triumphant. "Look at you. You don't belong with a man like him."

"Gracie," Hudson said, pushing Kelly off. "Please."

"Kelly?" James demanded, shoving me aside. "What is the meaning of this? Hudson, were you having your way with my fiancée? Call the police."

Astelle smacked James on the side of the head.

"Ow!" He grabbed his head.

"Don't be an idiot," Grandma Astelle thundered. "Once a cheater, always a cheater. You asked for it as soon as you proposed to her."

"Mazel tov, Astelle," Granny Murray said and raised her glass of vodka. "Broken clock is right twice a day after all."

"James, honestly." Kelly sauntered over to him, like she was wearing a full-coverage evening gown and not thong panties and her hair extensions. "Hudson's the type of guy a girl hooks up with. I didn't mean to fall in his arms. It's the pregnancy hormones."

I tried to contain my excitement as I waited for him to go for the kill, total annihilation, nuclear revenge, blow up the marriage and take James down.

But he didn't lay into anyone. Instead, he bowed his head and wouldn't look at me. "I'm so sorry, Gracie," he said quietly. "I better go."

"Hudson?"

Head still bowed, he walked quickly to the front door, through the crowd of my family, none of whom had wanted to stay at the country club when family drama was afoot.

The front door slammed behind him.

"Can't we all just go back to the rehearsal dinner?" my mother begged. "There's salmon."

"You're just going to sweep it under the rug?" James spat.

"Don't act like this is the first time you met my mother," I said, under my breath.

"It was a mistake, James. We didn't even do anything," Kelly purred.

James was wavering.

After weeks of planning a big, grand nuclear revenge, this was what I got. Three thousand dollars down the fucking drain. Fuck Hudson.

Fine. I'll do it myself.

"Are you seriously going to take her back?" I asked James, lacing a decade's worth of pent-up venom in my voice.

He jerked back.

"Are you seriously going to roll over and let her whip you? Let her drain your bank account, nag you in your own home, all while you know without a shadow of a doubt that she's bringing back men to fuck in your house? It's embarrassing how little self-respect you have. Hudson was right when he said you weren't a real man. We all literally heard her tell Hudson that she wasn't pregnant. And you still want her back?"

"Shut up, Gracie. I love you, James," Kelly begged. "I am pregnant."

"She's not," Connie called. "I heard it too."

"Kelly doesn't love anyone other than herself. Why? Because my parents enable her. She can do no wrong. She has and always will be treated as the baby of the family and allowed to get away with anything. So congratulations, Mom and Dad." I applauded. "You raised a woman who has no problem cheating on her fiancé two days before her wedding and lying about a pregnancy."

My voice rose, carrying through the house.

"You all have belittled me, berated me, used me, treated me like shit, ignored my mental health and sanity in favor of Kelly. I have put up with it way longer than I should have. James, I recommend that you learn from my mistakes and dump Kelly out in the cold."

"She's just jealous, baby," Kelly cried to James. "Mom, make her stop."

"Gracie, why are you acting like this?" my mother demanded.

I turned on her. "Because I'm tired of you treating me like my feelings and desires don't matter."

"You didn't have to go get pregnant out of wedlock from some boy from the wrong side of town to make your point," my mother snapped.

I drew myself up. "Hudson is not *some boy*. He is a grown, adult man, military veteran, and landowner. He works harder than anyone else in this family, and yes, I see all of you listed on payroll, yet never see you in the office," I told my cousins and extended family, who all looked around shifty-eyed.

"Be that as it may, Hudson is still an absentee father," my dad said with a frown. "At least James is here."

"You know what, James?" I threw up my hands. "Marry Kelly at your own peril. That?" I pointed to my mom. "Is your future and your kids' future. Good fucking luck. I'm not taking this anymore. I'm out."

Then James said, "I'm out too. The wedding is canceled."

"No!" Kelly cried, grabbing James's shirt.

"Boo. I wanted cake," Logan hollered.

I picked up Pugnog.

"Gracie, this isn't like you. Gracie, come back," my mom demanded, racing after me.

"No. It looks like there's a room free at the cute little boutique hotel downtown. I'm staying there tonight."

Granny Murray whooped and pumped her fist.

"You see?" Astelle berated my father. "I told you not to marry that Bethany. Look at the state of your children."

"Astelle," my mother shrieked, "there is nothing wrong with my children."

"Eh?" Granny Murray waved her vodka glass. "Two out of three ain't bad odds."

I felt like a queen as I walked out of the house, head held high.

My feet crunched in the snow on the walkway.

If only Hudson would roll up on his motorcycle and we'd ride off into the—well, not sunset, it was pitch-black—but into the snowy winter night.

Instead, there was James, his hand on my lower back.

"You were amazing back there," he gushed to me. "I wish you'd never given up on us, Gracie. It was heartbreak that pushed me back to your sister. Can you please forgive me, muffin?"

It was the pet name I hated.

"James," I said as he smiled at me, smug.

"Yes, darling?"

"Fuck off."

"Hudson ran off because he felt guilty," I told Pugnog when we were in the cozy hotel room.

I'd stopped at the country club first and asked the caterers very sweetly if I could make a to-go plate. They'd packed up a box of food for me and included a bottle of champagne and, of course, desserts. I'd planned that rehearsal dinner, goddamn it, and I had earned this food.

I'd done it! All—well, mostly all—by myself. I had stood up to James and my parents and my sister.

Some celebratory sex sure would be nice right about now.

I broke the rules and texted him.

Gracie: *The wedding is off!*
Gracie: *Whoo!*
Gracie: *I have food and champagne.*

I sighed as I waited for a reply.
… and waited.
Finally, I broke down and called him.
No response.
I rolled over on the bed, drawing the fluffy robe around me.

Gracie: *No hard feelings on my part BTW.*
Gracie: *Take no prisoners, right?*

I ate a bite of the cake. Why not eat dessert with dinner?
I flipped through the TV channels, hearing phantom pings from my phone. Hudson had to respond, right?
Maybe he was driving.
Maybe he thought I was upset.

Maybe he was with someone else.

No way. He was trying there at the end to ruin my sister's wedding, to try to help me, because *he promised.*

He wouldn't just disappear. I think he cares about me. I'm sure he cares about me.

Fuck it.

Gracie: *Will this make you come see me?*

I pulled back the robe, exposing my tits, and snapped a few photos and sent them to Hudson's number.

Then I sat on the bed and waited for him to respond.

Chapter 50

HUDSON

Should I show up to a dangerous billionaire's house in the middle of the night?

Probably not.

But fuck it. Fuck everything.

I pounded on the front door of the penthouse.

"What the fuck is wrong with you, coming here? You should have called me and told me to meet you somewhere more discreet," Grayson said when he opened the door.

"Why? You got some Rockette here?" I snapped at Grayson. "Throwing a rager?"

He shut the door behind me.

I'd been in his home before, though 'home' was probably inaccurate. Grayson Richmond lived in a sterile museum. There was hardly any furniture and none of the little homey touches like Gracie would have included.

Grayson's cold green eyes focused on the books in my hands.

"Follow me."

We headed through the dark, empty penthouse—no knickknacks, no pictures, no personal items.

This man has no soul.

Once in the study, I shoved aside the paperwork he'd been occupied with and slammed the books down on the desk.

"Look who's back on my good list."

Fuck him.

I would never forget Gracie's horror when she saw me with her sister, her shock as she stared at me as I walked out on her. I had to watch her heart break, and I couldn't even go to her when she begged me to all because of Grayson, because of this job.

He opened a notebook at random and made an appreciative noise.

"They're all like this," I told him as he flipped through the book. "Even a single page could bury EnerCheck Inc. And all the books together? It's a goldmine."

"She even time-stamped many entries. She also notes when the incident happened and when she wrote it down. You could use these as court evidence, they're so watertight." He whistled, a surprisingly casual move for him. He must be surprised.

"I told you, people underestimate her," I said, feeling proud of Gracie. It was hard to earn the respect of a man like Grayson. She'd done it without even officially meeting him.

"You really did deliver," Grayson said, green eyes glittering in the lamplight. "Now I need you to find some way of laundering this. Can you cross-reference her—"

"Already got you covered," I said. "You could just post all these on Facebook tonight if you wanted. If you have any concerns about the legality of it, well, a company whistleblower clued me in to them. Kelly's the one who told me about the books. She'll testify to it, I would bet, just to fuck over her sister."

"Huh," Grayson said, crossing his arms and leaning on his desk. "Her own sister? You sure?"

My heart clenched, remembering the text messages from Gracie I'd scanned in the elevator.

"Gracie blew up her marriage and made Kelly look like a fool in front of her entire family after she got caught kissing Santa Claus under the mistletoe."

"Sounds like you got both jobs finished just in time to be home for Christmas," Grayson said, deadpan.

"Fuck you. I don't care if you fire me, but fuck you."

"I'm not going to fire you. You're incredibly valuable to me." He stepped around his desk, sat down, and pulled out a checkbook. It wasn't the kind my mother used to use to write bad checks. This was the type with the big fancy checks and was a literally the size of a book.

Grayson opened the checkbook and pulled out a fountain pen that probably cost more than the truck I'd driven there in. The nib scratched on the expensive paper.

My phone buzzed again. It was her. I knew it.

After a mission, I destroyed my phones. I would have to do it tonight. Gracie would be out of my life forever.

Grayson handed me the check. "Merry Christmas. There's some extra in there since you went above and beyond. The whistleblower protection was a nice touch."

I felt dirty taking it.

This was what it was all for? I'd ruined Gracie's life for a piece of paper?

She was happy right now, but that was because she didn't know that Grayson Richmond had her in his sights. He was just waiting to pull the trigger.

I threw the keys to the truck on Grayson's desk.

"Thank you for your business."

My phone buzzed again.

"I'd get you a drink, but it sounds like you're busy." He nodded to the pocket with my phone.

"Probably my brothers," I lied.

Grayson gave me an assessing look.

"They're messaging your burner phone?"

I scowled at him and turned on my heel.

"Truck's parked in the public deck three blocks down. Oh, and one more free bit of advice," I said over my shoulder, "since it is Christmas."

"Yes, I suppose it almost is."

"You should consider hiring Gracie."

"Why, because if I don't, you will?"

"No," I said bitterly. "She's too dangerous to have around. She's going to figure out that I screwed her. She's too clever not to eventually figure it out. Then I'll have a weapon at my back. She has a hard-on for elaborate revenge schemes, you see."

"Why would I want her in my company if she's a ticking time bomb?"

"Because you're a billionaire. You can handle the risk better than I can."

"You feel guilty."

"I don't," I lied.

Grayson smirked. "It appears as if the cold-blooded mercenary grew a heart this Christmas. How sweet. I'll see you in the new year, Hudson."

"Yeah, sure."

I sat there in my office drinking, just so I wouldn't have an excuse to drive.

I looked at the picture blearily—her pretty mouth, her huge tits. In the photo, Gracie was lying back on the bed, her fingers down between her legs.

"She's not mad at you. You could go to her, be there in three and a half hours, three if you really pushed the bike."

I took another long swig from the bottle.

"You shouldn't," I reminded myself. "You're tired and stressed out. Ignore it. Ignore her."

There would be no happily ever after because this was about to blow the fuck up.

I stared at the photo again.

Another text message came from her.

Gracie: *Are you ok?*

No, Gracie, I am not okay.

Gracie: *I can kiss it and make it better.*

Elsa knocked on the doorframe of my office.

"Delivery from Santa's workshop."

Elsa set the shadow box with the bits of bridal lace, Gracie's great-grandmother's photo, a couple of little miniature items like a small dressmaker's doll, and a small handwritten note with the great-grandmother's name and what the items were from and the year. There were also a few other photos of Gracie's great-grandmother's wedding and engagement.

"Where'd you get that photo?" I asked, pointing to one in the corner. It showed two figures silhouetted by the light of a fire, the man holding Gracie's' great-grandmother's hand.

"The proposal photo? It was on Gracie's hard drive. I snagged it before Lawrence destroyed the evidence."

"Man, old-timey people really had it good, didn't they?" I took a swig from the bottle. "Chill by the fire, get a wife. That guy didn't even have to get on one knee."

"I think it's a sweet photo," Elsa said, poking at me.

"Thanks, Elsa." She took the shadow box back and rolled out some wrapping paper on my desk.

"Demarcus made tres leches cake, if you want something to soak up that booze," she offered as she expertly wrapped the present, a skill she'd learned from all her holiday retail jobs.

"Maybe."

My phone beeped again after Elsa had rejoined the party.

Gracie: *I miss you.*

There was only so much a man could take.

Fuck. I needed to be with her.

I hauled myself up off the couch.

"Where you heading, boss? We're having a Christmas party!" Talbot called to me.

"Whoo! Look at that bonus!" Jake was dancing on the table with Grayson's check.

"Give me that check before you ruin it," Anderson said, taking it from Jake. "I'm putting this in the safe. We need to deposit it first thing, Hudson. Hudson?"

I was slowly dragging myself to the door.

"Where are you going?"

"The bus station."

Chapter 51

GRACIE

The street in front of my parents' house was a parking lot when I walked up the next afternoon. The snowstorm had cleared out, and the sky was a crisp blue. The sunlight reflecting off the white snow was blindingly bright.

I grimaced as I headed up the walkway, bracing myself for nosy relatives. Everyone must want to know the latest gossip on Kelly and well, me, for that matter.

Pugnog snorted in his baby carrier as I let myself in through the front door.

"Roscoe Energy Solutions is here!" Dakota said, freaking out as she raced over to me.

"Here? Why? How?" I said in confusion.

"Didn't you see the news?"

"No." I had fallen asleep in a champagne-and-cake-induced stupor and only woke up when the cleaning lady demanded she be allowed inside for my dirty towels. Now I was ready for my afternoon snack and another nap.

"What happened?" I asked as I set Pugnog's carrier down on the floor in the foyer.

"It's really bad, Gracie," Dakota said as she ushered me inside. The motion-activated dancing Santa started singing "Jingle Bell Rock."

"What did you do, Gracie?" James demanded when I went into the living room where my family was gathered.

"I didn't do anything. I haven't even been here. Oh, hello, Mr. Roscoe." I weakly greeted the CEO of Roscoe Energy Solutions.

"Can I get you anything? Water? Tea? Coffee?"

"You can get me information on why these notebooks, *your notebooks*, are all over the news," he said, pointing at the TV, where a blond reporter on the national business news network was talking about shocking revelations about Roscoe Energy's subcontractor EnerCheck Inc.

The stock ticker on the bottom of the page showed Roscoe Energy shares dropping sharply.

"It's breaking news in the business world. The big hedge funds smell blood in the water. Svensson Investment is downgrading Roscoe Energy's rating, and Van de Berg Insurance has allegedly quietly been telling their clients to prepare for the worst and up their policy coverage. Still no word from the CEO of Roscoe Energy," one reporter said. "Back to you."

"Up next," the news anchor said. "Will there be a federal investigation? We have our legal expert here to join after commercials."

"This is a travesty. This is a disaster!" Mr. Roscoe thundered.

One of the corporate lawyers that flanked Mr. Roscoe dropped a stack of printouts in front of me on the coffee table.

"Where did you get this?" I asked, sitting down hard in a chair.

"A better question is why were you keeping a log of every little thing that could be used to take us down, Gracie?" James demanded.

"Because none of you were listening to me!" I shrieked. "I told you not to put all the family on payroll and have foreign unpaid interns"—I made air quotes—"to work for the company. I told you it was a bad idea. I told you not to invest the payroll in James's friend's cryptocurrency scheme. *I told you.*"

"If you knew it was a bad idea, why did you write it down? Didn't you think of how this would look?" my dad demanded.

"The notebooks were in my secret drawer. It was hidden." I pressed my hands to my throat. "No one knew about that drawer except for me and Dakota and … wait … *Kelly.* You went snooping in my room, didn't you?"

"Me? I don't even work at EnerCheck." My sister acted offended.

"According to these documents, you are one of the highest-paid employees," the VP of finance stated, pointing to a highlighted entry from one of my Festivus journals. The older man looked like he was going to have a stroke, he was so red-faced.

"Kelly, I swear to god." I raced up to my bedroom, Kelly running up behind me.

"It's not me. It wasn't me."

I tore off the window-seat cushion and opened the secret compartment in the built-in bookcase.

It was empty.

"You did this," I yelled, running back downstairs. "Dad, do you see this? She stole my journals just like she stole my toys when we were little and wrecked your car and stole my laptop. You did this because you were mad that I broke up your marriage, Kelly."

The CEO's lawyers had to hold him back.

"You tanked a multibillion-dollar international corporation over some girlish spat?" he hollered at us.

"To be fair, Kelly was banging Gracie's boyfriend in the kitchen," Granny Murray said as she headed out in her skimpy exercise clothes, wearing a shirt that said Yes I Strip!

The dancing Santa started screeching "Jingle Bell Rock."

"I don't care who was cheating on who—"

"Kelly. Kelly is the one who is cheating. There is no 'both sides,' there's just Kelly. She ruins everything."

"I count on you to be the mature one. You're the oldest. You have to watch out for your younger siblings," my dad scolded me.

"Kelly is a grown adult woman." I pointed at her. "Look at her. She was supposed to get married tomorrow."

"It doesn't matter. We are all going to prison, Gracie." My dad shook me by the shoulders.

"Prison?" I squeaked and sat down. "Kelly, how could you?"

My sister was defiant. "I didn't send anything to anyone. I don't know how the news got those notebooks."

"I believe you, Kelly," my dad said kindly.

"Seriously? This is all her fault. But of course you always give her a pass and punish me for what she does."

"This isn't about Kelly," my dad thundered. "This is about you."

In the corner, my mom was crying. "We're ruined."

"Damn right, you're ruined," the CEO snapped at her. "You all cost me billions. I'm coming after each and every one of you."

"There's no need for that," James said, puffing out his chest. "I take full responsibility for what happened, and we'll make it right. That's an EnerCheck Inc. promise. First off, you're fired, Gracie."

"*What?*"

"Fired," he repeated snidely.

"Fine. None of you know how to run this company anyways."

"The company's swirling down the toilet now," Dakota said, "so it's probably better you don't get sucked down that toilet of incompetence too."

"You're fired too then, Dakota," James snapped, "and you, Kelly."

"Me?" My sister screeched. "But Daddy, I need that money to pay for my Mexico trip."

"You're not fired, honey." My dad rubbed her back.

"How did it end up that EnerCheck Inc. was in charge of such a critical piece of our company's infrastructure?" one of the Roscoe VPs asked pointedly.

"Because Mr. Roscoe's daddy gave him that job," Granny Murray said, hustling back inside, "and he's incompetent. Forgot the cookies I was going to take to Janice."

We watched her grab a box from the side table.

"Carry on," she called and headed back outside, the motion-activated Santa wailing and dancing away.

"Here is what we can do," the CEO's lawyer suggested. "I have some contacts at TechBiz. We'll paint Grace O'Brien as having a mental breakdown due to her sister and ex's infidelities. We'll turn this into a tabloid story, not a business story. The stock will go back up. It will be something we laugh about at the next corporate retreat."

The door opened. The dancing Santa started singing again.

"Can someone lock that old woman outside?" the CEO bellowed as Granny Murray's voice filled the foyer.

"Amen," Grandma Astelle muttered.

But Granny Murray wasn't alone.

"Oh fuck," the CEO said when Hudson walked in. The older man's face went white, and his chest rose and fell. He raised a shaking hand, like he'd seen a ghost of Christmas past, as Hudson regarded him from across the room.

"You—you sold me out. You sold me out," Mr. Roscoe choked out. He turned to me, eyes wild. "Are you working with Grayson Richmond? After everything Roscoe Energy Solutions has done for your family?"

The VPs were freaking out.

Hudson let out a long breath.

"You know Hudson?" I was confused.

"Probably from the country club," Hudson drawled.

"The country club? Everyone knows what your company does," the CEO sputtered, looking like he wanted to bolt out a window.

"That data was clearly stolen. There will be jail time," the head lawyer barked. "And you, Grace, you're going away for a long time. Roscoe Energy will have its pound of flesh."

The CEO seemed to rally. "Call the police. I know the prosecutor. We have to get ahead of this before the quarterly earnings report."

"It's right before Christmas for maximum chaos. Everyone who can handle it is out of town," the VP of finance said in a low voice. "This couldn't have happened at a worse time."

"I don't care. Make it happen. All of them, Hudson included, are going to jail. We'll show the shareholders we have this situation under control."

Hudson clicked his tongue, sauntering into the room to stop in front of the CEO.

"Not so fast. Because your company takes federal money, the release of these notebooks falls under the whistleblower laws. Of course, the incriminating material was handed straight over to Pulitzer Prize-winning journalists."

"Hudson, what are you doing here? I don't understand," I begged.

He ignored me.

"Those notebooks were given to me by a concerned employee, a Ms. Kelly O'Brien."

"I knew it!" I shrieked.

"I didn't give them to you," Kelly argued.

"Yes, you did," Hudson said, leveling his gaze at her. "You told me all about them, where they were, and that I, quote, just had to read them."

"This ... this—" the CEO stammered, looking frightened. "I need to go. Tell my assistant to book us a flight to South America."

The men from Roscoe Energy Solutions practically ran out of the house.

Hudson's mouth turned down at the corners as he watched them leave.

"Gracie," he said, kneeling down in front of me. "Please let me explain."

"Don't even talk to me," I snapped, jumping up, sending the papers flying. "I don't want to hear you say it. I don't want to hear you say it's not what it looks like. Because it looks like you stole my private journals to what? Fuck with me? What the fuck is wrong with you?"

"We let you play hockey with us," my brother added.

My family, normally noisy, was quiet, subdued, in shock at what had just happened.

His silvery gray eyes were sorrowful.

"Gracie, I didn't mean to hurt you. I—It was—I'm sorry. I'll help you. You can come live with me. We'll find you a different job. I'll take care of you. You can come work for me if you want. You would be perfect for my line of work. You can bring your cousin, too, even your grandmother."

His expression was pleading.

"Your line of work," I said slowly. "What do you even do?"

"I solve problems," he said carefully.

"I'm a problem?" I spat.

He closed his eyes.

"No. You're the best thing that ever happened to me. I love you, Gracie. Please understand that. I don't want to live without you. We can be happy together."

"I am not working for you. You ruined my family's company," I screamed at him. "You stole from me. Wait." Things started clicking into place as I realized I had no idea who Hudson was this entire time.

"The maintenance men. They worked for your company. They were trying to get access to our servers. Did you hack the servers? Did you hack my phone?"

He winced.

"Don't lie to me."

"Yes," he admitted. "They work for me. And yes, we did access EnerCheck's servers, but there wasn't anything useful on there, Gracie, because you're the one who made that place run. I've never met anyone like you. From the moment I saw you on the bus—"

"The bus?" I shrieked at him. "You orchestrated our meeting on the bus? You planned this whole fucking thing. You were just using me. This was all one big lie. You're a monster!"

"I am a monster," he said helplessly, "but it's not a lie to say I fell for you, Gracie. I care about you, very much. I love you. I don't want to lose you. You are the best thing that ever happened to me."

"You're fucking delusional. I would rather spend Christmas on a tropical island getting sunburnt than waste another minute with you."

"I knew he didn't actually love you. I knew it," James crowed, chest puffed out like a cartoon rooster. "He wanted to take our family down, and you let him manipulate you."

"It wasn't like that, Gracie," Hudson begged me.

On the muted TV, breaking news was being announced that Grayson Richmond was about to start a press conference. I stared at the screen as a green-eyed man with an expensive watch and an Italian wool coat stepped up to the microphones.

"Oh my god." I turned to Hudson. "That's him. Grayson Richmond is your friend from the bar."

"We're not friends," he said quietly, standing up.

"So Grayson tried to ruin my company because he wants to, what, buy it? Make us pay for something? Did you insult him at a charity dinner or scrape up his car, Dad?"

"I've never seen that man before in my life," my dad swore.

"Maybe you were mean to him at the country club?" I needed some sort of explanation for why my family and I had been targeted.

"Gracie," Hudson said, crossing his arms, "none of this was about you or your company or your family. This was a stepping stone to ruin Roscoe Energy Solutions. You and your family are insignificant. You were collateral damage. It wasn't personal."

"Wasn't personal?" I choked out. "You pretended to be my boyfriend so you could steal my journals. You tricked me and lied to me. We had sex, Hudson. That sounds pretty fucking personal. Wait. That night at your apartment ..."

He looked away from me.

I was going to puke.

"I needed access to your laptop," he said, voice barely above a whisper.

"Hudson Wynter, you are the *worst* man I have ever met. You ruined my life. I hate you."

I started sobbing.

"Get out!" my aunt yelled at Hudson. "You're going to hurt the baby."

"The baby?" Hudson barked.

He grabbed my upper arm.

"Sugarplum, you think I ruined your life? You think you're the blameless victim here? You're the one who hired me to help you get revenge on your sister for sleeping with your ex-fiancé. You act like you're mad that I'm a mercenary, but you were all too happy about it when people you hated were the target."

He slammed an envelope full of money on the coffee table, the same envelope that had For Hudson written on it in my handwriting.

"News flash. Your life, Gracie, was already shit. Blowing up your dad's company? I did you a favor. Now you can actually go out and live your life, away from your parents' oppressive control."

"They're not controlling. They're family."

"Your family is fucking toxic," he snarled.

"Just because you hate your family doesn't mean that other people do. How's this for a hot take? Maybe if you'd been a better son, your family would still want to talk to you," I said hotly.

"You fucking—" He bared his teeth at me. "You don't know anything about me."

"No shit. Because you lie all the time."

"I'm a liar? I'm an awful person?" he spat, looking over me. "Sugarplum, you're the one who decided to fake a pregnancy."

"It's fake, Gracie? I'm not going to be a grandmother?" my mother asked in shock.

"Thank god," my father muttered.

"I knew she was just fat," my cousin Connie added.

I glared up at Hudson, chin trembling. Never had I hated anyone more in my life than Hudson Wynter at that moment.

Hudson shook his head.

"You're as fucked up and as toxic as me, but you hide it behind your poor little spoiled holiday Cinderella routine when you, Gracie, are the creator of your own misery. You let these people use you and walk all over you so that you can be the martyr and be holier than thou and play the victim."

"And you"—I stabbed my index finger in his chest—"walk around with a chip on your shoulder, the coldhearted bad boy who's too cool for Christmas and gets to fuck other people over just because they live in the nice part of town and like nice things."

"You're privileged and out of touch," he shot back.

"Says someone who is literally a landlord. What else do you own in this town besides the Canning Factory, hmm? Fine. Don't say anything. I'll find out. You run around pretending to be a poor, exploited working-class American when really you and I aren't so different after all," I continued.

"I am different from you," he shouted, slamming his hand down on the table. "You have happy Christmas memories. You want to know my last Christmas memory? My mom's shitty boyfriend, who was way too interested in my five-year-old sister, fell asleep smoking and burned down our fucking house. I had to throw my siblings out of a window to save them. Then the police acted like *I* had set the fire and threw me in prison, in adult fucking prison, Gracie. That's where I spent Christmas that year, and my siblings went into foster care. I don't have a fucking collection of toys in my childhood bedroom because I don't have shit from my childhood."

He was breathing hard.

"Everything I have is because I worked for it. I don't get caught up in petty shit like someone sleeping with my fiancé, because I have too much real shit I'm dealing with. You should have just taken a hockey stick to James's face and been done with it. But no, you wanted someone else to do your dirty work for you, so that you can stay the blameless, pure, good-girl virgin."

"Hear, hear!" one of my uncles shouted, setting off the singing, dancing Santa.

"You mean like how you made me do your dirty work so you could suck up to your nonfriend the billionaire? Now who's being a martyr? How much money did you make off of me?" I screamed at him. "Tell me."

He looked away, lips thin.

"Tell me," I demanded.

"Five and a half million."

"Five and a half—well. All right then. I guess I'd sell out a random stranger for that amount of money too," I said snidely. "Merry fucking Christmas. Go buy yourself something nice."

"Fuck you, Gracie. I hate my job, I hate Grayson, and I hate Christmas, and you better turn off that fucking singing Santa," he said, making a knife hand at the dancing decoration, "before I throw it out the fucking window."

"I don't hate Christmas, but I hate you. I hate your stupid jeans and your boots and the fact that you can't wear underwear like a normal fucking person. Also all your tattoos are trashy."

"Fine. I hate your flannel pajamas and all those mice in your bedroom—it's sick. I hate the Christmas cookies and those aprons you wear and all the desserts you bake. Who needs 3,000 Christmas cookies?"

"Oh yeah?" I screamed at him. "I wish I'd fucked your brothers instead of you. All of them. All at once."

"Fuck you," he roared.

"All your brothers are all hotter than you, and they smell better, and they're taller."

He flipped me off and grabbed his helmet, pushing through my stunned family members.

"Fuck you and your entire shitty family. Not you, you're actually cool, Granny Murray," he said to her.

"Right on." Granny Murray gave him a thumbs-up.

"Don't talk to him," I shrieked at her.

Hudson slammed the door behind him. The china in the cabinets shook.

I struggled to open the window to scream at him as he climbed on the black motorcycle.

"Fuck you, Hudson Wynter. I hope Santa drop-kicks you off a roof!"

Chapter 52

HUDSON

The motorcycle helmet clattered to the floor when I got back to my apartment.

"What the fuck?" I mumbled.

The whole place looked like I'd stepped into Santa's workshop at the North fucking Pole.

Wreaths decorated the windows, the Christmas tree had been decorated, there was garland over the doorway, stockings were on the unused fireplace, and a picture of Pugnog and Gracie in matching knitted Santa hats and sweaters was propped on the mantel. Strands of paper snowflakes twisted slightly above me, strung on the steel structure.

I reached up and tore the nearest one down, crumpling it up.

I was immediately filled with regret. I went to the coffee table to smooth out the snowflake on the tabletop, but I couldn't salvage it.

The lights on the Christmas tree sparkled softly, the tinsel reflecting the lights onto the ruined snowflake.

"Worst Christmas ever, huh," I said to the tree.

It glowed at me.

There was a single, solitary present tucked under the branches. I sat down on the floor in front of the tree and picked it up.

For: Hudson
From: Gracie

I pulled the present for her out of my bag and placed it there, feeling like I was in a waking nightmare.

What did I think was going to happen, though, when I'd gotten that late-night bus to Maplewood Falls? That Grayson, out of the goodness of his heart and moved by the spirit of Christmas, wasn't going to deploy the ultimate weapon to take down one of his rivals? That Gracie was going to wrap her arms around me when she saw me, tell me that she forgave me, smile up at me like I was her hero, and thank me for coming back to her? That I was going to give some sort of impassioned speech about why she and I were meant to be together, and she would tell me love conquers all?

I was as delusional as she was.

"I should burn this whole fucking place to the ground."

Instead, I went to the fridge, needing a drink.

Along with the bottle of vodka was a red Pyrex dish decorated with white Christmas trees covered in foil. I slowly pulled it out, placed it on the counter, and peeled back the foil.

Inside was a breakfast casserole Gracie had made and put in my fridge, probably expecting me to come home to her that morning.

I stuck it in the oven, letting the savory warm smells make the apartment feel like home. Like Gracie.

"I fucking hate Christmas."

"It looks even better in person!" I heard Elsa exclaim.

The floor vibrated under my cheek as my siblings piled into my apartment.

"Something smells amazing," Talbot said.

"Are you cooking, Hudson?" Lawrence called from the kitchen.

Elsa walked around, admiring the decorations while my head felt like it was going to split open.

"Aw. I wanted to know if she liked the present," Elsa said when she saw it under the tree. "I guess you didn't give it to her because you were waiting for Christmas, huh?"

Anderson snorted.

"Yeah. That sure looks like what happened," Elsa said, crouching down next to me.

I hated having her see me like this, see me like Mom.

"Go away. Please just go away." I rubbed my face. "You shouldn't have to sit through another Christmas with a family member too drunk to remember their own name," I slurred.

I didn't drink in excess when I was working a contract. But now it was over and the check deposited, so I drank and tried to forget about Gracie and the casserole and how she hated me and how she didn't believe me when I said I loved her.

I reached for the vodka bottle.

"Hey." Talbot grabbed it from me. "I think you had enough."

Lawrence stuffed forkfuls of Gracie's breakfast casserole in my mouth.

"This is the best fucking thing I've ever eaten," Jake groaned from his own plate.

"We're all thinking of going to Barbados for Christmas," Talbot told me.

"You're all going to get a sunburn," I mumbled.

"You shouldn't drink alone." Jake and Lawrence tried to roll me over.

"I have too many siblings. Get off of me." I swiped at Jake.

He force-fed me more casserole.

"We could have lost you, and then Grayson would never give us another contract."

"Yeah, you're his friend," Anderson said.

"I'm not friends with Grayson Richmond," I snapped.

"You always hang out with him."

"He ruined my fucking life."

"Come on, big brother." Anderson and Lawrence grabbed each one of my arms. They hauled me up, half carried me to the bedroom, and dumped me unceremoniously on the bed.

"She washed the sheets," I said deliriously. "She wanted to take care of me, and I ruined it."

Lawrence tried to make me sit up to drink a glass of water.

"Was $5 and a half million worth it to ruin what I had with Gracie?" I asked Elsa helplessly.

My little sister gave me a sympathetic look, a pitying look.

"You hate me."

"You're my big brother, and I love you," she told me soothingly. "You did what you thought you had to do. You were trying to look out for your company and us and …" She looked to Anderson.

He tapped in.

"It's the holidays," Anderson said carefully. "They make people crazy, give people existential crises. There's not a lot of sunlight. You start remembering the bad times with your family, thinking about another year over, another year possibly wasted. You'll feel like your old self in January."

My siblings looked worried, probably because they hadn't ever seen me this low.

Not that I had never been this low. I had just been better about hiding it.

"What you need to remember," Lawrence said, with forced cheeriness, "was you never actually had a relationship with her. You never had anything with her. It was fake, all fake. You can't ruin something you never had to begin with."

I curled up with a groan.

"You suck at this," Jake said, shoving him aside and lying down next to me. Elsa squeezed in next to me, and Talbot jumped on top of me, his elbow jabbing me in my ribs. Anderson sat near my head and put me in a headlock, and Lawrence lay crossways, draping his knees over my legs.

We lay there like we did when we were kids in the drafty old crumbling house, the leaking pipes forming sheets of ice on the walls in the winter.

In the living room, the clock Gracie had brought shrieked out a tiny Christmas carol, letting us know that it was now

11 p.m., and if you were tired of hearing the first few bars of "Jingle Bells," too fucking bad. Hope your alcohol cabinet was well stocked.

Anderson ruffled my hair.

"You have until New Year's to wallow, then we need you back in the game. Grayson Richmond is going to throw more work at us. You know he will."

I wasn't sure if I had it in me anymore.

I felt like this last job, Gracie had broken me.

Chapter 53

GRACIE

Ah, the wedding day.

This time last year had been the worst day of my entire life, including that time when I got my period on the third day of sixth grade, and I had been in a class taught by literally the only male teacher at the school, and he'd taken one look and fainted and hit his head, and the ambulance showed up, and everyone acted like I'd tried to kill poor, beloved, elderly Mr. Hollway.

He did not return to teaching, and everyone blamed me.

Last year's Christmas still gave me nightmares, especially the part where I had to tell everyone who didn't know that the wedding was canceled, and by the way, Kelly and James were engaged, and wasn't that nice?

I had wrongly assumed that the silver lining of that storm cloud of cheating, lies, and deceit was that I would never in my life have a day as bad as that Christmas.

Yet here we were, exactly one year later, with the new record for the worst day of Gracie's life.

Hudson Wynter had not just been lying to me, not just slept with my sister, but he'd been manipulating me and using me to ruin my father's company. And what was worse? It wasn't even personal. It wasn't some grand revenge plan to end a family feud. He had used me, pretended to care about me, pretended like we were partners in crime, had wormed his way into my heart, all so that Grayson Richmond could sacrifice EnerCheck like a pawn to win a chess match.

I was nothing to Hudson.

Just a check.

A big, fat Christmas bonus.

Hudson had never cared about me, had never loved me. In fact, he despised me.

I wiped my eyes with the apron that Hudson apparently hated.

"Aww." Dakota wrapped her arms around me.

"You were right," I said dully, turning back to the cream-cheese-and-pomegranate Danishes I was making. My cookie schedule had said I was supposed to be baking Italian Christmas cookies all day, but since there was no wedding, my baking plans were ruined. In this time of crisis, I needed leavened bread.

"You can't change a bad boy."

"Hudson wasn't just a bad boy; he's a terrible human being. Probably some sort of war criminal," my cousin said. "You didn't just dodge a bullet. You dodged a ballistic missile."

"It just felt so real."

Dakota picked up Pugnog, and he made snorting noises in her arms. She held him out so he could give me a doggy kiss on the cheek.

"I think," Dakota said delicately, "that maybe you wanted it to be real, and you ignored the red-flag-draped reindeer tearing up your roof? It sounded romantic on paper, right? Bad boy falls in love with wholesome good-girl fake girlfriend? I'd buy a ticket to see that movie. Well, maybe not buy a ticket, but at least renew my streaming subscription to watch it."

"He said he loved me," I reminded her. "That's all I wanted, was for him to say it."

"Hudson slept with you to get access to your laptop. He's a bad person."

I felt nauseous again. Dakota was right. I couldn't excuse that sort of behavior. It was a thousand red flags.

"My fake relationship with Hudson was probably the most beneficial," I said. "How ironic. He was always pushing me out of my comfort zone, encouraged me to stand up to my family, and made me feel like I mattered, made me believe I could take charge of my own life. He was always there for me."

"Stop rationalizing and excusing his behavior."

"Hudson's not all bad," I said. "I kept thinking about that little boy in the video, scared and alone and in jail on Christmas. No wonder he was so rough around the edges. I wanted to wrap him in knitted blankets and feed him soup."

"Sure, he's not all bad," Dakota agreed. "No one is all bad, but he's bad for you."

I wrapped my arms around myself.

"There's always a ton of dating events in January," Dakota assured me. "You'll find your Mr. Right."

"I don't want Mr. Right. I want Mr. Wrong for me in every way possible. I want the Christmas miracle. I wanted him to stalk into the kitchen, wearing all black. I'd scold him for tracking in snow. He'd sweep me up in his arms. I'd smell the warm leather of his jacket. He'd make some sarcastic comment about Pugnog but still sneak him a treat when he thought I wasn't looking. He'd tell me he made the biggest mistake of his life, that he's ripped up the check, told Grayson to get lost, and dissolved his security company, and he was there to whisk me off to our beautiful new life together."

"And how is this beautiful new life going to be funded if you're unemployed and he just set fire to a five- and-a-half-million-dollar check?" Dakota asked. "Why are you so hooked on him?"

I sighed and spread the sweet cream cheese filling on the dough.

"I want someone to love me," I said sadly. "I want someone to look at me and think 'that's my person.' That's what I've been waiting for my entire life."

"You're my person," Dakota said to me and grabbed my wrist. "Ever since we were babies, you know I'm always a hundred percent on Team Gracie. You don't need Hudson and his bad behavior. There are people here who love you."

I gave her a small smile.

"Eventually, some guy is going to see how amazing you are, and then I'll really be all alone." My cousin hugged me.

"Hudson made me feel seen," I said in her shoulder.

"Is this the Gracie appreciation party?" Granny Murray whooped, carting in a box of wine and a large steaming box of pizza.

"This is not enough for the whole family," Dakota said, taking the box.

"That's why I have this." Granny Murray pulled out her Taser. "We're going to get wasted then go get laid. Lots of lonely divorced men out there on Christmas Eve looking for a little love. It's not as easy to get laid as on New Year's Eve. That's like shooting sperm in a barrel, but we'll give it our best shot."

"I don't know whether to be depressed or disgusted," I said after a moment.

"You're hungry. Have some pizza." Granny Murray handed me a slice. "You on your period?"

"What?"

"Depends on which bar we go to. Some guys have certain kinks that obviously I can't fulfill."

"I think I'm just gonna remain single for the foreseeable future," I said hastily, giving Pugnog a bite of clam.

"Suit yourself. Good thing I bought vibrators for stocking stuffers."

"Gran, that's—You know what? Never mind. I didn't finish shopping for all my stocking stuffers, so what the hell."

"I even got ones for the men too." She cackled.

"Great. Dad's going to love a vibrating butt plug."

"We can still book a flight to Aspen," Dakota offered, waving her phone at me. "Girls' trip. Me. You. Pugnog. A ski resort. No cooking, no weddings, no family, no Christmas."

I felt a pang of sadness. No Christmas?

Would that be a bad thing? It wasn't like the holiday season was particularly festive.

My uncles were drinking. James and my dad were holed up in his home office pretending to problem solve. My cousins were working to spend as much money as they could on the company credit cards before they got shut down, because that was totally the right approach. Not that anyone had asked me. I was still fired.

"Gracie," I heard my mom call.

"If you don't bring me on the girls' trip, I'm ratting you out to your mothers," Granny Murray threatened.

"Fine. A girls' trip for three," Dakota hissed.

"Let's take the men something to snack on while they're working so hard to clean up your mistake," my mom said as she sailed into the kitchen, Kelly sulking behind her.

"Like Kelly's going to be able to put together so much as a bowl of carrots and ranch dressing," I snorted.

"Yeah. I don't cook," my sister said.

"Kelly," my mom chided her, "you need to do what you can to get James to take you back. Don't be like Gracie."

"What do you mean, don't be like Gracie?" I asked sharply.

"If you had just taken James back and forgiven him," my mother said shrilly, "none of this would have happened. Your dad would still have his company."

"No." I slammed down the metal tray. "No, he would not still have his company because I would have been busy having babies and Dad would have run EnerCheck into the ground. Actually," I backtracked, "that's not true. I would have *wanted* to stay home with my kids, but since I am the only one who has even a remote idea of how to make EnerCheck run, James would have manipulated me into keeping the company afloat, like I've been doing for the past several years. And what did I get for it? Shit on."

"You ruined my life," my mom cried to me. "I had the perfect life, and you had to destroy it. We're going to lose the house. We're going to lose everything, Gracie. Your dad won't talk to me, but I see it in his face. You ruined Christmas."

I felt horribly guilty.

Then I straightened up.

"Hudson is right. An asshole, but right. This family is toxic. I'm glad EnerCheck is dead. I'm glad that Dad and James aren't able to gaslight me and manipulate me anymore. If they had listened to me in the first place, the company would have been fine. There wouldn't have been anything for Hudson to report back to Grayson Richmond. Everything would have been fine."

"I don't understand how I raised such a selfish daughter." My mom was trembling.

"That's the problem," I yelled at her. "You *didn't* raise me to be selfish. Instead, you raised me to be compliant and put others' needs and feelings first. Maybe you should have made me stand up for myself more, to have more confidence. At the very least, I could have kept that company on the rails and told Dad to fire James. Shit, maybe I wouldn't have had the low self-esteem to think a man who used to call me muffin and pinch my stomach was my soulmate instead of just a loser. But sure, Mom, I'm the terrible daughter. I'm ruining Christmas. I'm the problem here."

I went to the fridge.

"You know what? Fuck you. Fuck Christmas. I'm taking Dad and James their cold, congealed turkey and then Dakota and me—"

"And me!" Granny Murray hollered.

"Are going to a ski resort, and I'm going to sleep."

"With what money?" my mom demanded as I slapped hunks of cold turkey on two plates. "We have no money. We're broke now."

"I'm not," Gran yelled at her. "I'm a wealthy divorcée with alimony, and we're going to get some hot tail in the hot tub."

Kelly slunk after us while I carried the dripping plates of meat down the hall, Pugnog snorting along after our sad parade.

"Granny, can't you give me some money? I'll go with you to find men to hook up with," Kelly whined.

"You will?" Granny Murray perked up.

"Gran!" Dakota protested.

She gave an apologetic shrug. "You're a little bit of a prude, you and Gracie."

"Kelly, why can't you find a nice man, a rich man, one with an in-law suite, because," my mom sobbed as they trooped after me down the hall, "we're going to lose the house."

"Gracie." My father looked up from where he and James were shuffling around papers on his desk.

Logan and several other cousins, who I had seen in the office all of ten hours over the past year, were also sitting around the home office in chairs, brows furrowed, trying to "fix" things. It was like an episode of *The Muppet Show*. All I needed was James to start parroting, "Business! Business!"

"We are trying to work," James said brusquely.

"We just wanted to bring you some lunch," my mom said, kissing my father on the top of his head.

"I thought Granny Murray brought pizza," one of my cousins complained when they saw the hunks of cold turkey.

"Business morons don't get pizza," I told them.

"I'm not taking food from traitors," James snarled at me and Kelly, who didn't seem at all upset that the guy she was supposed to marry today hated her.

"Shut up, James. You and Dad were running this company into the ground."

"Gracie, that's no way to speak to—"

"Who? *My boss?* Guess what. I was fired, so I don't have to be nice anymore." I slammed the plates of cold turkey breast on top of the papers.

"Watch out, Gracie," my dad warned.

"Those are the reports from last quarter which James created with bad information and then doctored. Turkey grease isn't going to make them any less useless than they already are."

My ex's face went red.

"You should have used the ones I made." I wagged my finger at them. "You're not going to blame me for your bad business decisions. Dad, I'm your daughter. I cared about EnerCheck. Yet you had so little respect for me and my contributions to the company that you'd rather listen to what amounts to a scam artist than someone actually trying to keep the company in the black."

My dad looked sad.

"I know, Gracie," he said. "I know that you were trying to help us, but I had to support the family. I can't just cut them off. You wanted me to cut off your cousins, your aunts, your uncles."

"Yes," I said. "Yes, I did because they did not work at the company."

"Bitch," James muttered.

"Cheating stupid asshole."

"Language! What happened to my sweet little girl?" my dad cried.

"She is sick of incompetent men being given all the credit and all the benefit of the doubt. New Year's resolution—I am not making myself small so that rude pompous men can feel better about themselves. Put up or get out."

"If you don't mind." Grandma Astelle appeared like the ghost of Christmas future in the double doorway that opened to my father's office. "We have company."

"Mr. Richmond?" my dad gasped when a familiar green-eyed man, flanked by another man in a suit, walked into the home office.

"Come. We'll let the men do business," my mom whispered.

"The hell? Is this 1950? I'm not leaving Dad in here alone with Grayson fucking Richmond so he can sell off what's left of the family assets." I shook off my mother.

"Mr. Grayson Richmond, the single, eligible billionaire with a penthouse?" Kelly perked right up.

Grayson was as unflappable as he'd been in the fight at the bar.

"Kelly, out," I barked. "And you," I spat at Grayson. "Get out of here."

"Grace O'Brien," the billionaire said, inclining his head slightly. "It's a pleasure to finally meet you." He gestured to the tall man next to him. "Marius, head of legal for Richmond Electric. We'd like to discuss your company."

"Actually, it's my company," my dad said, extending his hand.

Grayson took it. He was much smoother than Hudson, more cultured. Three weeks ago, I would have said he was just my type. Though now I just wanted someone to huddle on the couch with and call out how shitty this whole Christmas scam really was.

Maybe next year will be better.

Or maybe it will suck even more.

"May we sit?" Grayson asked.

"Of course." My dad pulled out a chair.

"No." I crossed my arms then uncrossed them and put them on my hips in a power pose. "Tell us what you want or get out."

"As you wish," Grayson said.

The good manners were grating. I was not in the mood for niceness today.

"Don't you want some cookies?" my mom offered.

"He hired Hudson to ruin our lives. He doesn't get Christmas cookies," I snapped at my mother.

Marius winced.

"Speaking of that issue. I'd like to buy EnerCheck for $1,000,000," Grayson announced.

"Done," my father said eagerly.

"You didn't even hear his offer," I hissed at my dad.

"It's a worthless company, so who cares what he's offering?" James scoffed.

"If it's worthless, he wouldn't offer anything," I argued.

"Very astute, Ms. O'Brien." Grayson gave me an assessing look.

Guess Grayson wasn't the type to call someone Sugarplum.

I wracked my brain, thinking about what Grayson could possibly want.

EnerCheck was a stepping stone, a pawn to sacrifice for a bigger fish.

"You want info on Roscoe Energy," I said abruptly. "That's worth a lot more than $1,000,000."

"I thought they stole everything from us already," my brother said.

"He needs the data free and clear," I said, narrowing my eyes at them. "Roscoe could sue him if they have proof he stole their data. That's not whistleblowing; that's just a felony."

Never write anything down.

I bet Hudson didn't even hand that data over to you, so that you could keep your hands clean.

"Ten million," Grayson said.

"Now that I know that's how much you're willing to pay, I can go to Roscoe Energy and let them make a counteroffer."

"They don't have money right now to buy you all out, and without them, you're worthless," Grayson said coldly. "Take my offer now, or I'll scoop you up in the New Year for pennies."

"Gracie, take the offer, please," my father begged.

"Shut up, Robert," Grandma Astelle told him. "Honestly. Sometimes you prove that old woman right."

"You are the CEO," Grayson said simply. "It is your decision."

My father was sheepish. "I think Gracie probably knows better."

"She is my granddaughter," Grandma Astelle said primly.

"No, she's my granddaughter." Granny Murray put up her hands like a boxer.

"Please don't get in a fight, and please put away that sword," I warned them.

Marius seemed alarmed.

"Thirty million," I counteroffered. "Or I could sell to Svensson Investment. Shoot, any of the hedge funds would take the company just for the data, once they know you want it so badly."

Green eyes flashed.

"Don't get all huffy," I said when he opened his mouth to protest. "This is a rounding error for your firm. I'm being very generous."

He worked his jaw then said, "Fine, but you will be the CEO."

"No thanks. I'm flying to Aspen with my share of the $30 million and finding a hot-tub boy. I might even get pregnant, buy a nice house, and raise a baby along with a dozen rescue pugs."

"That's my girl!" Granny Murray whooped.

"I need to lie down," my mother groaned, slumping against a bookcase.

"That would be quite the waste of your talents. You come highly recommended by my associate. He is very impressed by you. Per his information, you've been the one running EnerCheck all these years."

"Did Hudson ask you to buy EnerCheck because he felt bad?" I demanded, "Is this a pity offer? You two are friends, right? It was you he was hanging out with at the bar."

"I don't have friends." Grayson gave me an odd look. "Please understand. I'm not in the business of letting emotions cloud my judgment. You're valuable to me, regardless of Hudson's feelings toward you."

I scowled.

"I want a board seat, 25 percent ownership, and final say on all hiring."

"How about fifteen percent and a car?"

"How about you stop thinking I'm some brain-dead little girl you can buy off with toys? We're negotiating here. Man up or stop wasting my time."

Grayson sucked in an angry breath.

Was it smart to piss off a billionaire like that?

Probably not.

But who cared? After this meeting, I was going to go sit in my room and eat cinnamon rolls and drink bourbon hot chocolate until the New Year.

Grayson's lips thinned. Then his mouth quirked.

"Hudson was right about you. You are amazing."

"I'm not—he didn't—" I sputtered.

"He is quite enamored of you."

"He doesn't get to be enamored of me," I shrieked, causing Marius to wince.

Calm down.

This is a professional meeting, not a group therapy session about my ability to hitch my sleigh to some of the worst men on the planet.

"Twenty percent," Grayson said.

"Twenty-two, and a half a million sign-on bonus. And a parking space."

"A parking space? That's worth as much as rent."

"Shocking. A billionaire who actually knows how much something costs. Do a gallon of milk." I snapped my fingers.

"$2.89."

I applauded. "Congratulations! You will not be visited by a dead business partner and three ghosts tonight."

His mouth parted slightly.

"You know," Grayson said after a moment, "if Hudson Wynter wasn't so madly in love with you, I'd ask you out on a date."

"You would?" Marius was shocked.

"Hudson does not love me. And I hate him."

"Believe what you will, but he's so obsessed with you, I think he just might kill me if I was anything less than coldly professional."

"You're going to have to get over yourself because I don't do coldly professional. Come to the kitchen and let me fix you a plate of cookies while Marius preps the paperwork."

"Thank you, but I don't eat sweets."

"Fine. You can have brisket and garlic-herb mashed potatoes."

"After we sign the paperwork, Madam CEO." Grayson shook my hand. "I want all of the competitors' data in my office by this afternoon. I have a private plane waiting to take you to Manhattan."

"A private plane?" My cousins were excited.

"We're saved!"

"Let's go shopping."

Grayson's face was perfectly neutral.

He didn't even have to say it.

I whistled sharply. "I need everyone's laptop. Now."

I dumped out the box with the useless paperwork and shook it at the nearest family member.

"Put laptops and tablets in the box and pass it around. Those computers are company property, so I'm taking them with me to Manhattan."

Once I had all the electronics, I turned to my family.

"All of you except Dakota are fired."

"Fired?"

"Does that mean we don't get paid?"

"Way to ruin Christmas, Gracie." Kelly was furious. "I need to get my nails done."

"I'm trying to salvage something here," I snapped at them as Grayson picked up the box.

I opened the door while my cousins stormed after me, yelling at me about upcoming expenses they had.

"Pleasure doing business with you all. Merry Christmas," Grayson called.

"Wait! Take some cookies, hot stuff." Granny Murray shoved several in his pants pocket and dumped Pugnog in the laptop box.

"Did she just feel you up, man?" Marius asked under his breath.

"No take backs," I said as I herded Grayson and Marius out the door.

Chapter 54

HUDSON

"In a shocking turn of events, Richmond Electric has bought EnerCheck," the host on the business news channel was saying.

"It's not that shocking," the analyst replied. "After all, Grayson Richmond now owns the data of his biggest competitor. For $30 million, that's a steal. What's shocking is naming Grace O'Brien as the new CEO. Is this just a vanity position before he sucks the marrow out of the company, or does Grayson Richmond Electric have bigger plans for EnerCheck?"

I felt a rush of pride for Gracie for not backing down from Grayson. Then I felt sick.

If Grayson agreed to the price, that meant he probably did it because he liked Gracie, because he wanted her around him. There was no way she was going to be able to resist him. Grayson had stepped into the cultured billionaire persona like he'd been born for it. You wouldn't know upon meeting him that he came from an even worse background than I did. Women fell all over themselves for him.

At a nearby table, Grayson was chatting with several other suited Wall Street types. I turned my attention back to the TV hanging on the wall in the Lower Manhattan bar that was frequented by slick Wall Street bros.

I was wearing a suit to blend in. Some asshole had set the radio to play jazz renditions of popular Christmas carols.

I adjusted my tie. I felt constrained by the suit; I just wanted to rip it off.

"After the break, we're going to look at what this take-over means for stock prices," the TV anchor said.

"Let's just say the CEO of Roscoe Energy isn't having any kind of Christmas," her cohost joked.

Grayson was finishing his business meeting. He shook hands with the other suits and paid his bill.

I waited until they had left then grabbed Grayson as he was walking out and shoved him into a booth.

He didn't seem fazed as he straightened his jacket.

"You must really like this girl if you debased yourself enough to put on a suit just to harass me," he said, tone light. "Drink? They serve $500 glasses of whisky here. My treat."

"Someone's happy," I snapped.

Probably because he realized just how wonderful Gracie was. Grayson was one of the apex predators in Manhattan. He was in the market for the perfect mate, and I'd just delivered Gracie to him on a silver platter.

Of course she's going to want him more than you. What woman wouldn't?

"I like to win. Also Gracie is …" His smile seemed softer, less feral.

I wanted to kill him.

"You're such an asshole," I snarled.

"You knew what you were getting into with me." He sat back in the booth as the waiter set down two identical glass tumblers in front of us.

"Nothing like drinking in a bar on Christmas Eve," Grayson remarked, taking a sip. "Cheers."

"Did they wear gloves to pour this?" I asked, scowling at the sparkling glass, then drained it.

"You're supposed to savor it," Grayson said with a slight smirk.

He handed me his still-full glass. "You look like you need it."

"I don't." I drained it anyways.

"Now that you've called me an asshole, you going to call me a prick too?"

"I mean, you are a prick. You don't need me to say it."

"I'm an effective prick," he concurred.

"Was this your plan all along?" I asked him.

"As soon as you gave me the initial report, I had the outlines of the plan made," Grayson admitted. "When I met Gracie, I knew I made the right choice. You are correct—she is something else."

I closed my eyes, wishing I had more of that expensive whisky.

Grayson was an asshole, a coldhearted piece of shit, but he could also have moments of warmth. I knew with Gracie in his life, he'd be perfect for her. He'd give her everything she always wanted, and he wouldn't lie to her.

"Her grandmother tried to feel me up," he continued conversationally, "and her pug gets toted around in a baby carrier."

"Did its eye pop out?"

"Got pretty close in my office." He signaled for another round. "She brought a plate of brisket and mashed potatoes with her and insisted I eat it."

"Of course she did." My heart was breaking.

Kill him.

Or just let her be happy. You already ruined her life once.

"Please take good care of her," I choked out. "Gracie deserves someone who loves her."

Grayson crossed his arms and regarded me.

"The coldhearted military man in love. I almost don't believe it."

"Fuck you." My heart wasn't in it.

"She really did a number on you, huh?"

"Stop rubbing it in, asshole."

"Can't even complete his mission."

"What mission? I got you everything you wanted," I said bitterly. "Even the thing you didn't know you needed."

"We go way back, don't we? You did me a good turn once, you remember?"

"Hell, like I'm going to charge some snot-nosed kid a bunch of money so he can find his little brothers."

"You always looked out for me in the group home," Grayson concurred. "It's funny. If I was the type of person to have them, I might have called you a friend."

He reached out and set a small black box in front of me.

"You told me the plan was to get engaged at Gracie's sister's wedding, a nuke from orbit, as you put it."

"The wedding's already off," I said, running a hand through my hair.

"You know, my secretary has really been on point lately. I asked her to find a ring that looked like Gracie's great-grandmother's," he said, pulling an envelope out of his breast pocket. "It seems she found the exact ring. It has the serial number and everything, plus paperwork of when and where ownership was changed. I have, of course, written it off as a business expense already—no refunds, apparently. Unlike the car. Those Ford F-150s really do hold their value."

I frowned at the box.

"Gracie already left town," Grayson said pointedly. "So you'll have to forgo the cinematic race through the snowy New York streets. But you are free to take my plane."

I squinted.

"Or you can take the bus." Grayson smirked.

"Oh shit." It finally dawned on me. "But you don't— doesn't she—"

"We have a chilly working relationship."

"Damn right you do."

"It's shocking you're able to write your own name," Grayson said with a slight chuckle.

"Fuck you," I said and grabbed the ring box.

"Merry Christmas, Hudson."

"Yeah," I said. "Merry Christmas."

Chapter 55

GRACIE

Through the window, I saw pizza boxes stacked high. Dakota grimaced.

In his baby carrier, Pugnog panted. I'd swaddled him in sweaters and hats and might have overdone it.

"Maybe you want to lay low for a bit," my cousin said as the angry faces of my family appeared in the window.

"Right."

"I'll smooth things out. Granny Murray will too. You'll see."

I clutched Pugnog to my chest. Not too hard because of his eye.

"I'll let you know if it's cool for you to come to Christmas brunch tomorrow. Don't worry. When they all realize no one knows how to make your extra-special French toast, they'll be begging to have you back, firings or no firings. Why don't you go back to that cute little boutique hotel and watch Christmas movies?"

"Christmas alone? Sounds like a depressing way to spend Christmas Eve."

Though now that I thought about it, somehow I always felt alone on Christmas even though I had a huge family. Until Hudson. Hudson never made me feel lonely.

"I'm proud of you, Gracie. This has been a Christmas season of growth for you."

"Yeah," I said, feeling suddenly exhausted.

Dakota hugged me.

"Don't get too down. It's lonely at the top. You'll get used to it. That big, fat CEO paycheck will help sop up your tears."

I watched as my cousin went into the warm, well-lit house, to be hugged by parents, uncles, aunts, and cousins, while I watched outside in the cold.

Alone.

The Canal Club was practically glowing when the Uber dropped off me and Pugnog. I didn't want to go back to that hotel and sit there all alone. I felt stupid as I remembered how delusional I was, daydreaming that Hudson was going to come back to me and shower me with flowers and kisses.

Grayson said he was in love with me.

"You're a CEO now," I told myself sternly. "You have people who rely on you. You aren't just the girl in the kitchen making cookies. You don't need Hudson. You don't need anyone. Dakota is right. The top is cold and lonely."

Though my dream had always been to have a bunch of kids, a nice house, and a husband who came home at exactly

6 p.m. for dinner, plotting a new direction for EnerCheck was exciting. Grayson didn't want me to just dump the data and leave. He was actually interested in integrating our product into Richmond Electric's operation. The actual software service itself was still sound. Now that I'd be able to spend the money to make needed changes to it without having to do a whole song and dance to try to convince James and my father that it was necessary, I was raring to go.

I felt important and respected. I was even going to have my own corner office with a killer view.

All alone.

We are not feeling sorry for ourselves. There are tons of people worse off this holiday than you.

First, I was going to take back my decorations. I was renting a new apartment in Manhattan, and I was having Christmas in January, goddamn it, because I deserved it. Those Christmas trees would just have to hang on.

Inside, instead of the boxes of packed-up decorations, the staff was bustling about preparing for a three-hundred-person wedding.

"Oh no!" I cried.

The manager hurried over to me. "I'm so sorry. We're running a bit behind. How is the bride?"

"No, not that. No one in my family told you the wedding was canceled?"

"Canceled?"

"There was a last-minute end of the relationship," I explained with a wince. "And, of course, no one called you. I am so sorry."

The manager shrugged. "Everything was prepaid."

I felt terrible.

"There's no reason for you all to be here. It's Christmas Eve," I told the staff. "Please go home."

"But the food."

"Take as much as you want," I begged them. "Please spend Christmas with your families. I'm so sorry you all had to be out here for no reason."

I grabbed the box of goody bags I'd made specifically for all the staff to thank them for spending their holiday with us, and passed them out as the workers packed up leftover banquet food and desserts.

"Take some cake."

"Seems like bad luck to cut the bride's cake," the catering staff said.

"There is nothing you can do to curse that failed relationship," I promised. "I'll clean the rest of this up. Please go home. Merry Christmas. Have a wonderful holiday."

"Doors will lock behind when you leave," the manager told me with a wave.

I sighed and set Pugnog down.

Outside, I'd planned for a small ice-skating pond ringed by decorated Christmas trees for wedding guests to enjoy. At the edge of the frozen pond, candles burned, the glow reflected on the ice. It was a fairy wonderland.

I laced up my skates and stepped out onto the ice, gliding around in small circles, enjoying the feel of the wind and the smell of candles and juniper.

So what if I wasn't going to get everything I wanted this Christmas?

And let's be honest, this Christmas was kind of a net negative. My family hated me. I had no boyfriend, fake or otherwise, and I didn't even have a place to spend Christmas morning. However, some good things had happened. I'd stood up to my parents, finally taken control of my life, and accepted a new job.

I wished suddenly that Hudson had been there. I bet he would have been proud.

Or maybe he wouldn't have cared.

He probably wouldn't have cared.

He never really cared, had he? It was all in my head.

Pugnog was making his happy bark. I looked over toward the terrace that led to the ballroom to see him prancing around a tall man in all black. The figure was slowly making his way through the snow. I stopped to watch him slip off his skate guards at the edge of the pond.

Cautiously, he glided over to me, looking like everything I'd always dreamed of for Christmas.

And here we go with the delusions.

Hudson stopped in front of me, spraying ice chips from the blades of his skates. He dipped his head, watching me warily.

"What do you want?" I said finally.

He worked his jaw.

"I got you a Christmas present. It's at my apartment."

"You didn't have to get me anything," I told him.

"You got me something."

"I give people gifts because I like to give gifts. I don't expect anything in return."

He sagged. "I'll drop it at your parents' house then."

I barked out a laugh. "Better not do that. I'm blacklisted over there."

"You are?"

"Yeah. Turns out when you blow up the gravy train, people get upset."

"I'm sorry, Gracie." His expression was pained. "I know that doesn't cut it, but I am. I'm sorry for using you, and for the way I treated you, and for lying to you, and for stealing your stuff, and hacking your computer, and destroying your dad's company."

"You ruined Christmas." I crossed my arms. "But hey, the money's worth it, right? At least that's what I'm telling myself to make spending Christmas Eve alone not suck so much."

I looked down at my white skates.

His black ones moved closer.

"Yeah." He shrugged. "I guess."

We stood there in the flickering light from the candles. The blades of Hudson's skates scraped softly on the ice as he rocked on his feet.

"I should go," I said finally.

"Gracie, please." He reached for me.

"I can't just leave the venue like this. I don't want the staff to get in trouble."

"They won't." His mouth quirked. "I can put in a good word with the owner."

"You know the owner? Wait … For fuck's—of course you own this venue." I threw up my hands. "You're everywhere in my life."

"Gracie." He skated to face me again.

"What, Hudson?" My body suddenly ached, and all I wanted to do was lie down.

"I love you." It was awkward, sudden, abrasive.

"I don't believe you."

He closed his eyes like I'd stabbed him.

Then he opened them, his gray eyes the color of the ice beneath our feet.

"I know I lied to you."

"You didn't just lie. You made me believe that ..." My voice caught.

Do not cry, do not cry.

"It's not even about the company. I managed to patch that claptrap back up. Story of my life."

"I did not mean to do *that* with Kelly," he said quickly. "All I want is you." He rested his hands on my arms.

I looked up at the snowy night sky. "I don't care that you acted like a jerk. That's what you were supposed to do, and it would be hypocritical of me to be angry at you for it."

"I didn't mean what I said ..."

I shrugged sadly. "I said things I didn't mean. I'm sorry about the fire and foster care. That must have been horrible. I hate the thought of you trapped and alone and worried about your siblings on Christmas. It breaks my heart."

"Who knows. Maybe I deserved it," he said, dropping his hands. "Like the universe knew I was going to be a terrible person and was punishing me preemptively."

I shook my head. "I don't think that you're a bad person. Just maybe not the man for me."

"Please give me another chance. I won't hurt you again."

"I'm not even angry about the lying," I continued, wrapping my arms around myself. "I'm mad that you were nice to my dog and made a thousand Christmas cookies with me, and acted so perfect with my little cousins, and helped me decorate, and made me think that you were someone I could be together with forever, that I could build a life and a future with. I'm angry that you made me fall in love with you, and that I still am in love with you."

"That wasn't a lie. I am that man."

"Are you?"

"I want to be a good father and a good husband, better than my father was. I want to bake cookies with you and help you fill Christmas stockings and spend hours trudging around the woods to find the perfect Christmas tree. You melted all the ice on my heart, Gracie, and it's been there so long I don't know how I'm going to survive without it. But I think if I had you there, then I'd be okay."

He grabbed my hands.

"I'm not a billionaire. I can't offer you private planes, fancy trips, or a glamourous life, but I can offer you stability, partnership, someone who will always be there for you. I can offer you love, warmth, and undying support."

"I want that with you too. It just sounds too good to be true," I said sadly. "People can't change, especially not bad boys."

"I used to believe the same thing," he said. "But people can change, if they really want to, if they put in the work. I've changed, and so have you."

He skated back.

"It's fine if you don't want to give me another shot. I know I don't deserve another shot with you. Even if you say no, this right here with the snow falling and your hair framing your face and the smell of Christmas trees is perfect. You're perfect. Even if I never see you again, I'll always remember this, and it will be enough to keep me going on cold dark winter nights. And I think I'll always remember you like this."

In the black jeans, easily maneuvering on the skates like he was born in them, the leather jacket, his black hair falling over his forehead, the wary but hopeful look in his eyes, backdropped by Christmas trees and candles and snow, he didn't look like a bad boy. He looked like the man I'd want to spend the rest of my life with.

"It's funny." Those silvery gray eyes flicked down then back up to mine. "I never thought I'd ever like Christmas. But for the first time, being with you made me want Christmas every day—to have a family with you, a home with you, one of the big Victorians that you love. I'd build you a custom dining table and a bed, wake up before you and surprise you with breakfast, decorate a tree with you, hang stockings and pretend to play Santa with our kids. I want that now. I thought I never would, but now all I want is that with you. I want to marry you. I should just ask you to be my real girlfriend, but I don't want that. I want you to be my wife. And wasn't the plan to get engaged at your sister's wedding anyway?"

He gave me a crooked smile.

"You what?" I gasped.

Hudson dropped down on one knee and pulled a black box out of his jacket pocket.

"You're proposing to me?"

"Yeah. For real. If anyone had shown up, I'd have married you tonight, but I'll settle for a yes."

I started crying. "I can't. I can't marry you. Please stand up."

"Gracie, I'm begging you," he said, rising and cupping my face.

"I don't even know you. This is insane. You can't be asking me this," I said.

"Of course you know me," he insisted, taking me in his arms and kissing me wildly.

"My name is Hudson Wynter. I was in the Marines for six years, and then I started a security company and invested the profits back into my community, that, let's admit, I have a love-hate relationship with. I like to play hockey, and my siblings annoy me, but I still adore them. I hate wearing suits, but I'll wear one on our wedding day. Your brisket is the best thing I've ever eaten, and I actually don't mind baking cookies. I prefer German shepherds, but your pug is cool. I hate Christmas, but not when I'm with you. I can't resist a damsel in distress, but more than that, I love a woman who will go after what she wants no matter the wake of destruction and broken hearts in her path. I'm the man that loves you more than anyone else in the world. You know all of this. You know me."

"Hudson, I can't. Please go home."

"I love you, Gracie. I want to make you happy." He kissed the tears on my cheeks. "I want to spend the rest of my life with you."

"Hudson ..."

He knelt back down on the ice and said softly, opening up the box, "Please marry me."

"Oh my gosh," I sobbed. "It's the ring, the one that was sold. It looks just like that one. Did you have it made?"

He shook his head.

"This is that ring, her actual ring." He fished in his jacket with one hand then shoved papers at me.

"How did you find it?"

"Grayson has a very good assistant. Turns out being a hired gun does have some job perks. What do you say, Gracie? You want to make this the perfect Christmas ever?"

"How can you want to marry me?" I cried. "You only just met me."

He smiled up at me. "I feel like I've known you my whole life. I know you like the apron with the gnomes on it because the strings are long enough to tie it in the front, but you'll settle for the one with those demonic Christmas bunnies."

"They have antlers on. I embroidered that myself."

"I know you love your family and would do anything for them. I know you adore Christmas, and if the holidays would start in July, that would be just perfect for you. I know you're incredibly smart, that you can go toe-to-toe with some of the most cutthroat businessmen in Manhattan and come out on top. I know that you are the most beautiful thing I have ever seen, even in those flannel pajamas. I know that you're the woman I've been searching for my whole life. Gracie," he said, his skates scraping softly on the ice as he held up the ring, "will you please marry me?"

Did I want to marry him?

"Hudson," I said carefully. "I used to dream about spending my life with someone who loved me, someone boring, and low drama, who was content to lie in bed and watch movies. In my dreams, he'd have a steady job, maybe in accounting, and wear a suit and tie, and come home at six, and like casserole. He wasn't much in the looks department but was still a nice person."

I took a deep breath.

"You are nothing like the man of my dreams. You're aggressive, brashly overconfident, and obnoxiously good-looking. You don't wear underwear let alone a suit. You don't have a real job. Hell, I don't even know what you do, and you leave a trail of destruction and drama in your wake."

He was crushed.

"I know."

"But ever since I met you, I can't help but dream of a future with you, building a home, arguing about Christmas decorations—"

"I'd let you win any arguments," he promised. "Actually, you probably wouldn't even need me to let you win anything."

"I dream of coming home and curling up on the couch, baking cookies together while you get flour all over your black clothes and complain about it but still stay up until 5 a.m. in the kitchen with me. We'd raise little gray-eyed children who'd probably jump off the roof or steal a train or something crazy. Somehow, you're everything I never knew I wanted. I'm supposed to be the daughter who makes good decisions, safe decisions. Maybe being in love with you isn't the safe choice or the smart one, but it's the one I want to make. Or it could be the holidays."

He smiled. "I hear Christmas makes people crazy."

"You make me crazy."

"Marry me," he said solemnly. "Marry me, and I'll make sure all your Christmases are perfect."

"Okay," I choked out. "Yes, I will marry you, Hudson."

He slid the ring on my finger then stood up.

"I love you so much," I gasped before he kissed me, spinning us around on the ice, until I was dizzy and laughing deliriously.

"I love you more than you can ever know," Hudson murmured against my mouth as he slowed the spin.

"I can't believe I just did that," I said, gazing down at the ring sparkling on my hand. "Is this crazy?"

"You were going to give me a hand job in a bus, Sugarplum." He winked. "I'd say this is actually pretty mild for you."

Chapter 56

HUDSON

Gracie chattered on nervously as she helped me pack up the decorations, leftover cake, and remaining food from Kelly's canceled wedding.

I could tell she was anxious. She kept twisting the ring on her finger.

"Maybe this wasn't such a good idea," she said to me as I loaded the last box into the back of my actual truck, which was a little more down-on-its-luck than the one Grayson had lent me for the mission.

She regarded it critically.

"Hmm."

"What?" I tucked a piece of her hair behind her ear.

"Grayson offered me a car to convince me to sign on as CEO. If I'd known he was taking the truck back, I'd have told him to throw it in as a Christmas present for you," she said.

I grabbed her scarf, pulling her in for a kiss.

"The only thing I want for Christmas is you, as my wife."

She was warm and perfect in my arms.

She gently pushed away and gazed up at me. Her lips parted.

I used two fingers to close them.

"Sugarplum, I know you're about to give me an impassioned speech about why this is crazy and why you should give me that ring back. But how about before you nuke another engagement, you let me convince you that we're meant for each other."

⁂

I yanked my shirt off as soon as we were alone in my apartment.

Gracie wasted little time in running her fingers down my chest, her touch so tender and igniting such need for her in me.

I kissed her. Suddenly, briefly, sensually. We leaned into it more and more, tongues intersecting, and the adrenaline rush inside me building up more and more. I tugged off her sweater then her bra.

"Better than opening a Christmas present," I said.

She yanked my belt out of my jeans.

"I know what Christmas package I want to open first!"

I couldn't keep my hands off of her. Our clothes were tossed away in a heap of boots, denim, panties, and socks, until we were both on the plush carpet under the tree, only her skirt remaining.

Gracie was on top of me, her huge tits pressed against my chest. She slid up my body, shoving her tits in my face, me playfully suckling on them and getting a delightful sound in return. She scooted farther up my torso until her knees were holding my arms down.

"What are you up to, Gracie?" I said, in no rush to escape my situation.

"Just giving you a very merry Christmas, Hudson."

More squirming, and her skirt was over my head, her pussy right over my face.

I knew exactly what she wanted, and I was more than happy to give it to her.

With only my tongue available to me, I gave her what she desired. Sliding it into her folds, lapping up her juices, Gracie moaned and panted as I pleasured her, sucking her clit, teasing her with my tongue.

"Yes, oh ... yes, just like that, Hudson," she panted, her words stuttering and becoming less and less coherent by the moment. She was melting into me with just my tongue, and seeing her so pliable with so little made my imagination rush with wonder of what I could do to her with a whole lot more.

She came. Hard. She leaked her juices all over my face as she screamed for me, collapsing forward in a panting mess. I happily licked my lips and wiped my face off with my hands, only to look her way as I sucked my fingers dry of her.

"Oh, you're so insatiable."

"And you're such a bad little elf. What would Santa say if he knew you were being so naughty?"

"He'd probably give me a good spanking," she said, as she nibbled her lip coyly. "Likely bare-assed and over his knees."

"The way you're talking about it, it doesn't sound like much of a punishment, Gracie."

"Santa's never been the best at punishment anyway. He gives people coal and switches still. In the twenty-first century. Guy's kind of out-of-date in his practices."

I sat up. My cock throbbed with need.

Gracie smirked. "We should take care of that, shouldn't we?"

"Ever the little helper, aren't we?"

She scrambled to all fours in front of me, the skirt hiked up, her ass tempting me. "Come on. It's time to ride your reindeer, Santa."

I scowled. "One, Santa doesn't ride the reindeer directly. He uses a sled. Two, I thought you were an elf and not a reindeer? Make up your mind."

She rolled her eyes so playfully. "How about you stop being pedantic and fuck me, Hudson?"

I grabbed her by the hips, rubbing my cock up and down her ass as I found her pussy. She grinded against me, as if I needed further encouragement.

She was still dripping wet. She moaned as I teased her with my fingers, rolling on a condom.

I positioned myself behind her then speared into her, powerfully and suddenly. She was so fucking tight around my cock, squeezing me like a vise, so damn perfect for me. She cried out in pleasure as I slammed into her again.

As I took her harder and stronger, she ground back into me. One hand wrapped around her tits as I held her, massaging them, taking her as she bucked against me.

I was consumed with her.

She was whimpering and moaning, begging me to make her come. I reached down to stroke her clit, and it was enough to send her over the edge. I gritted my teeth as she came on my cock, not wanting this to end.

She moaned as I continued to fuck her, jackhammering into her, letting her feel every thick inch of me.

"I'm going to—" She cried out my name as she came again.

This time, I came with her, spilling into the condom. We collapsed into a wonderfully sweaty mess. I nuzzled up to her, pushed her hair out of the way, and kissed her on her swollen mouth.

"So that's the way you treat reindeer? You ride them that hard?" Gracie said, her voice weak from the exertion.

"You're a very special reindeer, Gracie. You only get the best."

More soft giggling. She turned to look me right in the eye. "I love you, Hudson."

"And I love you, Gracie," I said, without a moment's hesitation. "And? Was that convincing?"

"Very convincing," she purred. She cupped my face with her left hand and giggled. "The ring matches your eyes."

I picked her up and carried her to my bedroom. I kissed her, savored her.

"I love you. All I ever wanted was you."

"I'd say I can't wait to begin my life with you," Gracie murmured against my mouth. "But somehow it feels like you've always been here."

"I want to be your husband," I whispered to her in the dark. "I'll make sure every day is like Christmas morning."

"Not *every* day. Christmas morning is stressful," she whispered back with a smile. "Some days just need to be a lazy Christmas afternoon, after an early Christmas dinner."

"I can do that too," I promised, stroking her hair.

I made love to her until the ridiculous cuckoo clock she'd installed on my wall sounded out "Jingle Bells" at a deafening volume.

Gracie shot straight up.

"What in god's name?"

"Merry Christmas." I kissed her softly.

"Oh my gosh." She pressed a hand to her chest. "That is very unsettling and does not inspire Christmas joy."

"You gave me that clock," I reminded her, trailing kisses down her soft skin.

"You have my permission to smash that clock with a hammer." She smiled at me. "Sometimes there can be too much Christmas."

She nestled back against me and closed her eyes.

I nudged her.

"Gracie."

"Hmm?"

"Don't you want to open presents?"

"Presents?"

"It's Christmas."

She opened her eyes and grinned up at me.

"Someone's excited for Christmas morning."

"Not me," I scoffed. "I'm just looking out for Pugnog."

The dog was sound asleep on his back in a nest of Gracie's and my clothes on the floor.

As I heated up the oven, I took the dog outside. It was dark out, only me, the dog, and the falling snow. Still, I didn't feel alone at all. I had the love of my life waiting for me upstairs.

I made breakfast then started a fire in the ancient fireplace.

"I was going to make breakfast," Gracie said when she padded out, wrapped in a knitted red robe that sported a hood with Rudolph ears and antlers.

I carried the tray into the living room and set it on the coffee table. In the fireplace, logs crackled.

"I used to work in food service. I think I can handle a Christmas morning spread, though it's not as elaborate as your breakfasts."

"The best food is the kind you don't have to cook yourself," she said, taking one of the triangular bacon, egg, and cheese breakfast sandwiches.

I handed her a mug of coffee in one of the Christmas mugs she'd brought.

"Yum. Is that a hint of nutmeg I taste?"

"It is Christmas." I kissed her, tasting the spice on her mouth.

"All right. Who's first?" Gracie rubbed her hands together.

"Pugnog." The dog snorted awake when I wafted a sandwich under his nose. He sat up, spraying drool all over me.

Gracie giggled. "I'll shower you off. Don't worry." She ran a hand up my bare thigh.

I grabbed Pugnog's gift from under the tree. He stared at it. Well, one-eye stared—the other wandered up to the ceiling.

"Pugnog," Gracie cooed, "your new daddy bought you a gift. Isn't that nice? What do we say?"

The pug panted. Gracie gave him some bacon, and he scarfed it down noisily.

"I don't know if this is going to compete with bacon," I told the dog.

"Look, Pugnog," Gracie squealed as I opened the present for him. "It's a doggy water bowl you won't drown in."

"There is a lady in Harrogate who makes them custom," I explained. "I saw one when I was up there earlier in December and had Elsa buy one and bring it. It's tilted so that Pugnog doesn't have to stick his whole face in to get a drink."

"It's also decorated in pugs wearing Santa hats." Gracie kissed me. "It's adorable."

"Okay, now you."

Gracie handed me the carefully wrapped present and clasped her hands together in excitement.

I tore off the wrapping paper.

"What in the—" I unfolded what at first I thought was a blanket.

"It's a handmade knitted robe by yours truly that matches mine! Complete with Rudolph horns. We're twins!" she crowed. "Put it on. Pugnog has one too." She stuffed the dog into his outfit. "We have to take family photos in front of the tree."

She dragged me over to the tree, Pugnog clutched under one arm, and snapped selfies.

This was going on the Christmas card for next year.

She kissed me. "Thank you for being a good sport. You don't have to wear it, of course."

"Are you kidding?" I said, wrapping it around myself. "This is extremely comfortable. Now open yours."

"Yes! A present."

"It's not regifted shit like your family gets you either," I said.

"Someone's full of himself." Gracie picked up the last box.

"Hmm," she said. "This looks like you did not wrap this yourself."

"My sister did," I admitted.

"I cannot wait to meet her. This is an expert-level wrapping job."

"Elsa works holiday retail," I explained.

"Even better," Gracie said as she carefully unwrapped the present.

She was probably going to save the paper, I decided.

When Gracie pulled back the packing material keeping the shadow box safe, she let out a small sob.

"It's lovely, Hudson." She gazed down at the shadow box Elsa had helped me with, taking in the bits of antique lace, the photos, the miniatures.

"This is …" She traced it with her fingers. "This is so perfect. Wait is this …" Gracie looked up at me, eyes shining. "No way. Is this the actual lace from *the* dress? The real lace? How did you find this?"

"I do garbage collecting," I said gruffly. "Know the guys at the dump. You had said Kelly threw the scraps away. You dig through tons of trash, and you'll eventually find things."

Gracie threw herself in my arms.

"This is the best Christmas present ever! Well," she amended, "third best." She kissed me. "You're the second best."

"Damn. Demoted for a ring, huh?" I grinned against her mouth.

She grabbed my jaw.

"I can't believe you think I'm that materialistic. Pugnog was a Christmas present too," she said, giggling as I pretended to be offended.

"Let's go back to bed and start that lazy Christmas afternoon even though it's like 3 a.m. I have a gingerbread-house-decorating kit we can do later," I said after we had sat dozing in front of the fireplace.

I nudged her.

She laughed on my chest and looked up at me.

"You bought a gingerbread-house-making kit?"

"The gingerbread is premade, full disclosure, so I'm sure it's not up to your standards."

Gracie snuggled in my arms. "Maybe I'll just have to decorate your dick instead with frosting and gumdrops."

"That sounds …"

"Festive?"

On the coffee table, her phone beeped and vibrated. She reached for it and scoffed when she read the messages.

"Surprise, surprise." She ran a hand along my chest. "We're not going back to bed. I have a massive Christmas brunch for a hundred plus people to serve."

"Do you?"

She tapped me on the nose.

"Yes, because I'm inviting your siblings. Buck up, Hudson. It's Christmas. We die like men!"

I kissed her and sat up. "Then I guess I know how I'm spending Christmas morning."

Chapter 57

GRACIE

"You have some nerve," Kelly snapped when she came into the kitchen. It was still early, and no, I had not woken my sister up while happily singing Christmas carols while I made breakfast.

Kelly was in her party clothes, makeup smeared on her face, just returned from a night out.

"You ruin my marriage, my life, and the family, then just come back in here to use the kitchen."

"I'm making breakfast," I snapped at her and set down the spatula. "For the record, I'm not using anything, and I'm not taking advantage of anyone. You know, I really wish that we had been able to be closer as sisters. I'd like to be able to rely on you and for you to rely on me. Since it is Christmas, I'm willing to give you another chance."

"Give me another chance?" Kelly shrieked.

"Yes," I said forcefully. "You slept with my ex-fiancé, and you tried to sleep with my current one."

"What fiancé?" My sister crossed her arms.

"Hudson."

"Seriously? That's rich! Mom and Dad are going to flip."

"Maybe, but at least I have somewhere else to stay over Christmas now."

"Mom!" My sister stomped up the back staircase.

Ugh.

I hadn't thought of how my parents were going to take the news of my engagement. Did it really matter what they thought at this point? It wasn't going to change that I wanted to marry Hudson and spend the rest of my life with him.

"Gracie!"

"Why is everyone up at 6:30 in the morning?" I muttered as James swaggered into the kitchen. "Can't a woman make enough French toast for the Lithuanian army uninterrupted?"

"I just want you to know," James said, encroaching on my personal space, "that even though everyone in the family was angry I stood up for you, you're a regular boss babe, and I couldn't be more proud of you. I heard Mr. Richmond is giving you a very generous raise. I've taken the liberty of calling some of my real-estate contacts so that we can find the perfect condo." He whipped out his phone.

"Dakota's already got it covered."

"No, no. Dakota is not living with us."

"With us?" I said slowly. "There is no us."

James laughed. "Of course there is. You need a husband."

"Hmm." I tapped my chin. "Actually, I think I have that covered too."

"No man is going to date you, Gracie," James scoffed. "Especially not in Manhattan. They all want supermodels which, let's be honest, is not you. You have other talents. I know we went through a rough patch, but clearly your little revenge plan," he used air quotes, "was just because you secretly wanted me, and you were mad that you lost me to Kelly. Message received, Gracie. Let's start from where we left off. You made mistakes, I made mistakes. Let's call it even." He petted my hair.

I jerked away from him, but he didn't take the hint.

"I am not in love with you, James. That revenge scheme wasn't about winning you back. I don't want anything to do with you. I don't understand why you're still here. You're not part of this family. You're not marrying Kelly, and you're certainly not marrying me. So get lost."

"Gracie, of course we're getting married." James's hands rested on my waist. If I wasn't covered in egg, I'd have pushed him away. "I'm meant to be with you. You're a high-powered CEO now, and I want you to know that I'll be there to support you in any way you need. Well, obviously, you'd hire a nanny for the kids. I wouldn't, like, change a diaper or anything." He laughed.

"There is no scenario on earth where I have your baby then leave it with a nanny so you can mooch off me," I snapped at him.

"Stop being such a shrew. You're never going to find anyone as good as me."

The back door banged open, and Hudson pushed his way inside. He grabbed James by the collar of his shirt and slammed him against the pantry wall.

"Get away from my woman."

James stuttered, "What is he doing here? Someone call the police!"

I washed my hands off then I picked up the ring where I'd put it very far away from the sink by the window and slipped it on my finger.

"You can't just let him call you his woman."

"She can because she is. Gracie is going to be my wife."

Hudson wrapped me in his arms, tilted my face up, and kissed me like he'd just come home for Christmas.

"Now," he said to James, his arm still protectively around my waist, "get out of my sight."

James gulped and raced to the front door.

I turned back to my French toast while Hudson pressed his freezing-cold chest on my back.

"Don't you ever wear a jacket to run?" I giggled as he kissed my neck.

"I don't need to because you'll warm me up," he said, sliding his cold hands under my sweater, making me shriek.

"Let's just ditch Christmas brunch," he whispered in my ear. "We can go back to my place, and I can eat you out all afternoon instead."

I shivered against him.

"No can do. All your siblings and Grayson already accepted my last-minute invite. Do those people never sleep?" I said, turning my head and kissing him loudly.

He swore.

"Kelly woke up everyone," Dakota announced, trotting down the back staircase. She scooped up Pugnog and snuggled him. Then she took one look at my hand and screamed.

"You got engaged? To him? That asshole?"

I made a face, but Hudson stepped in before I could say anything.

"I promise," Hudson swore to Dakota, "that I love Gracie more than anything in the world, and I will always take care of her."

My cousin seemed unconvinced.

"And," Hudson added, "I'm not going to take her away from you. Not only that, but I will insist that we name our firstborn daughter after you, and you will be an honored godmother." He smiled that megawatt bad-boy smile at her.

Dakota narrowed her eyes.

"Damn, he's good."

"Also, guess whose ring this is?" I trilled, holding out my left hand and wiggling my fingers.

"*Oh my god!*" Dakota freaked out. "It's the ring. Are you freaking kidding me! Okay, yes, we accept your proposal, Hudson."

"Gracie!" several of my cousins cried, pouring into the kitchen.

"You got engaged!"

"Let's see the ring."

"Man, this is the spot on Christmas morning." My brother and Piper stumbled into the kitchen, yawning. "How can I help?" Logan asked.

"Merry Christmas," I called, hugging them all. "This isn't up to my usual brunch standards, but it should still be tasty."

I directed my cousins and brother to wash hands and form sausage patties as Grandma Astelle thumped into the kitchen, shawl around her shoulders. She regarded Hudson, who was gulping down water.

"I see she made an honest man out of you," Grandma Astelle said to Hudson.

"Yes, ma'am," he replied.

I handed him a tea towel.

Grandma Astelle looked like she'd eaten something sour.

"Let's see the ring. I hope it's real."

"It is very real." I held out my hand.

The elderly woman gasped. Her eyes teared up, and she gently took my hand.

"That's my mother's ring."

"Yes. The engraving is still inside," Hudson said.

"There's an engraving? I didn't even notice." I slipped it off.

Our love endures because you endure me. –H

"People were funny back then," Piper said, peering over my shoulder.

Grandma Astelle took the ring from me.

"My mother adored my father so. He could always make her laugh. He encouraged her to start her baking company, you know. She was quite the businesswoman. Julia Child had lunch with her often. Oh, I miss her so much." There was a slight sob in her voice. "What a wonderful Christmas present. Hudson, I believe I may have misjudged you."

I wrapped Grandma Astelle in a hug. Was it a Christmas miracle? Had she changed?

The elderly woman dabbed her nose.

"It's hard getting old. I'm surprised I haven't died waiting for you to get married, Gracie. You certainly took your time."

And there it was.

"I suppose you scraped something together at the last minute though, didn't you, Gracie. Don't let yourself go like James did, young man," she warned to Hudson. "No one likes buying a turkey then finding out it's mostly water."

Kelly stormed back downstairs followed by more of my male cousins, on break from college.

"Hudson's back!" they roared and ran through the house.

"Call Uncle Bic!"

"Hockey game after breakfast!"

They slapped Hudson on the shoulders and shook his hand.

"Congratulations!"

"Gracie, you locked him down. The star hockey player."

Violet grabbed the spatula. "Sit down, Gracie. Let me help you."

"You don't want to ruin your nails."

"You're a busy CEO now," my cousin exclaimed. "Put your feet up. Enjoy your sexy husband."

"Okay ..."

"By the way, are you hiring? I can be a receptionist."

"She's not even qualified to be the office sex toy."

"Connie, you bitch!"

My cousins went at each other.

"I was wondering," Bella said as she took the carton of eggs from me and started cracking them. "If you might be able to give me a small loan. Very small. Just to tide me over until February. I need to pay my gym membership."

"You can't ask her first. I'm asking her first," her sister snapped.

"Um?" A young blond man with gray eyes, darker gray than Hudson's, appeared at the back door.

"Where am I?" He looked shaken. "I think I was kidnapped?" The young man looked queasy. "Am I in New York?"

"What happened to you?" I hurried over to him, shoved him in a chair, and stuck a mop bucket between his knees. "Hudson, should we call the police?"

Hudson was frowning and studying the young man.

Kelly scoffed. "He's not kidnapped. I brought him home for Granny Murray."

The young man was staring at Kelly, mouth open. "I thought I was going to have sex with you."

"That woman!" Grandma Astelle thundered. "Call the National Guard, Hudson. She is a menace and needs to be removed from the state of Rhode Island at once."

"Oh shit," Granny Murray said from the doorway.

"Mom!" my mother scolded, her robe wrapped around her. "What is all this commotion? It's pitch-dark out. Who is this child that you brought home?"

"I'm twenty," the kid declared. He trailed off when he saw Hudson staring at him.

"Aren't you one of the Svensson brothers?" Hudson asked.

"Oh fuck."

"I'm calling Greg."

"No, no, no, let's not be hasty. No harm, no foul. I just woke up, and there was the old woman staring at me. She was wearing a Rudolph costume. I think I was drugged in the club."

"Drugged?" Granny Murray crowed. "He could barely hold his liquor."

"Tell Greg it wasn't my fault," the kid shrieked.

Hudson dragged him up by the arm.

"I was out volunteering. I'm innocent. I wasn't at a club. I'm only in college."

"Gracie!" my father greeted me. "Merry Christmas! How's my favorite daughter?"

"Daddy!" Kelly cried.

"Dad, you really shouldn't play favorites," I told him.

"What your father wants to ask," my mother said to me, "is if you might want to buy this house? We could all live here."

"I thought you paid off the house," I said.

My father grimaced. "The interest rates were just so good for a home equity loan."

"Oh my god."

"Hey," my dad protested. "I'm not asking for money, and you love this house. You're always in the kitchen."

"I'll have to talk to my fiancé."

My mother's eye twitched.

"Yes, your fiancé. We heard the good news." My dad gave me a pained smile.

"Your grandmother will be homeless," my mother cried.

"Don't do it, Gracie," Granny Murray said. "You can't start off a marriage by making your husband inherit all of his in-laws and their financial issues. Trust me on that one."

"I'll buy the house." My grandmother patted my mom on the shoulder. "You can live with me. Don't worry. I had money squirrelled away. I always knew your husband was a loser."

"How dare you?" Grandma Astelle went after Granny Murray, though it was a more of a slow-moving chase.

"They were out looking for him." Hudson came back inside, sidestepping the two elderly women. "Apparently, they put a tracker in his shoe."

"Look at you, returning lost siblings." I handed Hudson a mug of fresh coffee.

He took it then leaned down to kiss me.

"Can that man put on a shirt?" my mother begged.

"Boo! No!" my female cousins exclaimed.

"I gave Granny Murray's boy toy away," Hudson drawled. "She should get something for her troubles. It is Christmas, after all."

"Here, here! Ow!" Granny Murray complained as Grandma Astelle slapped her with her gloves. "Where's my Taser?"

"This place is a madhouse."

The doorbell rang.

Pugnog raced through the house.

"Merry Christmas!" Hudson's siblings called.

"I thought you said we had to dress up," Jake whined when he and the rest of the Wynter brothers shoved their massive six-foot-five bodies into the kitchen.

"Oh my god." Uncle Eddie gasped. "There are more Hudsons."

"Quick! Parcel out the girl cousins," my brother bellowed.

"Not Kelly," Connie snickered.

"Bitch!" my sister screeched.

Jake started to remove his tie.

"Stop it," Anderson hissed at him.

"It's fine," I said, throwing up my hands. "If he wants to change into a robe, he can, since apparently all sense of decorum has been lost in this house."

"You sound like Grandma Astelle," Violet told me. "But don't let that stop you from stripping down 'til you feel comfortable." She giggled at Jake.

"Keep your shirt on," a young woman said to him, shoving through her brothers.

"You must be—"

"Hi. I'm Elsa. I love Christmas and pugs and brunch, and we're going to be amazing friends, and I have a sister now, and I totally won't sleep with your fiancé because that would be really weird."

"She's been up all night selling Christmas trees then insisted we drive all night to be here," Anderson said. "Please excuse her."

"I have had so much coffee." Elsa grabbed Hudson's mug, drained it, and slammed it on the counter. "Hit me, bro."

"Can you all please act like you have some sense?" he said over the din of people packed into the kitchen.

I shoved past my brother, who was peeling potatoes.

"I'll make sure our house has an open floor plan," Hudson murmured to me.

"Lots of little rooms are fun."

"Is this fun?"

Jake pulled off his shirt.

Granny Murray wolf whistled, and my female cousins shrieked.

"Where is Dakota?" Aunt Babs hollered. "You're almost thirty. Get out there." She shoved my cousin, who still had her toothbrush in her mouth, into Jake's arms.

"I like older women." Jake waggled his eyebrows.

Dakota punched him in the abs.

"Ow," she said around the toothbrush.

"You're coming with me, sonny," Granny Murray told him.

Grandma Astelle drew her sword.

"Aw yeah! Fight fight fight!"

Logan started to chant. My family joined in.

"Did I come at a bad time?" Grayson Richmond said as he walked in. He handed me a bottle of wine.

Both grandmothers turned on him.

"Leave him alone. He's my new boss, so of course he should be invited."

"He's a billionaire," Kelly reminded my cousins. They swarmed him.

"Back! Back!" Grandma Astelle waved her sword at them. "None of them are good enough for you," she said to Grayson. "Gracie might be if she lost that last bit of baby fat. But since she's engaged to a hoodlum, she's off the market."

Grayson raised an eyebrow.

"My neighbor's daughter went to Harvard. She's a wonderful young woman. You'll like her very much. She is from a good family. I'll introduce you." Grandma Astelle escorted him to the sitting room.

"Does he play hockey? Do you play hockey?" my uncles demanded, following them.

Finally, the kitchen was clear.

"Wow," I said, ears ringing.

Hudson handed me a coffee.

"Merry Christmas," he said dryly.

I nuzzled my nose on his chest.

"I love you." The words came out slightly muffled.

Hudson picked me up, and some of the coffee sloshed on the floor as he kissed me.

"I love you so much, and this is the happiest Christmas I have ever had."

I closed my eyes, really letting myself bask in the perfect imperfection of this Christmas as I leaned into his embrace.

"Call me a bad elf," I whispered to Hudson, "but I'm seriously considering eloping!"

A SHORT HOLIDAY ROMANTIC COMEDY

BAD ELF GETS HITCHED

Chapter 1

GRACIE

"The stripper is here!"

"Gran," I hissed, "that is one of Hudson's brothers. If you can't behave, then you can't be at the couple's shower."

"I can behave," my grandmother cried. "I'm a wonderful guest." She handed me a pink gift sack festooned with penises in Santa hats.

"I said no gifts." I closed my eyes.

"These are sex toys. They're for your marriage." She patted my hand.

Five more months of wedding planning to go, five more months of wedding planning to go.

Since I'd had terrible luck with weddings, and because it probably would be a good idea to have a bit of a longer engagement since I had only known Hudson for about two weeks before getting engaged, I had planned on a spring wedding.

Here it was December.

Snow was falling, and a joint couple's shower was ongoing in my parents' house because never would I be able to escape it.

In my defense, all my stuffed animals were still here.

Hudson hadn't offered to move them into his apartment, and I didn't ask.

I set the gift by the fireplace.

Since I'd already had a couple's shower with James, and I was the new golden-egg-laying goose in the family, I'd told everyone no gifts. We were just going to have fun and enjoy each other's company.

"It's a pajama party," Kelly was telling Jake Wynter in a flirtatious tone. "You have to wear pajamas."

He waggled his eyebrows. "What if I sleep in the nude?"

My cousins made horny cat noises.

My sister had volunteered to host the shower. Dakota had said absolutely not. My mom had said I should let Kelly make it up to me.

The end result was Kelly and my cousins walking around in very skimpy lingerie. For whom you may ask? Weren't the majority of us related, you may ask?

Apparently, it was for this.

Connie, Violet, and the rest of my cousins had flocked to Hudson's brothers as soon as they'd arrived.

I stood there in my robe, flannel PJs, and oversized Rudolph slippers, wondering if this party was going to devolve into an orgy.

Hudson came over to me and kissed me.

"Where is your shirt?" I asked.

"You're lucky I'm wearing pants." He tugged the collar of my shirt. "This flannel is itchy."

"It's fireproof." I wrinkled my nose.

"Gracie," my mother tutted when she saw me. "Couldn't you have tried a little harder? At least brushed your hair?"

I clapped my hands on my head. "What's wrong with my hair?"

Hudson ran his fingers through my curls. "I love your hair." He nuzzled my neck. "I can't wait to marry you."

"Come on, Gracie, we're doing a PJ photo shoot." Dakota waved me over.

Hudson picked me up.

"Don't you have anything nice for Gracie to wear?" my mother asked Kelly. "These are family photos. I'm going to frame these."

"Are you even wearing a bra?" Granny Murray asked. She had jumped on the skimpy negligee sleepwear train.

"I'm turning down the heat," I called to no one in particular. That would convince everyone to put on a robe.

"Stand up straight, Gracie," my mother said as she tried to arrange everyone for the photo.

I didn't like having my photo taken. I did not take great photos or even good photos. If I got an okay photo, we were doing very well for ourselves.

"Gracie, you're the bride. Front and center, please. Can you please give me a nice smile? Shoulders back, head up. Look at how Kelly's posing."

My sister had her arm looped around Jake's neck. Her Santa hat propped jauntily on her head, she was posing like a Rockette. She winked at the camera.

"That's cute. Why don't all you girls wink for the camera? Gracie, a nice wink. Smile!"

"I do not want to have this wedding anymore," I hissed through my teeth.

"How many more wedding events?" I groaned and flopped down on Dakota's bed when we were back in our swanky-ish Manhattan condo.

Could I have just rented? Sure, but why rent when you could overextend yourself on a mortgage?

Also, I felt like I was a real adult now that I owned my own place.

Well, co-owned it. Dakota and I had bought it together because even with my fancy CEO position, Manhattan real estate was still expensive. Since Dakota and I were already so enmeshed, why not make it official? Most importantly, I didn't want her to feel like she was getting the boot when Hudson and I got married. I knew how it felt as a single, unmarried person to constantly be given the shaft, to be expected to sacrifice for the marrieds, and I wasn't going to be that person who shit all over their single friends and family members.

Dakota flopped down next to me.

"Let's see, there's the bachelor and bachelorette parties, there's the bridal shower, the bridal tea, the awkward evening when Grandma Astelle and all the aunts gather around to tell horror stories about sex, childbirth, and having a husband …"

"I went through that once. Never again. We have to cancel that one."

"You tell Grandma Astelle that," Dakota said, turning her head to me.

I ran my hands over my face. Dakota slapped them.

"That's how you get breakouts."

"I just feel like it's Groundhog Day. I already had all those events with James. Every time we have another wedding-related event, all I can think about is how naïve and stupid I was to believe that it was the start of a beautiful life with him."

"Look on the bright side. Now you can have the full experience this time with Hudson."

But I had my doubts. Hudson and I hadn't spent all that much time together. We didn't even live together. Both of us were busy with work. Last week, the only time I'd seen him in person was at the PJ party. One of his offices was right across the river in New Jersey, so it wasn't like we were that far apart. Still, it felt like he had been avoiding me these past few months.

"Yeah. I guess. I think he's just annoyed by the family. Maybe he regrets asking me to marry him so soon without us really getting to know each other. Now I'm so busy with work that we're still not actually getting to know each other."

Dakota patted my hand.

"Hudson isn't the type of man to do something he doesn't want to. If he's marrying you, it's because he doesn't want to marry anyone else."

"Mom was right. I should have tried harder at the PJ party. He saw me in the flannel, and he's having second thoughts."

"Why don't you take a bath?" Dakota suggested. "You're spinning out. Hudson loves you. Don't overthink it."

I woke up in the middle of the night to barking.

"Pugnog?" I mumbled, sitting up and pushing my hair out of my face.

"What's wrong?" I asked the pug. "Huh?" I looked down. Pugnog was on his back, snoring loudly in his basket.

The barking was far away and sounded desperate and frantic.

It also sounded very much like Pugnog.

"Dakota?" I whispered, pulling on my robe while I padded into my cousin's bedroom. "Dakota, do you hear that?"

"Is Pugnog stuck in the pantry again?" she mumbled.

"He's asleep."

"So someone's dog saw a moth or something. I dunno." She rolled over, eyes closed.

I didn't believe it. The barking sounded too frantic.

Pulling my robe around me, I headed out into the dim hallway.

The barking got fainter as I headed in the direction of the elevators, so I turned and went the opposite direction. I didn't hear it get any louder on our floor, so I took the stairs to the next floor, looked around, then went up another floor. Three doors down from the stairwell, I heard the frantic barking.

"Hello?" I knocked on the door. "Hello? Is that your dog barking? Is everything all right? Do you need any help?"

On the other side of the door, nails scraped on the hardwood floor and something wheezed.

I tried the doorknob. It was unlocked.

"Uh, sorry?" I called as the door swung open to an empty condo—empty except for an overweight pug sitting on the floor, looking up at me and drooling, his tongue lolling out.

"Hello, sweetie," I cooed, picking him up. "Where are your mommy and daddy?"

Cradling the pug to my chest, I took the elevator down to the lobby. The concierge smiled when he saw me.

"Hey, Pringle," the concierge said when he noticed the dog in my arms. "What are you doing here?"

"You know this dog?"

"It's the Krowoskys' dog," he said as Pringle whined in my arms. "They moved to Paris a couple days ago."

"You've been all alone by yourself," I cooed to Pringle.

The concierge picked up the phone on the desk and dialed a number.

"Uh-huh. I see. All righty, Mrs. Krowosky," he said. "I can find him a new home."

He hung up and gave Pringle a sympathetic look.

"They don't want him."

"They don't want him?" I clutched Pringle to my chest. "How? Even so, they just abandoned him there and didn't tell anyone?"

"Rich people." The concierge shook his head. "No offense."

"I'm not like that. I would never abandon an animal."

As I stood outside while Pringle did his business, I tried to compose a message to Hudson.

What could I say though? I knew pugs were not his dog breed of choice. He wanted a German shepherd. It didn't seem fair if I got another pug and he had no big dog to take hiking on long walks. Sure, he stoically carried Pugnog in his dog backpack when he got tired during long hikes on the trails up to the falls. But to have him cart around two pugs? That seemed like a lot to ask of a man you hadn't even officially married yet.

That sounded like a relationship-ending ask.

Chapter 2

HUDSON

"We see you when you're sleeping," my brother sang as we reviewed footage we'd stolen from the cameras from a high-powered executive who was certain the nanny was a plant from a rival company.

According to this footage of the nanny accessing the desktop computer, her suspicions were correct.

"Another merry Christmas," Anderson said.

"I feel like we are overqualified for this." I frowned.

"Some people don't want to mow their own grass or cook their own food or plan their own weddings." Lawrence elbowed me. "Speaking of, how's the very long engagement?"

"Long," I stated.

Maybe too long.

Gracie seemed distant with me. She worked all the time. I'd even got drunk one night and called Grayson to bitch him out. He had said that he didn't tell her to work that late and to calm the fuck down.

How could I be calm?

Maybe she's mad you pressured her into a wedding, I told myself. *Maybe she's having second thoughts and is avoiding you.*

Gracie certainly hadn't seemed happy at the last wedding event.

I shook off the doubts.

"Good work," I told my employees. "That will be a nice year-end chunk of change."

"Yeah, and will pay off that house you just bought."

My siblings trooped after me up the walkway to my new house in Maplewood Falls. This house was down the street from the Canal Club venue. I was slowly rehabbing the buildings in this area, trying to bring the Gulch back to its former glory. Once we had enough of the historic properties renovated, I was going to change the name back to the Canal District. Though to actually bring those canals back to life was going to be a feat.

I thought about the commercial properties I owned. Those were business decisions motivated by spite that the Gulch could be as nice as the rest of Maplewood Falls. This? This was a home. Or, well, it would be.

"Did you talk to her about this house before you bought it?" Elsa asked me carefully when my siblings and I were standing in the middle of the derelict living room.

Talbot made a face when water dripped on his head. "You can't show her this. It's a dump. She's going to run away screaming."

"In six months, when Gracie and I are really married," I said to my brother, "it will be our dream home."

"It has a sort of murder mystery vibe," Lawrence told me.

"You think Gracie's going to like it?"

I pulled out the long list of requirements she had for a home.

"It checks every single one."

"Except for it being actually, you know, livable," Lawrence remarked.

"I hope you all brought your work clothes, because we need to get some tarps on this roof."

As I carefully tugged a tarp over the roof, Elsa walked around harvesting pieces of the historic plaster that had fallen from the caved-in ceiling. I wondered if I'd made a big mistake. Not just the house, though now that my brothers and I were navigating the rotten roof, it looked a lot worse than I had originally thought.

Gracie's words at the party the other day haunted me.

She didn't want to have this wedding.

"Lunch break," Elsa called.

"What are we having?"

She shrugged. "I don't know, but I'm starving."

Half an hour later, we were wedged into a booth at the Philly cheesesteak place. Talbot and Lawrence were fighting over fries.

"Don't worry. Gracie is going to love the house," Elsa told me.

"Gracie doesn't like a lot of drama. The house might put her over the edge. I think I'll just sit on it and not tell her until I have it in better shape."

"Are you kidding me?" Anderson stated. "You can't keep this big of a secret from her. You're on shaky ground, remember?"

How could I forget? She and I had built our relationship on a solid foundation of lies and deceit. I had promised her and myself I wasn't going to lie to her ever again.

"I'll tell her about it, but make it seem like it's a big adventure," I said uncertainly.

"Tomorrow is Friday. Tell her you want to pick her up at the office early, that you have a surprise for her. We'll put up some Christmas lights and a wreath. She'll love it," Elsa said confidently.

"I guess so."

My phone beeped.

Gracie: *We need to talk.*

"Oooh fuuuck," Jake drawled.
I punched him in the arm.
"Ow!"

Gracie: *Sorry! Know you hate that, but we really need to meet in person.*

I felt sick.

Hudson: *Fine.*
Gracie: *Ugh. Sorry again. It's a surprise addition to our family.*

Elsa squealed. "Oh my gosh! You're going to be a dad. I'm going to be an aunt. We have to name the baby. It better be a girl."

"I've been sneaking pineapple into his food," Jake assured her, tapping his forehead. "So I think we're good."

"I'm going to be a father." I was stunned.

I started composing a message until I got her next text.

Gracie: *But we don't have to keep it. In fact, maybe it's better if we didn't.*

I slammed the phone down and crossed my arms.

"Well shit," Anderson said when he read the message.

"Just talk to her," Talbot told me.

"There's nothing to talk about. I want that baby."

The next afternoon, I stood in the lobby of the Richmond Electric skyscraper. I knew I looked out of place among all the people in suits.

She deserves better than you.

It was unfair to tie her to me when she was embarking on such a big life change. Even if Grayson swore up and down he was hands-off, there were other eligible bachelors in the office, as Astelle liked to say. They had the type of money to buy a perfectly renovated historic home, not one with half the roof missing and a thousand hours of work needed.

I saw her come off the elevator. She was laughing and smiling up at a man in a suit.

A surprise addition.

We had been very careful. Gracie said it would kill Astelle if she had a baby before getting married.

How was she pregnant now? She and I had been careful, but maybe she and whomever she was sleeping with in her office hadn't been.

Someone grabbed the back of my jacket and dragged me to an out-of-the-way alcove.

"You fucking—"

Grayson's green eyes narrowed.

"You look like you're here to kill someone. I've spent a lot of money to acquire and train my employees," he warned.

"I'm just—" I paced around. "Has Gracie been spending time with anyone at your office?" I finally choked out.

"You better not be implying me," Grayson said, voice dangerously low.

"Of course not. Just ... she's pregnant and—"

"She is?" Grayson frowned. "She was drinking at lunch."

"Then she really doesn't want to have a baby with me," I said miserably. "She still hates me. I think ..." I worked my jaw then admitted my worst fears. "I think she's concerned I'm going to be a terrible father, that she's going to have a kid who grows up to be a piece of shit."

Grayson gave me a sympathetic look.

"If you're worried that you're not going to be a good father because of your own parents, I understand that, believe me. It's a fair concern, but you also sound unhinged. You haven't even seen a positive pregnancy test."

"I know that's what she's going to tell me."

Grayson grabbed my jaw and spread one of my eyelids open.

"Are you on something? Have you been sleeping?"

I shoved him off me. "I don't need sleep. I have work deadlines."

I closed my eyes. "I need to talk to Gracie."

"You sure you don't want to sleep? Have a cooling off period, maybe eat something other than protein shakes."

"I'm fine," I spat.

Chapter 3

GRACIE

Hudson seemed angry when I finally found him.

"Where did you go? I thought I saw you in the lobby," I said in a rush, "then you disappeared."

"Had to talk to Grayson."

"Ah."

We stood there in silence.

He usually hugged me and kissed me when he saw me. Not today.

I rocked in my high-heeled shoes.

My fiancé was so tense.

"Are you okay?" I asked, resting a cautious hand on his arm.

"I'm fine." He jerked away from me. "What do you want to talk about?"

"Not here," I said weakly. "Let's go to my place. It's faster to take the train."

In the subway, I pulled my knitting out of my purse and sat there making a new hat for Pugnog while Hudson sat and stewed next to me. I had tried to ask him how work was, how his siblings were, but gave up after he just gave grunts or one-word answers.

I kept dropping stiches, I was so anxious. Hudson had to know about the dog. There was no other explanation for why he was so angry.

He was a silent presence next to me as we made our way out of the subway. No one hassled me or asked for money or a signature. One glare from Hudson and people parted for us, giving him wide berth.

I waved to the concierge and greeted the doorman when we arrived at my building.

Hudson nodded to the men.

We rode the elevator up in silence.

My mouth was dry.

Maybe I should have just called the pug rescue and not have said anything to Hudson.

"So," I said when I had unlocked the front door and stepped into the living room.

"I need to say something first," Hudson said, interrupting me. "Gracie, I know that I wasn't the best boyfriend and honestly haven't been a great fiancé. Please let me finish." He ran a hand through his hair.

"There is nothing I want more than to marry you and start a family with you. If you're nervous about it or concerned that I'll be a bad father or our kid will suck, I won't let that happen. I promise. I've been grooming several of my employees to take a bigger role in the company. I can step back so that you don't have to feel like you have to split your time. My hours are more flexible than yours. You can keep working as much as you want without worrying that I'll drop the ball." He took my hand. "I want to have a family with you, Gracie. I want that more than anything in the world."

I started to cry.

"Gracie, whatever it is, we can work through it," he said kindly.

"You're so perfect," I sobbed. "And now I feel terrible for not telling you the truth earlier."

"What truth, Gracie?" He sounded so hurt.

"I know you don't like pugs," I said.

"What?" Pringle and Pugnog chose that moment to trot out into the living room, having smelled Hudson. Well, Pugnog trotted. Hudson had insisted on putting him on an exercise regime. Pringle, however, waddled.

"Are they multiplying?"

"I adopted a pug without asking you," I said, trying to control my gasping sobs. "I know I should have just talked to you first, but now I'm really attached to him, and I know you wanted a big dog and not another inbred donut hole."

That made him snort.

"But Pringle is a great pug, and you're such a good dog dad."

"Gracie."

His face was relaxed, happy.

"I thought you were pregnant."

"Oh lord, I hope not. You're supposed to eat clean like six months beforehand, and I have soooo not been doing that. Also, I had a martini at lunch."

He leaned down to kiss me.

"You're such a Manhattan cliché. Next, you're going to tell me you were at a cigar bar smoking and plotting your enemies' downfalls."

"No. Just at the new bakery plotting how to convince you to adopt Pringle." I wiped my eyes.

The chubby pug flopped down on Hudson's boot.

He knelt down and scratched the dog behind the ears.

"His last family just abandoned him in their condo when they moved. I heard him barking one night. I can call the pug rescue to come get him."

Hudson picked up Pringle.

"He's already had too much trauma. Besides, only children are weird," he said as the dog chewed on the cuff of his leather jacket. "Pugnog needs a sibling. He's been too spoiled."

I threw my arms around Hudson, kissing him.

"Thank you, thank you, thank you."

"Besides," he purred. "I promised you as many babies as you wanted."

"I'd say let's make a baby right now, but I can't be pregnant at my wedding, and you don't know this, but all of these cabinets are filled with Sun Chips and Oreos."

I led him to my small bedroom.

He was right behind me, kissing me on the cheek.

"Got a thing for chicks in suits, don't you?"

He pushed me down onto the bed, his warm, powerful form right on top of me. "More like I got a thing for you, Gracie."

Soon I'm half naked, just wearing a professional blouse, still in the least professional situation I can imagine.

"I need to hear you come for me, babe," he whispered into my ear. "I've been daydreaming about it all day."

He chuckled as he ran his finger across my panties, stroking me through them.

I shuddered as he ran a finger over the lace. He held me down as he moved between my legs and kissed me through the fabric. He started to lick me a bit, poking at me, me murmuring in delight from what was coming my way. His finger pushed the fabric aside to touch me flesh to flesh, then tongue to flesh to build on the electricity more and more.

His licks slithered deep within me, hoping to hit all the right spots down there and drive me a bit more crazy. I cried out for him, everything boiling a little higher and hotter as his fingers worked my clit and pushed me harder. I writhed against the bed, struggling, wanting to simultaneously push away from him and get myself closer to him. The pounding orgasm rippled through me again and again, my entire form consumed with utter bliss.

I heard Hudson hastily undress behind me and a condom packet rip. I looked back enough only to have him back on top of me, that throbbing cock of his now poking against my lacy panties again, ready to thrust into me. His hands slid underneath my body to my blouse, worming their way toward my bra.

"Wish I could let you up so I could see how sexy you look in this, Gracie, but my cock wants other things."

"Does it now?" I joked as he brought his cock to my slit, my panties pushed out of the way just enough. "I'm sure there'll be plenty of other opportunities to enjoy the sights of me yet, Hudson."

"Then you agree, totally the right time to fuck you."

He thrust himself in, the pounding power of it all going right into me and making me gasp out, my body already aching and tender from the machinations of his tongue. I was dripping wet and so ready for him, and there was so little friction between us as he slid in and out of me again and again, setting a powerful pace for the fucking.

Pure, powerful need. It was what we both had for one another. It was so overwhelming, so passionate. I wondered how long this fire would burn, as I knew that they all started to flicker and fade eventually.

But for now?

I would enjoy every stroke of Hudson's cock inside me. Every moment of our insatiable lust. It was all too strong, too incredible.

I bucked into him. I squeezed his hips with my legs as much as I could manage in this strange position. The control he had, though, was undeniable. He hit me harder, stronger, and I was screaming at the top of my lungs for him, me trembling in a mess as I approached climax.

When I finally got there, it was a surprise, sudden and powerful as I screamed for him once more. His rhythm got more erratic, then he came with a curse.

Hudson collapsed next to me, pulling me into his arms, his cock still inside me. "You're fucking beautiful. Sexy. Wonderful. Countless other positive words, Gracie. And they're all true. I love you so fucking much."

I smiled, content and happy with the intensity of our love. I couldn't ask for a better man.

I lay there in his arms. "I love you," I murmured.

He hesitated.

"What?"

"I have a surprise for you as well. But I think it's a bad one, so brace yourself."

Chapter 4

HUDSON

"Can I open my eyes?"

"Not yet," I said, plugging in the Christmas lights that decorated the eaves of the old crumbling Victorian house.

In the dark, and with all the lights, it looked marginally habitable.

I went to stand behind Gracie. The pugs nosed around in the snow around her feet.

"Okay," I said in her ear. "You can open them."

I tensed, waiting for her reaction.

"Oh my god."

"Is that a good 'oh my god' or an 'oh my god my fiancé is insane'?"

Gracie turned around and kissed me lovingly, passionately.

"I love you so much, and you are insane, and oh my god, this is the most amazing house ever!" She jumped up and down squealing.

"The roof is half caved in, and it's leaking from everywhere," I warned.

"I don't care. I love it," she breathed. Her eyes were shining in the light.

I helped her up the rickety steps and opened the door.

"Is that the original skeleton key?" She was giddy as the two large wooden doors swung open.

"It needs a lot of work," I warned her.

"Look. The original wood paneling is here," she breathed.

"I think there's mold."

"And the old wallpaper. Look!" She peeled it back on a nearby wall. "It's here under the crappy '80s wallpaper."

She hugged me. "This is going to be a big, wonderful adventure."

I grinned at her then kissed her.

"I love you," I said softly.

"I love you too." She blinked back tears. "You really do know me, don't you? I love this house, and I can't wait for it to be our home."

"It's a big project."

She winked at me. "You know, I always love a project—chunky pugs, bad boys, crumbling houses, my sister's wedding—sign me up!" She spun around in the light coming in from the windows. "I want to get married here."

"For your spring wedding date, we might be able to make it," I said, "but don't get your hopes up. With these old buildings, you have to go slowly and carefully."

"No." She grabbed my hand. "Let's get married now."

"Now?"

"Yes. Here. Tomorrow."

"But your whole plan, your wedding festivities."

"I think I've had enough of weddings. I'm ready for marriage."

"Okay," I said with a laugh. "Let's get married."

She threw her arms around me, and I kissed her, savoring her.

"I'm going to call my grandmother to help. Otherwise we won't be able to pull this off."

"Which one?"

***

I positioned myself between the two elderly women.

"So," Gracie said to her two grandmothers after explaining the plan and showing them the house. "Do you think you can help me whip up some Christmas magic?"

"Do you think you can work together, more importantly?" I added. "Please?"

"No one can say no to that face," Granny Murray said.

"Gracie is adorable." I kissed her.

"No, I meant you, handsome."

"Gracie, I think you're breaking out," Astelle said to her granddaughter.

"She'll be in a veil," Granny Murray stated. "No one will see that big zit."

"New Year's resolution—I'm eating clean, super clean, nothing but raw vegetables," Gracie mumbled.

***

"Isn't it a bit early for a housewarming?" Anderson asked, wrinkling his nose.

"I think you mean a house cooling," Lawrence said, pulling down his wool cap. "Can't spring for a space heater, bro?"

"The ice sculpture is a nice touch," Talbot joked. "Feels like home."

I zipped up my jacket.

Gracie hadn't wanted me to wear anything different.

She was wearing a cream-colored 1950s-style cocktail dress with a flared skirt that didn't ring any wedding alarm bells, accompanied by a knitted shawl around her shoulders. Every so often she would catch my eye across the room and wink.

There was a bonfire outside and tables of food and drinks set up. I'd cleaned up as much as I could inside the house so people could walk around.

"I see you got it worked out after all," Grayson remarked, shaking my hand.

"I always close the contract," I reminded him.

He handed me a box with rings.

"They go on the dog."

"On the—"

Grayson sucked in a breath as Pugnog slobbered on his feet.

"You desperately need a baby."

When all the guests had arrived, Gracie and I took our places at the top of the curved staircase that was thankfully still structurally sound. She linked her arm in mine.

"We'd like to thank you all for coming this evening on such short notice," I began. "We're so excited to start our lives together, and we couldn't wait to show you all our new—well, old—home."

Gracie smiled up at me.

"As you all know, I was going to have a spring wedding," Gracie said, "but it's snowing outside, and now we have this beautiful old house, and the best time to start living is right now."

On the old organ, Astelle—stately in a high-collared gown—began to play "The Bridal March."

Chapter 5

GRACIE

There were screams from my cousins as the bridal music filled the cavernous house.

"You're getting married?"

"I didn't do my nails!"

"I'm having a moment!" I yelled at my family.

They continued to shout and yell over me.

"She's getting married. Shut the hell up!" Granny Murray finally shouted.

"Are you pregnant?" my father gasped.

"Uh, not that I know of. I adopted a pug though," I said as Grandma Astelle continued to play.

"Another pug?" my mom asked pointedly.

"You know what?" I said. "Cut the music. I'm just sick of all this wedding planning, and I didn't want to elope and not have you there. But you all are a lot."

"You can say it. We're awful," my brother told me. "I, for one, am happy that you're getting married because now we can have a wedding hockey match."

"Hockey! Hockey!" my male relatives cheered.

"Argh! Fine!" I threw up my hands. "I give in. Maplewood hockey match tomorrow morning. I'll bring the snacks. Now let's get hitched."

"Dearly beloved," Granny Murray began. "We are gathered here today to remember our dear friend ... Wait. Never mind. That's what I had for Bitsy's boyfriend's funeral. Don't be sad. He was a rat-faced bastard."

"Give me that microphone." Grandma Astelle stomped up.

The house shuddered ominously.

"We might want to hurry this along," Hudson said.

"I had all these vows," I protested.

Hudson kissed me.

"Wait wait wait." Granny Murray batted at him.

Some plaster fell from the ceiling.

I grimaced.

"We are gathered here to marry these two young lovers..."

"Gracie's not that young," one of my cousins heckled me.

I gave him the finger, to my mom's horror.

"Fine, these two early-middle-aged lovers. Any objections? No? Good."

"Marry her! Marry her!" my uncles chanted.

"Bring me the rings," Granny Murray said.

Pugnog trotted up, and Hudson bent down to grab the rings.

"Hudson," Granny Murray said, "do you take this good elf to be your lawfully wedded wife?"

"I do."

"Gracie, do you take this bad boy to be your lawfully wedded husband?"

"I do!" I said, jumping up and down.

"Please don't. You're going to go through the floor." Hudson grabbed me.

"I now pronounce you husband and wife. Kiss your bride!"

Hudson kissed me and picked me up in his arms.

"Evacuate carefully please."

Thankfully the house didn't collapse behind us as my family streamed out into the yard.

Hudson's brothers put up caution tape on the doors as our guests threw snow at us while we kissed on the porch.

"My beautiful, perfect wife. I love you more than anything in the world."

I wrapped my arms around his neck and my legs around his waist and kissed him.

"I love you so much."

"That's one child married," my aunt was telling my mother as we strolled around the yard, accepting congratulations.

"Man, he didn't even have to wear a suit for his wedding."

"Those are goals!" Uncle Eddie crowed, slapping Hudson on the back and handing him a beer.

Uncle Eddie saw my aunt glaring at him and winced. "Er … I mean you should wear a suit at your wedding. For shame, Hudson. I'm going to go take a turn at the grill."

"My daughter is all grown up." My dad sobbed and hugged me. Then he wrapped his arms around Hudson, who seemed a little taken aback then returned the hug.

"Dad, don't cry."

"I can't help it. I thought you would live with me forever."

"I mean ..."

"Oh, Gracie." My mother sighed and gave me a look.

"Stop it, Mom. It was a nice wedding," Kelly snapped at her. "Any wedding you don't have to plan is a nice one."

She put her hand on her hip and looked me up and down.

"You could have at least shaved that five o'clock shadow on your armpit. It's sexy on him, not on you. But congratulations."

"Thanks, Kelly?"

"Ignore her," Dakota said in excitement, shoving my sister away. "It's so dark you can only see that you missed a spot shaving when you're really close."

"Damn."

"Don't listen to them," Elsa said to me. "You should let your underarm hair grow out and dye it fun colors."

"She's twenty-two. She can do that, and it will look cute," Dakota warned me. "You are not twenty-two. Now, where are you going on your honeymoon? I'm free to dog sit."

I gave her a look.

"Here," I said, pointing to my glorious old house. "I saw historic wallpaper, and I'm going to spend all weekend carefully removing the '80s paper to get to that sweet, sweet historic goodness."

"You don't want to go to Aspen or a ski resort?" Hudson asked me.

"Nope, I want to be right here with you, my wonderful, sexy, surprise-house-buying, hockey-playing bad elf."

The End

Acknowledgements

A big thank you to Red Adept Editing for editing and proofreading.

And finally a big thank you to all the readers! I had a great time writing this hilarious book! Please try not to choke on your wine while reading!!!

About the Author

If you like steamy romantic comedy novels with a creative streak, then I'm your girl!

Architect by day, writer by night, I love matcha green tea, chocolate, and books! So many books...

Sign up for my mailing list to get special bonus content, free books, giveaways, and more!

http://alinajacobs.com/mailinglist.html

Printed in Great Britain
by Amazon

51474825R00324